Tear Down Heaven: Book 2

Rachel Aaron

Series Info

Hell For Hire
Hell of a Witch
Hell to Pay
Hell Hath No Fury
Tear Down Heaven

Publishing and Copyright Info

Hell of a Witch

Aaron Bach LLC
"Writing to Entertain and Inform."
Copyright © 2024 Rachel Aaron

ISBN Paperback: 978-1-952367-43-4

Cover Illustration by *Luisa Preissler*
Cover Design by *Rachel Aaron*
Editing provided by *Red Adept Editing*

Chapter 1

The warlock couldn't believe his luck.

He'd gone to his favorite wine store to peruse the newest inventory. Demons made scale-eyed humans nervous, so he'd left his slaves at home in order to have a productive discussion with the sommelier. It was the same routine he followed every Friday, but tonight, there'd been someone new. A woman, the most beautiful he'd ever seen, with golden hair and a smile that made him feel twenty years younger.

She was obviously a gold digger. There was no other reason a girl that young and lovely would be loitering inside such an old and exclusive shop, but the warlock didn't care. He'd liked her blatantness almost as much as he'd liked her scaled eyes. Scalies were much easier to impress.

This girl had been so easy she'd practically rolled into his convertible. Now she was climbing all over him, whispering all manner of dirty imaginings into his ear as he drove them back to his place at double the speed limit. Her suggestions were so distracting the warlock nearly crashed them into the moving truck that was parked in front of his Santa Clarita mansion. Another time, he would have sent his war demon after the minimum-wage idiots who'd parked on what was clearly a yellow curb, but the warlock was too distracted to care about anything except the blonde on his arm.

She had his coat off and was working on his shirt buttons by the time he deactivated his security wards and pulled the convertible into his three-car garage. He was about to ask if the girl—whose name he hadn't bothered to learn—wanted to go ahead and get started right here in the car when the knife touched his throat.

"What the—"

His panicked question cut off when his assailant—the one who'd been a smoking-hot, scale-eyed blonde not two seconds earlier—winked at him with their now *un*scaled eyes from a rugged, bearded, *masculine* face and slapped the hand that wasn't holding a blade over the warlock's mouth.

As if that would stop him. The warlock was already bellowing into the stranger's palm for his war demon. He heard the clatter upstairs as the lazy brute bolted from his pallet in the attic above the garage. The warlock was already leaning back in the driver's seat so his slave could tackle the assassin off him, but instead of leaping to his master's defense as he'd been ordered, the war demon froze as soon as his horned head cleared the edge of the attic.

For one confused second, the war demon stood perfectly still on the folding steps. Then, like an avalanche, the bronze-skinned beast threw himself down the stairs. The warlock wiggled his eyebrows at his assailant, who was surely about to get flattened by two hundred and eighty pounds of obedient demon, but his slave didn't jump into the convertible. He fell to his knees beside it instead, bowing his head so low that his flat horns scraped the garage's shiny epoxy floor.

The warlock screamed through the huge, hairy man-hand that was still covering his mouth, but it didn't do a thing. The thick-skulled idiot bowing his horns instead of helping his master didn't move a muscle. The warlock was about to try again when the car beneath him lurched like it'd been rear-ended.

The motion threw the warlock forward so suddenly he nearly slit his own throat on the sexy-blonde-turned-murderous-lumberjack's knife. He jerked away from the blade at once, wrenching around in his seat. But when he looked up to see which of his other demons had *finally* followed directions and come to his rescue, the triumphant smirk fell off his face.

There was a demoness standing on the trunk of his convertible, but she wasn't one of his. He'd never seen a demon with a human form that short, or with such enormous horns. Her pale hands clutched a thin black sword like she knew how to use it, and her eyes glowed like embers in the dark garage when she took off her sunglasses.

She looked nothing like her statues, but the rest of the warlock's household had made it to the garage by this point, and not one of them was running to help their master. They were all falling to their knees the same as his war demon, bowing before the strange demoness like she was Ishtar reborn.

And that was when the warlock knew for a fact that he was screwed.

"Up you go," Lys said in a deep, deadly voice, using their biggest, meanest male body to pry the terrified warlock out of his convertible. The man no longer looked like he wanted to fight, but Lys didn't remove their hand from his mouth or their knife from his throat as they led the wild-eyed human toward the kitchen door, which was currently blocked by bowing demons.

The warlock's slaves scrambled out of Lys's way at once. The lust demon nodded their thanks but kept their attention on the warlock, telling the human in a hard, calm voice that he was going to go to his computer and open his bank accounts, or Lys would start removing his organs in alphabetical order. Their enthusiasm for Option B must have been obvious, because the warlock started crying, nodding frantically against Lys's hand as the two of them vanished into the kitchen.

When they were gone, Bex pulled her sword back into its ring and turned to address the crowd of bowing demons. Drox had supplied their names the moment she'd laid eyes on them, but true-naming demons right off the bat set the wrong tone, so the Queen of Wrath smiled instead, hopping off the warlock's fancy car so she wouldn't have to talk down at them from on high.

"You're Anka, right?"

The question was directed at the demon kneeling in the middle of the group that had come into the garage from the house. Her human guise resembled a middle-aged Chinese woman, but her dark hair was wrapped around steeply downward-curved horns, and her eyes were the telltale deep blue of a sorrow demon when she raised them.

"I am called such, great queen."

Bex caught her wince just in time. The poor thing sounded terrified, and no wonder. It was one thing to send a text message to a tipline asking for help. It was quite another to have a figure from ancient legend show up in your master's garage.

"Don't be afraid," Bex said, giving Anka the warm, open smile she'd learned from Adrian. "Thanks to your bravery, your entire household will go free tonight."

The demons looked at her like she was speaking a foreign language.

"Free?"

Bex nodded and pointed over her shoulder at the moving truck she and Lys had jacked earlier that afternoon.

"That's your truck now. You have one hour to load it with anything you want to keep from this house. When you're done, I'll cut your slave bands and give you prepaid phones with directions to the safe houses that have agreed to take you in. You're free to stay with them or strike off on your own. Whatever you decide is fine, but right now, I need you to stop bowing and go pack. We don't have infinite time."

Giving orders to demons who'd been slaves all their lives left a bad taste in Bex's mouth, but she and Lys had done this dozens of times now, and they'd found that firm direction was the only thing that got folks moving. People expected a queen to be commanding, and the hour time limit was no joke. The clock was already ticking, so Bex led the way, striding into the warlock's ridiculously fancy kitchen as she started peppering the soon-to-be-freed slaves with questions about what to move first.

Once the demons realized she was serious, they got into the swing of things pretty quick. Only the war demon could lift as much as Bex, but all demons were stronger than the average human. This warlock had five in total, and they made quick work of his lavishly decorated home.

Anka especially knew where all the best stuff was. She kept the others moving, emptying hidden safes and grabbing all of the actually expensive decor while leaving the gaudy fakes and less valuable pieces behind. By the time Lys reappeared thirty minutes later, the moving truck was nearly full.

"Nice work," the lust demon said, carrying the warlock—who now looked much worse for wear—over the shoulder of their big, bearded male body.

"Nice work yourself," Bex replied, eyeing the battered human. "I take it he didn't cooperate."

Lys's smile grew bloodthirsty. "Nah, he coughed up everything like he couldn't wait to get it out. Whole process went a bit *too* easily, which is why my hand might have slipped at the end."

Bex arched an eyebrow at the warlock's broken nose. "Must have been some slip."

"It was more like several slips in a row," Lys explained with a shrug. "What can I say? Hitting warlocks is therapeutic."

"Just so long as you left some for everyone else," Bex said, turning to face the other demons, who'd started gathering in the garage the moment they spotted Lys.

"Good job getting everything packed so quickly," Bex told them while Lys dumped the bleeding warlock on the garage floor. "Step forward, and I'll cut your slave bands as promised. My companion"—she tilted her head toward Lys—"has convinced your former master to transfer his entire bank balance into a temporary anonymous account. You can access the money through your new phones."

"What about him?" asked Anka, glaring at the bleeding warlock on the garage floor with so much hate it rivaled Lys's. "What's his fate?"

"That's up to you," Bex said, planting her combat boot on the warlock's shaking shoulder. "You were the victims of his crimes, so his punishment is yours to decide. If you don't want to be bothered, I'll cut his head off right here. If you'd rather deal with him yourselves, we'll wrap him up for you like a present. The choice is entirely yours. Just as he once owned your lives, his future now belongs to you. Speak the word, and it shall be done."

The demons started whispering. It must have been a quick decision, because Anka turned back to Bex a few seconds later.

"We'll take him."

Bex nodded and pulled a half-empty bag of zip ties and a roll of duct tape out of the cargo pocket of her black fatigues. She taped the warlock's mouth shut before binding his tattooed fingers. She zip-tied his wrists and ankles next, pulling the plastic so tight his flesh bulged. When he was trussed up like a lamb for slaughter, she handed him to the war demon to load into the moving truck.

The warlock cried the entire time, his battered face gray with fear. Bex felt no pity, but she was relieved when the war demon shut the moving truck's rear door, sealing their pile of commandeered furniture and their old master inside with a metallic *click*.

As promised, Bex cut the demons' slave bands next. Just as she'd done in the Blackwood after the Spider's raid, she gave each demon the choice to keep the markings or not. Almost everyone chose to keep their bands, but Anka asked for hers to be burned away entirely.

"Are you sure?" Bex asked as she positioned her sword. "A clean neck will make you a target."

The sorrow demon looked her dead in the eyes. "I've been a slave to four generations of that warlock's family. I'd rather run from Gilgamesh for the rest of my life than go one more minute with their brand on my skin."

"As you wish," Bex said, touching Drox to the circle of cuneiform that ringed the sorrow demon's slender neck. "Be free, Ankanna."

She must have been an old demon, because her name hit Bex like a truck. It hit Anka even harder, causing the sorrow demon's whole body to seize up like she was being electrocuted. For a moment, Bex was worried something had gone horribly wrong. Then the sorrow demon's face split into a smile as the wings she'd clearly been forced to keep hidden suddenly unfolded, stretching nearly the entire width of the garage door.

"You have no *idea* how good that feels," she whispered, flashing Bex a look that was as close to giddiness as sorrow demons got. "Thank you, great queen."

"I'm the one who should be thanking you," Bex replied, her throat oddly tight. "You suffered four generations of warlocks waiting for me. Thank you for enduring so long. I swear to Holy Ishtar you'll never have to do it again."

That was a reckless promise to make, but Bex was feeling pretty reckless these days, and it made Anka smile even wider as Bex escorted her down the driveway.

"Make sure you withdraw all of the warlock's money before dawn," she warned as she helped the old sorrow demon into the moving truck's cab. "That's when the temporary account expires. I wish it was longer, but we can't afford to leave a trail."

"We'll get it all out," Anka promised, ducking her horns to Bex one last time. The rest of her household was already squeezed into the moving truck's front seat or the warlock's convertible, which the war demon had jumped to claim. They waved as they drove away, leaving Bex and Lys standing alone at the end of the warlock's fancy cul-de-sac.

"I don't think that's ever going to get old," Lys said cheerfully as they shifted back into their favorite genderless body. "Ready to put a nightcap on this?"

Bex had been ready since they got here. She knew exactly where to start, too, striding back through the warlock's empty garage and fancy kitchen into what was left of the formal living room.

The demons had taken all the easy stuff—the floor lamps and designer rugs and porcelain vases—but the obnoxiously huge leather sectional had been deemed too big to bother with. It was a surprisingly quality sofa, but it was still just wood, leather, and stuffing. All Bex had to do was press her burning hand into the cushions, and the whole thing went up in flames.

She did the curtains next, then the drywall, then the carpets upstairs. By the time Bex rejoined Lys in the driveway, the whole house was burning merrily, lighting up the wealthy subdivision like a bonfire.

"That is *definitely* never going to get old," Lys said with a grin, sliding the bag full of expensive wine bottles they'd snitched from the warlock's cellar onto their shoulder. "Ready to depart, your royalness?"

Bex rolled her glowing eyes and started running, sprinting down the dark street with Lys right behind her, both of them sticking to the shadows to avoid the neighbors spilling out into their yards to watch the warlock's mansion burn.

"And *that's* why you take the risks," Lys crowed, swatting pine branches out of their face as the two of them cut through the forest ten miles away from the warlock's still-flaming home. "That idiot should have known what I was the moment I touched him, but show 'em a pair of double Ds with a clean neck, fake scales, and some big hair to hide the horns, and they become as lust-stupid as the next human."

"Okay, okay, you were right," Bex admitted for the millionth time. "What do you want me to do, write a song about it?"

"That would be marvelous," Lys said, pausing to take a swig off the wine bottle they'd opened a mile ago. "'The Ballad of Lys, the Always Right.' A hundred stanzas, minimum, and you have to sing it in front of everybody."

Bex rolled her eyes. "You're going to have to be right a couple more times to get me enough material for a hundred stanzas."

"Only because you don't remember our previous lives together," Lys said, draining the last of the wine before chucking the empty bottle into the woods. "I've been right enough to fill a *thousand* stanzas."

Bex shook her head with a smile, but she didn't say anything else. They were approaching the edge of the Castaic Lake campground in the state park just north of Santa Clarita. This late in the season, the place was bumper-to-bumper with RVs full of tourists enjoying the final days of summer vacation. Since there were only a few hours left before dawn, most of the campground was asleep, but a few night owls were still talking around their fire rings. Bex pressed a finger to her lips, motioning for Lys to stay low as they slipped between the vacationers to their enchanted Winnebago, which was nestled among all the others like a pebble on the beach.

"Heya, kids!" Norma said when Bex opened the side door. "Did you have fun?"

"A blast," Lys replied, reaching over to turn off the cab light above the steering wheel, which put Norma into sleep mode. The construct was snoring the moment the bulb went out, slumped back in her driver's seat with a sleep mask over her eyes. Bex had no idea why the sorcerer who'd made their RV had chosen to make the old woman sleep in her seat rather than just having her disappear at night, but she was grateful for the silence as she flopped into the cushioned bench next to the dining table. Lys bustled farther into the kitchen, crouching in front of the netted cabinet beside the fridge to start unloading their stolen wine.

"You want first watch, or should I?"

"I'll take it," Bex said, trying not to sound too eager.

"Uh huh," Lys said, their voice full of innuendo. "Got a call to make?"

"Shut up," Bex muttered, glad the RV was dark enough to hide her face, which was uncomfortably warm. "Adrian is holding down our Seattle base. We need to communicate regularly to keep each other informed."

"Is that what the kids are calling it?"

Bex shot the lust demon a scathing scowl that did absolutely nothing.

"I'll just take myself downstairs, then," Lys said as they secured the last of their wine. "Have fun keeping Adrian Blackwood *informed.*"

Bex rolled her eyes, but she didn't say anything else as Lys strolled toward the RV's stairs, stopping every few feet to give Bex a wink.

When they were *finally* gone, Bex locked the RV's doors and went up to her room, which looked very different these days. Save for a few bottles over the door for emergencies, the gallons of deathly water that used to line the walls were gone, left behind in the Blackwood for safekeeping. In their place was a proper holder for Bex's guitar, a bolted-in chest of drawers so she wouldn't have to keep her clothes in a plastic box on the floor anymore, and a small grid of flat-screen TVs showing footage from all the new security cameras Adrian had helped her install on the Winnebago's exterior.

She should have done it ages ago. Setting up a closed-circuit camera system wasn't complicated, but Bex had been terrified to drill into the RV's walls for fear of damaging the magical whatevers that made their Winnebago a self-driving four-story palace. Fortunately, Adrian *hadn't* been terrified. He'd gone right in with a hand-cranked auger while Bex stood by to translate the cuneiform and hand him the cameras. Her ancient Sumerian wasn't as good as Lys's, but they'd muddled through, and now Bex could keep watch over the RV's entire perimeter from the comfort of her own bed.

There was another security station with bigger screens downstairs in the former client suite, which now served as their office, but Bex preferred to do her guard shifts up here. Her bedroom was cozier and, more importantly, out of range of Lys's excellent hearing. Not that Bex had anything to be ashamed of, but she still made sure the new curtain was pulled all the way over her door before she flopped onto her bed and dug her phone out of her pocket.

She sent a text first, just to be polite. Adrian didn't sleep much, but it *was* nearly four in the morning. Hardly an appropriate time for a nonemergency report, but she'd barely tapped Send on her message before her phone buzzed in her hands. Bex hit the Accept Call button just as quickly, clutching the phone to her ear for what had rapidly become the very best part of her day.

"Hey."

"Hey yourself," Adrian replied, his voice so warm and close that her eyes drifted shut.

Stop that, Drox ordered. *You're supposed to be keeping watch, and this is hardly behavior befitting a queen.*

"Why are you up so late?" Bex asked, tugging Drox's ring off her finger before the sword could ruin this for her.

"I'm up early, actually," Adrian replied with a yawn. "I'm repositioning all of the Blackwood's song sparrow nests into a more efficient matrix for the predawn portion of my new sound-dampening apparatus."

"Okay," Bex said slowly. "I don't know what any of that means."

"Let's just say that Heaven's forces should find it *very* difficult to ring a bell in my forest now," the witch informed her smugly. "Not that I have any way of testing the system short of a prince trying to force his way in, but there's no reason it shouldn't work."

"Have you had any trouble?"

"Not a thing," Adrian said. "It's driving me crazy."

Bex knew the feeling. It'd been over a month since she'd melted the prince in the Blackwood, and there'd still been no retaliation. The whole reason she and Lys were down in California freeing demons was to kick the anthill somewhere else while Adrian, Iggs, and Nemini fortified their position in Seattle. It was supposed to be a distraction even Heaven couldn't ignore, but they'd been tearing the Golden State's warlock population a new one for two straight weeks, and Bex still hadn't seen so much as a princess.

"Maybe Gilgamesh is just slow," she suggested as she placed Drox's vibrating ring on her new nightstand. "He has been in power for five thousand years. A month probably feels like a second when you're that old."

"Maybe," Adrian said, but he didn't sound convinced. "How'd tonight's raid go?"

"Not too shabby," Bex reported. "We freed five demons, scored a bunch of loot, and torched a warlock's house to the ground. You know—typical Friday night."

He laughed at that, and Bex grinned. Not that she'd ever tell anyone, but she loved that Adrian thought she was funny. No one had ever laughed at her jokes before him. Iggs was always too mindful of rank, and Bex was pretty sure the world would end if Nemini cracked a smile. Lys laughed *at* her, but that wasn't the same. It certainly didn't make Bex smile like this did.

"That's your twentieth hit since you got to California, isn't it?" Adrian asked. "Are you freeing every demon in SoCal?"

"Hardly," Bex said, careful not to scratch the plastic paneling with her horns as she propped her back against the wall. "Lys used their contacts to set up a tipline for demons who wanted out. We thought it'd be a faster way of finding targets, but the thing went crazy. I've got over two hundred help requests in my inbox right now, and the number gets higher every day."

Bex's smile faded as she spoke. She loved how many demons had jumped at the opportunity to be free, but that didn't keep the number from being overwhelming. She and Lys had been working nonstop since they got here, but they'd still barely made a dent. Bex hadn't realized there *were* that many demons in California until the pleas started piling in. Lys kept telling her the numbers were normal, but Bex hadn't done much slave freeing in this life since she'd ruined herself so early, which meant she'd never actually faced the true scale of the problem until now.

"There's just so many," she said, looking up at the dark windows of her skylights. "It's not only warlocks, either. Sorcerers keep house slaves, too, and there's tons of them. We've been prioritizing households with multiple demons since those are the biggest bang for our buck, but single slaves deserve freedom too." She trailed off with a sigh. "I don't know how we're going to get them all, and I *really* don't understand how we haven't pulled a prince yet."

"They must be up to something," Adrian said, raising his voice over what sounded like a whole lot of angry baby birds. "Gilgamesh is famous for not tolerating defiance, and you two have been slaughtering his people and freeing his slaves for weeks now. Add in the prince you killed up here, and there *has* to be a reason he hasn't brought the hammer down yet. Something else he's planning."

Adrian had been saying the same thing every night for the past week. As always, though, Bex didn't know what to tell him.

"What else can we do?" she asked. "It's not like we can hit him any harder."

There was a long pause, long enough that Bex started to worry he'd dropped his phone. She was about to hang up and call him back when Adrian's voice whispered over the speaker.

"What if we could?"

"What do you mean?" she asked, whispering too even though there was no one else around to hear.

"I mean what if we hit him where it *really* hurts?" Adrian said, his voice getting excited. "All this time, we've been punching at warlocks and princes. I'm sure Gilgamesh doesn't like that, but warlocks and princes are soldiers. It's their job to fight. Even freed demons can be replaced with new ones from the Hells, but what if we attacked something that *wasn't* made to take hits? Something *so* important its loss would be felt even up in Heaven?"

Bex frowned. "We already killed one of Gilgamesh's sons. What's more important than that?"

"The Anchors," Adrian said without missing a beat.

He must have heard her breath catch over the phone, because he began speaking very quickly.

"They're the perfect target. The Anchors are the biggest pieces of infrastructure Heaven has on earth, and the best guarded. We know Gilgamesh can revive lost princes, but Anchors are huge. If we wrecked one, I bet even the Eternal King couldn't just plop down a replacement without serious investment."

"Probably," Bex admitted. "But would he even care? Anchors are big, but they're just markets, and Gilgamesh has tons of them all over the world. If we blew one up, Heaven's spoiled citizens could just go somewhere else to buy their lobsters and chocolates."

The phone speakers rustled as Adrian shook his head. "I don't think that's all there is to it. Anchors are the only places I know of where Heaven and earth connect. They have markets because markets always pop up at crossroads, but if selling lobsters to Heaven was all they were good for, why would Gilgamesh have so many? There aren't *that* many people living in the Holy City, but there are four Anchors in southern California alone. Why have that many so close together if they're just markets?"

Bex shrugged. "I don't know."

"I don't either!" he said excitedly. "I've been digging into this for a few days now, but I haven't found any information about why Gilgamesh puts his Anchors where he does. I can't even find out why they're called 'anchors' instead of 'roads' or 'gates,' which would make more sense if connecting Heaven to earth was their only purpose."

"You think they have another?"

"I'd bet my hat on it," Adrian replied. "And that's why I think we should attack one."

"I don't know," Bex said, rubbing the back of her neck. "It sounds really risky."

"All the more reason we should go for it," he argued. "I don't know why Gilgamesh hasn't taken a swing at us yet, but the last thing you want to do in a war is let your enemy sit around and prepare. Attacking an Anchor will force Gilgamesh's hand while simultaneously cutting off his ability to send backup. The princes and princesses seem to move on their own system, but everything else from Heaven—quintessence, weapons, demons for the slave auctions—famously comes in via the Anchors. We've already cleaned all the warlocks out of Seattle. If we take down the local Anchor as well, Gilgamesh will lose his foothold here entirely!"

"Or he could come down on us with everything he's got," Bex pointed out.

"I hope he does," Adrian said fiercely. "If Gilgamesh strikes back for real, that'll mean we scored an actual hit. He clearly doesn't care about his warlocks or his princes, or he would have stopped you from killing them by now, but I bet he'll care about this."

"Why?" she asked.

"Because there's no information about them. Like I said, I've been looking into this for days. I've wiggled my way into every subreddit, forum, and hashtag for quintessence users on the internet, and I can't even find the name of someone who works at an Anchor."

"So?"

"So that's weird," he insisted. "Gilgamesh's spellcasters aren't exactly a humble bunch, and working at an Anchor is famously the most prestigious job a sorcerer can get outside of Heaven itself. Anybody who lands one should be lording it over his fellow sorcerers forever, but I can't find a single brag post. I can't find *anything*."

"Doesn't that just mean it's classified?" Bex asked.

"Classified from whom?" Adrian said. "With the exception of the Blackwood witches, every magic user on the planet either works for or gets their quintessence from Gilgamesh. Sorcerers guard their own spells, but all other information seems to be public knowledge. I can look up the binding for a demon or tonight's party schedule in the Holy City without even accessing the password-protected areas, but I can't find a single word about the Anchors—not who works there or what the qualifications are for a position or what the Anchors do, nothing. Just locations."

He lowered his voice back to a whisper. "If something's that important and sorcerers aren't bragging about being part of it, there *has* to be a killing secret involved. If we can find out what that secret is, it might help us destabilize Gilgamesh's control."

"That's a lot of *ifs*," Bex said.

"I'm working to find out more," Adrian promised. "Even if I'm totally wrong, though, and the Anchors really are just connectors, that still makes them good targets. No general ever went wrong destroying the enemy's highways."

Bex grabbed Drox's ring off the nightstand with a nervous breath. She was the rebel queen here, but what Adrian was suggesting was bigger than anything she'd ever attempted. Big enough to make her terrified, but maybe that was what they needed. The slave-freeing missions were going as well as Bex could ask, but it still felt like trying to empty the ocean with a teaspoon. It was also the same thing they'd always done. She'd *always* freed slaves, and while Bex was proud of that, even she could admit it had never changed anything. The slaves that made it to earth were just symptoms of a larger illness. If Bex actually wanted to change things for her people, she needed to attack the root of the problem. But while Heaven itself was out of reach, the Anchor Markets were right there, and unlike freeing demons, Bex didn't think any of her past selves had ever tried attacking an Anchor before.

You haven't, Drox informed her. *Because it's crazy.*

"It *is* crazy," she agreed out loud as she slid his heavy ring back onto her finger. "But you can't win a fight with a king no one's ever beaten by sticking to the same old tactics."

"It'll throw him off too," Adrian promised. "No one attacks the Eternal King directly anymore. He hasn't had to defend himself in thousands of years, which means he'll be *bad* at it."

That was music to Bex's ears. "Let's try it, then," she said, climbing off her bed. "Lys and I can leave for Seattle tonight."

"Great," Adrian said, his voice hitching as he hopped out of whatever tree he'd been sitting in. "I've already done all the snooping I can by myself. There's one more angle I can safely check on my own before I have to start sticking my nose in places it *really* doesn't belong, and I'm not doing that without you."

"My nose is a lot tougher than yours," Bex agreed, trying not to let her smile bleed into her voice. She knew Adrian was just being practical, but the idea that there was stuff he didn't want to do without her still made Bex giddy. It was a stupid, undignified, unqueenly way to feel, but the nice part about being a thousand miles away was that there was no chance of Adrian catching her grinning like an idiot as she started down the stairs.

"I'm going to get this rig moving," she told him. "See you in seventeen hours?"

"I'll be waiting," he said with a smile she could hear through the speaker. "Good night, Bex."

"Good morning, Adrian," Bex whispered, clutching the phone close to her face until he hung up. She was still staring at his name on her screen when Drox's voice sighed through her head.

Are you done making an idiot of yourself?

"I don't see what you have to complain about," Bex snapped, tromping the rest of the way down the spiral stair. "Adrian's done more for our fight against Gilgamesh in the last two months than anyone else has managed in fifty centuries. He's everything you've ever wanted, so shut up and let me have my crush in peace."

The Sword of Ishtar doesn't get to have crushes, Drox informed her pointedly. *This is your last life and therefore your last chance to defeat Gilgamesh and reclaim Paradise for your people. The witch has been an asset to our cause so far, but he could just as easily become a liability if you continue to foolishly allow his presence to distract you from your purpose.*

"Adrian isn't a distraction."

Says the woman who was supposed to be on watch but didn't look at her security cameras once.

Bex didn't have a good comeback for that one, so she settled for shaking her head, sticking the hand with the black ring into her pocket as she headed to the cab to wake up Norma.

The Crown Prince of Heaven, eldest son of the Eternal King, Gilgamesh's chosen steward and divine celestial adjunct of all royal affairs, was having a vexing day. He was alone in his office in the tallest tower of his father's palace, sitting at a golden desk stacked high with prayers. That in itself was not unusual, but the fact that all of the scrolls currently piled in front of him came from the same small corner of his father's empire was.

The situation in California was getting out of hand, and if there was one thing the Crown Prince could not tolerate, it was things getting out of hand. Fortunately, the solution was already on its way. He'd just witnessed his chosen tool's arrival through the eye he shared with his princess, which meant the knock should be coming any—

His thoughts cut off as the tap he'd been expecting sounded against his golden door. He still made the visitor wait—he was the Crown Prince, after all—but only for a few minutes before he called for the servants to open the door and let his brother in.

The wraith who entered his office was a shadow of the Divine Prince he'd once been. He was still resplendent with his golden armor and impressive height—the tallest of all the brothers—but his olive-skinned face was pinched, and his mirrored eyes were deep-set and red-rimmed. He'd lost twenty pounds since the last time the Crown Prince had seen him, but despite looking like a beggar, he was still a son of Gilgamesh, and he took his place before the Crown Prince's desk with all the haughtiness that divine bloodline demanded as the servants made themselves scarce.

"Welcome back into the light, Leander," the Crown Prince said when they were alone. "How fare the Hells?"

"Hellish," Leander replied, his dry voice edged with a malice that hadn't been there before. "But you knew that."

"It would hardly be a punishment if it were pleasant," the Crown Prince pointed out, furtively adjusting the eyepatch over his missing eye so he could face his younger brother properly. "I have an opportunity for you. After years of silence, the Coward Queen is back with a vengeance. She's been slaying our people, freeing slaves, and burning buildings all over California. The locals are getting quite restless"—he waved at the head-high stacks of prayers covering his desk—"so it falls to us to ensure that the Peace of Heaven is maintained."

"It's just the Coward Queen," Leander said dismissively. "She's nothing these days. Send one of the younger princes."

"She's already killed our youngest brother," the Crown Prince informed him. "Twice, actually. Father is most displeased."

"Then I would be happy to offer him satisfaction," Leander replied, perking up for the first time since he'd entered. "But I'll need my sword back if I'm to hunt the Coward Queen."

The Crown Prince shook his head. "You mistake my meaning. *You* won't be the one hunting her. We have a different weapon for that." He raised his voice. "Send him in."

Leander turned around with a scowl as another door opened at the back of the office, and a very different prince stepped into the room. Where Leander was tall, gaunt, and calm as a frozen lake, this prince was stocky, scarred, and radiating anger like a furnace. He stalked into the elegant room like an animal, baring his chipped teeth at the other princes.

If it weren't for his dark curling hair and mirrored eyes, the Crown Prince wouldn't have recognized him as a son of Gilgamesh, but the real madness was his princess. She trailed behind the newcomer like a beaten dog, her beautiful face lowered in fear, which was something to behold. The Princess of Greed was normally the clingiest of all the swords, but it seemed even she couldn't find a way to love the man in front of her. A troubling development but ultimately not an important one. Even when they were broken, princes were always useful, and the Crown Prince had a use for this one in particular.

"Leander," he said, knocking the gaunt prince out of his horrified gawking. "This is Damion, a hero of the purges and one of the strongest fighters our bloodline has ever produced. Alas, multiple deaths and centuries in the Sleep have left him... discombobulated. He hasn't responded as well to his rehabilitation as we anticipated, which is where you come in."

Leander's sunken eyes snapped back to his eldest brother. "Why me?" he demanded, pointing at Damion, who snarled like a feral dog. "Why *him*? It's just the Coward Queen. We don't need to resurrect a monster from the purges to—"

"That is where you're wrong," the Crown Prince interrupted, rising from his chair. "Things have changed while you were in the Hells. The Coward Queen has come out of the quiet portion of her reincarnation cycle early, and she's having quite the spot of activity."

Leander looked at him askance. "You make her sound like a volcano."

"An apt comparison," the Crown Prince said gravely. "She incinerated her last opponent, which means she's got her fire back. We suspected something of that nature when she defeated our brother the first time in Limbo, but that place has odd properties. Now that she's done it again in the living world, however, we must assume she's regained a measure of her old power."

"If that's the case, then a prince from the purges is too blunt a weapon," Leander said thoughtfully. "This isn't a rebelling army to be plowed under. Even in her weaker years, the Coward Queen was always a crafty opponent. It takes cleverness to defeat her, not brawn. If I had my sword—"

"If you'd used your sword properly, you wouldn't have been sent to the Hells," the Crown Prince reminded him. "Your opinion has been noted, Prince Leander, but I did not summon you to be a combatant. Damion should be sufficient for that task. Your job is to make sure he doesn't destroy any cities in the process."

Leander's expression turned surly, and the Crown Prince scowled.

"You are to be your brother's keeper," he explained. "Whatever sparked these new flames, the Coward Queen's revival has returned opportunities thought long lost to the table. Our divine father is most interested in her capture."

"If he wanted her captured, then he shouldn't have chosen a killer," Leander snapped.

"He chose exactly what was needed," the Crown Prince replied crisply. "The former Queen of Wrath is a monster, so Heaven must send a monster in reply. The Eternal King is aware of Damion's shortcomings, which is why he heeded my advice to bring you back from the Hells. With certain tragic exceptions, you've always been the most levelheaded of the princes, so here are your orders. You will accompany Prince Damion to the living world and ensure he engages the Coward Queen in a manner that does not endanger the Eternal King's peace. Once Damion finishes his work, you are to collect the Coward Queen and bring her and your brother safely back to Heaven. Do this, and I'll see that your sword is returned to you."

As ever, Leander's face betrayed nothing, but the Crown Prince didn't miss the hitch in his breath.

"You have your orders," the Crown Prince went on, sitting back down in his golden chair. "Mind your brother, make sure he does the job he was restored to do, and your punishment shall be rescinded. Your sword could be back at your side by the end of the week, and I'll stick someone else on Hells duty."

"You do me great honor," Leander said with a bow that was actually deep enough for once. "I shall see it done."

"Make sure that you do," the Crown Prince warned. "The Coward Queen represents a direct challenge to Heaven's control. I am extending a great deal of trust by recommending you for this task. Betray that trust, and your previous punishment will seem like a gift. Do I make myself clear?"

"Very clear, sir," Leander said in a tight voice.

The Crown Prince nodded and waved him away, pulling the stack of prayers back to the center of his desk to begin his replies.

Meanwhile, a few feet away, Leander spoke words of sorcery to cast a glowing chain around their mad brother's neck. Damion roared in fury when the leash landed, but Leander's strength had never been the sort that could be overcome with simple brutality. He'd already stabbed the mad prince full of conjured swords, using the pain to herd their broken brother into the hall while his princess trailed behind, crying into her white hands in great, pathetic sobs.

Chapter 2

Later that same day, at a well-rated brewery in northern Seattle famous all over the internet for its highly imaginative beer list, Adrian Blackwood was attempting to balance three trays of tasting flights on two arms. Each little glass only held five ounces, but there were six tasters on each tray. That added up to more beer than one person was wise to consume alone. Fortunately, Adrian had brought help.

"Oh, man," Iggs said excitedly as Adrian stepped carefully through the web of Nevermind spells he'd woven around their table on the brewery's tree-shaded patio. "You are my favorite witch *ever*!"

"Did you have to get so many?" asked Boston, who was sitting on the table wearing his harness, a sign of how very seriously he took tonight's business. "The spell only requires one libation."

"But it works much better if I like the libation being offered," Adrian countered as he set the trays full of miniature beer glasses down on the iron-mesh table. "And how am I supposed to know which one I like best if I don't taste them all first?"

"Well, *I'm* happy you're tasting," Iggs said, grabbing a glass at random and shoving it at Adrian so he could get started. "I haven't had a beer in forever!"

"Are you not allowed to drink?" Boston asked as Adrian dutifully took a sip.

Iggs shook his head. "Bex lets us do whatever we want so long as it doesn't interfere with the mission. Lys drinks all the time, but I never felt right about it. Beer is for celebrations, and it always seemed selfish to party when Bex never takes a day off."

As ever these days, Adrian's ears perked up at Bex's name. "She must take off sometimes," he said, passing the rest of the beer—which was far too hoppy for his taste—back to Iggs.

"Not unless she's sleeping," Iggs replied, accepting the little bulb-shaped glass like a sacred offering. "Those first two weeks we did guard work while you grew your forest were the most relaxed I've ever seen her, and even then, she was working. But I'm not working *now*."

The big demon brought the beer up to his nose with a deep breath, then he tilted the glass at Adrian. "Queen's health."

Adrian was still ducking his head in reply when Iggs downed the rest of the beer like a shot. He slammed the glass on the table when he was finished, his mouth opening in a sharp-toothed grin that took up his entire face.

"*Damn* me, but that is *good*!" he cried loud enough to draw looks from the other tables even through the haze of the Nevermind. Boston hushed him immediately, but the demon barely seemed to notice, pulling off his sunglasses instead to get a better look at the rest of the beers carpeting their table.

"How do they get it so clear?" he asked, poking the nearest glass of golden, bubble-lined liquid. "All the beers I drank before had chunks in them."

Adrian's hand paused on the next drink in the lineup. "Chunks?"

When the demon nodded, the witch and his cat exchanged a look.

"Iggs," Boston said suspiciously, "just how long ago was your last beer?"

"Before I got sent to Limbo," Iggs replied, watching the beer in Adrian's hand like a hawk. "Are you going to taste that or what?"

Adrian dutifully took a sip of what turned out to be a nice citrusy hefeweizen. He made a note next to the beer's name on the little sheet the bartender had given him and passed the rest to Iggs, who downed the second beer just as quickly as he had the first.

"So these are the first beers you've had in five thousand years?" Boston asked.

The wrath demon nodded as if this was no big deal, and Adrian whistled. "How do modern beers compare?"

Iggs was staring at the beers too hard to answer, so Adrian sipped his next drink—an IPA that was supposed to have banana notes but mostly tasted like beer—as fast as he could before handing it over.

"They're really different," Iggs said once the prize was in his hands. "They're watery and thin compared to the beer we brewed back home, but the taste is good, and I like that they're cold. I'd never heard of cold beer before I got here. I do miss the chunks, though. Can you even call it beer if it doesn't have chew?"

Adrian went a little green at the question, taking a thoughtful sip of the next—and mercifully chew-free—beer in the lineup.

"I can't believe you brewed beer in the land of the dead," Boston said, tail twitching thoughtfully. "How does yeast even procreate in—"

"Of course we brewed beer!" Iggs cried, insulted. "What kind of Paradise doesn't have beer?"

Adrian couldn't argue with that logic. Even so, "I thought demons didn't eat food."

"Not on this side," Iggs explained as he pushed another beer at Adrian. "But we ate all kinds of things back home. We had wheat, barley, millet, figs, olives, cattle, goats, everything you could want."

He said this as if it should be obvious, but Adrian was shocked. "I thought you ate wrath?"

Iggs gave him an impatient look, and Adrian quickly tasted his drink and passed it over.

"We did eat wrath," the demon answered, taking an actual sip of his beer this time instead of chugging it. "What do you think grew all that stuff?"

Adrian had no idea. Boston looked equally baffled, and Iggs drew himself up straight with a superior look.

"Ishtar created us to remove the world's sins," he explained, clearly over the moon to be the one in the know for once. "All demons drew water from the Rivers of Death, but each of us could only take out the sins we were made to cleanse. As wrath demons, we drew wrath from the rivers. That was what irrigated our crops and watered our livestock, and when we ate those things, we consumed the sin and removed it from the world."

"I see," Boston said, his green eyes bright. "You're like bacteria eating pollution out of the water!"

"We weren't *bacteria*!" Iggs roared. "It was a sacred duty!"

"He meant no offense," Adrian said quickly, though he secretly felt that Boston had the right of it. From Iggs's description, demons sounded like the liver of the afterlife. They filtered sins out of human souls just like the actual liver filtered toxins out of the bloodstream. He didn't think Iggs would appreciate that comparison either, though, so he changed the subject.

"What was it like?"

Iggs suddenly grew quiet. "What do you think it was like?" he muttered, staring into his beer. "It was Paradise. There was no hunger, no poverty, no sickness or drought.

We fought among ourselves occasionally, especially the war demons, but the queens kept it from getting out of hand. We mostly just lived in eternal summer under an endless blue sky."

His voice grew wistful as he trailed a big, black-clawed finger along the edge of his glass. "I grew up on a cattle farm right next to the River Styx. My entire family lived there: mom, dad, grandparents, aunts, uncles, and the cousins. *So* many cousins." He smiled. "My sister was the oldest. She used to run us kids like an army. Bex reminds me of her a lot. So much that sometimes I—"

He stopped, his finger freezing on the rim of his glass as he looked at Adrian in panic. "Don't tell Bex I said that."

"I won't," Adrian promised. "But I don't think she'd mind. Your family sounds lovely."

"They were fantastic," Iggs agreed. "But that doesn't mean I can compare my sister to a daughter of Ishtar. It's blasphemy! I'm lucky I haven't been struck by lightning just for thinking it."

He glanced nervously at the clear afternoon sky, and Adrian selected his next beer with a thoughtful scowl. "What was she like back then?"

"Who, my sister?"

Adrian shook his head as he sipped his drink. "Bex."

"Oh," the demon said, running a hand through the thick hair between his dark, ox-like horns. "Couldn't tell you, to be honest. Like I said, we were cowherds, and she was the *queen*. She'd come by our village sometimes for inspections and stuff, but she was always surrounded by elders and priests and other important people. My cousins and I used to climb up in the trees to watch her go by, 'cause how often do you get to see the real-life daughter of a goddess? But I'd never spoken a word to her before she freed me from Limbo."

Adrian's scowl deepened as he passed Iggs the next beer. "So you didn't know her at all?"

"Of course not," Iggs said, accepting the drink graciously. "Village life might sound quaint compared to modern cities, but Wrath was a big sin. We had hundreds of settlements scattered up and down the Riverlands. Bex was responsible for all of them, and that's not even counting the monsters she used to fight."

Adrian nearly spilled the next beer all over himself. "*Monsters?*"

"Tons of 'em," Iggs said, nodding rapidly. "This was back in the golden age of the gods. Ishtar was wise and responsible, but the other gods created all kinds of nonsense to test their heroes and harass each other. When those monsters died, they ended up in Paradise just like everything else, but since they were divine creations, we got the whole beastie instead of just the soul. We were constantly getting hit with dragons, chimeras, cyclopes, three-headed dogs, hydras, the works. Fortunately, Ishtar was a goddess of war as well as life, death, fertility, love, and beauty. Her daughters were born with Enki's sacred swords in their hands, and they knew how to use them. They defended Paradise from everything until Gilgamesh showed up, though if you ask me, Bex was the best. She was Ishtar's Wrath, and the moment something toothy started making trouble, she'd shoot across the sky like a flaming comet to stop it. She even protected other demon villages when their queens were too slow."

"I'm sure it was a sight to behold," Adrian said with a smile.

"It was," Iggs said, taking the beer Adrian handed him next without looking. "Though it feels weird to talk about. I don't remember anything from my time as a kick demon, so all this stuff is still recent history to me. Bex looks exactly the same as she used to back when I'd spy on her with my cousins, but she didn't even know our language when she cut me out of Limbo. I could understand what she was saying because she's my queen, but she didn't recognize a thing coming out of my mouth. I had to learn English just so I could tell her thank you without bringing in her sword to translate."

"Well, you've done an excellent job," Boston said. "You don't even have an accent."

"Thanks!" Iggs said, lighting up at the rare praise, but his face fell again a moment later. "To be honest, though, I didn't have much choice. No demons speak my language anymore except Nemini, and she's hardly chatty. Part of the reason I threw myself into English so hard is because I want to be ready to teach it to the rest of my people when we finally set them free."

"It'll happen," Adrian promised.

"Of course it'll happen," Iggs said proudly. "It has to, because we'll never kneel. When Gilgamesh struck our queen out of the sky, everyone said it was over, but we could still feel her. We *knew* the Queen of Wrath was still alive, so when the war demon traitors came to make us kneel, we spit in their faces. Not a one of us would bow to the false king, and without Bex, Gilgamesh couldn't make us. That's why he locked us in Limbo. It was the only way he could keep us under control, but Bex got me out, and I know she'll do the same for the rest of our people."

His big hand curled into a fist around the tiny beer glass. "She'll set *everyone* free, and when Gilgamesh is dead and things go back to normal, all of Paradise will sing praises to the wrath demons, the only tribe who never kneeled. Let's see those war demon traitors call our queen a coward after *that*!"

"No one who knows what Bex has done could ever call her a coward," Adrian agreed, lifting his beer in salute.

The sun was starting to set by this point. Bex would be coming home soon. Adrian wanted to be finished before she arrived, so he got to work on the task he'd set for himself. He tried to keep his sips small, but by the time he'd sampled every beer on the menu, he was feeling lightheaded. Iggs, by contrast, didn't seem affected in the slightest. Adrian didn't know if that was because the demon was huge or because modern beer couldn't measure up by the standards of Paradise, but it was nice having someone sober to keep an eye on things while he went back to the bar to settle their tab and purchase a growler of his favorite: a delightful coconut porter with just the right hint of sweetness.

Once the sixty-four-ounce jug of fresh beer was in his hands, Adrian stumbled back to strip the Nevermind off their table and collect the pair of shovels he'd set on the ground beside his broom. Boston, wise cat that he was, declined to walk with Adrian until he was sober, so Adrian handed his familiar's leash to Iggs, propped the shovels and his broom on his shoulder, and set off down the sidewalk.

As always, his witch hat and swirling coat drew plenty of stares, but not as many as they normally did. It was late August now, close enough to the Halloween season for most people to give him a pass, and the neighborhood around the brewery was pretty alternative. He, Iggs, and Boston were hardly the strangest things on the sidewalk, leaving Adrian free to enjoy the stroll on this lovely summer evening. He was studying the way the roots of the trees lining the street cracked the paving stones when Iggs cleared his throat beside him.

"So," he asked, taking great care not to pull on the leash Boston had deigned to wear for tonight's excursion. "Where are we going again? I know you explained everything earlier, but I kind of stopped listening after you said the word 'beer.'"

"You'll see soon enough," Adrian promised, pulling out his phone to check their location. It was still a bit of a walk, but the weather was fantastic, and Adrian needed time to lose his buzz. This was going to be a tricky bit of magic outside his area of specialization, but he was feeling pretty confident, especially after all that beer. This was just the gathering stage, so he let himself enjoy being tipsy as they followed the quiet residential street another several blocks until it dead-ended at a wall of cedars.

The daylight was nearly gone by this point. But while the sidewalk was well lit by streetlamps and porch lights, the area beyond the trees was almost black. It looked like a park in the gloom, but once he and Iggs pushed their way through the trees, the weathered rectangles set like paving stones into the grass told a different story.

"Wait," Iggs said, coming to a dead stop. "Is this a graveyard?"

"That it is," Adrian replied, pulling out his phone again to bring up the map he'd made earlier. "This way."

Using his glowing screen as a flashlight, Adrian led the way through the dry, late-summer grass toward the paved road that wove between the graves like a river. Iggs followed right on his heels, his red eyes surprisingly spooked for someone who'd been born in the afterlife.

"Why are you making that face?" Boston asked, looking over his shoulder from where he'd trotted ahead. "You were just bragging about how you used to clean the wrath out of people's souls."

"Those were glowing lights flowing in sacred rivers," Iggs protested, clutching the shovel Adrian had handed him like a spear. "These are dead *bodies*. Haven't you ever seen a zombie movie?"

"There's no Witch of the Bones skilled enough to raise a zombie in this area," Adrian assured him, tucking his own shovel under his arm. "The worst thing we have to worry about is a scale-eyed human calling the cops."

Iggs didn't look comforted, but Adrian wasn't paying attention to him anymore. He was glued to the map on his phone, following the marked path off the road to a line of newer graves at the top of a little crest.

"Here we are," he announced, double-checking the name on the last tombstone before he pulled the materials out of his pockets for another Nevermind. Not that there was anyone around *to* never mind now that night had fallen over the cemetery, but even the most cynical people reacted poorly to grave robbing, and given how much work he had left to do before Bex arrived, Adrian wanted to get through this part with minimal fuss.

Fortunately, Neverminds were one of the easiest spells to set up if you didn't need them to move. Five minutes later, he'd established a solid perimeter over this entire section of graveyard. It wouldn't keep out family members, but it should hide them from joggers, edgy teens, bored night watchmen, and other uninvested observers. He still put Boston on lookout, just in case, then he took off his coat, rolled up his shirtsleeves, and stabbed his shovel into the grass to start digging.

Iggs followed suit a moment later, turning up the dirt in small, nervous scoops.

"So," he asked with a swallow, "whose grave are we desecrating?"

"Jason Keller," Adrian replied as he heaved a fresh mound of dirt onto the grass beside them. "Devoted husband, respected member of the community, and sorcerer of Gilgamesh."

Iggs froze midshovel. "This is a sorcerer's grave?" he squeaked. "Won't we get cursed?"

"No, because sorcerers believe they go straight to Paradise when they die," Adrian replied, stomping his boot onto the shovel's edge to really dig it down. "Most of them don't even bother with graves, but this one married a scale-eyed Catholic woman who was pious enough to demand a proper funeral and put his obituary in the paper, thus providing us with a rare opportunity."

Iggs looked more horrified than ever. "Are you going to interrogate his ghost?"

"Of course not," Adrian said, flinging dirt over his shoulder. "His soul passed on ages ago. I'm going to question his bones."

This didn't seem to make Iggs any happier, but he got back to shoveling without further complaint.

Between Iggs's strength and Adrian's skill at digging, it took only half an hour to reach the casket six feet down. Clearing off enough dirt to actually open the lid took another fifteen minutes, but the corpse inside was in marvelous condition. It had skeletonized nicely, leaving only a few bits of flesh and hair attached to the skull when Adrian pulled it out.

"Ugh," said Iggs, cringing away. "What do you even need this guy for?"

"Information," Adrian replied, reaching out of the hole for his coat to retrieve a plastic bag, which he then wrapped carefully around the skull. "Knowledge of the Anchors seems to be a secret kept strictly to Gilgamesh's faithful, and unlike living sorcerers, a skull can't throw spells at me during an interrogation."

"Are you still on about that?" Iggs groaned, stabbing his shovel into the ground. "I keep telling you you're wasting your time. Bex is never going to agree to attack an Anchor."

"Actually, she already did," Adrian said, trying his best not to sound smug. "I explained my logic to her when she called this morning. She and Lys are already on their way back to Seattle."

Iggs's jaw was hanging open by the time he finished. "Bex said that to you?"

When Adrian nodded, the demon looked insulted. "Why didn't she call me? I'm supposed to be her point man in Seattle!"

"We were discussing magic," Adrian hedged to avoid admitting that Bex called him every night. Not because he was ashamed—their nightly conversations had quickly become the thing he looked forward to most—but because he didn't want Iggs thinking Bex had gone over his head. The demon *was* her point man in the city. Bex called Iggs all the time to discuss the safe houses they were setting up and how many new demons she was sending his way. She just called Adrian more.

That thought made him smile. Bex had been a fascinating puzzle from the moment he'd hired her, but getting to know her personally was something altogether more exciting. It wasn't anything he could put a name on yet, but Adrian liked the direction they were headed, which made tonight's business all the more important. He wanted to have something concrete to show off to her when she got back, so he climbed out of the hole to tuck the plastic-wrapped skull into his coat and got to work shoveling the mound of dirt back on top of the casket.

"Wait!" Iggs cried as earth began to rain down. "Don't you need the rest of him?"

"Nope," Adrian replied as he shoveled in another pile. "We're asking him questions, not inviting him to dance. A skull should be plenty for our needs, unless you want to deal with an entire skeleton?"

Iggs shook his head and got back to work, flinging dirt into the hole even faster than Adrian.

"I just hope you remember how to make it talk," Boston said, trotting to the edge of the pit they'd dug. "We can't exactly call home for help. Not after..."

Adrian sighed as the cat's voice trailed off. As his familiar, Boston's first loyalty was to Adrian, but while he would always follow his witch, he'd made it clear that he thought defying a direct order from the Old Wife of the Bones was a colossal mistake. Adrian didn't agree, which put them at odds.

It wasn't anywhere they hadn't been before. Agreeing to disagree was a cornerstone of their relationship, but this time was particularly frustrating. Adrian knew Boston was just trying to look out for him, but his normally brilliant cat seemed fundamentally unable to understand that crawling back to the Blackwood wasn't safety. It was just another prison, the same prison Adrian had come to Seattle to escape. They were all stuck under Gilgamesh's boot until someone flung it off, and with Bex in his corner, Adrian was in the perfect position to do so. He'd just have to keep going and hope that enough victories would make Boston see that eventually.

"How'd you find this guy, anyway?" Iggs asked, breaking the awkward silence. "It's not like his wife put his profession in the paper, right?"

"Of course not," Adrian said. "She probably had no idea what he actually did for a living. I only figured it out when I noticed Mr. Keller's name popping up next to a ton of spells in the sorcery database."

Iggs stopped shoveling to gape at him. "How did *you* get access to Gilgamesh's sorcery database?"

"I might have become a vocal commenter on the sorcery subreddit," Adrian replied smugly. "Their stuff looks like gobbledygook to normal humans, so sorcerers can get pretty blasé about secrecy on the internet. They're also prideful to a fault. All I had to do was imply that one of the moderators was lying about having spells published in the database, and he let me right in so I could see his genius for myself. Once I got access, I started checking every name I saw against the local obituaries until I found our guy."

Iggs whistled. "Nice work."

"Patience is the foundation of witchcraft," Adrian said with a smile, hopping back into the grave to stomp the latest layer of dirt they'd tossed in flat. "Help me pack down the ground layer. Once it's stable, I'll throw some grass over the top, and we'll be good to go."

Iggs started working double time at the mention of leaving. He had the rest of the hole filled up in minutes, using his giant boots to stomp down the dirt while Adrian put his hat and coat back on. When the grave was refilled to Adrian's satisfaction, he pulled some grass seed out of his pocket and tossed it over the upturned soil. A splash of water invigorated with an echo of the Blackwood's magic from his root-bound heart got it sprouting nicely, so Adrian left the rest to nature. He'd just gotten Bran into crow form to fly them back to Bainbridge when Iggs handed him his growler.

"If all we were doing was digging up a skull, what's the beer for?"

"The next step," Adrian answered, taking the jug reverently.

When the alcohol was secure in his arms and Iggs was seated behind him with Boston in his lap, Adrian assumed his usual position at the giant raven's head and tapped his foot, signaling his broom to rise silently into the clear night sky.

An hour later, it was full dark with a good moonrise, and Adrian was almost ready to begin.

He was standing at the center of his forest, which hadn't grown too much taller in the month since the Blackwood had stitched his heart back together and saved him from death, but had definitely gotten denser. The huge trees were more fluffed out, the moss thicker and greener, the animals bolder and more numerous. All that lushness and vitality made it the perfect environment for practicing his preferred craft, which unfortunately made it completely *in*appropriate for tonight's exercise.

"Okay," he said, plucking the final blade of grass out of the circle of barren dirt he'd been picking clean for the last forty minutes. "Time to be a Witch of the Bones."

"It's not too late to call your cousin," Boston called from outside the ring of red wax candles Adrian had set up around the deceased sorcerer's head. "She apprenticed under your Aunt Lydia, and skulls are her specialty."

"So is snooping," Adrian reminded him. "But I don't need to call anyone. A Blackwood witch is a master of all three branches, and I'm much better with the bones than the soul."

"Your divination *is* dreadful," Boston agreed, trotting over to take his position on the opposite side of the circle. "Ready when you are."

Adrian nodded and reached down to grab his growler. He walked around the candles in a slow circle, pouring the dark, frothy beer onto the ring of barren ground around the skull until the jug was nearly empty. He drank the last few swallows himself, focusing on how delicious, high quality, and—most importantly for a spell invoking a sorcerer—*expensive* the gallon of craft porter was.

When the final drop was gone, Adrian set the empty jug down on the ground with a *thunk*. He got on his knees beside it a moment later, reaching out to rub his fingers through the beer-soaked dirt, which he then rubbed across the skull. He had to rack his brain to remember the right motions, but he must have gotten close enough, because no sooner had he pulled back his hands than the skull at the circle's center began to shake.

"...at's all this, then?" it rattled, pivoting on its jaw before its empty sockets locked onto Adrian. "Who are you? Where's Mary?"

"Your wife said I could ask you a few questions," Adrian lied. "I'm a new sorcerer, and I was hoping to get a leg up on the competition by seeking the wisdom of the great Jason Keller."

That was a cheap way to open. Actual Witches of the Bones didn't need to resort to psychological tricks like this, but Adrian was moonlighting hard, and after reading everything he could find of the late Jason Keller's work online, he'd decided blatant flattery was the safest way to go.

It seemed to be working so far. The moment Adrian invoked his name, the skull perked right up, its face somehow managing to look gloating despite the complete lack of soft tissue.

"Well, well, my boy, if it's wisdom you want, you've come to the right place," Keller's skull said grandly. "Come closer, then, and let's have a look at you."

That was legitimately impossible. Whatever Iggs had muttered about seances and hauntings while Adrian was setting up, talking to a skull was nothing like talking to a ghost. Unlike the soul, bones couldn't think or acquire new information. They were pure memory, able only to ape what they'd already done in life. Even if its eyeballs had still been in their sockets, there was no magic in the world that could make this skull actually *see* Adrian. The bones still remembered seeing, though, and since he'd opened with such a flattering lie, the sorcerer's skull saw exactly what it wanted to.

"It's nice to finally meet a young man with some sense," Keller said with an approving nod. "Young sorcerers have gotten so cocky these days, always looking to reinvent the wheel, never listening to those of us who've already been there and done that. Fools, the lot of them, but you show promise. Now, what can I help you with?"

Adrian's smile slid into a smirk, and since the skull couldn't actually see him, he didn't bother to fix it. "It's a bit of a dream of mine, really," he said with all the hopeful wistfulness of a young man confessing his life's ambition. "I've just been informed that I'm under consideration for a position at the Seattle Anchor."

"Congratulations," the skull said with all apparent sincerity. "Anchor work is the most prestigious of all the magical professions. You'll be serving the Eternal King directly. How did you do on the written exam?"

"Well enough," Adrian hedged since this was the first he'd heard about an exam. "But I'm nervous about the next phase. Competition is fierce, and I know so little about what actually goes on at the Anchors."

"Naturally," the skull said, turning up the empty space where its nose used to be. "No one knows Anchor methodology before they're initiated. I was totally ignorant myself when I got my first position as a Chain Engineer."

"That's why I'm hoping you'll help," Adrian said with real eagerness. "Is there any information you can give me that would make it easier to impress the interviewers? For example, what do the Anchors anchor? Is Heaven going to fly away if it's not held down?"

He paused, waiting for the ridiculousness of that question to drive the dead sorcerer into an explanatory frenzy. None of the sorcerers he'd met online could stand it when anyone in their proximity was wrong, but to his great amazement—and even greater disappointment—the skull's jaw stayed shut.

"Can't you tell me anything?" Adrian pleaded. "Just one hint—"

"If you truly deserve to work at an Anchor, you won't need hints," Keller said with an air of insufferable superiority. "I certainly didn't get any, and I was the best Anchor manager on the west coast when I retired."

"But—"

"*No,*" the skull snapped, knocking one of its teeth out in the process. "The Anchors are the closest to Heaven we can get here on earth. Knowledge of their mysteries is a blessing that must be earned. Your questions will be answered when you are judged worthy and not a minute sooner. I certainly won't be saying anything. Do you know how hard I had to work for my position?"

Adrian rubbed his hands over his face with a completely legitimate sigh of frustration.

"Can you at least tell me who I need to impress?" he asked, trying a different angle. "The identities of the Anchor sorcerers are as guarded as the Anchor itself. I only know about you because you'd already retired and published your career retrospective, which was brilliant, by the way."

The skull nodded in acknowledgment.

"If you could tell me who's in charge now, I'd be able to study their work ahead of time," Adrian pressed on. "Your generation of sorcerers was known for its brilliance. If you showed me where to look, I'm sure I'd learn something impressive."

"You should learn for learning's sake," Keller scolded, "but I admire your ambition. We need sorcerers who do more than sit around in their towers and argue on the internet. If you're *really* serious about improving your understanding of the divine poetry, I suggest looking up the work of Dr. Hank Yearling."

Adrian couldn't write the name down fast enough. "Is he on the Anchor committee?"

"He was running the whole thing when I retired," the skull said. "Excellent sorcerer, Yearling. Threw fantastic cocktail parties, though he did tend to overuse the Seven Stanzas of Shaping. I kept telling him there were other verses better suited to..."

Keller was still going, but Adrian was no longer listening. He'd already whipped out his phone to look up Dr. Hank Yearling. Being both retired and five years dead, Keller's information was very likely out of date. That said, positions as important as head of an Anchor didn't seem like the sort that turned over often. He just needed a little bit of luck and—

There!

Adrian jumped back to his feet. There were two Dr. Yearlings with entries in the sorcery database, but only one of them mentioned Seattle in his bio. His profile picture was a refined-looking man in his fifties, though he could

have just as easily been ninety from what Adrian knew of
sorcerers. He didn't have "Anchor Director" listed next to
his name or anything so obvious, but all the spells he'd
published to the database's professional listings in the last
decade were marked as restricted, meaning that whatever
Yearling was doing with his career, Gilgamesh didn't want it
known.

That sounded Anchory enough to Adrian. Grinning
like a maniac, he reached down and tipped the still-talking
skull onto its side, cutting off a long-winded story about
Keller's own career beginnings midword. That rudeness
would have been a problem if the sorcerer had still been
alive, but bones never remembered anything that
happened to them postdeath. If Adrian needed to talk to
Keller again, they'd be starting the relationship over from
scratch no matter what, so he skipped the pleasantries and
shoved the skull back into its plastic bag, pausing only to
blow out the candles before rushing into his house.

He came out again a minute later carrying a large
paper sack full of peanuts still in their shells. Even this late
in the evening, the sound of the rustling bag brought the
local crows out of their roosts. By the time Adrian made it
to the bottom of his porch steps, he was surrounded by a
squawking flock.

"Ah, ah, ah, not yet," he said, keeping the bag of
peanuts pressed defensively against his chest. "There's a job
I need done."

He turned on his phone and used his fingers to zoom
in until the illuminated screen was filled with the profile
picture of Dr. Hank Yearling.

"I need you to find and follow this man," he said,
setting the glowing phone down on the ground so the crows
could look at it. "I want to know his movements throughout

the day: where he goes, where he sleeps, where he eats, all of it. Bring whatever you find to Boston. He'll translate."

"Hey!" Boston cried, loping over from where he'd been collecting candles. "I didn't volunteer to be your crow interpreter!"

"Do this as quickly as you can," Adrian went on as if the cat hadn't spoken. "Bring me good information, and you will be well rewarded."

To prove his point, he turned the paper bag upside down, dumping three pounds of peanuts onto the ground around his phone. This kicked off a feeding frenzy of epic proportions, forcing Boston to flee up Adrian's coat to avoid the beating wings and snapping beaks. Adrian couldn't actually see his phone screen through the chaos, but he was certain the crows could. They knew where their peanuts came from, and as soon as the ground was picked clean, they took off, squawking at each other as they winged their way through the night in the direction of the mainland.

"Why did you send them out so late?" Boston asked, hopping off Adrian's shoulder. "If this Yearling actually does hold a high position at the Anchor, he's probably in bed by now."

"Yes, but the crows will be spreading the word all night," Adrian said, bending over to reclaim his phone from the litter of empty peanut shells. "By sunrise, every crow in Seattle will know this face"—he tapped the picture that was still on his phone—"equals peanuts, and there's almost nothing a crow won't do for a peanut."

"Then I hope you're stocked up," Boston said as they went back into the house. "Because if you actually get every crow in Seattle, you're going to need a lot more than three pounds of—"

"Mr. Witch?"

Adrian jumped a foot in the air. Boston jumped even higher, nearly hitting the porch's wooden roof. His sharp claws dug into his witch's coat as he landed, pinning them together as Adrian whirled around to see Nemini standing right behind him.

"Great Forest," Boston gasped, collapsing onto Adrian's shoulder. "Don't *do* that!"

"There's no reason to be afraid," the demon told him gently. "Even if I meant you harm, death is inevitable for all beings, and there's no sense worrying about the inevitable."

Boston growled low in his throat, and Adrian decided he'd better move this along before his cat said something regrettable.

"Is there something you need, Nemini?"

"All needs are ego," the demon said with a shrug that caused the nest of snakes that formed her hair to hiss and slither. "I'm here because there's someone on the road."

"Is it Bex?" Adrian asked. Not that he actually thought Nemini would come to him like this if it was, but Bex was the only arrival he was expecting tonight.

Sure enough, the void demon shook her head. "It's a human woman. She asked for you by name."

That made Adrian go very still. "What does she look like?"

It was probably his imagination, but he swore Nemini smiled just a fraction.

"She looks like you."

Chapter 3

"**D**o you think it's one of your sisters?" Iggs asked eagerly, keeping pace with Adrian as he jogged through the dark forest toward the road.

"That's my guess," Adrian said, more curtly than usual.

That was rude considering how swiftly Iggs had shut down his video game and vaulted out of the nest he'd made for himself in Adrian's office to come along, but Adrian could have done without an audience tonight. After how he'd ended things with Aunt Lydia, it didn't take a Witch of the Future to guess this wasn't going to be a happy visit. The only reason he'd brought Iggs was because he'd promised Bex that none of them would go outside the Blackwood alone. Now that the big demon was here, though, Adrian could also admit it was nice to have backup—just in case.

"I hope it's not one of Lydia's apprentices," Boston whispered from his perch on his witch's shoulder. "They can be... upsetting."

That was one way of putting it, but Adrian didn't think he'd be lucky enough to get an apprentice. He was readying his forest to yank them back inside if things got dicey when he stepped out of the thick line of trees that marked the Blackwood's boundary to see a woman standing by herself in the middle of the road.

It looked like she'd dropped out of the sky. She had no car, no broom. If she hadn't been wearing the same black pointed hat as him, Adrian would have thought she was a local out for a nighttime stroll. It was too dark to make out her face at first, but as Adrian shuffled down the embankment, the moon came out from behind a cloud, revealing the truth.

"Mom?"

Even as he said the word, Adrian didn't believe it. His mother never left the Blackwood. *Ever.* For any reason. It was impossible, yet there she was, smiling at him the same way she had two months ago when she walked him to the forest's edge and sent him off to catch his plane.

"Hello, Adrian."

"Holy crap," Iggs said at the same time, gripping Adrian's arm. "That's your *mom*?"

Adrian shrugged helplessly. There wasn't anything else he could do. She might be called the Old Wife of the Flesh, but Agatha of the Blackwood was famously one of the most beautiful women on the planet.

Like her sister Lydia, she had piercing blue eyes and paper-pale skin. Unlike the wizened Witch of the Past, however, the Witch of the Present radiated vitality. Her round cheeks were pinked with life, and her bright eyes sparkled with hidden laughter. Her long hair was the same black as Adrian's, but where his was curly and unruly, hers fell as smooth and shiny as obsidian around her shoulders. Her practical black linen dress did nothing to hide a figure that had inspired countless volumes of erotic poetry, and her movements were as graceful as a dancer's when she reached up to pinch Adrian's cheek.

"You're thinner," she said disapprovingly. "Are you not growing enough food?"

"I have plenty of food, Mom," Adrian said, disentangling himself. "What are you doing out on the street alone? Where are your apprentices?"

"Oh, here and there," she answered in the dreamy, unconcerned voice that still drove him slightly crazy. "But I don't need an entourage to visit my son, or my favorite tomcat." Her smile widened as she reached up to pet the feline on his shoulder. "Hello, Boston."

Boston answered with a purr that rumbled through his entire body, and Adrian stepped back with a scowl.

"Stop buttering up my familiar," he ordered, moving Boston out of his mother's reach, much to the cat's dismay. "If you're here to tell me to go home, you can save your breath, because I'm not—"

"Adrian!" his mother cried, her lovely face appalled. "I would never impede your freedom. I'm here because I wanted to see you and your new forest. Now stop being rude and introduce me to your friends."

She leaned sideways to smile at the demons, both of whom Adrian had just now realized were standing on the road behind him. Nemini must have hopped down from the trees at some point when he was distracted, but while the void demon appeared the same as ever, Iggs looked like someone who'd just tasted cake for the very first time.

"Hello, ma'am," he said before Adrian could get a word out, shoving his way forward. "I'm Iggs. I saved Adrian's life."

"Then I am forever in your debt," Agatha said, her blue eyes shining through her dark lashes as she took the demon's offered hand in both of hers. "I like your horns."

The compliment had Iggs bouncing giddily on his heels, and Adrian decided he'd better move this along before the demon got any more wrapped around his mother's finger.

"This is Nemini," he said quickly, waving his hand at the snake-haired void demon, who was staring at Agatha with the same impassive, yellow-eyed look she gave everyone. "They're two of the four demons that helped me defeat the Spider's warlocks."

"Ah yes, Lydia told me about that," Agatha said, dragging her eyes off of Iggs's muscles to give Adrian a frown. "She's very cross with you, you know."

"I know," he said, lifting his chin. "But I'm not sorry."

"And that's why I'm *not* cross with you," his mother replied, letting go of Iggs at last to wrap her arms around her son with a beaming smile. "Oh, darling, I'm so proud of you! You took a stand for what you thought was right and stuck by your forest just like a witch should. Though I do wish you hadn't locked your roots against us. Even when we disagree, we're still family."

Adrian hadn't been trying to keep out his family. He'd had to lock his forest against *everything* because it was dangerous to leave openings when you were being hunted by princes, which was also why they shouldn't be standing out here in the open. Before he could explain that to his mother, however, a pair of headlights came around the bend.

The sudden flash was blinding in the dark forest. From the spacing and the height, they looked like the lights on a truck, but while Adrian, Iggs, and Nemini all stepped off the road, Agatha didn't budge.

This sent Adrian into a small panic. Despite how she looked, his mother was quite old, and she hadn't left the Blackwood in a *very* long time. He wasn't sure if she knew what a truck was, but she'd resist him on principle if Adrian tried to pull her out of the way. He was scrambling to come up with the right words to convince her to step off the road on her own when the truck screeched to a halt, and he realized it wasn't a truck at all. It was the RV, and the moment it slowed down, Bex leaped out.

Adrian jumped. They'd only been apart for a few weeks, but that was still long enough to forget how fast she was. His eyes had barely tracked her swinging out of the passenger-side window before Bex was standing on the road in front of him with the point of her black sword pressed against Agatha's neck.

"Who are you?"

The question was deadly, but Agatha just smiled. "I'm Adrian's mother," she replied sweetly, looking Bex square in her burning eyes. "And you're the missing queen."

Adrian felt Bex go still, and he took the chance to scramble in front of her. This put his shoulder dangerously close to the edge of Bex's smoking sword, but he'd much rather she cut him than his mother. Unlike Agatha, Adrian wouldn't bite back.

"It's okay, Bex," he said quickly, giving her a desperate look over his shoulder that he prayed she'd interpret as *Play along*. "Mom isn't here to drag me home. This is just a visit." He looked back at Agatha. "Right?"

"Only a visit," his mother promised, watching Bex with keen interest as the queen lowered her sword and stepped back to the edge of the road where Iggs and Nemini had already moved in to flank her. "Though I must say I'm delighted by the protective display. A mother likes to know her son is well taken care of."

Bex's eyebrows shot up at the innuendo in her voice, and Adrian winced. He briefly considered explaining that his mother always made things sound inappropriate, but that would only encourage her to do it more, so he let the whole thing go with a sigh and set about pretending he hadn't heard.

"Mother," he said formally. "This is Bex, the Queen of Wrath. Bex, this is Agatha, Witch of the Present and one of the three Old Wives of the Blackwood."

Bex stiffened slightly when she realized who she'd been threatening. Fortunately, Agatha seemed more interested in Bex's demons than in punishing slights.

Particularly, she was watching Lys, who seemed to have gotten stuck coming out of the RV and was now staring at Adrian's mother with an expression that was half horror, half dumbstruck awe.

"It seems you're doing *very* well for yourself," his mother said in a voice that made the hairs on the back of Adrian's neck prickle. "But delightful as the company is, I didn't come all this way to stand in the road. Take me inside, darling, and let's see this forest of yours."

Adrian wasn't feeling up for a tour, but there was no telling his mother no, and getting out of the street was a good idea for everyone. So, with a resigned sigh, he held out his arm to his mother, mentally nudging the trees aside to make a path as he led the way into his Blackwood.

"Well," Lys said in a shaking voice, "that's one way to come home."

Bex said nothing. She was too busy squeezing the steering wheel, staring through the windshield at the woman Adrian was leading up the hill. The terrifying, impossibly beautiful, impossibly *powerful* woman who was apparently his mother.

"Did you know his mom was the witch in charge of the entire Blackwood?" she snapped at Iggs, who was crouching on the floor between the RV's front seats.

"No," Iggs said in a dreamy voice. "She's so *pretty*."

"Too pretty," Lys muttered, peeking out from behind Bex's headrest like a spooked cat. "May I be excused?"

"Why?" Bex asked suspiciously.

Lys bit their lip. "You know when you see something that's *too* good? Something you instinctively know you need to stay away from, because if you get one taste, you'll be hooked forever?" They nodded at the Witch of the Present. "That's what I'm seeing, and if I don't remove myself from this situation right now, you're going to be down one lust demon."

Bex sighed and waved her hand. Lys was gone before she finished, shooting down the stairs to their room. This left Bex with only Iggs and Nemini, and since it was clear her wrath demon wasn't going to be good for anything for a while, she turned to the snake-headed woman sitting in the RV's passenger seat.

"What the hell was going on back there?"

"The usual," the void demon replied, holding out her dark-skinned hand to catch the leaves that were scraping over their RV. "Time passed, the slow decay of entropy continued unabated, bringing the universe that much closer to the inevitable end."

Bex squeezed the steering wheel a little tighter. "I meant why were you all standing out in the road with Adrian's mom?"

Nemini shrugged her narrow shoulders. "She said she was here for a visit."

Bullshit. The Old Wives of the Blackwood were the last great independent magical force on the planet. They still existed because their Blackwood was too dangerous for even Gilgamesh to mess with casually, but all those defenses meant nothing if one-third of their ruling council decided to go traipsing across the country.

There was no way one of the world's greatest witches would take a risk like that for no reason. Bex knew that one of Adrian's relatives had tried to make him go home during the prince fight last month, but he hadn't volunteered many details, and she hadn't wanted to pry. If he was the son of one of their leaders, though, that explained everything. A normal witch moving to Seattle was one thing, but an heir off on his own was a massive security vulnerability, and the Blackwood hadn't survived this long by letting those run loose. His mother must be here to collect him. That sneaky witch was probably luring him into the woods right now so she could—

Bex forced her runaway thoughts to stop, slumping down in her seat as the dark trees scraped past her window. This was stupid. She'd seen firsthand how powerful Adrian was inside his forest. No one could force him to do anything he didn't want to in here, and he certainly hadn't looked afraid. If anything, he'd seemed embarrassed that Bex had brought a sword into a friendly conversation.

Bex was embarrassed too. She'd flipped into kill mode the moment she'd seen her demons backing Adrian against a strange witch on the road, but the only emergency was her own paranoia. Adrian's mom was probably here for no more nefarious purpose than she was his *mom* and she loved him. Bex was the one who was too twisted up inside to understand something so simple.

You're not twisted, Drox said. *You are Ishtar's Sword, the last defender of her people. It is your nature to see threats and act upon them. I thought you made a credible security assessment when you put yourself between an unknown threat and your soldiers.*

For the first time in her life, Drox's approval didn't make Bex feel better. She normally liked when he reminded her that she was a sword because a sword's job was simple. Up until a month ago, Bex's biggest issue had been not being a good enough sword. That wasn't a problem anymore, thanks to Adrian, but when she looked at him walking arm in arm through his lovely forest with his lovely mother who'd cared enough to cross the entire country for him, all Bex could think about was how much she didn't fit into that picture.

The thought depressed her far more than it should have. One of the best parts about being the Queen of Wrath was that she'd never had to wonder where she belonged. Bex had known her duty for as long as she could remember. She struggled constantly to live up to it, but she'd never wanted to be anything else. All those late-night phone calls with Adrian must have done more damage than she'd realized, though, because for the first time in her life, Bex wondered what it'd be like to *not* be queen. To not have to fight and plot and see every shadow as a threat. To not greet Adrian's mom with a sword because that was her first instinct toward *everything*.

Don't be ridiculous, Drox scoffed. *That instinct is why you're still alive.*

"I know," Bex muttered, glancing at Nemini, who was still staring at the woods. "I'm just saying it might be nice to have something in my life other than war."

You have plenty aside from war, her sword assured her. *You have loyal subjects and a righteous cause, and when this is over, you shall have victory! You will return your people to Paradise in glory and rule over them forever as Ishtar made you to do.*

That was the dream. But when Bex thought of going home now, all her traitorous brain could think about was how Adrian wouldn't be going with her, and suddenly, that didn't sound much like paradise at all.

She could already feel Drox's anger spiking at that, so Bex took off her ring and dropped it into the RV's cupholder, silencing her sword before he could tell her anything she didn't already know.

Showing off his forest to his mother was both nostalgic and incredibly bizarre. Adrian had demonstrated his work constantly back when he'd been her apprentice, but even when he was the one who'd grown the trees, the forest had always belonged to the Three. Now, though, it was Adrian's own land they walked through, and it seemed determined to make a good impression.

Silvery moonlight streamed down through the canopy, bouncing across the burbling creeks and shimmering off the backs of owls as they swooped silently overhead. Thanks to the soundproofing measures he'd put in to disrupt Gilgamesh's bells, Adrian couldn't even hear the RV crunching along behind them. There was only forest: a beautiful, silvery, whispering wood flourishing at the end of summer.

"You always did grow lovely groves," his mother said wistfully, trailing her hands over the ferns that reached up to touch her. "I couldn't have done it better myself. Well done, Adrian."

Those were not idle words. His mother could be a shameless flatterer, but when it came to their craft, she was every bit as exacting as her sisters. A year ago, praise like that would have sent Adrian floating into the air. Now, it only carved his frown deeper.

"Why are you really here, Mom?" he asked, touching a pair of red flowering currants until the shrubs got the message and moved out of their path.

His mother brushed her fingers over the flower-covered branches with a smile. "Do I need an ulterior motive to visit my son?"

"No, but it's never stopped you from having one."

She laughed, a beautiful, silvery sound. "Sharp as ever, I see," she said, patting Adrian's coat sleeve. "I came here because I was legitimately curious. It's been a long, long time since we had a male Blackwood, and I wanted to see it for myself. But you're right, that isn't the only reason."

Adrian nodded and waited for her to go on, but his mother just kept walking, touching every shrub and tree all the way to the top of the hill. She insisted on seeing his house and garden as well, quizzing him over every plant choice and placement just as she had when he'd been her student. She spent a full ten minutes inspecting his heart tree, going over the Douglas fir's short needles one by one with a focused scowl.

By the time she started asking questions about the curses he'd used against the warlocks, Adrian felt like he was being put through the coven trials all over again. He was exhausted and impatient, but he'd been Agatha's student for almost as long as he'd been her son, and he knew it was pointless to rush her. The present could not be hurried. It could only be, which left him with no choice but to wait it out until, at last, his mother turned to face him.

"You've certainly met all my expectations," she said, smiling at him in the moonlight. "I'm happy to see you doing so well. I've been worried about you."

"I've been worried about me too," Adrian admitted, brushing the branches of his heart tree back into position. "But it's worth it. I know this is what I have to do."

"And that's why I haven't tried to stop you," Agatha said, reaching out to take his hand. "It's also why I came tonight. I wanted us to walk together like we used to, to see you once more before things changed too much."

Adrian scowled. It wasn't like his mother to speak of the past or the future, but before he could ask her what was wrong, Agatha stepped away.

She changed as she went. There was no grand transformation. She was still his mother, lovely and smiling in the blue-white moonlight, but when she met his eyes again, her face was no longer loving. It was cruel—the cold, hard, all-knowing visage of the Witch of the Present.

"I bring a message from my sister Muriel," she said in a voice that rang with all that was. "The Witch of the Future bade me tell you that when you see the crow, you should follow it."

The words of the prophecy rolled over him like boulders. As usual with such pronouncements, though, Adrian didn't understand.

"Which crow?" he asked. "I've got a lot of them out at the moment."

"I'm sure you'll know it when you see it," Agatha said, her motherly mask slipping back into place as she rose up on her toes to kiss his cheek. "It's going to get harder from here, Adrian, but always remember that you are a witch of the Blackwood. Just as no tree in a wood grows alone, you can never be truly separated from us. No matter how far away you go or how lost you feel, the forest will always be with you. Never forget that, my darling."

"Never," Adrian promised, but though she'd said them with love this time, the words still tied a knot in his stomach. "What's going to happen?"

The Witch of the Present didn't answer. She just gave him one last smile as she held up her hand to the owl that had been silently swooping overhead. The birds were so common in his woods these days Adrian hadn't even noticed that this wasn't one of his usual screech or barred varieties but a great horned owl the size of a toddler. It alighted on Agatha's fingers as silently as moonlight, and then the giant owl vanished, leaving behind his mother's broom.

Hers had been carved with an owl instead of a raven, but otherwise, it was the twin of Adrian's Bran. Both had been made by his Aunt Lydia, but where Adrian's broomstick still looked like fresh-cut wood, his mother's was ancient, the handle worn into grooves that fit her hands perfectly when she sat down.

"Take care, my little witchling!" she called as the broom lifted her into the sky. "And be careful with the queen. She's going to need your help. Don't abandon her!"

"Why would I do that?" Adrian yelled, but his mother was already gone, flying as silently as her owl into the night.

"That was more cryptic than usual," Boston observed from his shoulder.

It was, and that worried him. His mother had never been as straightforward as Aunt Lydia, but this was pushing it even for her. Something very important must be about to happen for her to deliver a prophecy in person. As with everything involving his Aunt Muriel, though, Adrian had no idea what.

"This is why I don't like witchcraft of the soul," he muttered as he stomped back toward his house. "It never makes any damn sense."

"At least she warned you," Boston said, hopping off his shoulder.

There was no "at least" about it. In Adrian's experience, Aunt Muriel's warnings were equally as likely to push you into trouble as pull you out, but there was nothing he could do. The only thing more dangerous than taking advice from the Witch of the Future was ignoring it. He just hoped this crow he was supposed to follow was obvious, because his record for solving his aunt's riddles wasn't very—

A sound at the edge of his hearing stopped him short. He'd been so busy with his mom he hadn't noticed that the demons had parked their RV back in its usual position across the clearing from his house. It was very late now, and the Winnebago was shuttered and dark. But just as he was starting to despair that he'd missed his chance to welcome Bex home, he spotted her sitting on her favorite tree branch just like she used to back when she'd worked as his security.

The familiar sight made him smile. Boston had already trotted into the house, but Adrian veered off the path at the last second, walking across the clearing instead to grin up at the queen.

"Missed your old perch?"

"Someone has to keep watch," Bex replied, sliding off the branch and falling fifty feet to land neatly in front of him.

That made him smile even bigger. He hadn't noticed before with everything going on, but now that Bex was standing in front of him, Adrian saw that she was wearing the clothes she'd bought during their shopping trip the day after the prince's attack. It was all still black, but her loose canvas pants actually fit her now, and her V-neck shirt was well cut, showing off her athletic figure beneath her ever-present leather jacket. Her long black hair fell loose and shiny around her horns, and the moonlight made her already pale skin glow like alabaster where it wasn't warmed by the firelight of her eyes.

It was enough to steal the breath right out of his lungs. Seeing her like this, Adrian understood why Iggs and his cousins had climbed a tree just to catch a glimpse. Bex really did look like the daughter of a goddess. But while Iggs had treated that with holy awe, Adrian eagerly leaned closer, breathing in the warm, fiery smell of her that he'd missed far more than he'd realized.

"I'm sorry about earlier."

"What?" he asked, blinking out of the daze she'd put him in.

"I'm sorry I pulled a sword on your mom," Bex said, dropping her glowing eyes with a scowl as she pushed a lock of smooth, shiny hair behind her ear. "I've been fighting a lot recently, which makes me react badly to surprises, and I... I'm just sorry."

"You have nothing to be sorry for," Adrian assured her. "My mom took no offense, and I was quite flattered."

Bex shot him a skeptical look, but Adrian just smiled. "Welcome home, by the way."

Her eyes widened at the words, and then she looked away again, her pale face going oddly dark in the moonlight.

"I'm glad to be back," she muttered, taking a sudden interest in the roots by her feet. "Thank you for letting Iggs stay at your place while we were gone. He told me you took him drinking?"

When Adrian nodded, she winced. "I'm sorry about that too, then. I'll pay you back."

"No need," Adrian said. "I brought Iggs along for my own selfish reasons. I needed somewhere to put all that extra beer, and he was a very eager bucket."

Bex laughed, forcing him to take another breath. Great Forest, she was pretty when she did that.

"What did you need beer for, anyway?" she asked, leaning against the tree trunk. "Iggs said something about you talking to a skull."

"A sorcerer's skull," Adrian replied proudly. "And while I didn't learn what I wanted, I did get a good lead. I won't know how good until my crows come back, but that's tomorrow's problem."

"I should let you rest, then," Bex said, settling more comfortably against the tree. "You get some sleep. I'll keep watch out here."

He shook his head. "My forest watches itself these days, and it's not your job to be my guard anymore."

"Somebody's gotta do it," Bex said stubbornly, but Adrian was already holding out his arm.

"Come inside," he coaxed. "I haven't had dinner yet, and I want to hear about California."

"There's not much left I haven't already told you," Bex said, looking at his sleeve as if it might contain a viper. "Are you sure you want to stay up? You got to work pretty early this morning."

"I'm positive," Adrian said. "I'm not missing our nightly conversation, especially now that I get to talk to you in person instead of over a phone."

Bex *definitely* blushed that time, but she took his offered arm with only a slight hesitation, letting Adrian lead her across the clearing into his brightly lit workshop.

Chapter 4

Bex woke up to sunlight streaming through her high windows.

On a normal day, that would have sent her vaulting out of bed in a panic over being late. Today, though, she just snuggled deeper into her comforter, staring up at the green leaves waving above the RV.

Hanging out with Adrian while he made dinner had turned into talking nearly all night with him. He'd insisted on making a plate for her as well even though Bex had already consumed her usual dinner of convenience-store sandwiches and whatever fruit they had in the basket by the register.

Of all the changes to her body, Bex resented her new need to eat the most. It was so inconvenient to have to stop and find food every few hours. The stuff she ate on the road didn't even taste good most of the time, but Adrian's cooking was different. She'd eaten his food just for the pleasure of it, then they'd sat on his front porch, talking and watching the moon as it crept across the sky. He'd been so close she'd been able to feel the warmth of his body through his coat, and when he smiled...

Her face broke into a stupid grin. Coming back was the best decision she'd ever made, and not just because of Adrian's plan to attack the Anchor, which they had talked about. Some business *had* been discussed, but Bex couldn't recall any of the details. All she remembered was that she'd been happy—giddily, ridiculously happy for no reason other than she'd been sitting next to him.

She was *still* happy. Bex didn't know what witchcraft Adrian put into his food, but the whole world looked brighter this morning. Even the black stains on her carpet didn't bother her like they usually did as she padded into her bathroom for a shower.

Unless she was cleaning up after a battle, Bex was usually in and out of the shower in under three minutes. Today, though, she took her time, washing her hair and buffing her black horns until they gleamed. She even used the fancy sugar scrub Lys had gotten her ages ago. Bex didn't understand how sugar made you clean, but it smelled nice, and she was in the mood for nice.

She hummed to herself as she toweled off and got dressed, choosing a purple shirt because Adrian had told her once that purple was her color. Lys had told her first, of course, but Bex had never noticed until today that they were right. It *did* make her skin glow, or maybe that was just her grin.

"Idiot," she told her reflection as she preened in the bathroom mirror, smiling so wide she could see her fangs as she grabbed her leather jacket off the towel hook and headed downstairs.

The main floor of the RV was empty when she got there. Nemini's book was in its usual place on the table, but the demon herself was nowhere to be seen. Norma was still deactivated from when Bex had taken over to drive them into the forest. They wouldn't be going anywhere for a while, so Bex left the construct off, leaning into the RV's empty cab to retrieve her black ring from the cupholder. She popped it back on out of habit, but when she turned around to head outside and see what everyone was up to, a roar of rage stabbed through her head like a spear.

WHAT DO YOU THINK YOU ARE DOING?

"Dammit, Drox!" Bex yelled, rubbing her temples. "Not so loud!"

You left me in a cupholder! the sword roared, biting down so hard that his ring drew blood. *Do you have any idea what could have happened?!*

"Not a damn thing," Bex snapped. "Because I can summon your ring to me from anywhere, and we're inside Adrian's Blackwood! There's nothing that can attack us in here."

That's the sort of thinking that gets you killed! Drox snarled, still gnawing on her finger. *A prince dropped into this exact clearing just a few weeks ago. Even if the witch has increased his security since then, you know perfectly well that a queen can never let down her guard!*

"Would you give it a rest?" Bex groaned. "There's nothing wrong with taking a night off once in a while, especially since *nothing happened*. Everything is fine. It doesn't deserve this level of freak-out."

You're right, Drox said in a cold, hard voice. *The fact that you actually believe that proves it deserves more.*

Bex rolled her eyes. "If you freak out any harder, we'll start stabbing the RV."

That was supposed to be a joke. Not that Drox ever got her jokes, but this was different. Her sword was radiating fury like nothing Bex had ever felt.

You are not taking this seriously, he growled. *We are at war, Rebexa! I know you are young, and I have done my best to be patient, but there is only so much negligence I can tolerate. Last night proved that things have officially gone too far. Your infatuation with the witch is clouding your judgment and putting us all in danger!*

"That's ridiculous."

Is it? Drox bit harder into her finger. *I am your sword, forged by the creator god Enki at Ishtar's request to serve only you. It is my duty, my* purpose *to help you be the best queen you can for your people, but I cannot do that when you sabotage yourself.*

"I'm not sabotaging myself!" Bex cried. "It was one night off!"

It was the biggest example yet of a disturbing pattern, Drox argued. *Have you forgotten that this is your last life? The fate of all Ishtar's children rides upon your now-mortal shoulders, but are you seeking out her enemies? Are you standing watch? Are you improving your skills for the fights to come? No! You're wasting your now very limited time sighing over a human. A human, Rebexa!*

"So what if he's human?" Bex demanded. "Have you forgotten what Adrian did for us?"

I have not, he said. *But you clearly have. You were given a miracle, a fire brought back from the ashes. I would have thought you'd be more committed to our fight than ever, considering what you gave up for it, but you forget your purpose and waste your time smiling and preening like a—*

"That's enough."

The quiet words came out with enough power to shake the RV. Even Drox was shocked into silence as Rebexa squeezed her fist, which was now a ball of white-hot fire.

"You're always telling me to act like a queen," she growled, "but a queen does not take orders from her sword. A queen does what she wants!"

A queen lives for her people!

"*I have lived for them!*" Bex cried. "I've lived and *died* one hundred and ninety-eight times for them! Up until a month ago, I spent all of *this* life doing nothing but living for my people. But, as you just pointed out, I don't get another reincarnation. This is now my *only* life, so in the few brief moments when we're not under attack, I would like the chance to actually live it!"

Selfish child! Drox roared through her mind. *You would choose idle, vacuous pleasure over your crown? Your sacred duty?*

"When have I ever not done my duty?" Bex demanded. "I'm the Queen of Wrath! Slayer of princes and soon to be death of kings! I have never once strayed from my path, and I never will, so I'll thank you to *shut up* before I cram you back in the cupholder."

I will never! her sword shouted. *I was forged to guard you from every foe, including yourself! I will* never *stay silent while you endanger our last chance at victory with this reckless, foolish, self-indulgent—*

Bex ripped off her ring. Drox fought the whole way, leaving bloody gouges down her finger, but Bex didn't care. She just shoved the buzzing ring into the pocket of her dark jeans and stormed out of the RV, throwing the door open with so much force, Iggs nearly fell out of the lawn chair he'd set up under the awning.

"What in the Nine Hells was that about?" he asked when he'd regained his balance.

"Nothing," Bex snarled, grabbing a leaf off the ground to wipe the black blood from her finger, which had already healed. "Where is everyone?"

"Nemini's watching the perimeter, Lys went into town to get breakfast, and Adrian's behind his house doing something with crows."

Hearing Adrian's name brought back a little of the good mood Drox had ruined. Bex was about to go see if the crows had found anything useful when Iggs spoke again.

"Are you okay?"

Bex looked over to see her demon watching her with a worried expression.

"I wasn't trying to eavesdrop," he said, lowering his red eyes. "But you got pretty loud in there, and I've never heard you yell at your sword like that before."

"Drox was out of line," Bex said, sliding her naked fist behind her back. "A sword's opinion isn't always what's best."

That made Iggs look even more nervous, but Bex stuck to her guns. She was sick of not getting a vote in her own existence. Drox expected her to act like one of Gilgamesh's doll princesses—a tireless, artificial monster—but Bex wasn't made of ivory and gold. She was flesh and blood, and as Adrian was always saying, this was her one precious life. Bex didn't see why making the most out of that and doing her duty as queen should be mutually exclusive. It wasn't as if she was going to stop fighting Gilgamesh because spending time with Adrian made her happy.

Feeling righteously justified, Bex put the whole mess out of her head and strode across the sunny clearing to find Adrian.

She heard what he was doing before she saw it. As Iggs had said, there were a *lot* of crows behind Adrian's house, and all of them were cawing at the top of their lungs. Bex knew Adrian had to be around somewhere, but she couldn't see anything through the storm of black feathers that had descended on the cottage's back garden. She was about to embark on a search when she heard Adrian call her name.

"Over here!" cried a crow-covered mass she'd thought was a young apple tree. Then the shape waved its arms, and the birds flew away to reveal Adrian standing with a giant bag full of peanuts under each elbow.

The gap was open for less than a second before more crows swarmed in.

"One at a time," Adrian told them sternly, batting the birds away. "I know you're eager, but I can't understand you when you're all talking at once. If you've got information, take it to Boston in the greenhouse. Once he notes it down, I'll feed you."

The crows croaked greedily and flew over to the glass-enclosed patio at the rear of Adrian's house, where Boston was sitting inside a wicker cage, presumably to protect him from the murder in the garden.

"I didn't know you could speak to crows," Bex said when Adrian was more or less debirded.

"I don't really," he admitted, shooing the last crow off his shoulders. "They're very vocal, but their logic is difficult for human minds to follow, and our ears aren't good enough to make out the subtle differences in their caws. That's why Boston has to be my interpreter. I can do the big stuff like 'peanut' and 'danger,' but he's the only one who can understand enough of the particulars to collect usable information."

That sounded promising. "Have you collected anything good?"

"Better than good," Adrian said as his face broke into an infectious grin. "We hit the jackpot! Turns out our target is a bird feeder. Throws bread to the seagulls on the pier every morning, which means they've been watching him for years. Sea birds are huge gossips, so the crows were able to get a full report."

"And?" Bex asked.

Adrian's grin got even bigger. "*And* if our Dr. Yearling isn't running the Seattle Anchor Market, he's definitely up to his eyebrows in it. Come look at this."

He led her over to one of the gravel paths that ran between his vegetable beds. The little stones were normally neat as a pin, but they were torn up this morning. Bex thought that was from the chaos of a billion crows fighting over peanuts, but as she got closer, she saw it was a map.

Scraped into the multicolored pea gravel was a five-foot-long drawing of Pike Place Market as seen from the sky. Peanut shells had been placed all over it like ants in a line, marking what was clearly a movement pattern that originated from a single point. But while all of that was obvious enough, something didn't add up.

"Where is that?" Bex asked, crouching to point at the place where all the paths came together. "It doesn't match any of the Anchor Market entrances I know."

"That's because it's not a public entrance," Adrian answered excitedly as he squatted down beside her. "According to the crows, there's a secret door in that wall that our target and a bunch of other serious-looking old men go into every morning, then out for lunch, then back in again in the afternoon, and then out one last time in the evenings."

"Like the entrance to an office," Bex said with a grin of her own.

"Exactly," the witch said, tapping the place where all the peanut shells came together with his finger. "There's no way to say for certain without going in ourselves, but I'd bet my broom that's the entrance to the Anchor Market's back end."

"What's the Anchor Market's back end?"

"I have no idea," Adrian confessed, his blue-gray eyes shining. "But it *has* to be good, or the entire sorcerous world wouldn't be conspiring to keep it secret. For all we know, there's a release lever in there that will detach the entire Anchor and send Gilgamesh's ugly gold statue spinning off into the void!"

Bex didn't think they'd get that lucky, but his optimism made her smile. "So how do we get inside?"

"That's the tricky part," Adrian said, digging into his pockets. "Fortunately, the crows came through on that score as well. Look at this."

He pulled his hand out of his pocket to show Bex a ball of something fluffy and brownish-gray. She thought it was rabbit fur at first, but then she caught the smell and realized she was looking at a large tuft of human hair.

"Is that—"

"Ripped right off his head," Adrian said smugly, sticking the hair back into his pocket. "I've got several, actually. It seems poor Dr. Yearling's morning commute was plagued by bird attacks. I've already told them to lay off so he doesn't get suspicious, but with this much hair, we're as good as in."

"How so?"

Adrian gave her his devilish smile, the one that made Bex's stomach do flip-flops, and suddenly, she was certain that she was going to like this plan very much indeed.

It took six days to get everything ready.

Adrian could have done it in four, but he was trying to conserve his remaining supply of bottled sleep, and he'd spotted something else that was... not mission-critical but still worth fudging the timeline for. It also didn't hurt that going a bit slower let him spend his evenings with Bex.

The job of being queen had gotten a lot more complicated now that she had more than three subjects to worry about. Bex spent her days working with Lys and Iggs to make sure their growing network of safe houses stayed secret and supplied. She also practiced with her sword, going full inferno on the gravel practice area Adrian had made for her at the edge of his clearing.

It would have been safer to build her a pier out in the inlet, which was both away from his trees and surrounded by water, but Adrian was far more worried about drawing attention than he was about accidental incineration. Bex was so good at controlling her fire now that she wouldn't have wilted a leaf, but light was another story. Even when she kept it small, Bex's bonfire stood out like, well, a bonfire, and there was only so much people could Nevermind when it involved large flashes of bright light.

His forest was the only thing big enough to keep her hidden when she went full burn. The commotion was distracting, but Adrian liked seeing her flashes while he worked. He also liked watching her practice while he waited for his potions to brew, though that one required borrowing Iggs's sunglasses. Even in full daylight, Bex was *bright*, but the best part came at night.

Since even the Blackwood couldn't hide huge flashes of fire in the dark, Bex was forced to stop practicing when the sun went down. The moment twilight fell, she knocked on his door, and Adrian invited her in to have dinner. Sometimes, Iggs joined them, but most nights, it was just the two of them sitting on his porch, eating whatever had come out of his garden that day. Bex always tried to give him money for groceries, but Adrian always turned her down. Feeding someone off the bounty of his forest was powerful witchcraft, and he loved the bashful way she smiled when he insisted. Demons might have showered her with gifts in the past, but his Bex was clearly a stranger to generosity, and it gave Adrian enormous joy to make her eyes light up.

By the time the day of the operation arrived, he was sorely regretting not telling the demons he needed two weeks instead of one. He could have spent a year getting off work early to sit on his dark porch, talking to Bex while she played her guitar without even looking at the strings. But he was the one who'd said they needed to hurry, and he had chosen Friday afternoon specifically, so Adrian forced himself to finish his potions on time.

According to the crows, who got it from the seagulls, Friday was the day Dr. Yearling left the office early. Boston had had a great deal to say about timing their plan off a game of bird telephone, but Adrian found it utterly believable that a man with a high-ranking managerial position would cut off work as soon as possible on the weekends. He was more surprised that Yearling didn't leave early every day, but working at an Anchor must have required serious dedication. According to the crows, Yearling was there from eight to six every weekday except Fridays, when he left at five, which was why the RV was on the ferry at four p.m. sharp.

Lys and Nemini were already in position. They'd gone across the water an hour earlier to locate Yearling's car and find a good hiding spot. Bex, Adrian, and Iggs were the second wave, though Adrian seemed to be the only one who was ready, sitting nervously in the front passenger seat next to Norma while the old construct studied her road maps and hummed off-key. He was double-checking his potions for the fiftieth time when he finally heard Iggs coming up the stairs.

"Damn, dude," the demon said when Adrian hopped out of his seat. "You look really different."

Adrian laughed. "That's kind of the point of a disguise."

He'd certainly put a lot of work into it. For the first time in over a decade, Adrian wasn't wearing clothes he'd made himself. He wasn't even wearing black. His look for the evening had been purchased entirely online and included a white button-up shirt, camel khaki pants, and a pair of dark-brown ankle boots that were supposed to be leather but felt more like hard plastic.

Adrian wasn't sure if that was because these were the first shoes he'd ever worn that hadn't been custom-made to fit his feet or if the website he'd gotten them from had lied and they really were made of plastic, but they'd do for one afternoon. It was certainly a lot more normal-looking than his usual outfit. He even had a wristwatch, which was actually kind of useful, though he *hated* not having his coat. The canvas messenger bag he'd bought to go with his outfit was woefully inadequate even after he'd embroidered expanding spells all over the inside. He also felt naked going out in public without his hat, and while he did have his broom, it was staying in the RV.

"You look like you're going on a date," Iggs teased.

"And you look like you're going to war," Adrian replied, casting a nervous look at the demon's riot-squad loadout.

Iggs was dressed head to toe in black body armor with sorcerous cuneiform painted all over it. The combat knives tucked into the tops of his tall boots were also enchanted, as was the short sword he wore in a sheath at the small of his back. The assault rifle slung over his shoulder looked normal, if very expensive, but the black canvas bags strapped to his hips were stuffed full of what appeared to be magical grenades.

"Where'd you get all that?"

"Little here, little there," Iggs replied with a fang-toothed grin. "Lys has sticky fingers and a talent for destruction. Our armory's full of stuff like this."

That explained why Bex had warned Adrian off it when she'd showed him around the RV the first time, but, "Why didn't you use any of it during the Spider's attack?"

"Because Bex didn't want to hurt your trees," Iggs explained, tapping the sword at his back. "This stuff isn't exactly collateral-damage-light. If we'd rolled our top shelf defending the Blackwood, you'd have had a whole lot of new clear-cuts. Only reason I'm loaded now is because I'm running backup for this mission, and our rule is if someone calls for backup, we throw everything."

"Good rule," Adrian said, slightly terrified at the idea of Iggs "clear-cutting" in a major pedestrian area.

The wrath demon nodded and walked over to take a seat on the U-shaped bench that surrounded the RV's built-in dining table. "Where's Bex?"

"I was hoping you could tell me," Adrian said, checking one more time to make sure his broom was ready in the storage locker beside the RV's side door. "She'd better show up soon. We've only got three minutes before—"

He cut off at the familiar sound of Bex's footsteps coming down the stairs. When Adrian turned to greet her, though, what he saw knocked the words right out of his head.

Bex was wearing a *dress*.

Not a full dress. This was more like a long shirt that hugged her waist before flaring out into a swirly hem above a pair of black biker shorts. She had her usual black combat boots on as well, but her dress was a beautiful plummy maroon, and she'd ditched her black leather jacket for a lighter acid-washed denim one that showed off her narrow shoulders. She was also wearing a necklace, which really threw him for a minute before he realized it was the leather string that kept Drox's ring dangling above the scoop neck of her dress. Part of him wondered why she wasn't wearing her sword, but the rest of Adrian was too busy grinning to care.

"Sorry that took so long," Bex said, tugging at her short skirt as she joined them by the RV's side door. "You said to dress like a normal person, and these are the most normal-person clothes I've got. I know the boots don't match, but I just realized I don't actually own any other shoes." She looked down at herself in dismay. "Is it too much?"

"It's perfect," Adrian assured her, taking her hand to spin her around so he could see the back. "You look fantastic."

Bex let him turn her in a circle, her cheeks coloring beautifully. "You look nice too."

Adrian grinned even wider, and Iggs rolled his eyes. "Yes, yes, we all look great. Now can we please pay attention? We're about to hit our window."

Bex jumped back into leader mode at once, snatching her hand out of Adrian's to go up to the RV's cab.

"How long until the ferry docks?" she asked, peering through the windshield.

"Two minutes," Iggs replied.

"You loaded for bear?"

"I'm loaded for a whole forest full of bears," the big demon told her proudly, spreading his arms so she could see for herself.

Bex came over to adjust a few straps and count his grenades. When she was satisfied, she pulled her phone out of her jacket pocket. "Lys says they're in position as well. Looks like we're good to go."

"Not quite," Adrian said, finally dragging his eyes off the swish of Bex's skirt to reach into his shoulder bag. "If we're going to be spying on sorcerers, we need to do something about your horns."

"There's nothing to be done," Bex told him with a shrug. "Even Lys can't shapeshift horns."

"I'm not talking about shapeshifting," Adrian replied, drawing two lengths of string out of his bag.

Bex arched a suspicious eyebrow. "What are those?"

"Forgetting strings," he explained, holding them up so she could see the silvery strands of spider silk woven into the cording. "You know how people used to tie bits of string around their fingers when they needed to remember something? These do the opposite. They make you forget anything they're tied to."

Her glowing eyes went huge. "You're going to make me forget my *horns*?"

"You and everyone else," Adrian said, smiling as her horror grew. "Don't look like that. It only works while the string's attached, and you can cancel the effect at any time by saying the breaking word."

"What's the breaking word?"

He squinted at the strings in his fingers. "I believe it's *bezelbrit*."

Bex wrinkled her nose. "Why would you pick a word like that?"

"I didn't," Adrian confessed, stepping up in front of her. "Forgetting strings are witchcraft of the soul, which is my weakest area. I stole these from my sister Olivia."

Her look of horror snapped back into place. "You stole those from a witch?"

"We steal from each other all the time. She stole Boston for a whole month once."

"She stole your familiar?" she asked. When he nodded, Bex's jaw fell open. "*Why?*"

"Because her cat was lonely," Adrian explained with a shrug, pinching the end of each string so he could tie them around the base of Bex's black horns from as far away as possible.

The distance made the work more difficult, but this was new territory for him, and Adrian didn't want to do anything untoward. For all he knew, horn-touching would get him slapped. It really was a shame, though. He'd been dying to touch Bex's horns since the first moment he'd seen them at the airport. Now was not the time or place to ask about such things, though, so Adrian behaved himself, keeping Bex at arm's length as he pulled the bows tight.

"There," he said, stepping back to admire his work. "That should do it."

Adrian could still see Bex's horns if he focused, but the magic was already tugging at his mind. Forgetting strings functioned a lot like Gilgamesh's scales. He knew the bows were there because he'd tied them, but his eyes were already skimming over the area above Bex's head like there was nothing to see, which meant the spell was working exactly as intended.

"That's crazy," Iggs said, squinting at Bex. "Even I can't see them, and she's my queen."

"Super weird," Bex agreed, reaching up to feel what appeared to be empty air above her skull. "My head feels so light."

"Because the string is making you forget the weight," Adrian explained.

Bex scowled as if that answer upset her, but then she shrugged and moved to the door. "Let's do this," she said, fishing her sunglasses out of her jacket and placing them on her face. "Ready?"

"Ready," Adrian said, stepping into position behind her.

"Make sure Norma gets a parking space close to the target," she ordered Iggs. "Keep your comm on, and be ready to scramble."

"Already done," the demon said, turning his head to show her the black bud wedged into his ear.

Bex put hers in as well, then turned around to hand one to Adrian. He recognized the compact combination mic-and-earphone from the fight in the woods, but he'd never put one into his own ear before. The fit was highly counterintuitive, and Bex had to help him get the device settled so it wouldn't fall out.

"There's a button on the outside," she explained once the little bud was in position. "Tap it when there's something you want to say. Otherwise, maintain radio silence."

"Got it," Adrian said, fighting the urge to fiddle with the hard plastic.

Bex checked his comm placement one more time before opening the door. She hopped out of the RV into the ferry's parking deck, which was already full of vehicles getting ready to drive out. Adrian followed right on her heels, keeping his hands on the strap of his shoulder bag with all its precious contents.

"Good luck," Iggs said as he shut the door behind them.

Bex waved in acknowledgment and started jogging toward the pedestrian exit. Adrian matched her a second later, both of them heading up the slip-proof steps to the ferry's main deck. The boat was already docked at the Seattle pier, and the deck was crammed with people waiting to get off, so Adrian took his chance and reached for Bex's hand.

She jumped when he took it, nearly clocking him with the horns he could no longer see as she whirled to look up at him.

"I don't want to get separated in the crowd," he said innocently as he gripped her fingers. "You're a lot harder to spot without your horns."

That was a blatant excuse, but while Adrian had the feeling she saw right through it, Bex didn't make him let go as the port workers finally unhooked the chain and let the hordes off the ferry.

"So where are we going?" Bex asked as they walked hand-in-hand down the shady pedestrian tunnel. "You said you had a stakeout location in mind."

"The perfect one," Adrian promised, forcing himself to pay attention to the mission and not the feeling of her warm, slender fingers wrapped around his. "It should give us a good view of both the secret door and Yearling's path to the garage. Unless he decided not to come into work today, there should be no way we can miss him."

"He's there," Bex said, checking her phone again. "Lys and Nemini are sitting on his car right now."

That was a fun mental image.

"Then we should be good," Adrian replied, squeezing her fingers a little tighter.

Bex responded by looking at her feet, but she still didn't take her hand back. She didn't rush him, either, leaving the two of them to stroll at a leisurely pace down the ferry dock's steps toward the sun-blasted sidewalk that ran along the pier.

With summer nearly over, the tourist swarms had died down. It was still a gorgeous Friday afternoon, though, and the waterfront was hopping with street vendors and people of all sorts. Despite having lived in Seattle for two months now, Adrian hadn't spent much time outside of his forest, and he found the experience fascinating. The sunny waterfront was hot, busy, and choked with tourist traps, but it had a fun energy, and the tree-shaded stairs up to the Pike Place Market—and the Anchor Market hidden beneath—were legitimately lovely. He spotted several restaurants he wanted to try when—*if*—things ever calmed down. But while it was exciting to finally be somewhere new, most of Adrian's attention stayed on Bex.

Unsurprisingly for the Bonfire of Wrath, the heat didn't seem to bother her at all. He could see her glowing eyes moving behind her sunglasses, noting the exits, marking their surroundings, evaluating threats. But while Adrian could feel her tension through their tangled fingers, she didn't pull away from him when the crowds thinned. She actually moved closer, walking so near to Adrian that their arms bumped.

That was fine with him. So far as Adrian was concerned, this was already a *highly* successful mission, and it was about to get even better.

Though its tourism zone stretched for blocks, the official Pike Place Market consisted of several buildings perched high on the hill overlooking Seattle's waterfront. The main market was a long multilevel structure that rose like a cliff from the tiny street that ran along the ridge below, but there were lots of other shops, restaurants, and sitting areas closer to the water. These outliers were connected back to the main market via a giant elevated skybridge filled with wooden tables that independent vendors could rent by the day to sell everything from handmade jewelry to local honey.

The place where all the crows' peanut shells came together was located directly below that bridge. Tucked into an alley that served as a pedestrian passthrough to the road the skybridge went over was an unassuming gray door. It looked like a maintenance entrance for the elevators that went down into the Pike Place Market parking deck—the same parking deck where Nemini and Lys were currently stalking Yearling's car. But while parking was a necessary evil for any tourism district, Pike Place had made the most of theirs by turning the top of the deck into a public sitting area with plants, picnic tables, and a sweeping view of the Puget Sound and the Olympic Mountains beyond. It was a fantastic double use of space and very convenient cover for their current objective.

"Is that our entrance?" Bex whispered as they walked past the door.

Adrian nodded. Even without the suspicious number of crows perched on surrounding buildings, he could feel the hum that always accompanied strong sorcery coming off the door's gray-painted surface like heat. Just walking near it was enough to make his hair stand on end, and from the way Bex's hand tightened around his, she felt it too.

"Where do you want to set up?"

Adrian answered with a smile as he led her out of the alley to the sunny public deck on the other side.

Like everywhere else on this fine afternoon, the cement deck was packed with people enjoying the views. All the public benches where they could have kept a casual eye on the door were already full, but Adrian wasn't aiming for benches. His target was the restaurant and brewery taking up the entirety of the converted deck's far end.

It was your classic tourist institution: a sprawling monument to Americana with simple, familiar dishes served beside beers brewed to appeal to the widest possible palate. It wasn't the sort of restaurant anyone went to on purpose but also not a place you'd be mad at if you got stuck there, though Adrian hadn't picked it for the food. He was here for the patio full of perfectly positioned picnic tables.

He'd already spotted the one he wanted. Grabbing Bex's hand tight, he pulled her across the sunny cement toward a red-umbrella-shaded table that was in direct view of the door they were here to watch. It also happened to be the only outdoor table not crammed full of customers at peak on a Friday, a feat managed only by the little plastic *Reserved* signs that had been placed all over it.

Bex gave Adrian a funny look. "You reserved a table?"

"I saw no reason for us to stand through the entire stakeout. This helps us blend in. We're just two more people enjoying a sunny afternoon."

She chuckled and took a seat on the wooden bench that faced their target. "Good work."

Adrian flashed her a smile as he reclaimed his hand. "I'm going to go tell the staff we're here. Do you want anything from the bar?"

"Why would I want something from the bar?" Bex asked, sounding legitimately confused. "We're here for a stakeout."

He lifted his shoulders in an innocent shrug. "Can't sit at a table with nothing in front of you."

"Good point," she said as she settled in to watch. "Get me whatever, then."

Adrian nodded and made his way through the crowd. He returned five minutes later, carrying two pints of bubbly golden liquid.

"Here," he said, putting one down in front of her. "Iggs said you used to drink beer in Paradise, so I went out on a limb. Sorry it's not chewy."

"Is beer supposed to be chewy?" Bex asked, bending over to peer at her glass from the side.

"Not in my opinion," Adrian said, setting his own beer on the table, "but tastes change over the eons."

He sat down on the bench beside her so he could watch the door as well. This also just so happened to put his arm flush against hers, which Bex didn't seem to mind.

"Are we actually going to drink it?" she asked, leaning a little closer. He was still enjoying that when Adrian remembered that questions generally required answers.

"It's part of our cover," he explained, forcing himself to pay attention. "But don't worry. This is a session ale, practically beer-flavored water. It won't get you drunk."

Bex stared at the beer like it might bite her. He was about to tell her she didn't have to drink if she didn't want to when she picked up the pint and took a sip.

"Ugh," she said, wrinkling her nose. "I definitely like the boba tea better."

"Is that your first beer?" Adrian asked.

"First I can remember," Bex said, taking another sip. "I think it's growing on me, though."

He smiled and took a sip of his own beer, which was much tastier than he'd expected. He took another sip right after, relaxing into the bench to enjoy the pleasant summer afternoon breeze. So far, his plan was working perfectly, and they hadn't even gotten to the best part yet.

Adrian's eyes flicked to the non-brewery side of the parking-deck-roof-turned-park where a scale-eyed man was setting up a pair of speakers on the cement square that served as a public stage. Bex's ever-watchful eyes had already spotted the man and moved on, but they snapped back again when the human unlocked the black case at his feet and pulled out an acoustic guitar very similar to her own.

"Wait," she said, turning to give Adrian a suspicious look as the guitarist began tuning his instrument. "Did you plan this?"

"I didn't leave it to chance," Adrian replied casually, hiding his smile behind his beer. "The website said they have live music on Friday afternoons. I figured if we had to stake out the door anyway, we might as well have music while we waited."

Bex stared at him for a moment, and then a beautiful smile broke over her face. She turned away at once, staring at the door they were supposed to be watching like she was trying to pry it off its hinges with her eyes, but the smile didn't go away.

"Mission successful," Adrian whispered into his beer.

"What was that?" Bex asked.

He shrugged and stood up, moving around to sit on Bex's other side so she'd have an unimpeded view of the musician and the Puget Sound beyond. He was congratulating himself on a job masterfully executed when the man actually started to play.

Adrian nearly spit out his beer. "Merciful Forest," he said as the music grated through the air. "He's *awful.*"

"He really is," Bex agreed, bending over her beer as she fought to hold in her laughter.

"I'm sorry," Adrian said, scrubbing his hands through his hair in frustration. "I didn't—"

"No, no, it's fine," she insisted, turning to grin at him. "I love it."

Adrian gave her a skeptical look. "Is your comm messing with your hearing?"

"I can hear just fine," Bex said, turning her attention back to the door. "And I can say with certainty that this is the best concert I've ever attended."

It was probably the *only* concert she'd ever attended. Adrian could see her wincing behind her sunglasses when the playing skewed even more out of tune. Before he could say anything else, though, Bex scooted closer on the picnic table bench, resting her head against his arm as she settled in to watch the door.

Adrian forgot all about the music after that. The musician could have been murdering the audience with his guitar and Adrian wouldn't have noticed. The sphere of his senses had shrunk to Bex's warm body pressed against his. He was so busy enjoying having his face so close to her hair, he entirely forgot why they were there until Bex suddenly sat up.

"There he is."

Adrian was too addled to follow. "What?"

Bex nodded ahead of them, raising her barely touched beer to her lips so she could stare over the rim of the glass. "Coming out the door," she whispered against her cup. "Looks like your crows had it right. That's Yearling, though he's looking a little worse for wear."

Yearling looked *terrible* when Adrian finally managed to shift his attention. The picture he'd shown the crows had been of a refined, middle-aged man with graying, well-kept hair and a somber, serious face. The sorcerer standing in the doorway was piebald, scratched up, and furious-looking. He raised his briefcase over his head like a shield as Adrian watched, glaring at the wall of crows waiting on the power lines like he wanted to curse the lot of them.

The crows cawed madly in reply, calling excitedly to Adrian with *Here is man!* and *Give food now?*

Adrian obliged at once, reaching into his canvas bag to grab the large packet of shelled peanuts hidden inside. He ripped the plastic under the table and shook the bag with his hand, sending nuts scattering all over the pavement.

The crows descended in a frenzy, causing the other restaurant patrons to shriek as birds swooped under their tables like black-feathered missiles. Yearling gave the feeding frenzy the evil eye, but he didn't so much as glance at Adrian or Bex as he slammed the metal door and scuttled to the elevator right beside it, pounding the down button repeatedly with his thumb.

"And there he goes to the parking deck," Bex said, reaching up to press the button on her comm. "Lys," she whispered, her voice louder over the speaker in Adrian's ear than it was in real life. "We've got confirmation on the doorway. Target's headed your direction."

"Ready and willing," the lust demon replied in a purring voice. "See you in ten minutes."

Bex let go of the button and turned to Adrian, who'd already stood up, though he had to lean right back down again to make himself heard over the racket of the frenzied crows.

"I'm going to go settle the tab," he whispered next to her ear. "Are you ready for this?"

"Are *you* ready for this?" she whispered back.

That was a good question. Technically, Bex was only here in case things went bad. The actual execution of the plan was all him, but Adrian knew better than to let his nerves show. The magic he was planning required confidence to work correctly. Fortunately, being a witch involved a lot of bravado, giving Adrian a wealth of experience to draw from as he flashed Bex his surest smile and started weaving his way through the crows—and the crowds of people taking pictures of them—toward the register.

Chapter 5

Bex rested her elbows on the picnic table, staring at the door she was supposed to be watching with a dreamy expression. Somewhere to the right, the horrible guitarist started playing even more ferociously in an effort to drown out the shrieks of the restaurant patrons as Adrian's crows finished their peanuts and started hopping up on tables to help themselves to French fries. A man tripped over a crow right behind her, dropping his beer in the process. Bex caught the falling glass without looking, handing it back to the confused human with a dazzling smile.

Adrian had taken her on a date.

Not a *date* date. Even Drox couldn't have argued this wasn't a stakeout, but that didn't change the fact that Adrian had arranged for said stakeout to take place on a lovely patio with music. Terrible, terrible music, but still as sweet as Ishtar's own singing to Bex's ears, because it proved that Adrian had been thinking of her—her, *Bex*, not the Queen of Wrath. He'd taken a job that could have been done from a park bench and turned it into the most magical afternoon of Bex's life. He'd dressed up, he'd held her *hand*, he hadn't pushed her away when she'd leaned her head on his shoulder. If a crow hadn't been pecking the last crumbs of a peanut out from under her boot at that very moment, Bex would have sworn she was dreaming.

She could feel Drox rattling furiously on his leather cord. He'd been doing that every moment they weren't training since their fight in the RV, but for once Bex didn't care. *Nothing* could ruin this moment. She'd always thought Adrian was handsome, but the way he'd looked today, smiling in the sunlight just for her. The way he'd walked next to her, so tall and so close. The way his calloused hand had gripped hers so readily, like he couldn't wait to touch her. The way she could feel every muscle in his long, lean arm when she'd pressed her cheek against—

The wooden picnic table rocked as someone plopped onto the bench beside her. Bex whipped around immediately, hand going for the ring around her neck only to pause when she realized it was Adrian. He smiled wickedly when their eyes met, making her heart skip a dozen beats as he leaned closer.

"Hello, beautiful," he whispered, reaching out to stroke her cheek with his long, clever fingers. "Miss me?"

For one breathless second, Bex was certain she was going to die. Just burn up into a pile of ash right there at the table. Then she spotted the pair of small, pointed horns sticking up through Adrian's dark hair.

"Dammit, Lys!" she cried, smacking the lust demon's arm as they began to cackle. "That's not funny!"

"That's where you're wrong," Lys snickered, shifting their shape just enough that they no longer looked exactly like Adrian but not *so* much that the crow-obsessed crowd would notice and start kicking. "It was, in fact, *hilarious*."

Bex crossed her arms over her chest with a huff. "What are you doing up here so early, anyway?"

"Actually, I'm late," Lys said, grinning wider than they had any right to. "You've been spacing out for a good fifteen minutes." Their voice dropped to an innuendo-laden murmur. "Must have been some stakeout."

Bex shoved them away and pressed her hands over her face, which was so hot she was surprised she hadn't gone bonfire yet. She was still trying to get a hold of herself when Lys wrapped their arm around her shoulders.

"Calm down, baby queen," they cooed, rocking Bex back and forth. "I'm just teasing you."

"Well, *don't*," Bex snapped, dragging her hands off her face. "Drox has been on my case enough about Adrian being a distraction already. He doesn't need you giving him more ammunition."

Lys snorted. "You already work every hour of the day. What's he worried Adrian's going to distract you from? Training in your sleep?"

"He'd make me if he could," Bex said, secretly happy that Lys was on her side. Still. "He's not entirely wrong, though," she whispered, looking back at the door she was supposed to be watching. "I *was* distracted. You just snuck up on me in the middle of a job, for Ishtar's sake."

"No one expects you to be perfect all the time," Lys said, running a hand through Bex's hair to untangle the ends. "The mission is fine. It was just a joke. Don't worry about it."

"I have to worry about it," Bex argued, clenching her fists. "I'm the queen. If I start missing things because of Adrian, then Drox is right."

"Drox is a sword," Lys reminded her. "Of course he only cares about fighting, but queens have to rule in war and peace." They stopped untangling Bex's hair to brush their hand against her cheek. "There's so much more to you than fighting Gilgamesh. Don't let Drox bully you into forgetting that."

Bex lowered her eyes guiltily. "I'm surprised to hear that from you."

"Just because I've dedicated my life to Heaven's downfall doesn't mean I'm a one-trick pony," Lys replied in an insulted voice. "I fight so that all of us can be free to do what you're doing right now."

"Screwing up a stakeout?" Bex grumbled.

"Being happy," Lys told her with a smile. "Gilgamesh stole Paradise from us. He took our home, killed our gods,

and damned us to eternal slavery. Living free and enjoying
the hell out of it is how we shove that back in his face, so if
you want to have a drink with your witch or screw him
right here on the table, go for it."

"*Lys!*" Bex cried, looking around frantically to make
sure Adrian hadn't overheard that while the lust demon
stole a sip off her beer, completely unrepentant.

"Relax," they chided. "Adrian's a Witch of the Flesh.
I'm sure I'd have to dig a lot deeper into my dirty talk
arsenal to shock him, but I'm happy he makes you blush.
He's by far the highest-quality guy I've caught you spacing
out over."

Bex stared at them in horror. "You mean I've done
this *before*?"

"Once or twice," Lys said, pausing to take another
swallow of Bex's beer. "And before you ask, they were
terrible. I was seriously starting to worry about your taste,
but Adrian's handsome, powerful, not a jerk, fantastic body,
and his forest is a priceless strategic asset. If I wasn't so
ridiculously happy for you, I'd gobble him up myself."

Bex had no idea how to reply to that, but she was
certain she was going to implode from embarrassment if
this conversation went any further.

"What about the target?" she asked, frantically
steering them back to the much safer topics of assault and
espionage. "Did you get what Adrian asked for?"

Lys gave her an exasperated look that was still far
too close to Adrian's for Bex's comfort. There must have
been a merciful bone somewhere in the lust demon's body,
though, because they let the subject change lie and started
emptying their pockets.

"That looks like all of it," Bex said when Yearling's ID
badge, wallet, fresh hair sample, and silk bag full of

quintessence were lying on the table. "What made you late, by the way? Did the sorcerer give you trouble?"

"In a manner of speaking," Lys replied with a wistful expression. "Yearling was very loyal to his husband, so I had to scuttle the seduction. Even if they're Gilgamesh's stoolies, I never break up a couple."

Bex smiled. "I guess even the bad guys aren't bad all the time. But if you didn't seduce him, how'd you get his stuff?"

"Good old-fashioned mugging," Lys said cheerfully. "Nemini's still got him locked down in his car if you need anything else."

"I think this should be it," Bex said, pulling out her phone. "But let me ask—"

She stopped, her lips curving into a smile before she could think better of it as she spotted Adrian making a beeline back to their table.

"Sorry about the wait," he said as he sat down on the opposite bench. "The crows caused a bigger commotion than anticipated. I practically had to put my money in the register myself before..." His voice trailed off as he finally registered Lys wearing a near duplicate of his face. "Um, did I miss part of the plan?"

"Nothing important," Lys assured him, pointing at the pile on the table. "Is that everything you need?"

Adrian's eyes lit up as he started sorting through the take. "This should do it. Thank you, Lys."

"My pleasure," Lys purred, giving Bex a slow wink as they stood up. "Don't let him get away ungobbled."

Adrian watched the demon leave with a confused look while Bex just focused on not sinking under the table. "Never mind Lys," she said at last, giving herself a firm shake. "What's next?"

"We go change," Adrian replied, his voice all business as he swept the sorcerer's effects into his shoulder bag. "Follow me."

Bex latched herself to his side as he took them back into the crowded restaurant. She assumed they were going through the building and out the back, but Adrian led her into the kitchen, where one of the busboys was waiting. He was a scale-eyed human, but he nodded at Adrian like he knew him and motioned for them to follow him past the dishwashing station to what appeared to be a broom closet.

Adrian murmured his thanks and passed the man a bill, then he put his hands on Bex's shoulders and steered her into the tiny room, locking the door behind them.

"How did you get that guy to let you in here?" Bex asked as Adrian yanked on the chain that turned on the bare, dangling light bulb.

"Same way I got them to reserve the table," he replied, slinging his bag off his shoulder. "Bribery. People in the service industry are usually very helpful if you pay them for their efforts, and I needed somewhere no one would see. This spell relies on perception. If I did it in the men's room and someone walked in at the wrong moment, it could blow the whole operation."

"Should I be in here, then?" Bex asked nervously.

"Yes, because you're part of the spell," Adrian said, looking at the space above her head. "*Bezelbrit.*"

Bex gasped as a weight landed on her head. Her hands shot up next, grabbing the familiar, smooth curve of her horns. Holy Ishtar, how had she forgotten her *horns*?

The forgetting strings were already shredded from the breaking spell, but Bex couldn't pull the remnants off fast enough. Meanwhile, Adrian unfolded a square of leather on one of the supply shelves beside them and began laying out a pharmacopeia of different-colored potions.

"These are for you," he said, placing a metal flask and what appeared to be a bag of dust on the left side of the leather. "And these are for me."

His collection was much bigger: five stoppered bottles and a glass eyedropper filled with something that looked like glowing yellow slime.

"Okay," he said when everything was laid out. "Ready?"

"No," Bex replied sharply, pointing at the bottles. "I thought we were dressing you up as the target. What does all that do?"

"Exactly what you just said," Adrian explained, unstopping the first bottle in his lineup. "Despite what the Harry Potter franchise would have you believe, you can't just drink a potion to look like someone else. The flesh has many factors, each of which must be addressed with its own concoction, and they can't be combined until they're in your body. There's also the issue where we're sneaking into one of Gilgamesh's most secret sorcery facilities, and I'm not a sorcerer. It doesn't matter how much I look like Yearling if I don't know the spell that lets me in."

Bex hadn't considered that. "Does one of those potions make you a sorcerer?"

"Not exactly," Adrian said, picking up the glowing eyedropper. "The hair the crows took from Yearling has gone into every potion, but this one is special. It's a copy of his muscle memory."

"What does that have to do with anything? It's not like you'll need his ability to ride a bike."

"Muscle memory's much more than that," Adrian assured her with a wry smile. "There's no potion or spell that can transfer knowledge, but our bodies do common, repetitive actions on their own all the time. Actions like opening the door of the same facility every day, for example."

He picked up the new hair sample Lys had just stolen from Yearling and began feeding single strands into each of his potions.

"Given how long he's been doing this, I'm betting Dr. Yearling can go to work in his sleep. Once I drink all of these, I'll look, sound, smell, and feel exactly like the pecked-over Yearling we just saw for approximately fifteen minutes. That should be enough to sneak past any cameras or magical checks, but I'll be counting on his muscle memory to actually get us to where we need to be."

"Is that safe?" Bex asked, her eyes darting to his half of the shelf. "Not to question your skills, but that looks like a lot of potions to take all at once."

"Bex," said Adrian, clearly trying not to laugh. "We're about to sneak into the heart of one of Heaven's best-kept secrets. *Nothing* about this is safe."

That didn't strike Bex as something to laugh about, but Adrian had already turned to point at the flask and powder he'd put aside for her.

"The liquid starts the spell while the powder sets it," he explained. "Once they both get going, you'll be invisible, untouchable, inaudible, and undetectable by magic, but only when you're within arm's reach of me. *My* arm, not yours. Leave that radius at any time, and all the potion's effects will stop. They won't come back, either, so make sure to stay right on my heels."

Bex was about to swear she would when she realized Adrian wasn't finished.

"I also need you to stay close for another reason," he said, tilting his head at the wall of bottles he'd set out for himself. "You're my emergency brake. None of these potions affect my mind, but changing the body so completely can be very disorienting. I'll need you to stick right behind me so that I don't accidentally get stuck wandering around the Anchor office in a dissociative fugue."

The look on her face must have been awful, because Adrian rushed to reassure her. "I'm sure it won't come to that. But taking multiple potions at once increases the instability of all of them. If things go bad, they'll go bad quickly, and I'll need you to be there to pull me back."

"I won't leave you," Bex promised. "But what do I do? *How* do I bring you back?"

"Just remind me that I'm me," Adrian said, putting the potion to his lips. "Ready?"

He tossed his head back before she could answer, drinking the first bottle in one gulp. He drank the rest in rapid succession, getting paler with each one. By the time he got to the glowing eyedropper, he looked like he was going to be sick, but Adrian didn't stop. He just picked up the dropper and peeled his eyelids back, dripping three drops of yellow glowing slime into each eyeball.

He'd barely finished squeezing out the last drop when the change slammed into him. He dropped with a gasp, curling over his knees in a ball on the broom closet's dirty floor. For three long heartbeats, he sat as tight as a knot. Bex was about to squat down beside him to see if he was okay when the man on the floor suddenly shot back to his feet.

A man who wasn't Adrian.

He'd been absolutely right about the multiple factors thing. The man who was suddenly in the closet with Bex didn't just look like the angry, piebald sorcerer they'd seen scuttling away from the crows who'd become his nemeses. There was nothing of Adrian left in him at all. The way he breathed, the way he stood, the way he smiled at her before glancing down to survey his limbs, they were all the actions of a stranger, so much so that Bex actually took a step back before she realized what she was doing.

"That was less pleasant than I remembered," the man said in what she could only assume was Yearling's voice. "Take your potion. We don't have much time."

Even the way he talked was wrong, clipped and superior, like a boss ordering around an incompetent subordinate. That alone was enough to put Bex's back up, but she forced the reaction down and did as she was told, drinking her potion in a single draught, the same as she'd seen him do.

Given how Adrian had reacted, Bex was braced for the worst, but the liquid didn't taste like anything. It didn't feel like anything either. If not for the pressure in her throat, Bex wouldn't have known she was drinking at all. She was wondering if the flask had actually been empty when she looked down and saw that her body was gone.

The stranger who wasn't Adrian grabbed the bag of dust off the shelf next, opening the top and throwing the contents over the spot where Bex had just been like he was blessing it with holy water.

"That will set the invisibility," he announced as he upended the last of the bag over her head. When it was completely empty, he shoved the bag and the empty potion bottles back into his shoulder bag, the only part of him that didn't look like Yearling.

"There," he said in the stranger's voice. "Even I can't see or feel you now, so please stick close."

Bex started to say she would only to discover she couldn't speak. Her feet didn't make any sound, either, and Yearling's blue Oxford shirt didn't wrinkle when she put her hand on what had been Adrian's shoulder. It felt like she'd been turned into nothing, which was far more terrifying than she'd been prepared for. But as freaked out as she was feeling on the inside, Bex had a mission, and she stuck to it tight, following the fake Yearling as close as a shadow as they strode out of the closet and back into the busy restaurant.

Adrian had never felt more wrong in his life.

He rode in his body like a passenger. Everything still followed his commands, but it all felt disconnected, like he was puppeteering someone else's biology. That would have been uncomfortable under any circumstances, but for a Witch of the Flesh, it was downright horrifying. The only thing that kept Adrian from going to pieces was how much work it had taken to put all of this together and the knowledge that Bex was right behind him.

He couldn't feel her thanks to the magic, but he *knew* she was there. Bex never abandoned anyone. She wouldn't abandon him. She was doing her part and trusting him to do his, so Adrian forced himself to keep going, walking his alien-feeling body across the sunny patio—which Yearling's senses perceived as oppressively hot and overcrowded rather than exciting and new—to the door that still looked just as gray and unassuming as ever.

Here goes nothing.

Putting his trust in his witchcraft, Adrian blanked his mind and let his copied muscle memory do whatever it wanted. This turned out to be grabbing the knob and flicking his thumb down to press a hidden cuneiform marking. The moment his skin grazed it, the locked knob turned in his hand, and Adrian stepped out of the heat into a freezing-cold white room.

He stopped, glancing around for the trigger that would spur his body into doing whatever came next, but the room was empty. There didn't even seem to be a door other than the one he'd come in through, just smooth white walls, ceiling, and floor. He was still looking for the way forward when the alley door finished closing behind him with a final-sounding *click*, and a golden eye opened on the other side of the room.

Adrian cringed inside his shell. That eye absolutely had not been there when he'd come in. There hadn't even been a line in the stone on that side. It was open now, though, the metallic iris turning inside the base of the golden eyeball to constrict the pupil like the aperture of a camera. It reminded Adrian of the princess's eyes but bigger and without any humanizing elements. At least the princess's golden eyes had been set into a face. This eye was the size of a watermelon and moved entirely on its own, the iris turning with a mechanical clicking noise as it focused on him.

That was enough to send Yearling's piebald scalp crawling. Thankfully, the sorcerer's body knew exactly what to do, bowing Adrian's head so fast he worried he'd broken his neck. His hand shot up at the same time, presenting the giant eyeball with the ID badge Lys had swiped. That must have been what the eye was looking for, because it snapped closed again a second later, and the floor vanished from beneath Adrian's feet.

He fell with a yelp, plummeting through the dark for a single second before Yearling's polished leather shoes hit the floor. What kind of floor and where, Adrian had no idea. Every direction he looked was covered in soup-thick darkness. He tried to move, but his feet stayed rooted, his knees locked tight by years of habit. His hand twitched for the same reason, so Adrian let it go, fumbling in the pocket of Yearling's gray golf pants for something that wasn't there.

It checked his other pockets in an increasing panic before Adrian realized the problem. The hand was looking for Yearling's bag of quintessence, which Adrian had stuck into his shoulder bag. He got it out at once, using his left hand since Yearling always seemed to do this with his right. The moment he slid the bag into the pocket Yearling's muscle memory expected it to be in, his hand seized upon it, opening the tie to pull out five coins of quintessence.

Adrian almost jumped out of the spell when he saw them. Five coins was a *huge* amount of quintessence and four coins more than he'd ever taken. He'd only used quintessence once before in his life, and only then because the Spider had forced it down his throat. That memory alone would have been enough to make him hate the stuff, but Adrian also loathed quintessence on its own merits. It was basically the cocaine of magic: so pure and concentrated that it went through your brain like a lightning bolt, destroying everything in its path.

He wasn't sure he could survive five coins at once, but Yearling's muscle memory was already shoving them toward his mouth. If he refused now, he'd disrupt the chain of habit and leave himself and Bex stranded in this awful dark, so Adrian pushed aside his fear and opened his jaw, popping the coins into his mouth and crunching all five in a single bite.

The result was every bit as bad as he'd feared. The quintessence burned through his body like a grass fire in a high wind. But while Adrian was fighting back panic, Yearling's muscle memory was already raising his hand, opening his mouth to speak a slew of words so old and sharp he couldn't remember what they sounded like after they were gone. The speech just poured out of him, taking the burn of the quintessence with it. When the last word was spoken, the all-consuming blackness vanished, leaving Adrian standing in an office that was even more terrifying than the dark.

Growing up in the Blackwood, Adrian had zero experience with corporate work environments. He'd seen them in movies, though, and this place looked like it had been lifted straight out of the worst. *Everything* was yellow beige: the carpet, the drop ceilings, the fluorescent lights, the cubicle walls, the molded plastic desks, the rolling chairs with their rubberized arms. It was hideously ugly, but at least the furniture was still relatively normal. The true horror came when Adrian looked past the immediate area by the water coolers where he'd come out.

He had to grab the wall to keep from falling over. Just beyond the cluster of cubicles in front of him, the office changed direction—*vertical* direction. The carpeted floor went straight up like a hinge, leading to a new open office space filled with even more cubicles. There were cubicles above him as well. Also cubicles on the walls, cubicles turning sideways, and cubicles with little steps leading to yet more cubicles. They were all connected by beige pathways that ran up, down, and sideways, creating an M.C. Escher-like maze that his brain couldn't begin to make sense of. It was as if the whole office had been built on the surface of a Gordian knot. He was still working on staying upright while his sense of balance readjusted when a middle-aged sorcerer in a pink polo shirt and the same gray golf pants as Adrian's version of Yearling suddenly stopped in front of him.

"Hello again, sir," the man said with a nervous smile. "Did you forget something, or is it the crows again?"

"I forgot something," Adrian said in Yearling's voice, forcing his eyes away from the madness that was the sorcerer's office to the relative safety of the ugly beige carpet. "Excuse me. I'm in a hurry to get home."

The man nodded as if this curtness were normal and continued on his way. Adrian started walking the other direction before he remembered he didn't know where he was going. Yearling's muscles did, though, so he blanked his mind again, trusting his stolen feet to follow their usual path to wherever it was they were supposed to be.

It took a *lot* of trust. Looking at the sorcerer's brain-breaking office was nothing compared to trying to navigate through it. The floor always stayed under his feet, but Adrian himself flipped directions half a dozen times just following Yearling's habits down the corridor. If he'd been more connected to his body, he would have been sick. Thankfully, his stomach was one of the many things he couldn't feel right now, leaving him more or less able to keep it together as Yearling's muscle memory walked him into the only office he'd seen that *wasn't* a cubicle.

The door was at the intersection of three hallways positioned like an X-Y-Z axis. Looking at it hurt Adrian's brain, so he closed his eyes and let Yearling's body find the knob by rote. He opened them again once he got inside, holding the door for the invisible Bex while he looked around the room.

If he hadn't known Yearling was important already, his office would have sealed the deal. It was palatial, a high-ceilinged chamber big enough to hold a wide, paper-covered desk, a conference table with six chairs, and a sitting area with couches. Everything was the same ugly yellow beige as the cubicles outside, but the furniture in here was much nicer, though what really caught Adrian's attention were the windows.

He thought they were TV screens at first. The back corner of Yearling's office was made up of two large panes of ink-black glass. They were positioned like a corner window, but they didn't seem to be looking out at anything. When Adrian walked Yearling's body over to the glass, though, he saw that was highly incorrect. They didn't just look out at something. They looked out at *everything*.

The entire Anchor Market was spread out below the windows like a diorama. Looking down, Adrian could clearly see the rolling green hills, the merchant tents, even the giant golden statue of Gilgamesh. It was all there, but the scale was far too small. If it wasn't for the obviously living people walking between the vendors, he would have said he was looking at a model. It even had a dome over the top of it to show the sky, and beyond that dome was the same ink-black nothing Adrian had fallen into when the giant eye had dropped the floor out from under his feet, leaving the Market looking like a diorama floating in an endless void.

Adrian pressed Yearling's face against the window, trying to figure out how that made sense. He knew the Anchors used the same space-stretching magic that enabled the demons' RV to be four stories tall, but the market portion couldn't be *actually* floating in nothing. Magic, like all natural systems, abhorred a vacuum. A sorcerer could turn a closet into a stadium with enough quintessence, but it still had to be filled with something. Empty pockets collapsed from the weight around them, which meant all that nothing couldn't actually *be* nothing. There had to be something else going on, something all that blackness had been put there to hide.

The more Adrian thought about that, the more right it felt. If Gilgamesh's sorcerers could make the Anchor Market look like it was sitting in the endless hills of

Paradise, covering whatever it was *actually* sitting on with an impenetrable wall of blackness would be easy. The most plausible explanation was that he was looking at a cover, a curtain meant to hide whatever it was the Anchors actually did. Adrian didn't know if this was to maintain Gilgamesh's secrecy or if the darkness was hiding something mortal eyes couldn't handle, but he hadn't come all the way down here to stare at nothing.

He pushed away from the window and strode back to the door. Whatever was hidden behind that curtain, he wouldn't find it up here in the offices. He needed to get into the actual mechanics of the Anchor, which meant he needed to go down. The muscle memory he relied on couldn't be triggered by thoughts like "Go down," but he had passed an elevator on his way here.

That was good enough to start. Adrian whirled around, trusting Bex to keep up as he jogged out of Yearling's office. According to the watch on his stolen wrist, he had seven minutes left before his disguise became unstable. Thankfully, the elevator was only a few nauseating direction flips away.

Yearling must not have left this floor much, because Adrian didn't feel a single twinge when he stopped in front of the beige-painted doors. Fortunately, he didn't need to be a sorcerer to use an elevator. He mashed the down button all on his own, shooting a murderous look at the obviously junior employee who was also in the hall to make sure the man didn't try to get in with him. The other sorcerer must have gotten the hint, because he made an immediate about-face and practically ran the other direction, leaving Adrian mercifully alone when the elevator's plastic down arrow lit up with a *ding*.

Adrian knew he was headed somewhere good the moment the doors rolled open. The outside of the elevator was yellow beige just like everything else in this hellscape, but the inside was the same relentless white as the first room. There were only two buttons—up and down—so Adrian hit the lower one and moved to the center of the elevator, folding his arms over Yearling's slight potbelly as the doors trundled shut.

The elevator dropped like a stone the second the doors were closed, sending Adrian stumbling into the cold white wall. The trip down was far longer than the black view from Yearling's window suggested. Adrian plummeted for a solid thirty seconds before the elevator slid to a quiet stop, opening its doors again to reveal a very different place.

It was a stone tunnel—a deep, *deep* channel carved into the bedrock with chisels and dynamite. The industrial lights and exposed wires running along the walls made it look like a mine shaft, but the door at the tunnel's end was like nothing Adrian had ever seen.

It looked like it was made from solid gold. The tunnel was only ten feet high by the elevator, but the door at the end was clearly much larger. Adrian could only see the bottom from where he was standing. He started walking closer, hoping to see more, but Yearling's body fought him for every step. Whatever that golden door was, the sorcerer didn't want to go near it, which meant that Adrian did. He pushed against Yearling's instincts, dragging his body forward like he was walking underwater until he was standing directly in front of two giant slabs of gold.

The tunnel opened up as he got closer, the roof rising like a cliff to finally fit the golden doors, which turned out to be fifty feet tall. Their faces were covered with cuneiform markings spiraling around the reliefs of two golden lions, one for each door. The lions were facing each other on all fours, their maned heads looking down at two white disks set into the gold where the door handles should have been.

Those must be what opened it, Adrian reasoned. He glanced nervously over his shoulder, but the stone tunnel was as empty now as it'd been when he arrived. He told himself that Bex was there, but it was hard to believe when he felt so alone. Yearling certainly wasn't helping. The man's body was groaning around him like a tree in a storm as Adrian reached out to press his stolen hands flat against the white disks.

Nothing happened.

Adrian dropped his arms with a frown, then he reached into Yearling's pocket to pull out his bag of quintessence. Just touching the stuff gave him a massive headache, but nothing in Gilgamesh's empire worked without it. It made sense that the giant doors wouldn't either. He didn't like it, but he didn't have a better idea, and time was running out on his disguise, so Adrian popped five more coins of quintessence into his mouth and bit down.

The concentrated magic popped like firecrackers when his teeth landed, flooding his body with power. Unlike the last time he'd done this, though, Yearling's muscle memory had nothing to give him. The sorcerer had either never touched these doors before or did so so infrequently that his body had no idea what to do. Adrian couldn't just stand there burning with quintessence, though, so he made a guess and pressed his palms back against the white disks.

The experience was very different this time. The moment he touched his quintessence-soaked fingers to the door, magic bit back into him like a viper. It stabbed straight through his disguise, leaving Adrian—*just* Adrian— hanging in blackness between two enormous golden lions. The great beasts stared at him with golden eyes that turned and clicked just like the one in the wall. But while Adrian couldn't feel it anymore, his disguise must have still been working, because the lions lowered their heads a second later, and Adrian slammed back into his stolen body just in time to see the giant golden doors swing open.

He stumbled out of their way with a curse, his heart thundering in the roots under his forest. There was darkness on the other side of the doors, but it wasn't the flat, inky blackness he'd seen from Yearling's window. This was something else, something *horrible*.

Body shaking, Adrian reached a hand over the threshold. The light changed noticeably when he crossed the line between the stone tunnel and the golden door, cloaking his fingers in shadow like he'd stuck them underwater. It didn't feel great, but it didn't bite his fingers off. He was working up the courage to step all the way inside when something grabbed him.

Adrian jumped a foot in the air, whirling Yearling's body around to see Bex standing behind him with her hands wrapped around his arm.

"Stop!"

"What are you doing?" he hissed, looking frantically down the empty tunnel. "You can't take your invisibility off yet! How are we going to get you out?"

"This is more important," Bex insisted, her fingers biting into Yearling's cuffed sleeve. "I've been trying to get your attention since before you put your hands on that stupid door, but you couldn't hear me or feel me, so I had to come out."

She looked up at the wall of blackness in front of them, and her fingers gripped down even harder.

"You can't go in there, Adrian."

"But this is why we're here," he argued, but Bex just kept shaking her head, which made no sense. She hadn't looked this scared when she'd faced the prince, but something about the darkness beyond the doors had her terrified.

"What are you so afraid of?"

"I'm not sure," she admitted. "Maybe one of my past lives had a bad experience with a door like this, or maybe it's the sin iron, but I just know something terrible will happen if you—"

"Wait," Adrian interrupted, desperate to understand. "Sin iron?"

Bex reached past him, pointing at the strange darkness he'd just stuck his hand into. But where his fingers had gone through the blackness like he was dipping them into water, hers stopped at the threshold, her hand flattened against the dark like she was pushing on a wall.

"You see?" she asked, closing her fist to rap her knuckles against what was very clearly a solid black surface. "I don't know how you put your hand through it, but this whole door is blocked with sin iron."

She said that the same way he'd say "cyanide," but while Adrian had heard the term before, he didn't actually know what sin iron was.

"It's all the evils of mankind baked into a brick," Bex explained when he asked. "Gilgamesh forces demons to forge it in the Hells and then uses it to make their control collars and slave cages. It's highly toxic, especially in its raw form. I can tolerate it because I'm a queen, but I'm surprised you're not already feeling sick." She tugged his arm again. "You should get away from it as soon as possible. Nothing good ever comes from sin iron."

Adrian frowned. He didn't feel sick in the slightest, but he was extremely curious. He didn't know what kind of magic he'd activated inside the doors to let his body pass through what was apparently a wall of poisonous metal, but it had to be powered by quintessence. He could still feel the coins he'd taken burning inside his veins like acid, but the pain was already fading. If he waited too long, it would burn out entirely, and then he'd have to do this all over again.

"I'm going to take a look."

"Adrian, *no,*" Bex said, pulling on his hand.

"I won't go all the way in," he promised, looking up at the wall. "But we didn't come this far just to turn around at the finish line. Gilgamesh's secrets are on the other side—I can feel it! I'm just going to stick my head in real fast, get a look around, and then we'll go."

He could tell from Bex's face that she thought that was a *horrible* idea, but Adrian's mind was made up. If he hadn't believed the Anchors held Heaven's secrets before, the giant golden treasure doors would have put all doubt to rest. He *had* to do this, quickly, before the quintessence and his Yearling disguise wore off. So before Bex could stop him, Adrian turned and stuck his head through the black-filled door.

Just like before, he passed through what should have been a solid wall of sin iron like a fish slipping into dark water. He didn't even perceive the metal. It just felt like passing through a shadow, a slow blink of darkness before the world burst into dazzling light.

Blindingly dazzling light. He froze where he was, squinting so hard that his eyes were practically shut. Eventually, his pupils adjusted, and Adrian cracked his eyelids to see he was staring into a desert.

At least, it looked like a desert. The sky was huge and pale, pale blue, but he couldn't see a sun, and the sand was like no desert he'd ever seen. It was black as volcanic soot but not dusty. The dark grains were long and thin, like metal shavings, and they were piled in huge dunes around a great black pillar that seemed to stretch all the way to the sky.

A few seconds later, Adrian realized there was no "almost" about it. The pillar *did* go to the sky, and it wasn't a pillar. It was a chain—a black metal chain as wide as a four-lane highway running from the ground into the sky straight as a spear.

It wasn't alone either. Now that his eyes were adjusting, Adrian could see the black lines of other chains far in the distance. How far was impossible to tell across the black dunes, but there were five just in what he could see directly in front of him. He was staring at them in wonder when he heard a man's low voice.

His head whipped toward the sound before he could stop it, and Adrian's blood ran cold. Two figures, a man and a woman, were standing at the base of the nearest chain, their heads bent toward each other in conversation. They were both filthy with the black grit that covered everything here, but no amount of grime could hide the man's gleaming golden armor or the woman's carved ivory skin.

It was a prince and his princess for sure, but something was wrong. Unlike the creepily perfect princess who'd tried to kidnap him in the Blackwood, this princess looked disheveled, and not just because she was dirty. Her ivory body was cracked and chipped all over like she'd been thrown down a mountain, and her prince wasn't any better. Every part of his golden armor was scuffed and dented, and his curling hair was caked in black grit, making him look like he'd been wandering out here for months.

It definitely wasn't the usual level of Heavenly immaculateness, but that just made the pair more fascinating. Neither prince nor princess had noticed Adrian yet. They were too busy studying the chain, their faces grim as they held a whispered conversation. Adrian couldn't hear what they were saying, which was a *real* pity, because that was a technical discussion if ever he'd seen one. He was leaning closer to try to catch at least a few words when the prince reached up and knocked his golden-gloved knuckles against the enormous chain's lowest link.

The moment he touched the metal, the whole chain rang like the deepest bell Adrian had ever heard. The sound shook the metal links like a plucked string, sending a shower of fresh black dust falling over the landscape. It pattered to the ground in front of Adrian like rain. Some of it even landed on his face, making him gasp. The shavings had the same metallic smell as the sin iron wall, but they were burning hot.

They must have come from the chain, he realized in a rush. The desert wasn't a desert at all. It was a sea of metal filings that had fallen off the giant chains. Giant *sin iron* chains! But why? What were the chains connected to up in the sky? And why was a prince doing what looked like maintenance work with his—

"Yearling!"

The shout rang through the air like a shot, and Adrian's head snapped up to see the prince's mirrored eyes staring straight at him.

"What in the Nine Hells are you doing?" the prince yelled, stepping away from his battered princess, who was smirking like she knew this was going to be good.

"I—I'm sorry, my prince," Adrian said, doing a quick emergency check of his disguise as he bowed his head in what he hoped would be taken for terrified reverence. "I was just... That is..."

"Save your excuses," the prince snarled. "You knew you were *never* to open those doors. No wonder this chain started going haywire!" His mirrored eyes narrowed.

"You're lucky the Eternal King forbade connecting the Hells to this place, or I'd damn you right here and now."

"You can always send him away and damn him later," his princess suggested eagerly.

"Of course *you'd* suggest that," the prince snapped, glaring over his shoulder. "You're the Princess of Envy. You live to watch others suffer, but I have to be practical. If Father found out I let a mortal walk away after glimpsing one of his sacred spaces, even if I damned him later, he'd harvest me for parts and stick me in the Sleep!"

The princess shrugged as if that didn't concern her, and the prince turned back to Adrian with a glower.

"I'll just have to shut you up another way."

"That really won't be necessary," Adrian said, struggling to pull back through the door only to find he couldn't. The wall of sin iron looked like a shadow from this side, but now that most of the quintessence had burned out of his body, it held on to Adrian like the metal it was, leaving him stuck like a bug in tar as the prince grabbed his head with a grime-smeared glove.

"I'm sorry about this, Yearling," he said, sounding as if he meant it. "You've been a damn good Anchor manager, but I can't let this slide. You understand. Now, hold still."

Adrian did nothing of the sort. He thrashed wildly in the prince's grip, pulling with all his strength as the prince began chanting a spell. Since Adrian didn't speak ancient Sumerian like Bex, he had no idea what the prince was saying, but it sounded *big*. He could feel the prince's hand growing hotter against his scalp as his voice built to a crescendo. Then, just when Adrian thought the building magic was going to incinerate him on the spot, the prince said something final, and a wave of light crashed out of his hand, knocking Adrian backward out of the door.

Chapter 6

"*A*drian!"

Bex had grabbed him the moment he stuck his stupid head through the stupid wall like an *idiot*, but it hadn't done any good. He'd made it as far as his shoulders before his body had stopped cold. She'd tried to pull him out, but the metal he'd passed through like a shadow felt as hard as any demon cage under Bex's hands. Hard and *painful*. The toxic sin iron burned her bare skin like stinging nettles, and Adrian was trapped *inside* it.

Bex ignited with a scream of frustration. She'd been keeping a tight hold on her flames since going full bonfire in the enemy's basement was almost as stupid as sticking your head through a sin iron door, but there was no point holding back now. Adrian was going to die whether the sorcerers caught them or not at this rate, so Bex threw all of her anger onto the fire, stoking her flames white-hot as she locked her arms around Adrian's disguised body.

It was a good thing she'd been training. Bex was mad enough at Adrian right now to scorch him to the bone. But the fear that fueled that anger also allowed her to hold it back, because the last thing she ever wanted to do was hurt him. Bex focused on that as she slammed her glowing shoulder into the wall of sin iron beside him.

Thank Ishtar, it worked. She'd never tried melting sin iron before, but the black metal began to hiss and pop the moment her fire touched it. She probably could have melted the whole wall, but then Adrian would be stuck inside a slab of *molten* sin iron. That was even worse, so Bex focused her heat instead, keeping one arm wrapped around Adrian's waist while she dug her fingers into the metal directly above him, heating it just enough to bend the sin iron away from his body.

It was slow going, but she didn't dare burn hotter. Bex could control her own heat, but she couldn't do anything about how hot the sin iron itself was getting. If she wasn't careful, she could cook Adrian before she got him out. Now more than ever, she needed to be steady and precise, but it was hard to stay focused when the fumes from the melting sin iron were hitting her in the face, making even Bex lightheaded.

That was bad. Since they'd been made to eat sins, demons had a fair amount of resistance to sin iron, but Adrian had nothing. Between the heat and the fumes, Bex had no idea how he wasn't dead yet, but she could feel his pulse racing under his skin. He was still alive in there, so Bex pushed herself to burn hotter, prying the black metal away from his body inch by inch. She'd almost gotten him loose when the whole sin iron wall shook like it'd been hit by a truck, and a wave of force blew them both backward.

It felt like being kicked. That was the only invisible thing Bex knew of that hit this hard, but they didn't get knocked into Limbo. They flew down the tunnel instead, crashing into the stone floor with Bex on the bottom and Adrian gasping on top of her.

"Adrian!" she cried, snuffing out her fire as she scrambled out from under him. "*Adrian!*"

She grabbed his face and pried his eyes open, almost crying in relief when she didn't see any black. No sin iron poisoning. That was a miracle, but while he was alive, things were definitely not well. His Yearling disguise was melting off of him like wax, but Adrian still hadn't stopped gasping, and his dilated eyes didn't seem to see her at all. Was this where she was supposed to remind him that he was himself?

"Adrian," Bex said, grabbing his shoulders. "It's me, it's Bex, and you're you. You're Adrian Blackwood, Witch of the Flesh, and I need you to snap out of this so we can..."

Her voice trailed off. Bex didn't know what a dissociative fugue looked like, but she didn't think this was it. Adrian didn't look confused. He looked like he was having some kind of attack. His chest was heaving like a bellows, and his pulse was pounding so fast that she could see the blood pulsing under his skin. His heart must have been going crazy under the Blackwood, but maybe that was the cause of this. Maybe something had happened to him inside the Anchor, and now his forest was fighting to keep him alive.

Bex didn't know if that was right, but getting Adrian back to his Blackwood was never a bad idea. Having a goal also helped snap her out of her panic, sharpening Bex's focus to a diamond edge as she shot to her feet.

"Hang on," she said as she grabbed Adrian's arms. "I'm getting us out of here."

He didn't react when Bex hoisted him onto her shoulders. She took a second to get him balanced, cursing yet again that the Blackwood's magic had left her so damn short and that he was so damn tall. All that handsome height she'd sighed over earlier was making her current life very difficult as Bex swung Adrian into a fireman's carry and took off down the tunnel.

She cleared the distance to the elevator in seconds, but the doors didn't open when she mashed the button. Bex didn't know if that was because she was a demon or simply wasn't a sorcerer, and she didn't stop to find out. She just hauled back and kicked the doors down, sticking her head through the wreckage to get a look at the empty elevator shaft.

It was a *long* way up. She couldn't even see the elevator itself, just a dark hole going up forever. But while there wasn't anything as convenient as a ladder, there were rails set into the smooth stone walls, which would have to do.

"Hold on tight," she told Adrian as she dug her fingers into the slippery metal rail. "This might get a little hairy."

He didn't react to her voice. She could still feel his heart thudding against her shoulder, but his breaths had stopped heaving, leaving his body terrifyingly still. There was nothing Bex could do about that down here, though, so she just focused on getting them out, bracing her boots against the elevator's smooth-bored walls as she started climbing.

Adrian would fall if she let go of him, so she had to pull them up one-handed. It was tricky going, but Bex had always been stronger than she looked, and she'd never been more motivated. She was *not* going to let her first date end in death. She was going to get them both out of here, and once the Blackwood fixed him—because it *had* to fix him— she was going to tear Adrian a new one for scaring a thousand years off her life.

That was the thought that kept Bex going as she hauled them up the elevator shaft. Every move was a complicated dance of wedging her boots against the rails hard enough to hold her weight while she slid her single hand up then holding onto the rail with her fingers while she levered her feet as high as she could get them before bracing to do it all over again. It was slow, arduous work, but eventually, Bex's horns bumped against the bottom of the elevator.

Keeping Adrian steady on her shoulders, Bex wedged her feet under the lip of the greased rail and reached up to rip open the bottom of the elevator with her free hand. No sorcerers fell out, which was a pity, because Bex was killing mad at this point—mad and scared. Climbing the elevator shaft had taken way too long. Adrian's body felt like a deadweight across her shoulders, and his breaths were so slow and shallow they barely registered. She needed to get him out of here twenty minutes ago, but now that she'd finally achieved her goal of making it back to the office level, Bex realized she didn't know how to get out.

That was enough to send her into a panic. The tunnel with the golden door had been scary, and going up the elevator shaft had taken way too long, but at least there'd only been one path to follow. Without Adrian leading the way, Bex had no idea how to navigate the space-folding labyrinth that was the Anchor's office. Worse, it sounded like they'd be doing it under fire. She could already hear voices shouting on the other side of the elevator's creepy white doors in English and Sumerian, laying down spells for when she came out.

Bex wasn't normally afraid of sorcerers. All the poetry they had to recite before they did anything usually left plenty of time for punching, but that advantage didn't work if there were enough of them. Even if she hadn't had Adrian's body to worry about, Bex wasn't fast enough to take down all the sorcerers she could hear outside the elevator before one of them got a spell off, and those were just the threats she was aware of. If the office had had time to set an ambush, then someone had undoubtedly already called for a prince, which meant things were about to get really, *really* bad. Bad enough for Bex to do something she'd never done before in this lifetime.

She called for backup.

"*Iggs!*" she hissed, mashing the button on her comm with her free hand while she backed herself and Adrian into the elevator's front corner where they hopefully wouldn't get hit if someone opened fire on the doors. "We need evac!"

For a moment there was nothing, then Iggs's voice came over her earbud like a blessing from Ishtar herself.

"Where are you?"

"Sill inside the Anchor," Bex whispered frantically, setting Adrian down for a second to take off her jean jacket so she could use it to tie him to her back, a clever plan she should have thought of a thousand feet of elevator shaft ago. "Adrian's down, and there are sorcerers everywhere. I need you to go to the door we were staking out and make us an exit. I'll carve my way over from this side and meet you."

That wasn't the greatest plan she'd ever come up with, but finding Iggs sounded a lot easier than spotting the watercooler where she and Adrian had entered this hellhole, and adding another attacker would divide the enemy's attention. It might also get Iggs killed if he was in the way when the prince arrived, but Bex couldn't worry about that right now. Iggs certainly wasn't. She could already hear him throwing open the RV door and jumping onto what sounded like a sidewalk full of surprised people.

"I'm on my way!" he yelled over the angry shouts. "Just hold tight!"

Bex let go of her comm to check the knotted sleeves of the jacket she'd tied around Adrian. When she was sure he wouldn't slide off her shoulders, she took a deep breath, said a prayer to her holy mother, and kicked out the elevator doors.

She hadn't refired her flames since she didn't want to make herself an even bigger target, but her boot still hit the metal doors like a battering ram. Bex jumped the second the kick finished, using the exploding doors to cover her flanks as she crashed out of the elevator and into the polo-shirted sorcerer who'd been chanting just outside. The man went down with a pained yelp, the glowing magic he'd been working on falling to pieces in his hands as Bex kicked him into a cubicle and took off down the hall.

Not getting caught was more important than speed or destruction, so Bex ignored the rest of the attackers, running in a low crouch to make them as small a target as possible as she wove through the topsy-turvy maze of the sorcerer's office. She tried her best to follow the path Adrian had led them down earlier, but the yellow-beige everything made it hard to tell one cluster of cubicles from another, and she didn't dare slow down to get a better look. She could already hear sorcerers chanting in the hallway behind her, rattling off the long litanies that told their magic to shoot her with lightning or whatever.

It sounded like the incantation for lightning, at least. Her Sumerian was usually pretty good, but translating poetry while running for her life was a stretch Bex couldn't make right now. Whatever it was, she didn't want it hitting them, so Bex whipped around the next corner she saw and took off down, then up, then down the hall on the other side.

By the time the flipping stopped, Bex was pretty sure she was going the wrong direction, but she didn't dare turn around. Her restored body could take a lightning spell, but Adrian's would get cooked. Her only chance of keeping him alive was to stay ahead of the firing squad until she found the way out.

It had to be here somewhere. The sorcerer's office was a dizzying three-dimensional maze, but Bex didn't think it was a very big one. There couldn't be *that* many sorcerers working here, and they didn't run very fast. All she had to do was stay ahead of them until she found the exit.

That was her plan, anyway. It started off pretty good, but the hallways seemed to go forever. Bex was wondering if Gilgamesh made his office workers walk for miles every day out of spite when she passed the same half-dead snake plant for the third time and realized she'd been running in circles.

She skidded to a stop, clutching Adrian as she turned in a circle, but it didn't do any good. She was thoroughly lost, and the sorcerers knew it. One stepped into the hallway ahead of her as she watched, the quintessence glowing in his hands as the spell he'd been reciting reached its conclusion.

"Lament of the Polished Desert!"

Bex nailed the translation that time, but she still didn't know what the spell did until the sorcerer opened his fist and sent a hail of shining glass knives flying at her face. One sliced her cheek open before she managed to dive sideways into the nearest cubicle. She rolled as she landed, twisting her body to save Adrian's and nearly crashing into a metal filing cabinet in the process.

The urge to go bonfire right then was overwhelming. Bex hated this place with a literal burning passion. But as satisfying as torching it all to the ground would have been, trapping herself and Adrian inside a burning labyrinth before she found the exit was a suicidally dumb idea. She also couldn't afford to make herself a beacon. If a prince *was* here, her flames would bring him right to them, and there was no way Bex could keep Adrian safe through a fight like that. So fire was out, but running clearly wasn't working, either, which meant Bex was going to have to come up with a third option.

With a string of curses that would have made Lys proud, Bex shifted Adrian's weight to free the leather cord that held her ring. She broke the string with a jerk and crammed the black metal band onto her finger, shoving the ring down hard to preemptively knock Drox out of the tirade he'd no doubt been building up since the last time she'd taken him off. Bex wasn't sure if that actually worked or if her sword could instinctively sense that now was not the time, but Drox's voice was steady as an iron palace when he spoke inside her head.

What is going on?

"Sorcerers," Bex said, rolling Adrian's weight entirely to her left shoulder to free her sword arm. "We're cutting our way out."

True to its nature, her sword didn't bother with silly questions like "Cutting what?" or "Out of where?" Drox simply appeared in her hand, his black blade already moving to slice the closest cubicle wall in half.

Bex leaped through the opening as soon as it appeared, dodging the glowing net one of the sorcerers had managed to get off above her head. She wasn't as lucky with the next spell, which appeared as a stone directly under her feet. The rock shot up the moment she stepped on it, throwing Bex off balance just in time for the next rock—which had formed on the cubicle wall—to slam her in the face while a sorcerer chanted from underneath the conference table in the upside-down meeting room directly over her head. The words were flying by too fast for Bex to make sense of them. Fortunately, her sword was on it.

Cobbles of the Sinner, Drox translated. *Witness, all ye faithful! The earth itself rises against those who defy Heaven's King. Curse the feet of the unworthy that they may—*

"I don't need the whole thing!" Bex yelled, swinging her sword through a red-painted, cuneiform-covered urn that looked like the ancient Sumerian equivalent of a fire extinguisher. "Just tell me how to avoid it!"

How would I know that? Drox snapped as the urn exploded in a cloud of freezing mist. *Gilgamesh invented sorcery after we were cast out of Paradise. The only way I know what a spell does is if I listen all the way to the—*

His explanation cut off when Bex swung his smoking blade up to slice through the conference table above her head. She'd been aiming for the sorcerer who was chanting at her, but her wild swing missed and cut through the beige-carpeted floor beside him instead.

This turned out to be *way* better. The Anchor sorcerers didn't seem to care about saving each other, but the moment Bex started cutting into the infrastructure, they stopped yelling spells at her and started yelling them at the walls.

Grinning at her discovery, Bex turned and swung Drox into the wall on her left, slicing clean through what looked like a support beam into a bathroom on the other side. She must have hit something load-bearing, because the whole architecturally impossible office started to tilt, sending desks, chairs, and chunky computers with cuneiform-modified keyboards sliding across the floor in a beige avalanche. Bex had to jump to avoid getting swept up in it, transforming Drox back into his ring so she could grab onto the nearest hanging light—which was actually a floor lamp in the office above her—without dropping Adrian.

She pivoted the moment her fingers locked onto the hot metal, swinging her feet until up became down and she was standing on the floor of the room that had just been the ceiling. As soon as her brain finished processing that, Bex took off running again, her boots grinding into the hard beige carpet as she raced toward the busted elevator she'd just spotted at the end of the hall.

This, of course, meant that she was right back where she'd started, but at least the elevator was a marker Bex recognized. She was already planning to reset and try the maze again when she heard something roaring down the hall.

The sound almost made her cry with relief. That was Iggs's voice! Bex spun toward it at once, slicing cubicles in half with her sword to clear a path until she spotted him. He was only a few direction flips away, red-faced but not yet fully transformed, though he looked like he was right on the edge as he threw a beige server rack into a pack of sorcerers that had been attempting to chain him down with glowing manacles.

"Iggs!" Bex yelled as he ripped his legs out of the chains. "Over here!"

Her voice was lost in the destruction, but it didn't matter. Iggs was a wrath demon, *her* demon. Sure enough, his head snapped toward her shout the second it left Bex's lips, and then he was plowing through office furniture to reach her, blasting desks and cubicles out of his way with jabs from the explosive short sword they'd stolen from the same sorcerer who'd made their RV.

"Are you okay?" he yelled when he finally made it over, his red eyes darting from Bex's face to the witch's body tied across her shoulders. "What happened to Adrian?"

"Nothing we can fix here," Bex said, readjusting Adrian's weight. "How far to our exit?"

"Not very," Iggs said, slapping a fresh handful of quintessence against his sword blade as he led Bex back down his path of destruction. "But this damn place is a maze crossed with a hornet's nest. I took a lightning bolt to the face on my way in."

Bex glanced at Iggs's fried hair with a wince. "Thanks for running to our rescue."

"I was worried I'd be too late," he confessed, grabbing a beige stapler off the closest desk and winging it like a bullet at the sorcerer who'd just stuck his head around the corner. "It took ten minutes and my entire bag of grenades to bust through the creepy white room at the beginning."

"At least you made it," Bex said, starting to breathe easier when she spotted the gaping hole in the ceiling over a destroyed water cooler that must have been Iggs's entry point. "What's the situation outside?"

"Little good, little bad," Iggs reported, sliding his glowing sword back into its sheath at the small of his back. "On the upside, none of the scalies outside thought the explosives I used to bust in here were magical, so I didn't get kicked. Downside, they thought I was a terrorist, which means we're about to be up to our necks in cops."

"Better than a prince," Bex said, jumping herself and Adrian through the hole in the ceiling to land in the remains of the white entry room, which did indeed look blown to hell. The creepy metal eye was in pieces on the floor, the gold glinting in the dusty sunlight streaming through the huge hole that now opened to the alley outside.

"Nice work," Bex said appreciatively as Iggs hauled himself up behind her. "Where's the RV?"

"Super close," Iggs promised, shooting past her to take the lead as they ran into the deserted square where she and Adrian had been listening to terrible music not thirty minutes ago. "I scored a great parking spot. Follow me!"

They took off at a run, vaulting over the toppled picnic tables and scattered trash cans the fleeing people had left in their wake. Bex thought they were headed toward the parking deck, but Iggs led her up the wide pedestrian stair behind the restaurant she and Adrian had used for their stakeout. Bex was about to ask Iggs where in the Nine Hells they were going when she spotted it.

Iggs had left their Winnebago in the middle of the damn sidewalk. It was parked sideways at the top of the cement stairs they were running up. No wonder people had thought he was a terrorist. It looked like he'd powerslid the RV off the road and charged down the stairs, fully armed, into a patio full of tourists. Bex could already hear sirens closing in from all sides, but they'd deal with that later. Right now, all that mattered was getting Adrian back to his forest before he died for real.

Goal in sight, Bex put on a burst of speed, leaving Iggs huffing to keep up as she raced up the stairs toward their RV. The normally busy road in front of Pike Place Market was deserted when she reached the top. Bex was praying to Ishtar that was because of the explosions and not because the cops had already set up a roadblock when she saw them.

Across the empty street, standing as still as statues in the long evening shadows, were two men. Two handsome, olive-skinned men with golden armor and eyes that shone like mirrors. One was short and stocky with a scarred face and a white sword at his side. The other was tall and thin with no sword, but Bex didn't think he'd need it.

"Shit," Iggs swore as he slid to a stop beside her. "*Two of them?*"

Bex took a cautious step backward. She'd never seen two princes together at the same time before. Funny enough, her first thought was that this proved Adrian's theory that the Anchors were important. He'd be excited about that when he woke up, but only if Bex could keep him alive that long. She was about to tell Iggs to run back down the stairs when the shorter prince, the one with the scars and the mad-dog snarl, stepped off the curb and started walking across the empty street.

His slow pace scared Bex more than any charge. He kept his mirrored eyes on her the whole time, waiting for her to move. Even more unnerving, his brother hadn't budged. Bex didn't know if that was because he thought his help was unnecessary or if he was saving something nasty for when she ran. If she didn't run, though, the prince was going to walk right into them.

"Bex," Iggs whispered, edging back toward the steps.

She was about to give the signal to run when a cop car came over the hill. It was going so fast that its tires left the ground, sirens wailing and lights flashing as it shot down the middle of the empty street to slam into the prince who'd been slow-walking toward them.

For one glorious second, Bex thought they'd just been saved. The black-and-white patrol car hit the prince at full speed, its front end crumpling like tinfoil around his golden-armored body. But just as Bex was starting to believe they'd been on the receiving end of a legitimate miracle, the cop car flipped up onto its nose, stopped cold by the prince, who hadn't moved an inch.

The airbags went off inside the crumpled cop car a second later. Its tires had just slammed back to the ground when five more police vehicles came screaming over the top of the hill. They screeched to a halt when they saw the wrecked patrol car wrapped around the prince, who was still standing there like a golden post. For a long moment, everyone just stared at each other, then Bex saw a barrage of impacts hit the prince's golden armor.

The rush of joy almost made her drop Adrian. That idiot had just gotten himself kicked! Even princes couldn't escape their father's automatic ticket to Limbo, and with all the cops watching, his brother couldn't do anything about it unless he also wanted to get the boot. The demons were in the same boat, but Bex felt a lot better about her odds running from a bunch of mortal donut munchers than fighting two princes. She was about to tell Iggs to book it when the prince who hadn't been hit by the car called her name.

"Queen of Wrath."

Bex glanced up to find him smirking. His face was surprisingly thin and haggard for someone who lived in Heaven, but his mirror eyes shone with the same malice as all of Gilgamesh's spawn when he pointed his golden finger at the spot where the kicked prince had just disappeared.

"My brother is a monster resurrected from the purges," he announced in a hard, challenging voice. "Are you sure you want to leave him alone for five minutes with your people?"

Bex's stomach dropped to her feet. She'd thought they'd gotten saved, but this had been no accident. That prince had gotten himself kicked into Limbo on *purpose*, to hurt her demons.

That was as far as Bex's panicked brain got before she shoved Adrian into Iggs's arms.

"Run."

"What about you?" Iggs cried as Bex charged into the street. "I can't just—"

"*Run, Iggerux!*" Bex commanded as she grabbed the police car that had crashed into the prince. "*Now!*"

The demon erupted in curses, but Bex couldn't spare him a look. She'd already hoisted the totaled patrol car into the air and thrown it as hard as she could at the second prince. The vehicle was still sailing past the watching cops when the hail of kicks landed in her chest, punting Bex out of the living world.

Chapter 7

Prince Leander sidestepped the hurled vehicle with ease, smiling at the local authorities, who were still blinking in confusion. Humans were always bewildered after administering a kick. The prince happily took advantage of this fact, crossing the empty street faster than their poor scaled eyes could see to go after the demon who'd taken off running back toward the market with the mortal man the Queen of Wrath had been carrying.

He was surprised the demon hadn't gone for the house on wheels. It had been many, *many* years since Leander had visited the living world. Its contraptions got stranger every time he returned, but it was obvious the boxy metal wagon was sorcerous in nature. He'd been planning to crush the thing with its own quintessence the moment the demon stepped inside, but the beast had denied him the easy kill, fleeing down the stairs toward the water instead.

Perhaps the demon felt he had a better chance of losing the prince on foot, or perhaps he was running toward the Coward Queen's other allies. Either way, it made no difference. Leander might not have his sword, but he'd been overseeing the Hells for centuries. There was no demon in existence who could escape him.

"Fifty Steps of the Pilgrim," he said, drawing on the quintessence in his blood to shoot fifty paces forward, directly next to his fleeing quarry. "Band of a Thousand Irons."

The sorcery fell from his lips as naturally as breath, the ancient words giving form to quintessence's limitless potential as an iron band the size of a log appeared out of thin air to wrap around the demon's legs, causing him to pitch forward. The giant curled his body as he fell, protecting the human in his arms. Curious behavior for a demon, especially one of this size. It wasn't a war demon, so what...

The prince leaned down, grabbing the tripped demon's ox-like horns to have a look at his eyes. *Ah hah.* This must be the wrath demon the Coward Queen was rumored to have freed from Limbo, the one everybody in Heaven thought she'd died for.

How inconvenient. Until the Queen of Wrath bowed her horns to Gilgamesh, her wrath demons could not be named and commanded like the others. This one was already snapping his fangs like an animal, his body growing huge and red as he fought Leander's sorcery. The prince watched him struggle for a moment before placing his hand on the demon's head with his two front fingers pressed right between the beast's black horns.

"Hammer of the Eternal King."

A great *gong* rang out as the golden will of Gilgamesh slammed into the demon's skull, flinging him off the raised square. He landed with a crash on the waterfront road down below, which was disappointing. Leander had intended to knock him into the bay, but the demon must have been heavier than expected. Still, it was enough. He was about to head back to the road above to await his idiot brother's return when he noticed the human the Queen of Wrath's demon had dropped.

The prince crouched down, grabbing the young man's jaw in his golden grip. His face had a deathly pallor, but breath still flickered inside his throat. It looked like he'd been cursed with one of the Royal Verses, which made no sense. There wasn't another prince on this mission.

Leander leaned closer with a frown, taking off his gauntlet to press his bare hand against the man's cold cheek. Something was wrong. The curse should have killed him instantly, but a strange magic Leander didn't recognize was pushing it back. The man's face looked oddly familiar as well, almost like...

The prince snatched his hand back, cursing in his mother's tongue. This was no ordinary human. The man was a witch, and not just any witch—a Blackwood witch. Leander's mirror eyes narrowed. A *male* Blackwood witch.

He could be someone else's son, reason cautioned. *Many witches still hide in the forests. He could be one of theirs.*

But Leander already knew it was not so. Now that he'd noticed, there was no unseeing the thick, black, curling hair that was nigh identical to Leander's own. But how was that possible? How was he *here*? How was he still free and not—

Leander's hand dropped back down to wrap around the witch's throat. He should kill him now. Snap his neck quickly while he could still reasonably claim ignorance. It would be no more than his scheming mother deserved, yet the prince's hand did not move.

For ten long heartbeats, Leander stared at the witch's unconscious face. Then, slowly, he removed his hand from the young man's throat.

He lifted his body off the pavement next, tucking the witch under his arm like a package to carry him back up the stairs.

Bex arrived in Limbo with her sword ready in her hands. The force of the kick was still rolling through her insides, but she didn't have time to deal with it. She had to find the prince, had to stop him, but all she saw was Limbo's gray nothing. Where—

Behind you.

Drox's warning came with a tug inside her head. Bex followed it instinctively, whirling around so fast that her boots left skid marks on Limbo's gray floor, then she breathed a sigh of relief.

The prince was only five feet away. There were no dead demons at his feet, either, which meant she wasn't too late. But while Bex already had her sword up, the prince was just standing there, staring at her like he couldn't understand what his mirrored eyes were seeing.

"This is it?" he rasped, his voice creaking like it hadn't been used in centuries. "This is the monster they're all so afraid of? This *child*?"

"Try me and see," Bex taunted, her eyes flicking to the prince's wide-open left side.

Do it, Drox ordered. *While he still thinks you're weak.*

Bex shook her head. Bloodshed would just draw her demons faster, but all princes seemed to love the sound of their own voice. If she could keep this one talking, she could burn their five minutes without endangering her people.

"Have I killed you before?" she taunted. "I can't tell. All you golden jackasses look the same."

She paused there, but the prince didn't take the bait. He just kept staring at her, his golden-gloved hand opening and closing above the hilt of his white sword, which, for some reason, was still sheathed at his side rather than fawning at his feet.

"This is all your fault," he whispered as his body began to shake inside the shell of his armor. "You're the reason they woke me up. It's because of *you* that I was taken from the Sleep and forced back into this torture." His face contorted into a mask of hate. "*I will beat you until there is nothing left to reincarnate!*"

He'd just started lurching toward Bex when the sword vanished from his side, and a white figure appeared to throw herself between them. It was the same princess Bex had fought last time, the one whose hand she'd almost grabbed: the remains of the Queen of Greed.

"My prince!" she cried, wrapping her arms around his armored body. "I beg you, still your anger! Remember the Crown Prince's orders! I know you wish to destroy her, but the Coward Queen *must* be brought to Heaven intact! If you do not obey—"

Her pleading cut off with a yelp as the prince slammed his fist into her face. The punch landed hard enough to crack the princess's ivory nose. When she staggered away, he hit her again, cratering her white body into the gray ground with a scream of rage.

"*He brought me back!*" the prince roared, bringing his golden boot down on the princess's torso. "I purged his enemies, did everything he asked! He promised it was over, that I could rest, but then he drags me back to—"

His tirade cut off when Bex's sword crashed into his helmet.

"*Don't touch my sister!*"

The prince hadn't been paying attention, so she'd managed to get him right above the ear. The strike should have sliced his skull in half, but this prince was much faster than the one she'd fought in the Blackwood. Bex barely felt her sword touch his helmet before he dodged away, turning his mad snarl off the princess onto her.

Bex snarled back, showing him her fangs as she swung again. She went for his legs this time, putting her body between the prince and her sobbing sister. He dodged the second blow as fast as he had the first, but at least she'd driven him back. Bex was preparing to drive him all the way to the edge of Limbo when a hand grabbed her ankle.

"You will not hurt my prince!" the princess screamed, her cracked face contorting in rage as she yanked Bex off her feet.

The prince kicked her the moment she went down, sending Bex skipping across Limbo's gray emptiness like a stone. By the time she pushed herself up again, the princess was kneeling at her prince's feet.

"Please," she begged, pulling off her glove to offer him her dark-skinned hand. "Please, my love, use me. We'll defeat her together and return to Heaven in glory! We'll—"

"There is no glory," the prince snarled, looking down at his princess with so much hate Bex actually felt sorry for her. "You're as much a part of this farce as the rest, but I don't need you. I'll destroy the Coward Queen on my own. I'll destroy her demons. I'll destroy this hideous cell. I'll destroy the city outside. I'll destroy and destroy and destroy until all of creation is as broken as my father left me!" He bared his white teeth. "He wanted a monster? *He can have me!*"

He reeled back as he finished, but there was no time to move. There was barely even time to watch as his golden boot landed in the crying princess's stomach, sending her white body hurtling into Limbo's gray nothing. Bex was about to go after her when Drox spun in her hand.

Eyes front!

Bex braced just in time as the screaming prince slammed into her like a golden train. He was only a few inches taller than she was, but his fury made him seem enormous, his body a golden blur that was striking everywhere at once. If Bex's sword arm hadn't had five thousand years of muscle memory to guide it, she would have been dead in the first two seconds. Instead, she was driven back, focusing everything on defense as the prince's fists slammed into Drox like golden anvils.

She tried blocking on her cutting edge to slice his arm. A Blade of Gilgamesh was the only thing that could stop Drox. Slicing the prince should have been easy now that he'd thrown his princess away, but while his golden gauntlets were destroyed in seconds, the scarred skin beneath was harder than anything they'd ever hit.

Bex had no idea how. Princes couldn't be injured by normal weapons, but Drox had always been able to cut them. They should have been carving this unarmed rage junkie to pieces, but something was letting him block her sword strikes with his bare hands.

The quintessence has crystalized inside his body, Drox said, twisting in Bex's grip as he tried in vain to saw through the prince's calloused fingers. *It happens with very old princes.*

Now that he'd drawn her attention to it, Bex realized she could feel the uneven hardness of the prince's knobby, swollen hands through her blade. It looked incredibly painful, but while Bex would never feel sorry for a prince, she was in trouble if she couldn't cut him.

He can't be calcified everywhere, Drox told her patiently. *Try stabbing other parts.*

Bex nodded and shifted her stance, whipping her blade away from the prince's hardened hands to go for the meaty part of his leg instead. This left her center open, but if she couldn't hurt him, the fight was already lost. She just had to keep him away from her demons for five minutes. That'd be a lot easier if he couldn't move, so Bex took a risk, putting all of her strength behind the strike that would hopefully take off his—

A blow to her stomach knocked Bex's plans—and all her breath—right out of her. She'd thought she'd have time to at least land the cut before he struck back, but the prince was so fast. Fast and *strong*. He'd hit her in the gut with a quick jab from his bare fist, but it was still enough to send her rocketing backward.

Straight into a kick demon.

The impact took them both out. The gray wrath demon was one of the big ones, but Bex still knocked him off his feet. They landed in a tangle several dozen feet away with Bex on top, but she couldn't breathe. The impact had collapsed her lungs, and black blood was everywhere. Bex didn't know if it was hers or the kick demon's, but there was way too much of it, and she couldn't—

Calm down, Drox ordered as he flew back to her hand. Bex hadn't even realized she'd dropped him, but her sword was suddenly right there, filling her mind with his iron calm.

Your regeneration will fix your lungs in four seconds. You need to get off the demon before he gets caught up in this. Once you're clear, ignite and go for the prince's left. His movements looked marginally slower on that—

"I can't ignite in Limbo," Bex wheezed as her lungs shuddered back to life, just like Drox had said. "You know what happened last time."

This isn't like last time, her sword promised. *But it will end far worse if you don't light up.*

Bex had no argument there. The prince was too fast, too strong, and every bit of his body she'd managed to hit felt like a rock. She had no chance of beating him without her bonfire, but her hands were shaking. She didn't remember how she'd burned herself to a crisp the last time she'd fought a prince in Limbo, but her body must have, because she was suddenly trembling uncontrollably. Just thinking about fire made her heart start racing so fast she felt lightheaded, dumping ice water on the rage she needed to ignite.

You must *ignite,* Drox ordered, his black blade heavy in her hands. *Or every demon around us is dead.*

He forced Bex's head up, turning her neck to make her see the ring of gray-skinned kick demons that was already closing in. Sure enough, the smell of her blood had brought them in droves. The prince was already slaughtering them, tearing into her starvation-maddened people so wildly, his golden armor was painted black with their blood.

The horrific sight was enough to break through Bex's fear, curling her shaking hands into fists. Those were *her* demons being torn to pieces. *No one* should hurt them while she lived, especially not one of Gilgamesh's golden puppets.

Righteous fury filled Bex in a torrent, fueling the bonfire that had never gone out. She leaped off the kick demon the prince had knocked her into with a scream that shook Limbo. Fire exploded over her as she flew, turning her into a blazing comet as the Queen of Wrath crashed into the prince's left side.

He was so caught up in slaughtering her demons that he never saw her coming. Bex took advantage of the lapse to drive Drox's smoking blade deep into his ribs. It felt like pushing her sword through a rock, but she was blazing with the fire that was her true form now, and it made her stronger than her human shadow ever could be. She drove Drox in to the hilt, cooking the prince's flesh from the inside with his smoking blade. She was about to yank up and slice the monster in half when the prince reached back to grab her burning shoulder.

His hardened hands started charring before he'd even touched her, but the mad prince was beyond pain. He ripped her off him with a roar of rage, throwing Bex at the ground so hard her bones cracked.

She was *not* beyond pain. Bex screamed as her body shattered. Her fire-fueled regeneration healed the damage in seconds, but the shock still dulled her reflexes long enough for the prince to reel back and kick her in the ribs.

At least she didn't fly as far this time. The ring of kick demons was thick around them now, their hunger-fueled madness driving them relentlessly toward food even though the gray ground was black with their blood. They snatched Bex out of the air and dragged her flaming body toward their mouths. One actually got his fangs into her before she kicked him away, calling Drox back into his ring so she wouldn't cut her own people as she wrestled out of their claws.

You must cut them, her sword counseled. *Pain is the only feeling that gets through their starvation, and you can't fight the prince and all of Limbo at the same time.*

"I won't use a queen's blade on my own people!" Bex shouted as she shoved her way out of the horde of kick demons. "It's not their fault they're like this!"

I respect your resolve, he said. *But if you don't start doing actual damage soon, your own people will eat you alive.*

As always, Drox spoke the truth Bex didn't want to hear. Even after she'd fought her way out of the cluster the prince had kicked her into, kick demons were all she could see. Their gray bodies filled her vision, their tongues glistening wetly in her firelight as they licked the black blood—hers and theirs—off the ground. Even now that she was lit up, there was no recognition in their gray eyes, only hunger. Endless, maddening hunger that had turned her proud, noble people into monsters.

The rage that hit her then was like nothing Bex had ever felt. Fire exploded out of her in a blast of superheated air strong enough to knock the kick demons backward, buying her precious room to charge the prince, who was still tearing demons apart in his own mad rage. The heat coming off her was so intense the prince actually looked up from his slaughter, lifting his head just in time for the fireball that was Bex to crash into his chest.

"Burn!" she screamed, taking them both to the ground in an inferno of white-hot flame. "Burn like the flames in your father's Hells, you gods-damned son of a—"

Her cursing cut off when something grabbed her horns. Bex's first thought was that one of her demons had sneaked in from behind, but when she looked up, the princess was standing over them. Her ivory face was cracked down the middle, and her white body was splattered with black demon blood, but her golden eyes were gleaming with fury as she tightened her fists around Bex's tall horns and wrenched sideways.

The move nearly tore Bex's head off. But she was flaming hard now, and she spun with the princess instead, releasing the prince to swing her black sword like an ax at the princess's torso. It should have been a clean cut through the ribs, but even in this form, the princess was still a sword. Drox's blade bounced right off her side, leaving the princess free to toss Bex away and throw herself at her scorched prince.

He tried to beat her off, but the princess latched onto him like a lamprey, healing the flesh Bex had managed to char. The Queen of Wrath, meanwhile, landed among her people, who instantly tried to eat her.

Burn them off! Drox roared, turning back into a ring as he desperately tried to stay on her hand. *It's the only way!*

Bex knew that. The kick demons were biting her all over, tearing her flesh and spilling her blood faster than even her fire could heal. But though their teeth were buried in her flames, the Bonfire of Wrath controlled what she burned, and she couldn't burn them. These were the people Ishtar had made her to protect. The people who'd refused to kneel even when Gilgamesh had damned them to this cold, empty hell because they knew their queen was still alive. They'd believed in her, put their hopes in her. She could never hurt them.

You are a good queen, Drox said. *But you will soon be a dead one if you don't bend on this. Who will save your people if you let them eat you?*

Bex's answer to that was to turn all her fire inward. She didn't have to beat the prince here. She just had to keep him occupied until the kick was over. Their five minutes had to be nearly up. Once they were back on the street, Bex could scorch him to ash just like she'd done to his brother. She just had to survive long enough to make it.

Easier said than done. Demon teeth might not leave never-healing wounds like the Blades of Gilgamesh, but there were still a lot of them. Even with all her fire going to fuel her own body, Bex's regeneration wasn't able to keep up with the gallons of blood her demons were spilling.

Desperate, she turned to her people, grabbing their gray heads in her bloody hands as she begged them to see her, to know her. As ever, though, no recognition flickered in their glassy eyes. Only endless, ravening hunger and the ghost of something else, a dim sliver of the same crazed light she'd seen in the prince's mirrored eyes.

Bex went still, her hands freezing on the jaws of the demon she'd been weakly attempting to shove away. Of *course*, why hadn't she seen it earlier? Her wrath demons weren't crazed just because they were starving. They were angry, *furious*. They'd been suffering in Limbo since the fall of Paradise, unable even to die. Their eyes shone with the same pain-maddened rage that drove the prince to throw away his sword and blindly attack whatever was in front of him, but unlike Gilgamesh's son, her demons had not been abandoned to their fate. Their queen still fought for them, bled for them. Their wrath was hers, and Bex would burn with it until she died.

That's more literal than you know, Drox warned. *These demons have been raging for five thousand years. I know you care deeply for them. You've always cared, but this is bigger than both of us. If you take their wrath upon yourself, I won't be able to—*

Bex didn't wait for him to finish. She'd already grabbed the fangs the closest demon was attempting to sink into her chest and shoved her fire down its throat. The flames passed through the demon's body harmlessly, because Bex's fire only burned those she raged at, and she wasn't angry at her people. She was angry *for* them, though not as angry as they were. She was used to burning at this point, but the rage she fed into her fire had always been her own—a queen's wrath to be sure, but still just one lifetime's worth, which was nothing compared to the inferno she touched now.

The blast hit her like a bucket of kerosene thrown on a campfire. Wrath was what Ishtar had made her to burn, but the scope of her people's fury was bigger than even Bex could comprehend. She'd only touched her spark to one demon, but the flames roared out like a forest fire, leaping from demon to demon until all of Limbo was burning with Bex at the center.

Not again, Drox groaned, getting a stronger bite on her finger. *Control it, Rebexa! Before it consumes you!*

Impossible. There was no controlling this explosion as five thousand years of her people's pent-up wrath went up in flames around her. The demons' rage fed her like gasoline, building her bonfire so hot and high that even Bex was swallowed, leaving nothing but an inferno that roared to the sky.

The kick demons fell to their knees at the sight. One by one, they bowed their heads, offering their fury to flames that were rapidly turning Limbo's gray to red. Even the prince stopped to watch, his mad eyes confused as he stared into the hell burning above him.

Stop this, Rebexa! Drox roared. *You'll lose yourself again!*

The Bonfire of Wrath did not care. There were no more thoughts in her head, no more fear, no more plans. All was consumed by the fire, leaving only a righteous, punishing fury as she reached down her arm—which was now the size of a mountain—to enclose the prince in a burning cage of a thousand fingers.

His princess screamed when she realized she was locked outside. She rammed herself against the burning cage, scorching her white body black, but it did no good. The Bonfire was already closing her fist, incinerating the prince inch by inch. Making him suffer as they had suffered. Making him *burn.*

He welcomed her with open arms, embracing the fire even as his melting armor ran off his charred body in golden rivers. His princess screamed in terror at the sight and rammed herself even harder against the Bonfire's prison, ignoring the cracks its heat opened in her ivory arms as she fought to touch her prince in any way she could. Every time a part of her brushed him, his body healed, the blackened flesh knitting back together, and every time, he bashed her away, screaming at her to let him die.

The princess refused. She kept fighting, throwing herself into the Bonfire over and over until her carved body was as brittle as a charred log. Even when her blackened limbs cracked off and fell away, she never stopped trying to reach her prince, beating herself against the fire until nothing was left of her but a hand.

A woman's dark-skinned hand, lying limp on Limbo's blackened floor.

In the heart of the inferno, the Bonfire of Wrath stopped. There was more to be burned, eons of rage, but even when everything else was lost to the flames, the Bonfire knew that hand. The prince was sobbing on the floor next to it, begging for death as the molten gold of his armor left blistering trails down the face his princess had just healed, but the Bonfire did not care about him. She'd already bashed him out of the way, reaching down to clumsily grab the princess's small hand in her giant burning ones.

The prince grabbed it back with a roar. His body started healing again the moment he touched it, but as much as that seemed to enrage him, the chance to finally die must have been more important. He'd already seen that the Bonfire cared more for the hand than for him, so he dropped it on the ground and stomped it under his boot, screaming at the flames that they'd have to burn him first to get what they wanted.

The Bonfire of Wrath was happy to oblige. She fell on the prince like a burst dam, drowning him in a river of flame that even his princess's healing couldn't keep up with. She'd nearly burned him down to his quintessence-

crystalized bones when the prince's body suddenly
vanished.

Consumed by her wrath, the sky-spanning Bonfire
could only stare in confusion, but Bex was finally beating
her way back to the surface, and she knew. The prince's five
minutes were over, dropping him out of Limbo. Since Bex
had gotten herself kicked right after him, she only had a
few seconds before she was forced out as well. She used
them to go for her sister's hand, which was still lying on the
ground where the prince had dropped it. She was still
struggling to get her thousand fiery fingers around it when
a voice cried out in her head.

Reboxa!

The queen stopped. That was Drox's voice, but it was
panicked and raw, as if he'd been screaming. She felt the
rush of his relief next, but only for a moment before her
sword snapped back into her hand.

You can't leave like this, he said in a rush. *You're still
burning with five millennia of your people's wrath. If you fall
out of Limbo like this, you'll take all that rage with you and keep
burning until there's nothing left. That's what happened last
time! If you don't want to burn to a cinder again, you have to cut
yourself free before you drop!*

The fear in her sword's voice filled Bex with terror.
The Bonfire of Wrath flared up in response, trying to
consume the fear as it did everything else, but Bex refused
to let it take over again. She sliced Drox down instead,
cutting through the sky-consuming flames. It hurt like she
was cutting into her own flesh, but Bex could see the gray of
Limbo again and her sister's hand lying on the blackened
ground. She fell toward it like a stone, grabbing the familiar
fingers just in time as Limbo shattered around them.

Her people howled as it broke. All around her, wrath
demons were rising from their knees, reaching up to the

once-again flameless gray sky with bellows of thwarted rage. Bex felt their anger echoing inside her own body, but she couldn't reach them anymore. Limbo had already spat her out, crashing her back into the real world so hard she cracked the pavement.

Bex lay where she'd fallen with a wince. The bonfire had healed the holes the demons' teeth had punched through her, but while her physical body had repaired itself perfectly, the rest of Bex was a wreck. Her mind felt as fragile as scorched paper, and her insides were hollow and aching. She felt like a used-up, ash-coated shell of a person, but she was alive. She was *alive* with her sister's hand still clutched against her chest.

Congratulations, Drox said, his voice brimming with pride. *You burned the wrath of your people and didn't get consumed. It would have been better if you hadn't lost control in the first place, of course, but that was still a vast improvement over last time, and you got the Queen of Greed's hand!*

She had, hadn't she? Bex had finally rescued one of her sisters! Only her hand, but that was still more than she'd ever managed before.

It's better than that, Drox said, his eagerness marching through her like an army. *That hand is more than just a piece of Ishtar's daughter. It is a Blade of Gilgamesh, a weapon of the enemy!* His voice grew louder. *This is the chance we've been waiting five thousand years for! Gilgamesh can't replace his swords like he does his princes. With this hand, we can begin to turn the tide. All that's left now is to finish the enemy, and our victory will be complete!*

Bex was too ash-brained to follow that last part, so Drox turned her eyes to the prince's blackened carcass lying on the shattered pavement beside them. He looked like a burned wooden carving, but Bex could see the faint movement of his breath stirring the ash flaking off his charred nose. He was still alive.

Not for long, Drox promised gleefully, turning back into a sword inside her clenched fist. *He killed your people. He hurt your sister. Draw on that wrath and burn once more. Quickly, before the other one finds us.*

Bex nodded and pushed up, keeping her sister's hand pressed tight against the blood-soaked ruin of her purple date dress as she lifted Drox above the scorched prince. She could see the whiteness of his quintessence-calcified bones through his blackened skin, which meant she'd need her fire to cut him. Bex wasn't sure she could muster that again whatever Drox said, but her sword was insistent. He chanted in her head, reminding her of all the wrongs the princes had done until Bex's flames flickered back to life once more.

And Holy Ishtar, did it hurt. It hurt so damn much, like running on a sprained leg. Nothing good ever came from pain like that, but Bex forced herself to ignore it, swinging Drox's smoking blade down for the strike that would split the monster prince's quintessence-hardened skull right off his—

"I wouldn't do that if I were you."

Bex froze, fumbling the sword in her hands from attack to defense. She knew that voice, and it was *far* too close. She'd been so focused on the hand, the prince, and the pain, she hadn't noticed that she was back in the middle of the street where she'd thrown the police car—the one that had been swarming with scale-eyed cops only five minutes ago. Now, though, the humans were on the ground, their heads twisted backward as if something had broken all their necks at once. Bex was still trying to figure out how that could have happened when she spotted the second prince standing in the long shadow of a building not ten feet in front of her.

He looked exactly the same now as he had when she'd thrown the car at him: tall, gaunt, swordless. He'd clearly been waiting for her to drop out of Limbo, but while Drox was screaming at her to ignore the unarmed newcomer and finish the enemy in front of them, Bex couldn't tear her eyes away because the new prince was holding an unconscious man under his arm. A tall, handsome, dark-haired man that made her heart seize up in fear.

Adrian.

"Put him down," she ordered, ignoring the terrifying pain inside her as she fired Drox's blade as hot as it would go and pressed the smoking edge against the unconscious prince's charred temple. "Now, or I stab him through the head."

Don't bargain with him! Drox roared. *Just stab me down and run! Finish the prince we've got and get back to your demons before your body gives out!*

Bex wasn't sure it hadn't already. Her flames were still burning for the moment, but the rest of her was collapsing. It was the same exhaustion she'd felt after killing the prince in the Blackwood, but infinitely bigger. The only reason she was still standing was because she was too afraid for Adrian to let go. The prince clearly knew it, too, giving her a superior smile as he reached down to wrap his golden hand around Adrian's throat.

"Lower your weapon," he ordered, his mirror eyes gleaming in her firelight, "or the witch dies."

Don't you dare, Drox snarled, but it was too late. Bex had already pulled her sword back into his ring and stumbled away from the burned prince to give his brother room.

"Good," the tall prince said, moving closer. "Now his sword."

"No," Bex snapped, clutching her sister's hand against her chest. "*Never!*"

"The princess as well," he told her in a hard voice, "or I break the witch's neck."

He turned his hand as he finished, wrenching Adrian's head sideways. Another inch, and his neck would break, leaving him as dead as the cops on the ground. Adrian was going to die in front of her, and she couldn't—

"Stop!"

The prince stayed his hand, staring at her with eyes that looked more like polished swords than mirrors as Bex unclenched her fist from her sister's hand.

No! Drox roared in her head. *Queen Rebexa, think of what you are doing! That is a Blade of Gilgamesh, an irreplaceable weapon of the enemy. If we can keep it, the Eternal King will be limited to six active princes instead of seven. This is the only chance we've ever had to do permanent damage to the enemy! You can't just—*

The yelling stopped when Bex ripped Drox's ring off her finger. She gripped him tight in her right fist while her left tossed the princess's hand—her sister's precious, irreplaceable hand—onto the burned prince's chest.

"There," she said when it was done. "Now give the witch back."

The gaunt prince smiled politely and let go of Adrian's neck. He placed his body on the ground next, laying him out like a corpse on the cracked street. The moment he let go, Bex darted forward and grabbed her prize, clutching Adrian in her arms as she turned and fled as fast as she could back toward the RV.

The street with all the dead cops turned out to be surrounded by a sorcerous barrier that kept the rest of the arriving humans spellbound. All the cops who'd come to back up the first wave were standing on the street like statues, their faces dumbstruck as they stared slack-jawed into the barrier's undulating patterns. That struck Bex as significant—she'd never seen a prince use sorcery before—but she was too panicked to investigate.

Adrian looked *terrible*. Bex didn't know if the prince had done something to him or if his body had run out of whatever had been keeping it going during the five minutes she'd been in Limbo, but he seemed to be clinging to life by a thread. His skin was as gray as the afternoon rain clouds rolling in overhead, and his breaths came in short, irregular pants. Bex didn't know what any of that meant, but she knew she had to get him back to his forest *right now*, so she pushed what was left of her fire as hard as it would go, shooting across the street toward the RV.

She kept an eye out for Iggs as she ran. She didn't see any sign of him, which was better than finding a body, but Bex didn't believe for one second that Iggs had given Adrian to the prince willingly. Praying to Ishtar that he was only hurt and not evaporated, Bex released her grip on Adrian for a split second to tap the button on her comm, which, by the same miracle that had spared most of her dress, was somehow still in her ear.

"Lys!" she cried when the mic clicked on, shifting Adrian to her shoulder so she could yank open the RV's side door. "I need you to find Iggs! I think he—"

"Already on it," her lust demon interrupted grimly. "We saw him go flying all the way down here. He hit the road pretty hard, but I'm reasonably sure he'll live. Nemini's hauling him into the parking deck right now, but there are cops everywhere. What happened? Are you—"

"I'm fine," Bex lied, finally letting her flames die out as she grabbed Adrian's broom out of the storage cabinet next to the RV's cab. "I'm sending Norma your way. Load up, and find somewhere safe to lie low. I've got to get Adrian back to his forest."

It was a sign of how long they'd worked together that Lys didn't ask any questions. They just told her they'd take care of it and hung up, leaving Bex in silence as she turned to face Norma.

Iggs must have put the construct in emergency mode when he jumped out, because their normally cheerful grandma looked as serious as an ambulance driver eight hours into a hell shift. Her mood matched Bex's, in other words, which made the next step much easier as the Queen of Wrath began barking orders.

"Drive to the first floor of the Pike Place public parking deck," she commanded, keeping her fist tight around Drox as she marched down the steps with Adrian's body tossed over one shoulder and his broom balanced on the other. "Avoid cops and roadblocks, but otherwise, go as fast as you can. Get a parking spot and wait for Lys to find you. They're in charge until I return."

"Yes, ma'am," Norma replied, revving the engine as Bex slammed the screen door shut behind her.

She charged down the cement stairs next, refusing to feel grateful that the prince's barrier was still keeping the cops occupied as she raced across the deserted patio where she and Adrian had been so happy. The panoramic views of the Puget Sound were still there, but rain clouds had rolled in while they'd been in the Anchor, hiding the islands and the police helicopters she could hear thumping in the distance. Bex *really* didn't want to be around for that, so she set Adrian down on a bench and started searching for his phone.

She found it in the front pocket of his khakis. Hauling Adrian back into her arms, Bex unlocked his screen using the security PIN she'd seen him enter a thousand times and dialed the number for his house. Boston was there right now, holding down the fort, and if anyone would know what to do, it was him.

Unsurprisingly, the familiar picked up on the first ring. "Adrian!" he cried in relief. "Thank the Forest! I felt something horrible happen to your—"

"I need you to tell me how to activate Adrian's broom," Bex interrupted.

There was a long, terrified silence as Boston realized what Bex's voice on Adrian's phone meant. But the cat was a consummate professional, and he snapped into business mode only a few seconds later.

"Bran knows what to do," he said in a too-tight, too-calm voice. "Just put him on the ground. He'll take care of the rest."

Bex nodded and dropped the broom just like she'd seen Adrian do. It fell so fast she didn't think it was working at first, but then the broom stopped just above the pavement, hovering back up near her knees as it waited for Bex to get on.

She did so immediately, plopping onto the broom like she was sitting on a bench with Adrian clutched in her lap. The moment they were seated, Bran shot into the sky, streaking toward the clouds that had turned the sunny waterfront gray.

Good thing, too. The long summer evening wasn't dark enough yet to activate the broom's bird illusion. If the storm front hadn't been there, they'd have been kicked out of the sky for sure. But the universe must have owed them after this horrible day, because Bex didn't feel so much as a twinge before they were safely hidden inside the obscuring fog.

"I'm preparing medical on this side," Boston's harried voice said over the phone as the broom zoomed through the misty swirls. "How bad is it?"

Bex looked down at Adrian, whose face was the same gray as the clouds around them.

"Bad."

"I'll throw everything I've got, then," the cat said. "See you when you arrive."

Bex nodded and hung up, curling her body protectively over Adrian's as the broom went faster, shooting across the cloud-choked bay at speeds she hadn't known it could go. If she hadn't been a desperate demon queen, they would have been thrown off for sure, but Bex's grip was strong. She held them on tight, gritting her teeth against the needle-sharp pricks of the light rain that had just started to fall when Bran swooped them to the ground in front of Adrian's house.

Boston was wiggling out of the thick branches of Adrian's heart tree when Bex jumped off.

"I've gotten everything as ready as it can be," he said as she carried Adrian over. "What sort of injury did he suffer?"

"I don't know," Bex said, trying not to let her voice crack. "The Anchor did it."

"The *Anchor*?" Boston repeated incredulously.

"He stuck his head inside it," she explained. "By the time I got him out, he was like this."

Boston's face grew grim as he looked the witch over. "I wish you'd gotten him here sooner," he muttered, ducking inside the heart tree. "Follow me."

Bex did as she was told, carrying Adrian under the thick branches and laying him in what looked like a shallow grave. The roots rose up to grab his body the moment it touched the dirt, winding around him like tentacles to pull him into the earth. Boston had already vanished back up the fir tree, so Bex took her chance, leaning down to press a kiss against Adrian's freezing lips.

"Thanks for the best four weeks of my life," she whispered, brushing her fingers through his soft hair as the forest dragged him under. "Goodbye."

The barely audible word was still on her lips when Adrian's face vanished beneath the twisting roots. Bex knelt there a moment longer, listening to the rain pattering against the silent forest, then she pushed back to her feet. She collected Adrian's broom from where she'd dropped it in the grass and moved it under his porch, where it would be safe from the weather. Then, wrapping what was left of her tooth-gored, black-blood-soaked dress tight around her body, Bex turned her back on the flower-filled clearing with its giant heart tree and cozy witch house and walked away.

She waited until she reached the edge of the Blackwood before unclenching the fist she'd wrapped around Drox's ring. He went onto her finger like a circle of teeth, but his rage quieted when he realized where they were and that they were alone.

You left him?

"I had no choice," Bex said, turning her face up to the rain. "You were right, Drox. I let myself get too attached, and when the time came to make the hard choice..."

You failed.

There was no condemnation in his voice, which made it even worse.

"I had everything," she whispered, shoving branches out of her way as she pushed through the dark, wet forest. "A prince's life, a Blade of Gilgamesh, a piece of my sister. The victory we've fought five thousand years for was *right there,* and I just..." She waved her hands furiously. "Threw it away."

Drox sighed. *My queen—*

"That's not even the worst part," Bex warned as she slid down the muddy embankment toward the road. "The *worst* part is that I'm not even sorry. If I had a chance to go back and do it all over, I'd *still* choose to save him."

She stopped when she reached the pavement, tilting her head down until the raindrops ran off her horns to land on her bloodstained boots.

"I failed," she whispered. "Failed my duty, failed my people, failed myself. I chose my own wants over what was right. I never would have done that before I met Adrian, but now I can't promise I won't do it again, which means I have to leave."

A wise conclusion, her sword agreed. *I'm only sorry it cost so much to learn.*

"So am I," Bex said as she started down the dark, rain-soaked road.

Chapter 8

In the palace of the High Heavens, Prince Leander dragged his burned brother down the white stone halls. Servants cowered against the walls, but no one said a word as Leander bashed his way into the Crown Prince's office and threw the charred carcass down in front of his brother's desk.

The Crown Prince looked down from his thronelike chair at the blackened flesh flaking onto his white carpet and sighed.

"What is this?"

"The result of your leadership," Leander replied coldly, brushing the ash from his golden gloves. "I told you he couldn't do it. I handed this idiot the Coward Queen on a platter. I even got them both trapped in Limbo where your 'champion' wouldn't have to hold back since Heaven knows *that's* not his strong suit. I thought I was doing him a favor, but five minutes later, what gets dumped on the street?"

He pointed accusingly at the burned body, which was barely breathing.

"I almost didn't get that much," Leander went on. "The Queen of Wrath isn't just having a 'spot of activity.' She's *fully* restored, a true demon of Ishtar. Why was I not informed?"

"You knew as much as we did," the Crown Prince replied, scowling at the burned man leaving black bits all over his floor. "She did that to Damion?"

"She would have done it to me as well had I been foolish enough to face her without my sword," Leander said angrily. "I was forced to bargain for my brother's life and the return of the Princess of Greed because you sent me into battle unarmed."

"Bargain?" The Crown Prince's single mirrored eye narrowed. "What did *you* bargain with the Coward Queen?"

"Nothing of consequence," Leander said, guarding the secret he'd discovered in the unconscious witch's face in case he needed leverage later. "But the fact that any of this happened is an insult to the Eternal King. We never would have landed in this mess if you'd had the common sense to arm your soldiers. Now a prince from the purges has been damaged, possibly beyond repair."

"We can fix his body."

"But not his mind," Leander insisted. "He is *broken*, brother."

"Most of us are," the Crown Prince said with a shrug. "The quintessence is strong. Not all our brothers can handle it as well as you and I do, but new princes don't grow on trees."

"Then make better use of the ones you've got," Leander suggested, placing his hands on the Crown Prince's desk. "Give me back my sword. Let *me* lead the mission to capture the Coward Queen, and I swear on our father's name I will make her kneel."

His brother scowled, considering, but Leander knew it was all for show. The Crown Prince kept as much from their divine father as he could get away with, but this was no slave-freeing mission gone wrong. The Coward Queen had attacked an Anchor this time. If the princes did not mount a swift and crushing response, Gilgamesh himself would get involved, and no one wanted that. Least of all his eldest son, which was why, though he clearly didn't want to, the Crown Prince nodded his head.

"So be it," he said reluctantly. "Princess?"

"Yes, my prince?"

Leander stopped himself from jumping at the last second. The Crown Prince had been alone at his desk when Leander dragged their failure of a brother into the office, but the moment he called for her, the Crown Princess was suddenly at his side. No matter how many times Leander saw it happen, he was always shocked by how swiftly she could appear, but what else could he expect? His brother had bound his princess closer than any of them, as evidenced by the mirrored eye he'd sacrificed from his own head to place inside her skull.

"Prince Leander is now leading the mission to subdue the Coward Queen," the Crown Prince announced, lifting his one-eyed gaze to his towering other half, who stood an inch taller than even Leander. "Return his sword, and give him access to whatever other resources he requires. I'll inform the king."

"It shall be so, my prince," the Crown Princess replied, bowing low. "But what would you like done with Prince Damion?" She glanced down at the charred body that had yet to stir on the floor. "Shall I return him to the Sleep?"

"After all the quintessence we spent waking him up?" The Crown Prince shook his head. "We'll get some use out of him yet." He turned back to Leander. "He's your weapon now. Use him however you see fit. Just make sure you recoup our investment. You know how particular Father is about wasting resources."

Their father was a skinflint who couldn't stand to let a gram of quintessence go unaccounted for. He'd come down on all of them if Leander didn't make use of a tool as expensive as their brother. So, though he wanted nothing more to do with the mad idiot, Leander bowed his head.

The Crown Princess bobbed her head politely back and waved her gloved hand at the door.

"Shall we go fetch your sword?"

Leander was moving before she finished. His brother's towering princess followed one step behind, as befit her station. It might have gone faster if he'd let her lead, but despite having been through this part of his brother's labyrinthine tower only once before, Leander recalled all the turns by heart. The hardest part was keeping himself from running up the endlessly intersecting stairs until he reached the small golden door at the very top.

Like all doors that led to the Eternal King's hidden places, it was set flush into the wall and sealed with a white stone circle where the handle should have been. The handprint pressed into the disk was masculine, clearly belonging to his brother, but the Crown Prince and his princess shared all things. Her white hand was able to do the job nicely, opening the door's enormous clockwork lock with a series of clicks. The moment the wheels finished turning, Leander elbowed his way past the Crown Princess and burst into the room.

"Cell" would have been a better word. The space beyond the golden door was completely bare, nothing but smooth white stone and a gold-barred window overlooking the dust bowl that had once been the Riverlands of Paradise. Few places in the Holy City were high enough to see over the walls into that desolate waste, but this was the Crown Prince's own tower. No secrets under Heaven were hidden from him, and he no doubt considered the bleak view fitting. Leander himself had seen the Goddeath Wastes only once before, but he didn't spare them a glance now. His gaze, his everything, was locked on the woman who was sitting on the window ledge.

She was as beautiful now as the first time he'd seen her—a flawless, pure-white figure with a delicate face, long hair that flowed down her body like a river, and large, intelligent eyes so expressive they were barely lessened by the gold inside. She was still wearing the shawl he'd given her the night they were separated: a royal-blue square of the finest silk draped across her delicate shoulders.

Leander was astounded they hadn't made her take it off. Princesses never wore clothing other than what had been carved into their bodies, but this was no normal princess. She was *his* princess, the light that made his Heaven bright, and the sight of her after so many years nearly sent him to his knees.

"Mara," he whispered, staggering forward. "*Mara.*"

"Leander!" she cried in that beautiful voice that still whispered in his dreams as she ran to him. "My prince!"

He threw his arms around her, pressing his face against the hard fall of her carved hair. "There are no words for how much I've missed you."

"And I you," she sobbed, her ivory cheek clacking against the breastplate of his golden armor. "There is no Paradise unless you're with me."

"I told you I'd return," he whispered, squeezing her tighter. "I'm sorry I made you wait so long, but I swear we will never be parted again."

Never. Mara was the only thing that made Leander's life worth living. It was for her sake that he'd gone to the Hells, for her alone that he bowed his head and held his tongue, but no longer. His princess was in his arms again, and there was no force on Heaven or Earth that would take her away from him.

He was still reveling in the feel of her after so long when the Crown Princess cleared her throat.

"I am overjoyed to see you so content, Prince Leander," she said from her position at the door. "But for your brother's sake, I must implore you to be mindful of the mistakes of the past." Her mismatched eyes slid to Mara, who cringed in Leander's arms. "A princess is expected to love her prince, but there are limits. Take care you do not forget again where your ultimate loyalty lies, sister."

"I forget nothing, *sister*," Mara replied, lifting her chin in the proud way Leander had missed so much. "Now leave me to my prince. You owe me that much after keeping me locked up in this vault for so long."

"You are due a boon," the Crown Princess admitted, stepping back into the hall. "You are granted one day's rest before you return to your duties. Until then," her white lips curled into a smile that would never touch her eyes, "I wish you happiness, Princess of Sorrow."

Mara scowled and made a shooing gesture, but the Crown Princess did not leave. She turned instead, fixing her gold-and-silver gaze on Leander.

"Do not forget that this reunion happens only by your brother's benevolence," she said quietly. "He is showing you great trust, Prince Leander, as he did once before. Fail him again, and there is no limit to what you will lose."

His princess's hands tightened fearfully behind his neck, but Leander stood tall.

"I will not fail," he said, casting a cold look at his brother's sword. "Return to your master, Princess of War, and do not interrupt us again."

The Crown Princess bowed her head and closed the door, leaving Leander alone at last with the only person in all the worlds who mattered.

Adrian hadn't felt this bad in a long, long time.

He drifted in and out of consciousness. Sometimes, he saw Bex carrying him, other times, he saw nothing at all. Mostly, he felt sick. His veins burned under his skin like his blood had turned to acid, and his stomach churned so badly he never wanted to eat again. His muscles ached, his eyes felt dry as sandpaper, and his head hurt like someone was using it to hammer nails.

The only good thing he could say was that at least he never had to suffer for long. Every time the pain grew unbearable, he'd pass out again. He was starting to worry he'd be stuck in this cycle forever when he felt the familiar embrace of the Blackwood rise up around him, and the endless up-and-down agony was replaced by the cool rush of rain.

Adrian had never been so happy to be wet and muddy in all his life. He opened his eyes groggily, pushing the roots and dirt out of the way to see Boston's furry face hovering right above his.

"Finally," his familiar groaned, sounding more worried than Adrian had ever heard him. "I thought you'd become worm food for real this time."

"What happened?" Adrian croaked.

"I was hoping you could tell me," Boston said, scooting back to give him room.

Adrian sat up groggily, looking around to see they were underneath the boughs of his heart tree. It must have rained at some point, because everything was soaked, including him. The date clothes he'd bought were ruined by mud, and though the moon was shining, no other lights pierced the forest, which looked as dark as midnight.

"It *is* midnight," Boston informed him as Adrian began the long, slow process of crawling out of the ground. "Bex brought you back on your broom just before sunset. You had the worst curse on you I've ever seen. It's a miracle you aren't dead."

Adrian touched his forehead with a wince. He could still feel the pressure on his skull where the prince's fingers had dug in, but the rest of him felt surprisingly normal.

"How long was I out?"

"Five hours," his cat said. "Two for the forest to draw the curse out of your body and another three to heal the damage. I'm not sure what all that magic was supposed to do, but I'm pretty sure it only failed because your heart was outside your body. It did a number on the rest of you, though. If your flesh wasn't bound so closely to the Blackwood, we never could have repaired your nerves."

Adrian winced. Nerve repair was tricky business, but Boston had done a marvelous job. He felt as light as a feather, which was good, because he had work to do.

"Thanks for patching me up," he said, giving Boston a smile as he finished freeing his legs from the muddy ground. "You won't believe what I found inside the Anchor. Let me get Bex so I can tell both of you at the same time. Where is she?"

"I'm not sure," Boston confessed, trotting ahead of him into the dark, wet clearing. "I was too busy saving your life to keep track of visitors, but the forest has been empty for hours, so I assume she went back for her demons."

That made sense. Adrian didn't remember anything from their trip out of the Anchor, but he couldn't imagine it'd been easy. He felt guilty about putting Bex in that position, but she'd gotten them out just like he'd known she would, and it had *worked*. He'd seen behind the curtain! He wasn't sure why there was a black desert or what the chains he'd seen were used for, but Adrian was certain he'd figure it out. First, though, he needed to check in with Bex and make sure everyone was safe.

His plan made, Adrian hobbled to the relatively dry shelter of his front porch and pulled out his phone, which was fortunately still in his pocket. The comm Bex had put in his ear was gone, as was his shoulder bag, probably lost during the chaos. His phone still worked, though. It was muddy and damp, and the interface was sluggish, but the screen still responded to his commands as he pulled up his contact list and hit Bex's number.

She didn't pick up. Adrian frowned and tried again, then again. When she failed to answer the fourth time, Adrian checked his news alerts to see that all of downtown Seattle was on lockdown due to a suspected terrorist attack.

The dire headlines made him smile in relief. Bex was probably just busy dodging cops. Ferry service was suspended as well, which explained why she hadn't come back yet. Adrian wasn't sure how she'd gotten off the island since the broom Boston had said she'd flown them over on was sitting right next to him on the porch, but Bex was nothing if not resourceful. She'd get back in touch when she was free, so Adrian sent her a text asking her to call him and went to take a shower.

Ten minutes later, he was clean and back in his usual black. Bex still hadn't answered his text, so he grabbed his broom and went outside to inspect his forest. He wanted his Blackwood to be ready in case the demons came back with trouble, but there wasn't much to do. His forest was already on maximum alert, so Adrian left it to its work and went back inside his house to prep his medical supplies, just in case.

When he'd laid out and inspected every piece of his triage set, made himself a sandwich from the heels of yesterday's bread, read every news report he could find, and Bex *still* hadn't replied to any of his messages, *that* was when Adrian started to get worried.

"Why isn't she calling me back?"

"She's stuck in the middle of a police lockdown," Boston reminded him, looking up from the squirrel he'd caught for his supper/breakfast. "It's also nearly four in the morning. She's probably asleep."

Those were both perfectly reasonable explanations, but Adrian couldn't shake the feeling that something was wrong. He fought it for another twenty minutes while he relit his stove and made a pot of strong black tea, but by the time the tea was cool enough to drink, his patience had eroded enough that he gave up and called Iggs.

Unlike his queen, the wrath demon picked up on the first ring.

"Adrian!" he cried, his voice weirdly muffled, like there was a cloth over his face. "Dude, I am *so* happy to hear your voice! I'm super sorry about dropping you, but it was probably for the best. That prince whacked me like a croquet ball! We're talking serious pavement crater. I don't think your poor human flesh could have survived."

"Wait, wait, wait," Adrian said, gripping his phone. "There was a *prince*?"

"Two of 'em," Iggs replied with a shudder. "Bex smoked the first one in Limbo. I was supposed to take you and run from the second, but he caught me before I made it down the stairs. I've never seen anyone use sorcery that fast! They normally have to recite a damn sonnet to cast anything good, but this guy was ripping off spells like—"

"What happened after that?" Adrian interrupted, pushing his tea away.

"I don't know," Iggs confessed. "I got knocked out when the prince flicked my forehead like a rail gun. I must have dropped you before I went flying since Lys didn't find you splattered next to me, so I guess Bex picked you up after she was done in Limbo."

"You *guess*?" Adrian said, much sharper than he'd meant to. "Give me to Bex, please. I need to talk to her."

There was a lot of muffled rustling followed by a long silence, then Iggs came back on. "Sorry, Adrian, she can't talk right now."

"Why not?" he demanded, suddenly terrified. "Is she hurt?"

"No, not hurt," Iggs said, his voice oddly hesitant. "She's just... busy. Yeah, she's busy."

"Okay," said Adrian, very worried now. "Well, when she gets *un*busy, can you ask her to call me?"

"Sure," the demon said, sounding supremely uncomfortable. "I gotta pass out again. We'll be headed your direction as soon as they stop blocking the ferries."

"I'll be awake," Adrian promised, keeping the phone to his ear until he heard Iggs hang up. He stared at the End Call screen for a long moment, then he set his phone down on the worktable and turned to Boston.

"What happened?"

"Don't ask me," his familiar said, licking the last of the squirrel off his face. "I got left behind to hold down the fort, remember?"

"Exactly," Adrian said. "You were here when Bex brought me in. What did she look like? Was she okay?"

"She looked fine," Boston said. "Her clothes were ripped to shreds, but her body looked perfectly healthy beneath the holes, certainly better than yours. She made a decent landing and didn't seem to be in any pain when she helped me get you under the tree, but I was too busy saving your life to keep track of her after that."

Adrian drummed his fingers against his rapidly-cooling mug of tea. It all sounded normal enough, but his instincts were screaming that something wasn't right. He should have realized sooner that getting his unconscious body out of the Anchor would trigger a massive response, but how had she escaped? Since Iggs had been in the fight, Adrian knew she must have called for backup. That was the only smart thing to do against two princes, but if Iggs had gotten knocked out early, what had happened to the prince he'd been fighting? Even if Bex had "smoked" the first one in Limbo, she would have come out straight into the sword of the second.

The thought made him wince. Adrian had near-religious faith in Bex's abilities by this point, but fighting two princes in a row on top of saving him was a very tall order. Boston had said she looked fine, but he hadn't done a thorough inspection, and Bex's record for self-reporting injury left much to be desired. He'd thought they were past her hiding wounds from him, but Adrian didn't see how anyone could do what she'd done without getting hurt, and if she wasn't answering her phone, it was probably bad.

"Or she could legitimately be busy," Boston pointed out, reading the thoughts right off his witch's face. "I heard Iggs tell you she was fine. Do you think he would lie to you?"

"No, of course not," Adrian said, scrubbing his hands through his damp hair. "I'm just..."

Worried. Worried sick, but until Bex called him back, there was nothing he could do except wait. Fortunately, patience was a skill every witch was required to master. Adrian didn't exactly manage it with grace, but he was able to keep himself from checking his phone more than once every ten minutes as the interminable night wore on.

168

Chapter 9

Two days later.

"**W**e need to talk."

Bex sighed and dragged her eyes away from the pile of reports she'd put together from all their various demon safe houses. Reports she'd printed out using the new LaserJet in the RV's office because having everything in front of her made it easier to manage and definitely not because using paper meant she didn't have to look at her phone.

"Can't it wait?"

"I think it's waited long enough," Lys said in a dangerous voice, checking to make sure they were alone before dropping their currently genderless body onto the opposite bench across the RV's dining table so they could glare at Bex properly. "How about we start with why we're still driving around Seattle like a Winnebago full of sitting ducks."

"The police aren't letting anyone onto the ferries yet unless they can prove residency on one of the islands," Bex explained with queenly patience. "We can't do that, so we're holding tight."

"Bullshit," Lys said. "I could shimmy us past any blockade, and you know it. You're *avoiding* going back, and I want to know why."

"I'm not avoiding anything," Bex lied as she tapped her printouts into an even neater stack. "You're the one who's always warning us that Gilgamesh's sorcerers routinely bespell local authorities. The Seattle police have got to be crawling with spies right now, so I'm playing it safe and lying low while the storm blows over, just like you taught me."

"Don't throw my lessons back in my face," Lys snapped, dropping their voice to a whisper as they leaned over the table. "Bex, what is going on? Why aren't you returning Adrian's calls? You're freaking him out."

"Adrian is fine," Bex said, pointedly not looking at the front of the RV where she'd left her phone. "He's a witch inside his fully grown forest. He doesn't need us babysitting him anymore."

"Doesn't need us?" Lys repeated with a scowl. "Did that prince stab you in the brain?"

"Staying away is the best strategic decision," Bex insisted, clutching the papers so hard they ripped a little. "The princes know we've based out of the Blackwood in the past, so it's safer for everyone right now if we're not there. We need time to recover, anyway. The whole city's a mess, and Iggs is still healing from—"

"Iggs is fine," Lys insisted. "You're the one making it worse by keeping him cooped up in here. You know he doesn't do well when he's indoors too long."

"It was pure luck I didn't get him killed!" Bex yelled, slamming the papers down so hard she rocked the RV. The motion made them both freeze, and then Bex rubbed her empty hands over her face with a sigh.

"The princes are still out there," she muttered into her fingers. "I didn't kill either of them, and they won't let us escape twice. Staying under the radar is the only safe way to do things right now."

"Then why aren't we doing it in the place where we actually have protections?" Lys demanded. "The RV is cover, but that's it. If you're really worried about princes, we should be in the Blackwood where we have the advantage, not parked out on the street where anyone can get the drop on us!"

"Driving all the time burns too much quintessence," Bex argued. "But I've ordered Norma never to park us in one place for more than four hours. That should be good enough to—"

"Dammit, this isn't about the parking!" Lys cried, grabbing Bex's hands and squeezing them hard. "What is going on with you? For real this time."

"Nothing!" Bex insisted, prying her hands out of Lys's grasp.

Lys grabbed them back. "Don't 'nothing' me! I've raised you from a baby *three times.* You think I can't tell when something's wrong?"

"I've got it under control."

"That's exactly what I'm worried about," Lys said with a pleading look. "Talk to me, Bex. You were so happy before you went into the Anchor. Then you have this big fight you refuse to talk about, dump Adrian in his forest like a bad habit, and then *swim back to Seattle* to help us sit around?"

"It was only ten miles," Bex assured them. "And I stole a boat for the first half. I would have sailed the whole way, but I had to jump ship when I hit the Coast Guard's blockade. Honestly, though, it wasn't that bad."

"It's ridiculous!" Lys cried. "This whole mess is ridiculous! And I'm not letting you go until you tell me *why*. What happened with those princes, and why is it making you avoid Adrian like the plague?"

"I'm not avoiding him."

Lys gave her a scathing look. "That's not what he thinks. I know because he called me this morning trying to figure out what's wrong. So if you're *not* avoiding him, you'd better get on your phone right now and tell him so because

Adrian is part of our team. More importantly, he's a good guy who doesn't deserve this kind of treatment."

Bex pulled her hands back and crossed them over her chest. "I'm not calling him."

Lys's scowl could have cut sin iron, but Bex didn't give them a chance. "This conversation is over," she announced. "You will not speak of this again, Lysanae."

The command landed hard enough to make Lys flinch. Bex saw their mouth moving as they tried to fight it. When that failed, they stood up with a curse.

"This is *not* over," Lys snarled, stabbing a sharp-nailed finger at Bex's face. "You can use your royal name-me bullshit all you want, but don't think for a second that I'm letting this go. I didn't sign up to follow a coward."

"I'm not being a coward," Bex snapped. "I'm *trying* to do what's best for every—"

She cut off with a hiss. Lys was already stomping out the RV's door, and Bex couldn't exactly call them back after declaring the conversation finished.

That was poorly managed, Drox observed.

"Shut up," Bex grumbled, going back to her reports. "You're the one who wanted this."

I wanted you to stop obsessing over the witch so your mind would be free to make objective field decisions, her sword replied scornfully. *I thought we were on the right track when you left the Blackwood, but now you're obsessing over not thinking about him, which is equally unproductive.*

Bex lowered her head to the RV's built-in table with a sigh. "There's no pleasing you, is there?"

I am exceedingly easy to please, Drox informed her. *All I ask is that you act in a manner befitting your station, and that's not this.*

"You're the one who told me to leave him!"

I told you to focus, he argued. *A queen puts her people first, and yours need the Blackwood's support. Witchcraft is what got us this far. We can't keep going without it.*

"So you want me to go back?" Bex demanded. "Undo everything I just did?"

You didn't think you could just run away, did you?

That was exactly what Bex had thought. Not in those specific words, of course, but a clean break followed by never seeing Adrian again had been a critical part of her plan. As always, though, Drox's strategic assessment was on the nose. Even if it had all gone wrong at the end, Adrian had gotten them into the heart of an Anchor, which was ten times farther than Bex had ever managed on her own. If she was serious about making this last life the one that beat Gilgamesh, she needed him, and that *sucked* because it'd taken everything she had to leave him the first time.

Bex didn't know if she had it in her to do it again, or while he was awake. She already missed Adrian like an ache, and the wall of messages he'd left on her phone wasn't helping. How was she supposed to pretend to be indifferent in the face of so much caring?

Figure it out, Drox ordered. *Being queen is about more than killing princes. Ishtar made you to lead her people, and a leader must always take the position that provides the greatest chance for victory. Lysanae was correct when they accessed that as the Blackwood. We should be there planning our next move with the witch's power, not wasting our time hiding in the open because our queen can't control herself around a human.*

Bex banged her head against the table with a *thunk.* Drox was right. She really, *really* hated it, but she was going to have to do the right thing. That's what being a queen was: taking the punches so your people didn't have to. Bex normally took pride in that, but all she felt right now was bitter. Bitter and scared, because if they were going back to the Blackwood, then she was going to have to tell Adrian to his face that she didn't care, and Bex wasn't sure that she could do that.

You'll manage, her sword promised. *This is what you were made for, Rebexa. Ishtar would not have forged a sword that was not equal to the battle. You have been the unyielding blade of your people for thousands of years. This life will be no different.*

"Thanks for the vote of confidence," Bex muttered into the table. She was still working up the courage to call Lys back over and tell them they were right when Bex heard someone call her name.

She turned her head on the table to see Nemini poking her snake-wreathed face through the curtain that hid the RV's cab.

"Have you been there the whole time?" Bex snapped, fighting the urge to hide under her papers.

"Nothing is everywhere," Nemini replied in a monotone, watching her with those eternally calm yellow eyes as she held out Bex's phone. "You have a new message."

"I've got a lot of messages," Bex grumbled, dropping her head back to the table. She'd just accepted she was going to have to go back to the Blackwood. Dealing with Adrian's texts on top of that felt excessive. She was trying to think of something to say that wouldn't sound like the cowardice it was when Nemini rendered the whole issue moot.

"It's from the demon tipline."

"Oh," Bex said, too relieved she'd dodged the Adrian bullet to mind that Nemini had apparently been snooping through her messages.

"Didn't Lys suspend the tipline when we returned to Seattle?" she asked as she heaved herself off the padded bench and walked up to join Nemini in the cab.

"That doesn't stop people from calling," the void demon replied, careful to keep her fingers from touching Bex's as she handed the phone over. "We have no control over the future. The worm can struggle for hours crossing a dry sidewalk only to end up eaten by the bird on the other side. Everybody knows this, yet they still fight desperately to survive and better their lives. These efforts do nothing to change the final outcome—death is still inevitable—but without them, life would not exist. Watching the messages pile up on the closed tipline reminds me of that."

"Okay," Bex said, not sure how else to respond.

"I find it comforting," Nemini assured her. "I wouldn't have bothered you with my hobby, but I recognized the name on the last message that came in, and I thought you'd want to know."

"I *do* want to know," Bex said, really curious now as she tapped her bulging inbox. "Who was it?"

"A fear demon named Desh. He was part of your crew two reincarnations ago. He helped us kill a prince once."

Bex whistled. She didn't remember anyone named Desh, but that didn't mean much since she didn't remember ninety-nine-point-nine percent of the shit that had happened to her. If Nemini remembered him, though, he must have been important, and someone who'd helped kill a prince sounded pretty useful right now.

"He wants a meeting," Bex said, reading the message. "Tonight. That's pretty short notice."

"Short and long are matters of perception," Nemini replied with a shrug. "Were you planning to spend the finite measure of your life on anything else this evening?"

Only going back to the Blackwood, which Bex was more than happy to put off.

She looked at the message again, drumming her black nails against the top of the RV's passenger seat above Nemini's snake-covered head. She didn't like meeting people from her past. It was stressful trying to live up to whatever version of Bex they remembered, but with two princes in the field, she was feeling the need for extra muscle, and a new demon would give her a great excuse when she had to explain to Adrian why she'd been avoiding him.

"Let's see what he wants," she said, typing out a quick reply. "A queen can't afford to turn down allies."

Nemini's snakes swiveled their flat heads up to look at her, but the demon herself said nothing. She just sat there silently, staring out the windshield as Norma started the RV to move them to their next random location.

"You're sure it was Desh?" Lys asked.

"That's what the message said," Bex replied, adjusting her oversized black T-shirt. She was back in her baggy black jeans again as well, because if she was going back to an Adrian-less life of discipline and duty, then dammit, she was going *all* in.

"And you didn't think to talk to me about this *before* you agreed to a meeting in the middle of nowhere?" the lust demon said irritably, waving their hand at the empty Redmond commuter lot. "Not everyone we used to run with is good news, you know."

Bex fought the urge to roll her eyes. "I'm not afraid of a demon, Lys. And I could hardly ask you anything while you were stomping off."

"Don't play the blame game with me," Lys warned, shifting into a dangerous-looking male body with a shaved head and brass knuckles. "Let's just get this over with. The sooner he shows his fear demon face, the sooner I can tell him to go play in traffic."

"Whoa," Bex said, surprised. "What's with you?"

"Oh, you want my opinion now?"

Bex gave them a look, and the lust demon sighed.

"Desh was on our crew for ten years. He was one of the best fighters we ever recruited, but his judgment was poor."

"What does that mean?" Bex asked.

"He was reckless," Lys explained. "He pushed us to take risks and go after targets we had no business messing with."

Despite knowing better, Bex smiled. "He sounds like Adrian."

"Desh is *nothing* like Adrian," Lys snapped. "Adrian always has a plan. He's not afraid to go big, but there's always a strategy behind what he does, and he cares about our safety. Desh didn't do any of that. He just threw himself at the enemy, and he dragged you down with him. His foolishness is what got you killed that time."

Bex frowned, wishing she could remember. She didn't have enough information to say if Lys was overreacting, but that's what it felt like. From the stories Bex had heard, she didn't need anyone else's help getting herself killed, but Lys wasn't finished.

"That's not the worst of it, though," they said, glaring up at the cloud of moths swarming the parking lot's single blue-white floodlight. "If I hated everyone who got you killed, I'd have to hate myself as well, but the *worst* thing Desh did was he ran away."

"You can't hate him for that," Bex said. "I'd just been killed by a prince. If I was in his shoes, I'd run away too."

Lys shook their head. "I'm not talking about the fight. I meant later. Desh knew all about your reincarnations, but when I called to let him know I had the next you, he told me he was out."

Their lips pulled back from their teeth, showing the little fangs Lys normally kept hidden. "He left me and Nemini alone with no money, enemies on our trail, and a newborn baby. I'd already raised you once at that point, so I was able to handle it, but it was still a dick move that I *will* be taking out of his hide the moment he shows his stupid—"

"Hello, luvs," said a Cockney-accented voice. "Talking about me behind my back? That's not very polite."

Bex stopped herself from jumping at the last second, cursing fear demons under her breath. Scaly bastards were *always* sneaking up on you. Lys had already whirled around with their knife in their hands, pointing the shining tip at the demon who was suddenly standing only one parking space behind them.

His human guise was pretty good for a fear demon: tall and rangy with white-blond hair and zero sign of the black-scaled, scythe-clawed terror that was his true form. His eyes were the classic fear-demon orange and glowed menacingly in the dark, but his black horns had a lovely curve to them, sweeping back above his head like two crescent moons. He actually looked surprisingly handsome in his white motocross jacket and broken-in jeans. He clearly knew it, too, strutting toward them with his arms out like he expected Bex to leap into them.

"Ishtar bless me," he said, looking legitimately happy as he eyed her up and down. "If it isn't my darling come back from the dead. You look just like I remember, minus a few inches."

Bex scowled. Why did *everyone* have to pick on her height? But while she was getting miffed over the little things, Lys looked on the verge of going nuclear.

"You've got a lot of nerve crawling back to us," they said in a cold voice. "What makes you think you deserve the queen's attention?"

"The fact that she's my queen too," Desh replied, pulling down the high collar of his jacket to reveal his unmarked neck.

That made Bex pause. The only way a demon got to Earth without a slave band was if she burned it off.

"You really are one of mine."

"From the day you set me free," Desh replied, giving her a soft smile before turning back to Lys. "You can drop the guard-demon routine, Lyssy. It ain't your show anymore now that she's all grown up."

"And what would you know about that?" Lys spat.

"I know I wasn't willing to put a hold on killing warlocks for eighteen years to help you play house," Desh said with a shrug. "You always accused me of running out, but I signed up to be a soldier, not a babysitter, and it wasn't as if you needed me. Just look how lovely she turned out! Though this version is a bit younger than I expected." He tilted his head. "Just how many times did you let her die while I was away?"

"Lys didn't 'let' me do anything," Bex said before her lust demon decided to use their knife instead of their words. "My deaths are my own business, as is everything that happens with my crew." She crossed her arms over her chest. "You said you wanted a meeting? This is your chance. Talk or go. Seattle's no place for catching up on old times right now."

"That's why I'm here, actually," Desh said, sauntering closer. "Is it true you're the one who janked up the Seattle Anchor?"

"It is," Bex said, annoyed that she had to glare up at him. "We were looking for a way to destroy it, but we were unsuccessful."

She thought so, at least. Bex hadn't actually talked to Adrian about what had happened inside the golden doors yet—one more reason she needed to suck it up and take them home. Despite her just telling him they'd lost, though, Desh's grin got wider.

"Wanna try again?" he asked, wiggling his pale eyebrows.

"Not with you," Lys said, stepping between them. "He always does this, Bex. He *always* sticks his hand in the hornet's nest and then drops it in our laps."

"Least I pushed us to *do* things," Desh snapped, shooting Lys's glare right back at them. "If the queen only listened to you, we'd still be driving around the countryside, freeing house slaves while the princes killed Bex until she started reincarnating as a hamster."

Bex almost chuckled before she caught herself, stepping up to stand beside her seething lust demon instead.

"I will not tolerate you speaking badly of Lys in my presence," she warned. "But you're not entirely wrong. We attacked the Anchor precisely because it was time to do something different, but that doesn't mean we're accepting new candidates. You want to fight Gilgamesh?"

"I live for nothing else," Desh said. "Other than your ravishing company."

He finished with a wink, which Bex ignored.

"Then show me what you've got," she challenged. "Working with us in the past doesn't give you a free ticket back onto the team. I only take demons I can trust. Lys says you ran out on us, and I certainly haven't seen you during all the years the rest of my crew and I have been putting in the less glamorous work. What makes you worthy of a place in our ranks now that we're pushing the top?"

"Because I know you," Desh said with a smile that was far too intimate for a stranger. "You've always cared about results over methods, and I've got something none of your obedient lapdogs can boast."

She was opening her mouth to tell him not to insult her crew when Desh reached into his motorcycle boot and pulled out a knife, which he presented to her handle first.

Bex couldn't jump back fast enough. The black blade was only four inches long, but she could feel the malice rolling off it from three feet away. She'd never seen one before in this life, but Bex's body knew what it was even without the hints Drox was whispering into her mind.

"That's a sin iron dagger."

"Get out," Lys said, forgetting their enmity as they swooped in to get a better look. "Sin iron is the most controlled substance in Paradise. Every gram is tracked by Gilgamesh's holy bean counters. Where in the Hells did you get a piece that big, much less in that shape?"

"Nicked it from a sorcerer," Desh said proudly, turning the knife over to show them how the pitch-black blade didn't shine at all in the floodlight's glare. "Nastiest piece of work I'd ever seen, so naturally, I had to have it. Cuts through anything from a demon's sin iron manacles to a prince's golden armor." He smirked. "Or so I'm told. Haven't had the opportunity to try it on a prince yet, though now we're back together, I'm hoping to remedy that."

He flashed that intimate smile at Bex again, and she was embarrassed to admit it worked a lot better this time. It might have been small, but Desh's sin iron dagger represented a *very* big advantage. A knife like that on their side meant Bex wouldn't be the only one who could stab princes anymore. They could split into teams, hit multiple targets, attack from two sides at once! She was still buzzing with all the strategic implications when Lys grabbed her arm.

"You're not actually considering this," they whispered in her ear.

"Why not?" Bex whispered back, glancing at Desh, who blew her a kiss. "If Iggs had had that dagger at the Anchor, everything might have gone differently."

"Or he might've gotten bliffed even harder," Lys argued. "Iggs only survived that fight because the prince didn't bother coming down the hill to finish him. You think that would've been the case if he'd had a sin iron dagger?"

"Okay, bad example," Bex said. "But this is still huge. Sin iron is the most toxic substance known in life or death. Forget cutting through their armor. If we stabbed a prince in the heart with that thing, the poison alone might be enough to drop him."

"Assuming we could survive long enough to get that close, which no one but you can do," Lys reminded her. "I'll admit it's tempting, but unless we get the drop on them, a knife that small is functionally useless against an opponent with a sword. We're more likely to poison ourselves by accident than hurt a prince, and the price is too damn high." They shot Desh a deadly side-eye. "I say we tell him to shove his dagger and leave him in the dust."

"And I say we take him," Bex countered, pulling off her sunglasses to glare Lys down. "The whole reason we've been running is because we're facing two princes with one sword. Now, a demon you just said was one of our best fighters shows up with another prince-killing weapon, and you want to turn him down because his knife's too short?"

"I'm turning him down because he's dangerous," Lys argued. "We can't trust him."

"I'm not trusting him," Bex whispered. "I'm using him."

"That's even more dangerous!"

"Everything's dangerous now," Bex snapped. "Our first stab at the Anchor was a bust, but we've all agreed to keep pushing as hard as we can. That means multiple princes might be the new normal, and there's only one of me." She put her sunglasses back on. "It's a queen's job to choose the position that provides the greatest chance of victory. If Desh's knife puts another piece on our board, I can't afford to turn that down. We're taking him."

Lys turned away with a glower. They didn't argue with her again, but Bex could feel the displeasure radiating off of them like electricity.

That was fair. Reincarnation meant Bex got to leave her regrets behind while Lys was forced to carry all of theirs, but there was too much at stake to turn down a strategic advantage over bad blood. That was Bex's official reasoning, anyway, but another, more shameful part of her was leaping all over this because having Desh and his dagger around meant she'd have someone to throw at the enemy who wasn't Adrian. If she could keep him safe in his forest, away from the fighting, then she'd never have to make a horrible choice like the one on the road ever again. And while that thinking wasn't noble or queenly, Bex was desperate enough to take it, especially since Desh had already volunteered.

"Welcome back to the team," she said, offering the fear demon her hand. "You'll start on a provisional basis. Help us bring down the Anchor, and we'll talk about expanding your role. Until then, you'll be under Lys.

Answer to them as you would to me, and if I hear any bad reports, you're out."

Desh arched an eyebrow. "That's a lot of asterisks for someone who's bringing you a priceless weapon, but I suppose it can't be helped." He leaned down to tuck the dagger back into his boot. "I accept on one condition: the dagger stays with me. A demon's gotta protect his worth, and I need something to keep Lyssy over there from slitting my throat in the night."

"As if I'd wait until you were asleep," Lys muttered.

Bex shot them a pointed look, and the lust demon bowed their head with a defeated sigh.

"Your terms are acceptable," Bex said, pulling her hand back since this clearly wasn't a shake-on-it sort of bargain. "Do you have any baggage?"

"Loads," Desh said with a chuckle. "But if you mean material possessions, everything I own at the moment is already on my person." He spread his arms with a self-deprecating smile. "It's been a hell of a time for me these last few years."

Bex felt a twinge of pity before she shoved it down, motioning for Desh to follow as she and Lys escorted him across the dark commuter lot to the RV, which was parked around the corner.

Chapter 10

Fifty-two hours after their infiltration of the Anchor, Adrian had worked himself into a very black mood indeed.

Bex still hadn't come home. She hadn't called, hadn't texted, hadn't given him the damn time of day. The only reason he hadn't gotten on his broom and flown out to find her was because Iggs was sending him regular updates on their status and the status of the city.

Apparently, Heaven was taking their explosive exit from the Anchor *very* seriously. Sorcerers were being brought in from all over the country to increase the Eternal King's hold over mortal security forces. Not that a sorcerer would be caught dead actually working for the police, but they had enchantments and bespellments active in every department, especially on the port authority officers who were tracking travel. But while this explained why Bex hadn't risked getting on the ferry yet, it didn't explain any of her other behavior.

He'd tried his best to stay calm and rational. As far as Iggs knew, the plan was still to come back to the forest when it was safe, which meant Bex would have to speak to him eventually. Until then, Adrian spent his time trying to figure out what he'd seen inside the Anchor.

The black desert was clearly some kind of pocket dimension. The black lines he'd seen in the distance had looked like other chains, so Adrian's current theory was that all the Anchors were connected through a back area that was monitored by a prince the same way Bex had told him Limbo was. Given how dirty his armor and princess had been, he was clearly in there a lot, but he'd also known

Yearling on sight, which meant he must come out and speak with the Anchor managers on a regular basis.

The whole thing reminded him of a municipal infrastructure system with multiple independent facilities run by managers who all report to a single civic authority. That made the most sense given what he'd seen, but Adrian still didn't understand what all that infrastructure was for. What did the Anchors *do*? Why were there chains, and what made them so important that Gilgamesh kept one of his own sons on permanent watch? What was so secret about what they were doing in there that the prince had been willing to kill a loyal company man like Yearling just for seeing behind the curtain? What in the world was going on?

Adrian had no idea. He couldn't seem to get an idea either. The publicly available information about Anchors already wouldn't fill a nutshell, but there was nothing at all about the golden doors, sin iron, or the black desert. He couldn't even find a reference for how the place he'd seen might have been constructed. The sorcery database had plenty of spells for stretching your closet into a casting workshop or creating hidden doors but nothing close to expanding space on the scale he'd witnessed. Whatever he'd stuck his head into down there, it was clearly for royal eyes only, which made Adrian even more determined to crack it. He was writing up a plan to microdose himself with fractured coins of quintessence in an attempt to figure out how eating the stuff had allowed him to phase through sin iron when his phone finally buzzed.

Adrian snatched it off the table at once, turning on the screen to find a message from Iggs that they were finally boarding the ferry. A second text came in immediately after informing Adrian that they were bringing a guest. He was still trying to figure out if that was code for something when his phone started ringing in his hand, and Bex's name popped up on the screen.

Adrian couldn't hit the Accept Call button fast enough. He slapped the phone against his ear, holding his breath until her voice sounded over the speaker.

"Hey."

Adrian closed his eyes. He'd known she wasn't dead, but hearing her voice after so much worry was still an enormous relief.

"Are you okay?" he blurted out. "Did you get hurt?"

"I'm fine," she said, her voice oddly flat.

"Fine?" he repeated sharply, struggling to control the anger that was suddenly boiling inside him. "Bex, you've been ignoring me for two days. You haven't called, haven't answered any of my texts. If it wasn't for Iggs, I wouldn't have known you were alive! I don't want to hear you're 'fine.' I want to know what's actually going on."

"Nothing," she insisted, still in that strange, flat voice. "I've just been busy."

"Too busy to take five minutes to tell me you weren't dead? Or to check if *I* wasn't dead?"

Her sigh gusted over the speakers. "I'm sor—"

The word cut off so abruptly, Adrian thought the call had dropped. It hadn't, but when Bex spoke again, the words came out very, very carefully, as if she were talking her way along a cliff.

"It was not my intention to make you worried. I got swept up in work and did not consider how you would see the situation. You're an irreplaceable ally, and I promise to be more mindful of your feelings in the future."

Adrian supposed he should be happy there was a future, because this sure sounded like a breakup.

"Bex," he said, gripping his worktable. "What happened after I passed out?"

"Nothing you need to worry about."

"Is this because I put my head in the Anchor after you told me not to?"

"Of course not," she snapped, sounding a bit more like herself. Then she sighed, and the feeling vanished. "You did what you felt you had to, same as the rest of us. But that's not why I'm calling."

There was nothing polite he could say to that, so Adrian just waited for her to go on.

"My crew's picked up a new demon," she said after a very long silence. "He used to fight alongside one of my previous incarnations, and he's brought a weapon that could be a game changer for our cause. I know it's assuming a lot, but I was hoping you'd let him stay in the Blackwood."

"It *is* assuming," Adrian said irritably, "but I put myself on your team, so as your majesty wishes."

Normal Bex would have gotten angry at that, but this new, cold Bex just sounded relieved. "Thank you. We're on the ferry right now, so we'll be at your place in about thirty minutes."

"I'll open the trees," he said. "Goodbye."

Adrian hit the End Call button and sank down with his elbows on his worktable and his head in his hands. He heard a little thump beside him a second later, and then Boston whispered, "Well?"

Adrian sank lower with a sigh. "I think I just got dumped."

Even as he said it, Adrian rejected the idea. He couldn't get *dumped*. They weren't even dating! He didn't know what to call the beautiful, unspoken thing he and Bex shared, but he absolutely refused to let it end like this.

"Adrian," Boston cautioned as his witch stepped away from the table. "Let it be."

"When has 'letting it be' ever helped anything?" Adrian snapped, grabbing his hat off its hook.

"You can't force her to talk to you."

"Maybe not," Adrian said as he stormed out the door, "but if she's going to keep using my forest as her base, then I can damn well force her to look at me."

"What is that going to accomplish, other than making you both miserable?" Boston demanded, galloping after him. "I'm sure Bex has her reasons for acting this way. You just need to—"

"Boston," Adrian said through clenched teeth as he strode across the clearing, "I know it's your job to give me advice, but I'm not going to listen, so you might as well save your breath."

His familiar heaved a long sigh, but Boston had been with Adrian long enough to know a lost cause when it was stomping away. He didn't say another word, just ran silently after his witch as Adrian stormed down the hill.

"So this is a witch's forest," Desh said, bending low between the RV's front seats to get a better look at the leaves rolling over the windshield like a parting sea. "Never been inside one before."

"It's a priceless refuge maintained by an excellent ally whose good faith keeps us all from dying," Lys said, glaring daggers at the fear demon from the passenger seat. "That means keep your lips zipped."

"But of course, oh great second-in-command," Desh said with a mock bow that somehow moved him closer to Bex, who was gripping the steering wheel like it was the only thing keeping her from being hurled into space. "But I gotta ask, how'd you find a *boy* witch?"

"He found us," Bex replied in a hard, clipped voice. "And this is his territory, not ours, so don't insult him."

Desh snorted. "Why're you both acting like I'm going to start pissing on his trees the second you let me outside? I *am* housebroken, you know, and I'm certainly not daft enough to insult a witch. He'd probably turn me into a newt."

"I'd pay to see that," Lys said. "Though I always thought you'd make a better toad myself."

"Now who's being rude?" Desh replied with a sniff. "How did we ever work together?"

Lys shrugged. "You were a lot more likable before you got our queen killed and ran out on us. Nothing like a little betrayal to take the fun out of a relationship."

"Rude *and* bitter," Desh said, rolling his orange eyes. "I'm amazed you can find anything to eat with that attitude."

"Enough," Bex said, unwilling to deal with the bickering even though putting them together had been her idea. She'd hoped having authority over Desh would make Lys chill out, but all they'd done the whole drive over was fight like cats and dogs, and she wasn't sure how much more of it she could take on top of everything else.

"Go run the spell thingy that checks for bugs," she told Lys just to get them away from each other. "We've been in the city for two days. I don't want to ruin Adrian's security by bringing in a magical tracker."

Lys looked supremely miffed at being assigned such obvious busywork, but they did as Bex ordered, hauling the huge male body they were wearing out of the passenger seat. Desh stepped out of their way at once, but that didn't stop Lys from shoulder-checking him on the way by.

"I'm only going to the back of the RV," Lys warned, glaring down at the fear demon from their current massive height. "Don't say anything to Bex you wouldn't want me overhearing, Desh-hole."

"Yes, commander," Desh said, hopping into the seat Lys had just vacated.

"Don't listen to Lyssy," he whispered to Bex as soon as the lust demon was gone. "They're giving you entirely the wrong impression of me."

"Wasn't aware it was wrong," Bex said, keeping her eyes on the wall of trees rolling out of their way.

"You really don't remember me at all, do you?" Desh asked, sounding almost sad.

"I don't remember anything when I come back," she replied apologetically. "It's nothing personal. Even Lys has to reintroduce themself every time, or so I'm told."

"That must gall," the fear demon said, looking over his shoulder toward the back of the RV, where Lys was banging on a panel. "They always wanted to be your favorite. That's why they hate me so much." He leaned in close, dropping his voice to a conspiratorial whisper. "*I* was your favorite."

Bex highly doubted that. She was actually starting to wonder if Desh was the reason she'd always been weirdly prejudiced against fear demons. There was *something* about him, though. Her mind was in chaos over coming back to the Blackwood, but her body felt oddly relaxed, as if she and Desh had already sat like this a thousand times. It was a confusing disconnect Bex didn't have the capacity to deal with right now, especially since she was about to hit the clearing. Just another few feet and she'd be able to see—

Her fingers tightened on the steering wheel so hard they left dents. Adrian was standing right beside where they usually parked, and he looked *furious*. Not that Bex had expected anything different after that disaster of a phone call, but the sight still stung. She really was the Coward Queen, giving him the cold shoulder instead of telling him the truth.

He deserved better from her, but Bex didn't see any other way. Her witch had never met a problem he didn't think he could solve. If she tried to explain that she liked him too much to make objective field decisions—assuming Bex could even get those words out without dying of embarrassment—Adrian would just start coming up with reasons why that logic didn't apply to him. And since Bex didn't actually want to lose him, she'd end up agreeing, and all the work she'd put into creating distance would be for nothing.

Not that Bex had much to show for her efforts. She'd buried herself as deep in her queenly duties as possible over the last two days. She'd read reports and talked to safe-house managers, discussed security strategies and secured weapons shipments, anything to show she was committed to the life of service Ishtar had made her to lead. She'd thought she was doing a credible job, but one look at Adrian was all it took for her brain to turn traitor.

Even when he was glowering like a vengeful witch in the moonlight, all Bex wanted to do was throw her arms around him and prove to herself that he was safe. She wanted to bury her face in his chest to feel his heartbeat when he wasn't dying, wanted to sit next to him and eat his food and talk like they always did. She wanted so much, and she couldn't have any of it, because she'd already made her decision. Bex knew exactly what she had to do, and if she didn't get a grip, she was going to end up right back where she—

"Is that the witch?" Desh asked, leaning over the dashboard with a grin. "Wouldya look at him! Got the pointy hat and the cat and everything. Give him a broom, and we'll have bingo."

"He has a broom," Bex said stiffly, locking her eyes back on the path before she drove them into a tree.

"Does he?" Desh asked in a knowing voice Bex did *not* appreciate. "I think I see why Lys didn't want me coming back now."

"What does that have to do with anything?"

"Because he's your type," Desh replied authoritatively. "And I'm sure Lys would much rather you hook up with a human than come back to me."

Bex hit the brakes so fast, the fear demon nearly went through the windshield. "You don't know anything about me," she snarled. "Your Bex might have tolerated this crap, but I don't know you from that tree, so keep your assumptions to yourself."

"Can't be that different," Desh said as he hauled himself back into his seat. "You're still touchy as a—"

"*Desh*," Lys snapped, appearing between them so suddenly that even Bex was startled. "What did I say about keeping your mouth shut?"

"Sorry, Mummy," Desh said, hopping out of the passenger seat and offering it back to Lys with a flourish. "Or is it Daddy?"

"It's about to be your funeral," Lys said, stabbing their finger at the table where Nemini was reading her book. "Go sit down and wait for orders."

Desh gave a mocking salute and traipsed out of the cab. Lys yanked the curtain shut the moment he was gone and flopped into the seat beside Bex.

"Sorry about that."

"It was bound to happen," Bex said, turning the steering wheel by fractions as she maneuvered the giant RV over the Blackwood's giant roots. "So was he telling the truth?"

"About what?"

"About him and me being together."

Lys heaved a long sigh. "Unfortunately," they said, changing into a smaller female body so they had room to kick their socked feet up on the dash. "I told you you had terrible taste."

Bex leaned back in her seat with a sigh, and Lys arched an eyebrow.

"Is that going to be a problem? Because it's not too late to kick him out."

"No, I can handle it," Bex said. She was far more worried about her reaction to Adrian, but she was curious. "How did it end? With Desh, I mean. Did we break up?"

"No," Lys said quietly. "You died."

Bex supposed that was better than getting dumped, but Lys's hands were clenched in their lap.

"You died trying to save him," they whispered. "It was his fault. He helped us kill one prince, and it went to his head. He pushed you to bait another into coming down, and when the fight went south, he kept attacking after you said run. You went back for him, shoved him out of the way just in time for the prince's sword to cut your head in two." Their clenched hands tightened to bloodless fists. "You *died* for him, and he couldn't be bothered to stick around and help you back up."

Bex sighed. At least now she understood why Lys hated Desh so much. She would've hated him, too, but it was hard to feel that level of venom for someone she'd only met an hour ago. Bex was far more concerned to hear that her weakness for Adrian wasn't a one-time quirk of her current reincarnation. If letting personal feelings get in the way of her duty was a recurrent personality flaw, Bex was going to have to be even more careful not to fall back into the trap.

Speaking of which, she'd fiddled with the parking for as long as she could. It was time to stop stalling, so with a breath big enough to lift her shoulders, Bex cut the RV's engine and opened the door to see Adrian standing just a few feet away.

Even with the moonlight washing out all his color, she could still see the beautiful blue-gray of his eyes cutting into hers. His normally smiling mouth—the one she'd shamefully stolen a kiss from the last time they'd been together—was pressed into a hard line. Even Boston looked angry, his green eyes narrowed to slits from his perch on Adrian's shoulder.

It was quite the impressive display, and the fact that Bex still wanted to wrap herself around him despite it was a warning sign big enough to see from space. If so much hadn't been on the line, she would've thrown the RV into reverse and driven away from this problem at top speed, but Bex had been enough of a coward for one week. She'd made this bed. She'd lie in it as a queen should: with her horns held high. Bex held hers so tall she nearly clipped the RV's roof as she slid out of her seat to land in the grass in front of the witch.

"Adrian," she said—with impressive calm, Bex felt— "thank you for letting us in."

He didn't reply, just stepped forward to close the distance. Bex was scrambling for something else to say when Desh suddenly popped up between them.

"So you're the famous Blackwood witch," he said, looking Adrian up and down before dropping a fancy little bow. "Desh, at your service. Thanks for taking me in as her majesty's plus-one. I promise to be on my best behavior."

Adrian stepped back in surprise, and Bex let out the breath she hadn't realized she'd been holding. She'd been contemplating hating Desh back in the RV, but she could have thanked the fear demon on her knees right then. That would have ruined the Get Out of Jail Free card she'd just been handed, though, so Bex rolled with it instead.

"Desh used to free demons with us," she explained in a quick, businesslike voice. "He heard about our attack on the Anchor, and he wants to help."

"Oh, well, nice to meet you, Desh," Adrian said. "We could always use another pair of hands."

"My hands are *quite* the asset, I assure you," Desh replied with a wink over his shoulder at Bex. One Adrian clearly noticed and did *not* approve of, not that that was any of Bex's business anymore. Thankfully, Iggs chose that moment to come outside and take over the conversation.

"*Adrian!*" he cried, sweeping the witch into a bear hug. "I'm so glad you're okay! You were looking terrible the last time I saw you."

"Thanks for carting me around," Adrian said, grinning at Iggs with a warmth Bex already missed terribly. "So does this mean someone's finally going to tell me what happened while I was knocked out?"

The question was fair and not aimed at Bex, but she stifled a wince just the same.

"The princes were the most important part," she said, retaking control before this conversation went somewhere she couldn't allow. "Nothing we've done has ever pulled a double before, so I think that proves your theory about Gilgamesh valuing the Anchors over all his other earthly assets."

"They might be way more than just assets," Adrian said, his face getting that bright, excited look it always got when he was talking about magic. "You won't believe what I saw in there! After I stuck my head into the sin iron, I—"

"You stuck your *head* into sin iron?" Desh demanded. "How are you still alive?"

"I'm a Witch of the Flesh," Adrian replied, looking at him askance. "If we weren't sturdy when it comes to poison, we couldn't survive our own witchcraft."

"Sin iron isn't a poison," Desh argued, looking surprisingly serious. "It's death made solid. A dose in the blood can take down a raging war demon on the spot. It's not something you can just 'sturdy' your way through."

"He didn't," Bex said quietly. "That door nearly killed him."

She'd never forget the sight of his body being swallowed by that blackness if she lived another hundred and ninety-eight lifetimes, but Adrian was shaking his head.

"It wasn't the door that did it," he insisted. "It was the prince that—"

"Prince?" Iggs cried, his tanned face going pale. "There was *another* one?"

"He was doing work inside," Adrian explained. "I was still in disguise, so he thought I was Yearling." His face got even more excited. "He hit his own sorcerer with a killing curse to keep the Anchor's secret! Thankfully, witches are hard to kill, because I *saw* it."

He turned back to Bex. "There's a whole other world down there. I think it's an artificial space like Limbo that connects the insides of all the Anchors, and it's full of enormous chains! I don't know what they're for yet, but if Gilgamesh has a prince standing guard to kill anyone who sees them, I think we've finally found one of Heaven's weaknesses."

"A weakness we can't exploit," Lys pointed out from where they were leaning against the RV's bumper. "You two barely survived the trip when they didn't know you were coming. Security's going to be much tighter now, and if there's a prince waiting at the bottom as well—"

"We'll take him," Adrian said, breaking into a grin. "Don't you see? This is the opening we've been looking for! Those chains are obviously extremely important to Gilgamesh. If we can figure out why, we might be able to strike a blow to Heaven's entire infrastructure."

"Or we could die," Lys said. "I'm all for taking risks, but there's a fine line between bravery and stupidity."

"The same could be said for caution and cowardice," Bex argued, giving her lust demon a pointed look before turning back to Adrian. "What do you need to make this work?"

"Knowledge," he answered without missing a beat. "No matter how much of a weakness they look like, I don't want to touch those chains until I'm certain of what's on the other end. For all we know right now, they could be holding back a world-eating monster from the Age of Gods."

"That'd be fine with me," Iggs said, cracking his knuckles.

"How do we find out?" Bex asked at the same time.

Adrian's grin fell into a scowl. "Ideally, another trip inside the Anchor. Barring that, I'm not sure. I could try doing some experiments, but what I really need is information."

"You could talk to the skull again," Iggs suggested.

"Maybe," said Adrian, but he didn't look convinced. He did, however, look at Bex. "I'd love to hear your side of what happened in the Anchor after I passed out. If we can't go back immediately, we should at least make use of the information we've got." He flashed her a smile. "Come sit with me while I make dinner. We can get the whole story and figure out what to do next."

That was a perfectly reasonable and incredibly tempting request. Sitting with Adrian like she used to sounded like paradise, as did the prospect of an actual meal. Bex had been living on convenience-store food since the Anchor. Her stomach was already rumbling at the prospect of real sustenance, but Bex knew a trap when she saw one. Just being in arm's reach of Adrian was already shaking her resolve. If they went back to eating together and talking under the moonlight, all of Bex's noble intentions would crack before the sunrise.

"I can't," she said, proud that her voice only wobbled a little. "There are other things I need to take care of at the moment. Leave your questions with Iggs. He'll pass them on to me."

Iggs looked extremely surprised by this, but he nodded like the good soldier he was. Adrian, on the other hand, looked like she'd just punched him.

Don't falter, Drox warned.

Bex clenched her fist around her ring. She didn't need her sword to tell her that. She was the Queen of Wrath, dammit. She could hold the line against anyone, even when the enemy was her own stupid heart.

"We'll see about getting another opening to return to the Anchor," she went on, her voice clipped and authoritative, just as it should be. "I'm going to check in with some of our people in the city. Lys, make sure Desh has somewhere to sleep. I know we turned the client suite into an office, but the mattress should still be in storage."

"I'd rather find my own accommodations if it's all the same to you," Desh told her before turning to Adrian. "You got a guest treehouse anywhere in this nature preserve?"

Adrian hadn't even answered before Desh sauntered off.

"Didn't think so. No worries, mate. I'm used to roughing it, and I'd rather sleep in a squirrel's nest than share a magical camper with a lust demon who lusts for my grisly demise. Just show me where I can stretch out without crushing any magically important blades of grass, and I'll be out of your hair."

Bex liked Desh better with every rude word. Adrian clearly wasn't ready to leave yet, but the fear demon just kept *talking*, pulling the witch away with a vortex of conversation, questions, and problems until Bex and her demons were left alone in front of their RV.

"Poor Adrian," Lys said, pushing off the bumper. "I'm going to help him."

"I'll take first watch," Iggs volunteered, stretching his arms over his head. "It feels so damn *good* to be outside again! I was starting to hate that RV." His eyes lit up. "I wonder if Adrian would make me dinner instead."

Bex's stomach clenched at the reminder of what she'd be missing, but she forced herself to wave Iggs off without another word. She'd just opened the driver's door to flee back inside when she found Nemini waiting in the passenger seat.

"Do you need something?" Bex asked nervously.

The void demon shook her head, never taking her eyes off the book she was reading. All her snakes were staring at Bex, though, which was usually a sign she had something on her mind. Bex was about to tell her to just spit it out when Nemini asked, "Is that all you're going to say to Adrian?"

"What else would I say?" Bex muttered as she shut the door behind her.

"Anything would do," Nemini said, turning a page in her book. "He's only going to get more upset if you keep ignoring him."

Bex sank down on the armrest of the driver's seat with a sigh. "I'm surprised you noticed."

"Just because I don't waste my time attempting to control the uncontrollable doesn't mean I don't notice what's happening around me," Nemini informed her in a calm voice. "And I'd have to be blind not to see that you're miserable."

"I'm fine."

Nemini's yellow eyes narrowed in the closest thing to a scowl Bex had ever seen on the void demon's emotionless face, and she slumped over in defeat.

"Okay, I'm miserable," she admitted. "But I'll get over it. It's just stupid personal drama."

"All suffering is personal," Nemini replied quietly, turning around in her seat to look up at Bex with all her snakes. "I'd like to aid in relieving yours, however subjective and fleeting the results must be."

It took Bex several seconds to realize this was Nemini's way of offering to talk.

"Thank you," she said. "But there's nothing to talk about. I've already made my decision. Now I just have to live with it."

"Actions are only as significant as the meaning we ascribe to them," Nemini said. "In my admittedly imperfect judgment, you've placed more weight on this one than can be managed alone. As your friend, I would offer my assistance."

"It's *really* okay," Bex insisted. Then she smiled. "But I'm happy to hear you say we're friends. I was worried you only stuck with me out of pity."

Nemini looked as close to insulted as Bex had ever seen. "How could you doubt? We value each other's well-being despite knowing that life is meaningless and everything will end. There is no name for that folly other than friendship."

"I care about you too," Bex said, because she was touched. She really, really was, but, "I still don't want to talk about it."

"You would feel more peace if you did," Nemini offered, closing her book and placing both her hands atop it to give Bex her full, unblinking attention. "I've known you for a long time, long enough for experience to suggest that no happiness will follow your present course of action."

Bex crossed her arms over her chest. "So you're an expert on me now?"

That response was pure sullen rudeness, but to her surprise, Nemini nodded.

"As much as anyone can be. You and I have kept company since before the fall of Paradise, though I did not fully appreciate our relationship until after. You helped me through some difficult times before I learned to accept what could not be changed. I would like to return the favor if I can."

She said this as if it were common knowledge, but Bex was dumbfounded. No one had ever told her she'd known Nemini for that long, but then, who could have? Bex forgot everything every time she died, and Drox barely noticed the void demon even when she was standing right in front of them. Nemini was the only one who could have remembered.

Bex knew she should be excited to discover someone who could tell her about the lives she'd forgotten, but honestly, all she felt was bitter. Hearing how wise and noble her previous incarnations had been just made her current mistake-prone self feel like a cheap knockoff. She was so tired of never being good enough, but Nemini was still looking at her expectantly, so Bex decided to switch tactics.

"Tell you what," she said, forcing a smile. "If you really want to help, keep Adrian out of the RV. I need some distance, and this is the only place I've got."

"Isolating yourself will not fix the problem," Nemini warned. "But if that's all you can ask of me, I will do my best to give it."

"Thanks, Nemini," Bex said with real gratitude, reaching out to squeeze the demon's hand. She got a blast of emptiness for her trouble, but the void felt nice for once. It was a relief to feel something other than anger and loss, and Bex took a moment to savor it before fleeing through the RV toward her bedroom like the coward she'd apparently become.

Chapter 11

Adrian wouldn't have said it was possible, but the next five days were even worse than the previous two.

Bex was still avoiding him, only now it hurt more because she was doing it in person rather than over the phone. She was never rude or dismissive, she just always managed to be somewhere else whenever he went outside. Iggs had no idea what was happening and just wanted the whole situation to be over. Lys was furious but apparently under orders not to say anything. Even Nemini was acting stranger than usual, getting in Adrian's way every time he tried to go inside the RV like she'd been put on guard.

The only demon who was willing to talk about Bex was Desh, though after a few of *those* conversations, Adrian started avoiding the fear demon as hard as Bex was avoiding him. It wasn't really fair—Desh had never said anything truly insulting in his presence—but the way he talked made Adrian feel like the butt of an inside joke. He also made no secret that he and Bex's previous incarnation had been closer than merely queen and soldier, which was just obnoxious.

"You could curse him with tongue swelling," Boston suggested from his sunny spot on the windowsill. "That's a fun one."

"I'd rather turn him into a snake," Adrian replied darkly, tapping a few more mouse claws into the potion he'd been brewing all afternoon. "People with swollen tongues can still make noise. Snakes are silent."

Boston shot him a surprised look, but Adrian just kept working on his potion. He knew he was being petty, but Desh annoyed him on a level that was difficult to describe. He was just so flippant about things no one should be flippant about, and he was *always* watching Bex. It seemed to be the demon's number-one pastime when he wasn't bothering Adrian about when he was going to finish his Anchor research. The only good thing about the situation was that Bex seemed too busy to notice.

She'd been consumed with royal duties since she arrived. Every time Adrian caught a glimpse of her, she was getting supplies for the demons she'd freed, practicing with Drox, or working with Lys to monitor the situation at the Anchor, which was getting stickier by the day. Pike Place Market had finally reopened to the public, but the national cabals had been flooding Seattle with warlocks in response to the attack, which made movement inside the city dangerous. Bex had her hands full getting all their safe houses relocated to the suburbs, even going out herself to protect the demons as they moved. It was all very queenly and heroic, and if she hadn't seemed so happy to leave him behind, Adrian would have loved it.

"At least we won't have to put up with the situation much longer," Boston said, rolling over to better enjoy his sunbeam. "Desh doesn't seem like the patient sort, and we're no closer to cracking the mystery of the Anchors now than we were a week ago. I give him three more days before he gets fed up and quits."

Adrian made a noncommittal sound and pulled down a bottle of dried ginkgo leaves, which he began dropping into his cauldron one by one.

"What are you brewing, anyway?" Boston asked, lifting his head off the sun-warmed wood.

"A different approach," Adrian said, adding a final leaf before he put the bottle back on the shelf.

That was enough to make Boston sit up. "What approach?"

"Nothing too fancy," he said, grabbing his homemade tincture of belladonna and adding three drops, which turned the whole bubbling cauldron purple. "Just a memory potion."

Boston's green eyes narrowed to slits. "*Which* memory potion?"

Adrian sighed. *Here we go.*

"Walking."

"*Adrian!*" his familiar yowled. "Are you out of your skull? The Walking Memory is incredibly dangerous!"

"But also incredibly effective," Adrian argued. "I've chased every lead I can think of on this, and they've all come up blank. I even hired a hacker to get me a data dump from the classified sections of Gilgamesh's sorcery database, and I couldn't find a single mention of the golden door or what I saw behind it."

He put up the belladonna and reached for the alligator teeth that would bite into his mind like a steel trap. "At this point, my options are to put everyone in danger by going back into an Anchor that's on full alert or drink a memory potion and take another look at what I already saw without the distraction of a prince trying to kill me."

"I have no fault with your logic," Boston said. "But why *this* potion? There are safer formulas that will let you relive your moments inside the Anchor as many times as you like. The only thing the Walking Memory does differently is enable you to leave your body and experience your past as if you were an outside observer, but there's no need for that unless you were specifically looking for something you wouldn't have been able to see at the time. Like if you were unconscious, or…"

Boston trailed off, his black fur bristling. "This isn't about the Anchor at all!" he cried. "*You* want to know what happened after you passed out!"

"Of course I want to know!" Adrian yelled, throwing the alligator teeth into the bubbling mixture like daggers. "Something happened after the prince cursed me that made Bex cut me out of her life! It must have been dreadful, because she hasn't told any of her demons about it and named Lys into silence just for asking."

"If it's that bad, then maybe you should leave it alone," Boston argued. "She's a *demon queen*, for the Blackwood's sake! Did it never occur to you that her secrets might be the sort we don't want to poke?"

"Not when I'm the one who's paying for them," Adrian said, swirling his hand over the bubbling cauldron to get the purple vapors moving in a spiral. "I *like* her, Boston, and I'm pretty sure she likes me. That's a rare and wonderful thing. Too wonderful to lose over something I wasn't even awake for."

"So you're going to take one of the most dangerous potions in existence?" Boston stomped his fluffy paw. "You can't use witchcraft to solve all your problems! Just go talk to her."

"What do you think I've been trying to do?" Adrian snapped. "I've been trying and trying, but she won't even tell me why she won't look at me!" He turned back to his potion with a scowl. "Short of grabbing her RV with my trees and holding her hostage, this is what I've got. I need to go back and take another look at the Anchor anyway, so why not kill two birds with one stone? Maybe if I can discover what happened to make her act this way, I'll have something to say that Bex will actually listen to."

Boston heaved an enormous sigh. "I'm not talking you out of this, am I?"

"Not after the fortune in ingredients I just used."

The cat sighed again. "Did you at least use the right number of alligator teeth? You didn't look like you were counting earlier."

Adrian waved for him to come and see for himself. Boston did so with a huff, hopping onto the cauldron's edge to give the boiling concoction a sniff.

"Everything seems right," he admitted grudgingly. "But why did you make so much? You don't need a whole cauldron for one potion."

"You do when you're going to be concentrating it."

The cat shot him a horrified look, and Adrian crossed his arms. "I need to walk through an hour's worth of memories I wasn't conscious for. That takes a strong dose even before accounting for my built-up tolerance to belladonna."

"Your aunts are going to kill me," Boston muttered, then he shook his head. "All right, let's get to it."

Adrian grinned and reached up to grab the silver chalice from his collection of potion vessels. It wasn't strictly necessary, but silver kept magic pure, and if there was ever a potion he didn't want to risk contaminating, it was this one. Boston was already waving his paw over the brew, urging the purple fumes to spin faster and faster until they looked like a miniature tornado. When the whole pot was caught in the spiral, Adrian dipped his chalice into the center.

When he pulled it out again a second later, the cauldron was empty, and there was a tablespoon of liquid at the bottom of his chalice that was so dark purple it looked almost black.

"Pungent, isn't it?" Adrian said, rolling the purple sludge around the silver as he carried the potion into his bedroom. Boston hopped onto the bed while Adrian closed the door and pulled the curtains over his windows, leaving the room in darkness as he placed the chalice on his bedside table.

"Remember," he told Boston when he sat down to pull off his boots, "I'll be under for at least sixty minutes. If I don't wake up on my own after that, splash some water on my face. If that doesn't work, there's an adrenalin shot in the top drawer of my nightstand."

Boston blinked at him. "Why do you have a—never mind, I don't want to know. Just don't make me use it. Even in my big form, I'm all paws with needles."

"It won't come to that," Adrian promised as he lay down on top of his quilt. "I'm good at this, remember?"

"So's your mother," Boston reminded him, "and even she doesn't take the Walking Memory lightly." He hopped up on top of his witch's chest with a worried scowl. "Don't get lost."

Adrian flashed him a smile and lifted the chalice to his lips, downing the contents like a shot. As with all powerful potions, it tasted dreadful, but that was how you knew it was working. Sure enough, sleep grabbed him before the liquid could make it all the way down his throat, dropping Adrian through his bed and into a memory.

The Walking Memory was a dangerous potion for a whole host of reasons. It trapped the mind in a waking dream, most of its ingredients were poisonous, and its formulation was extremely easy to get wrong. All highly valid causes to treat it with respect, but the true danger of the Walking Memory was the "walking" part.

The first thing Adrian felt was a sensation of waking up. He opened his eyes and stretched his body as usual, only to see that he wasn't *in* his body. He was beside it, though it was hard to tell because the man standing next to him didn't look like *him* at all. He'd gone back to the moment right after he first opened the Anchor's golden doors, the exact time he'd written on the dried hawthorn leaf he'd used to start his potion this morning, which meant past-Adrian was still in his Yearling costume.

He'd done a really good job with that. The man beside him looked *exactly* like Yearling, the memory so real and clear that Adrian could smell the residual potion on his breath.

Everything was like that. Adrian's "body" in the Walking Memory was merely an echo of his residual self, but he could still feel the cold, damp air of the stone tunnel in his lungs and hear the soft hum of the electric lights over his head. The sensations felt even more real than they had at the time, probably because he was actually paying attention now. Past-Adrian had been too focused on the golden door to notice little things like air temperature. His body remembered, though, and those memories were what the Walking Memory potion dragged up, giving him a complete recreation of the moment exactly as his senses had perceived it, whether his mind cared about those sensations or not.

That was one of the truly lovely things about being a Witch of the Flesh. The brain was a liar. It took in an enormous amount of sensory input but chose to focus on only a fraction, which was why multiple people could remember the same event in wildly different ways. With the Walking Memory, though, Adrian could recreate any moment *exactly* as his senses had perceived it. He could even move around inside the bubble of his perception, hence the "walking" part.

He could also walk right out of his mind if he wasn't careful, but that wasn't a danger so long as he stuck close to his original memory self. To be safe, Adrian positioned his current body directly in front of his old one, ensuring the best possible view of what came next as he waved his hand to kick time into motion.

What happened from there went exactly as Adrian remembered. Bex shed her invisibility spell and told him not to touch the sin iron, then he ignored her and did it anyway. He still didn't regret finishing the mission, but Adrian was better able to study Bex's face this time, and the look on it made him wince. He hadn't realized she was so scared. He also hadn't realized how creepy he'd looked with his head stuck through the sin iron wall like he'd been decapitated.

Adrian slowed the memory down to get a better look at himself from this side. There was no sign of what was happening beyond the door from out in the hall, but he could feel the sin iron much better now that he wasn't being distracted.

No wonder Bex had been so afraid of the stuff. It was like someone had taken the deathly feeling of a really bad poisoning and compressed it into a solid mass. Even through the translation of the Walking Memory, being near the black metal made Adrian feel sick and weak, which was odd since he didn't remember feeling either of those at the time. Maybe the quintessence he'd taken to open the door and pass through the wall had also shielded him from the sin iron's poison?

Adrian chewed on the mystery for a while before deciding it wasn't worth his time. He had a lot of investigating to do and only an hour to do it in, so he wound the memory back to the moment when he'd first stuck his head through the sin iron. This time, though, when the memory of Adrian went inside, current Adrian went with him, stepping his entire body through the wall of sin iron to get another look at what was on the other side.

This, too, was exactly as he remembered. He was standing in a black desert full of sin-iron shavings. Above him, the black chain of the Anchor rose into the pale-blue sky, its huge links grinding against each other with a faint ringing sound. The prince and princess were there as well, talking beside the chain in their hushed voices.

Adrian gave himself one deep breath to celebrate his success, then he dropped down to have a look at the ground. Since this was only a memory, he couldn't actually move the black dust, but he could study how the shavings piled on top of each other in the still air. He also noted how flat the area around the chain was compared to the rolling dunes that surrounded it, almost as if the Anchor were sitting on a plate.

Or it *was* the plate. Since this was a memory, he couldn't dig down to check, but looking at the odd flatness and the way the chain seemed to vanish into the ground, Adrian bet he was standing on top of some kind of buried structure. It must have been enormously heavy, because while the chain was twisting and groaning above him, the ground wasn't moving at all. A giant weight attached to a chain would definitely qualify as an anchor, so that lined up as well, but anchoring *what*?

Putting his hand over his eyes to shield them from the blinding light, Adrian tilted his head back and looked at the sky. It was the same empty pale blue he remembered from his first trip, but the more he thought about it, the less sense that made. Low-humidity places like deserts normally had deep-blue skies, or at least the ones on Earth did.

This place clearly didn't follow those rules, but he didn't see a giant white city either. He'd never made the trip himself, but it was common knowledge that every Anchor had a giant statue of King Gilgamesh holding a golden chain that connected back to the Holy City. That was how denizens of Heaven traveled to Earth to buy their lobsters and handbags. It was even called "going up the chain," but Adrian didn't see anyone traveling on these chains, nor did he see where they connected. The black lines—both the huge one above him and the half dozen fainter ones he could see in the distance—just seemed to vanish up into the too-pale sky.

Tapping his foot in frustration, Adrian rewound the memory again and turned his attention to the royals. Unfortunately, he couldn't make out the prince and princess's whispered conversation any better now than he had the first time. It'd just been too soft for his ears to hear, and reliving a perfect memory didn't change that. He was replaying the moment where the prince had knocked the black dust off the chain in slow motion to see if he could spot anything new or useful when Adrian noticed something that made the memory of his blood run cold.

A bird was flying above him in the pale-blue sky. Adrian didn't remember seeing a bird the first time, but this one was as plain as the nose on his face. It swooped gracefully through the still air, flapping its black wings as it landed in the hollow of the giant chain's third link. Since the sin iron structure was so huge, this put it way above Adrian's head, but he still had no trouble seeing what it was.

It was a crow—a common black American crow just like the ones he'd bribed with peanuts to track down Yearling. It looked down at him as he looked up at it, swiveling its head from side to side to study him with each of its beady eyes in turn. Then, with a caw, it took off again, swooping down to land on a large dead tree just beyond where the black chain met the ground.

Adrian squinted through the dusty glare. He *definitely* didn't remember any trees being here the first time, but maybe he'd just missed it? Past-Adrian certainly looked more concerned with the prince who was yelling at him than with the scenery, but the crow didn't seem to mind Gilgamesh's servants at all. It just got more comfortable on its tree, waving its wing at current-Adrian like it was beckoning him over.

Adrian's feet stayed rooted in the black dust. His first thought was that this was a hallucination. Walking Memory potions contained dozens of potentially psychedelic compounds, and plants were notoriously variable in their potency. It was possible he'd gotten a stronger dose than intended, but nothing else had been strange.

He almost wished it had. Adrian would much rather be tripping off his rocker than face the alternative, which was that this was the crow his mother had come to Seattle to warn him about—the one she'd promised he'd recognize if he saw. A mysterious crow cawing at him from a place no living animal should be definitely fit that bill, but was the prophesied visit happening *now*, or had it happened back in the actual Anchor and he'd just been too focused on the prince trying to kill him to notice?

Adrian legitimately didn't know. The whole point of the Walking Memory was to provide a totally accurate re-experience of past events, and the prince *was* just about to smack him with the curse. If ever he was going to miss a portent, it would be here, but Adrian strongly felt that this was new. If he was right, though, that was a problem, because following the crow now was a bad, bad, *bad* idea.

He stopped the memory again, just to see. But while his old self and the prince who was trying to murder him froze like a paused video, the crow kept waving, putting Adrian in a dilemma. The dead tree where the crow had landed was on the other side of the giant chain, well beyond the Walking Memory's safe zone. If he followed it as the Witch of the Future had instructed, he'd be walking out of his mind with no guarantee that he'd be able to get back in. It was the one thing you were never *ever* supposed to do inside a Walking Memory, but Aunt Muriel wouldn't have told him to do something if it was going to get him killed.

Right?

Adrian was still going back and forth on that question when the crow cawed again, angrily this time. It was clearly losing patience, so with a deep breath of air that wasn't actually there, Adrian stepped away from the memory of his body.

It felt terrifyingly like stepping off a cliff. He didn't actually fall, which was good, but the ground felt less solid with every step. Sight was the farthest sense, so everything still looked the same, but Adrian couldn't smell, hear, or feel any part of the desert by the time he made it to the base of the crow's dead tree.

"All right," he said, planting his feet on the shifting sin-iron shavings that felt like nothing. "I'm here. What do you want?"

The crow cawed again and flapped its wings. It flapped harder and harder, sending black feathers flying. Adrian was wondering if it was trying to lift the whole tree when the bird suddenly wasn't a bird anymore.

It was a woman. A tall, terrifying woman with hair as dark as night and skin as pale as death. Her leather armor was stained with old blood, and her brow was crowned with human finger bones. She carried a spear and a shield, both damaged from battle, and her eyes were the same hard, beady black as the crow's. She sat on the dead tree as if it were a throne, looking down at him with a face that was as dreadful as it was beautiful, though her bloodless lips curled into a smile when Adrian threw himself on the ground.

"Clever witch," she said in a raspy crone's voice that reminded him of a crow's caw. "You know who I am?"

Adrian had no idea. He'd bowed because he'd read enough stories to know that great and powerful beings didn't react well to human arrogance, and he didn't want to get cursed again.

"I do not have the honor of your name," he said at last, opting for flattery since that seemed like the safest path. "Please, tell me who blesses me with the glory of her presence."

That was probably laying it on a little thick, but the woman seemed amused rather than punishing, hopping off her branch to land on the ground in front of him with a smirk.

"You certainly are your mother's son," she said, reaching down to grab Adrian's head with her hand, which felt more like a crow's claw. "Agatha always did have a pleasing tongue. I wonder, little witch, will you serve as well as she?"

Adrian swallowed, struggling for an answer that promised nothing but still couldn't be interpreted as a rejection. The terrifying woman let him go before he could think of one, and Adrian risked lifting his head to see her studying him. She must have liked what she saw well enough, because she motioned for him to rise.

"I have many faces and even more names," she said, hopping back up into her dead tree as he got to his feet.

"Some are more flattering than others, but your family knows me as the Morrigan."

Adrian cursed himself for a fool. The Morrigan was the triple-faced goddess his ancestors had worshiped back before Gilgamesh burned every grove except the Blackwood. From the weapons and the bloody armor, she was leaning hard into her war-goddess aspect today, though considering how he'd come to be here, she could also have been a goddess of fate. Many faces, indeed. Adrian just had to cross his fingers and hope he hadn't gotten the death goddess as the Morrigan looked him over.

"You're early," she informed him, her croaking voice thoughtful. "Blackwoods don't normally see my crow until their heart trees are old and gnarled. My sweet Muriel must be desperate indeed to toss you at my feet so soon, or perhaps she meant you as an offering?" The goddess tilted her head with a bloodcurdling smile. "I do so like them young and tender."

Sweat sprang from Adrian's brow. Fortunately, the Morrigan didn't seem interested in eating him just yet.

"I will grant you the same terms as all the others," she announced, lounging against the dead branches like an empress reclining on her divan. "You may ask me three questions. If I find your queries pleasing, I will answer. Fail to keep my interest, and I will eat you: bones, flesh, and soul." The unsettling smile curled back across her face. "I know which outcome *I* prefer, but fair is fair, so go ahead, little witchling. Begin."

Adrian looked down at his boots to hide his panic. He'd come here expecting to answer questions, not ask them. He was normally good at solving riddles, but everything he'd heard about the Morrigan was too ancient and distorted by fiction to be reliable. He hadn't even realized she was still around. He'd always heard that

Gilgamesh had killed all the gods when he conquered Paradise. The Morrigan looked plenty alive, though. Alive and quickly losing patience, her clawlike nails scraping against the branches of the tree like little knives.

The sound brought him back to his senses. A witch never panicked. She'd given him precious little to work with, but the Morrigan's challenge was no different from every other test he'd overcome to earn his place in the Blackwood coven. Adrian would clear this hurdle, too, and gladly, because how often did you get guaranteed answers from a goddess? This was a once-in-a-lifetime opportunity, and not just because it might actually be the end of his life. After days of postulating in the dark, Adrian was *finally* in front of someone who had insider information, and he knew exactly which answer he wanted first.

"What are the Anchors?"

"Heavy things meant to hold something down," the Morrigan replied. "Next."

He gaped at her, but the goddess just raised an eyebrow. When it was clear that was all he was going to get, Adrian gritted his teeth and asked his second question much more carefully.

"What is the intended purpose of Gilgamesh's Anchors?"

"I already told you," the Morrigan said, kicking up her bloody sandals on a branch. "You'd do better to ask what they're anchoring."

She paused, waiting, but Adrian crossed his arms over his chest. Oh no. She wasn't tricking him out of his third question that easily.

"Good to see you have *some* sense," she said, chuckling with a series of hoarse croaks, like a chuffing crow. "The Anchors of Gilgamesh are exactly as they are named, and they're something of a wonder. Their very existence defies the gods, but then, Gilgamesh *is* human. Defying us seems to be what your species does best."

"I heard Gilgamesh killed all the gods," Adrian said. When the Morrigan's face curled in a smile, he lifted his hand. "Not a question."

"There's a clever witch!" she cackled, her pale lips splitting to show her sharp teeth. "You're not wrong, but you're not right either. Gilgamesh went on quite the bloody spree, but he couldn't kill us all because not all of us were stupid enough to let him. Paradise was a fool's errand only the most meddlesome gods bothered with. I enjoy a good meddle myself now and again, as evidenced by the fact that I'm talking to you, but there are limits. Some gods forgot that. They thought they could fix mankind, and like all acts of hubris, it destroyed them. Gilgamesh was merely the one who brought down the ax."

She paused again, but Adrian had learned his lesson. He stared right back at her, patiently waiting. Crows never could say quiet for long, and sure enough, after a few minutes, the Morrigan continued.

"We didn't even call ourselves gods at the beginning," she said. "We simply were: a tribe of wanderers in a forest full of life that lived and died as we did not. Some among our number found humans especially entertaining. You were such dramatic, loveable little creatures, but so *bad* at learning from your mistakes. You kept making the same tragic decisions over and over, and you died so quickly. Even when you produced the rare specimen with enough vision to try to lift your species out of the mud, they invariably keeled over before any actual progress got made."

She heaved a sharp sigh. "It was so *frustrating*. But where some of us accepted human failure as a fact of life, others thought they could do better. Ironically, it was Anu, god of wisdom and kings, who fell hardest into this folly. He convinced himself that if you had guidance, you would do better. To this end, he gathered Ishtar and Enki and all the other gods who would listen, and together, they built a new land and strung it upon the wheel of reincarnation like a bead on a circle of string. This way, every human soul would be required to pass through their hands and thus be improved."

"Paradise," Adrian said.

The goddess harrumphed. "That's one word for it. No one can say they didn't mean well. They sought to tumble humanity like rocks in a river, cleansing your sins and giving you gifts so that each soul could return to the living world a little better than it left. A noble effort, I'll give them that, but they were so blinded by their own good intentions that they forgot what you are. They treated you like little dogs, cleaning your fur and giving you treats when you pleased them, but you are not dogs. You are humans: cunning, malicious, violent creatures. The more power they heaped upon you, the more they ensured their own demise when one of your ilk did what humans do best and bit the hand that fed you."

Adrian frowned. He'd never heard it from that perspective, but the Morrigan's version wasn't actually different from what Bex had told him about Gilgamesh's conquest. It also didn't answer his question.

"That was a very interesting story," he said, looking up at her. "But you still haven't told me what the Anchors do."

"Isn't it obvious?" the Morrigan asked, her black eyes narrowing. "You have a very high opinion of yourself, telling me what I do and do not say. What part of my answer failed to meet your lofty standards? I know you are young, but I hadn't realized Agatha's children had grown so stupid they required everything to be drawn out like a picture book before they could comprehend it."

She looked down her sharp nose at him, but Adrian was too busy thinking to be offended. The way she'd responded just now was exactly what his Aunt Lydia did when she wanted Adrian to figure something out for himself. Given how familiar the Morrigan seemed to be with his family, he wouldn't be surprised if Lydia had learned the technique from her. That worked in his favor, though, because Adrian had done this dance before. Now that he better understood the context he was working in, he could stop worrying about meeting the Morrigan's arbitrary standards and start thinking about what she'd actually said.

She'd told him that anchors were heavy objects that held things down, but what did Gilgamesh have to anchor that was so big it needed thousands of weighted chains scattered all over the planet? It had to have something to do with the story she'd told about the gods because their inclusion made no sense otherwise. But the only new information he'd gleaned from her version of Gilgamesh's rise was that the gods had made Paradise to "fix" mankind. Adrian had always assumed it was a natural part of life and death, but if Paradise was an artificial construct built onto the cycle of reincarnation specifically so the gods could meddle with human souls before they were reborn, and Gilgamesh had conquered that construct, then the chains had to have something to do with—

"It's the cycle," he said abruptly, eyes going wide. "Gilgamesh is using the Anchors to hold back the wheel of reincarnation!"

A huge smile spread across the Morrigan's face as she pointed a clawed finger at the sky. Adrian followed it, confused. He'd already looked up several times, and he hadn't seen any—

He staggered, feet sliding in the black dust he could see but not feel. Standing in the shadow of the giant chain, the sky had looked like merely an oddly pale shade of blue. Now that he was on the other side and able to see the whole sweep of the sky at once, though, Adrian realized the sky wasn't pale at all or even blue.

It was the bottom of a wheel.

He was looking at the rim of an *enormous* blue wheel set against the star-spangled backdrop of the infinite cosmos, and wrapped around the wheel's spokes were the chains. They looked no thicker than black threads at this distance, but there were *thousands* of them holding the wheel in position, their links grinding together from the strain of stopping it from turning. *That* was why the desert was full of black dust! It probably wasn't even a desert at all. It was just where the grit of the constantly eroding chains collected, piling into drifts over millennia.

"Are you satisfied with your answer now, little witchling?" the Morrigan asked when Adrian finally lowered his head.

He couldn't begin to answer that. Everything he learned about this place only seemed to spawn more questions. Why had Gilgamesh chained the cycle of reincarnation? If the wheel wasn't turning, did that mean no one had been reborn since the fall of Paradise five thousand years ago? And if so, what had happened to all those souls? Did they vanish? Fall off into the void? Pile up in Heaven? And why would Gilgamesh want any of that? He'd always presented himself as humanity's champion, but what kind of champion conquered death and then locked the only way back out?

"I like the look on your face," the Morrigan said, leaning down with a smirk. "Ready to ask your last question?"

Adrian was ready to ask a million questions, but eventually, he settled on just one.

"What happens if the wheel turns?"

The goddess scoffed. "What kind of question is that? It's called a wheel of reincarnation. What do *you* think will happen if it starts spinning again?"

Adrian supposed he'd walked right into that one. But while part of him was pissed that he'd wasted his last question, the rest of him was too deep in the puzzle to care. If the wheel of reincarnation turned, the dead would obviously be reborn, but despite his "champion of humanity" propaganda, Adrian didn't think Gilgamesh cared about random human souls. If he'd gone through this much trouble to stop one of the great cycles, then there must be someone or something he absolutely couldn't allow to come back, and given how much trouble the worn-down nubbin of their last queen was causing him, Adrian could guess who.

"The gods," he said, looking back up at the wheel. "If the cycle turns, the gods he killed will be reborn."

The Morrigan chuckled. "That's the trouble with betrayal. You can only catch your victims by surprise once. If the rivers of Paradise are allowed to flow again, Ishtar and her ilk will return, and they will not be charitable toward their old favorite."

"Then that's what we have to do," Adrian said, getting excited as he pointed at the giant chain rising over their heads. "Even with thousands of Anchors, it's obvious Gilgamesh is holding that wheel back by a thread. We might only need to cut a few chains to shift the power balance, and the cycle of rebirth will start spinning again on its own!"

This was it, the opening they'd been searching for! Heaven was Gilgamesh's territory, functionally unassailable, but the Anchors were on *Earth*—still not soft targets, but infinitely more reachable. All they had to do was figure out how to destroy an Anchor, and they'd have the key to bringing down everything Gilgamesh had built! Victory was closer than he'd ever imagined, but the Morrigan wasn't smiling.

"What's the catch?"

"That's one more question than you've got left," the goddess said, sliding off her tree to land in front of him. "But you've entertained me well, son of the Blackwood, so I'll answer with a question of my own. What do you know of the gods?"

"Um," Adrian said, scrambling to think. "I know Bex's mother was one. I know that you're one, and you're very powerful."

"And vulnerable to flattery," the Morrigan agreed, but while that could have been a joke, her face was deadly serious.

"We all were," she continued grimly. "Every culture in your world has stories about it: the arrogance of the gods. How we judged every mortal soul but never suffered to be judged in return. How we birthed monsters. How we sent floods and played favorites. How we answered prayers with cruelty." She leaned closer. "Tell me, young Blackwood, do you think those stories are false?"

"Mythology has a tendency to exaggerate," Adrian said cautiously. "But no, I don't think they're *all* false."

The Morrigan moved closer still, leaning down until their faces were almost touching.

"Do you think Gilgamesh was wrong to kill us?"

"That doesn't matter," Adrian insisted. "He's wrong *now*. He built the Hells and damned the demons through no fault of their own. Hundreds of generations have lived and died in slavery, and it's all his fault. He's stamped out every other magical tradition, including ours. The Blackwood is all that remains of what was once a great forest—*your* forest and mine. He's what gives warlocks the power to act like tyrants. I don't care what Gilgamesh did in the past. He will be judged by what he does in the present."

"And what about you?" the Morrigan asked. "If the wheel spins and the Age of Gods returns, what do you think will happen to humanity?"

"I don't know," Adrian confessed. "We'll deal with that when we get there, but I refuse to allow Gilgamesh to continue his crimes out of fear of what will happen if he's forced to pay for them."

"Good answer," the Morrigan said, straightening back to her full height with a smile. "I see now why Muriel picked you. You are a sharp spear, Adrian of the Blackwood, and very much like your father."

Adrian froze. "You knew my father?"

The Morrigan nodded. "He stood right where you are and said the same things to me once. I wished him luck at the time, though later, I worried I'd made the wrong decision. Meddling almost never helps, but it seems humans aren't the only ones who repeat their mistakes, because here I am, meddling with you."

"I'm happy you did," Adrian said. "You're the first one who's ever given me actual information about how to bring Gilgamesh down. I promise I won't disappoint you."

"You haven't so far," the Morrigan said, pulling her cloak around her shoulders, which Adrian just now realized was a pair of black wings.

"I've enjoyed our time together, Adrian of the Blackwood," she said as her wings began to beat. "I'm curious to see how far you'll run with this, so I give you leave to call on me again."

"Thank you, but how do I do that?" Adrian said. "The Walking Memory isn't exactly something I can take every—"

"It is the Blackwood that connects us, not the potion," the Morrigan replied. "Offer to the Blackwood and I will answer, assuming your price merits my attention."

Before Adrian could ask what kind of offering she had in mind, the Morrigan's human form collapsed in a storm of black feathers. When the chaos cleared, all that was left was a crow flying away, its caw ringing hollow through the tight silence of a memory stretched far, far past its limits.

Heart suddenly hammering in his chest, Adrian turned and began racing through the black dust back to his body. He'd left time paused, which meant everything was still right where he'd left it—including the prince, who was still standing over the disguised past-Adrian with his fingers pressed into Yearling's piebald scalp. All was as it should be, but the edges were starting to go fuzzy, like a camera going out of focus.

The Walking Memory was losing strength. Adrian didn't know how long his conversation with the Morrigan had lasted, but even in memories, time didn't like to hold still. He'd burned the potion's magic by pinning things in place for so long. If he didn't get back inside the sphere of his perception *right now,* his body would fall out of the past without him in it.

That lit a fire under his tail. Adrian leaped past the prince toward the black shadow that was the sin iron door on this side. His senses came back with every step, but they were all fuzzy, like his vision. The distortion didn't go away when he reached his body and let time snap back into motion. Then he had to run again to chase after himself when the prince's curse sent him flying.

He reached his own side just as Bex wiggled out from under his unconscious body and started yelling at him in a panic. Somewhere far away, he could feel Boston's paw batting at his face, but Adrian ignored the sensation. The Morrigan had given him more than he'd known to ask for, but knowledge of the Anchors was only one part of why he'd risked the Walking Memory. This was the other. He *had* to see what happened after he'd passed out, so though it went against every survival instinct he had, Adrian ignored the pull of the thinning potion and stuck tight to the past, clinging to Bex's shoulder as she grabbed his unconscious body and began to run.

Chapter 12

"**T**hree, two, *one*."

Adrian gasped as the needle entered his arm, his body arching off the bed like a bow. He collapsed back down a second later, pulse thundering in his ears as he opened his eyes to see Iggs standing over his bed with a very worried Boston perched on his shoulders and the spent adrenalin shot in his hands.

"Easy," the demon said, dropping the needle to grab Adrian's shoulders. "You're fine. Just breathe."

"He is *not* fine," Boston snapped, leaping off Iggs to land like a cannonball on Adrian's heaving chest. "You were in the Walking Memory for nearly two hours! What did you do? Walk all the way back to your birth?"

"No," Adrian panted. "I saw it. All of it. I saw—"

He was shaking too hard to explain. He'd fought the Walking Memory's decay the whole way, using the potion to its last dregs until he'd seen everything: the escape from the sorcerer's office, Iggs's incredible rescue, the princes. Merciful Forest, he'd never seen anything as terrifying as those two golden figures waiting like wolves on the empty road, but Bex had been incredible. The way she'd dived into Limbo without hesitation to save her demons, the way she'd thrown that police car at the gaunt prince's *face*.

He might have fallen in love a little then. Too bad everything had gone wrong immediately after. Iggs had already told him the next part, but actually being there for the second prince's assault, to see him using all that sorcery with only a handful of words and no breaks to take quintessence...

Horrifying didn't begin to describe it. The second prince hadn't even needed a Blade of Gilgamesh. He'd swatted Iggs like an insect, then he'd picked Adrian's body up off the ground as if it weighed nothing and stared at him with those creepy mirror eyes full of hate.

Adrian had no idea what he'd done to deserve such a look, but he was shocked that the prince hadn't killed him. The man had certainly looked like he wanted to, but then he'd tucked Adrian's body under his arm and walked back up to the street where Bex and his brother had disappeared, slaughtering police along the way.

If it'd been possible to throw up inside a memory, that would have done it. The prince had killed the humans without even touching them. All he had to do was speak a word in Sumerian, and their heads twisted backward like screw caps. The prince didn't even stop to watch it happen. He just calmly kept walking to the center of the road and settled in to wait, tapping his golden boot impatiently on the pavement until, with a flash that lit up the street, Bex had returned.

The sight was still seared in Adrian's mind. Bex had looked more like a goddess than the Morrigan when she crashed back into the world with her fire roaring around her like phoenix wings. She went out immediately after, but she still looked formidably divine when she pushed up to finish the other prince's smoking corpse. Before she could swing her black sword, though, the sorcerer prince had shown her his hostage, and everything became clear.

Back in the present, Adrian ground his palms into his eyes. No wonder Bex didn't want to look at him. She'd traded her victory—the win she'd fought a hundred and ninety-eight lives to achieve—for *him*. She gave up her sister's hand, a Blade of Gilgamesh, to save his foolish life, then she'd flown him back to his forest, put him under his heart tree, and kissed him goodbye.

Adrian's hands slid down to press his shaking fingers to his lips. He'd imagined kissing Bex several times over the past two months. It'd become a bit of an obsession if he was honest, but not like this. This was all wrong. He needed to fix it, to make it up to her, but he didn't know how. Was it even possible to make up for—

"*Adrian!*"

Adrian's wild eyes snapped back to Boston, who was starting to look panicked. "I said, did you find out what you needed about the Anchor?"

It took his scrambled brain an embarrassingly long time to remember what the cat was talking about.

"Yes," he wheezed at last, forcing himself to sit up. "Yes, I found it."

Boston looked both surprised and pleased, but Iggs started grinning from ear to ear.

"That's awesome!" he cried, slapping Adrian on the shoulder. "I told Bex you'd figure it out. So what do we gotta do to shut that sucker down? Blow up another office? Raid some sorcerers?"

Adrian nodded, then shook his head. "I don't know," he said, forcing himself to sit up. "There was... It was a lot. Give me a few hours to sort it out."

"Of course," Iggs said, backing off at once. "Take all the time you need. I'm just glad you didn't lose your brain or whatever."

"Thank you for helping with the shot," Boston said as the demon walked out of the bedroom.

"Yes, thank you," Adrian repeated, but his teeth were chattering. The aftereffects of the Walking Memory potion were starting to hit, along with the exhaustion brought on by the fading adrenalin. Adrian knew his body as well as any living creature could, and he gave himself five minutes before he was a complete mess. As always, though, Boston had his back.

"Come on," the cat said, hopping off his lap. "Let's get you into the bath."

Sweeter words had never been spoken. "Did you put in the—"

"I put everything in," Boston said. "Now get moving before the shakes take out your legs and I have to call Iggs back to carry you."

Adrian ducked his head and did as he was told, stripping out of his clothes as he followed his cat through his workshop into the steamed-up greenhouse where his stone bathtub was already stewing with Boston's favorite selection of medicinal plants.

Bex sat on a piece of driftwood, staring down the muddy stretch that was Adrian's beach at low tide. It was a muggy evening full of bugs, but the narrow saltwater inlet that bordered the Blackwood was still full of boaters stubbornly enjoying the sunset. The nearest boat was only fifty feet away, but thanks to the forest, no one even glanced in Bex's direction.

She watched them instead, shuffling and reshuffling the stack of papers she'd brought down here to get away from the RV. She'd planned to do another round of safe-house calls, but she'd already called this morning, and her managers were starting to make noises about her not trusting them, which was totally untrue. Thanks to her new zeal for queen work, Bex had gotten to know all the leadership of their new demon underground, and she had nothing bad to say. They were all great at their jobs, so good that they could have run the whole operation without her. She was the one who was flailing.

You could practice again, Drox suggested. *Your fire has been burning low lately.*

Because it was hard to get red-hot mad when you were miserable.

Bex flopped over on the driftwood log, resting her cheek against the smooth wood as she stared at the inlet's lapping brown water. Nemini's prediction had been spot-on. Exactly zero happiness had followed her chosen course of action, but Bex wasn't doing this to be happy. She was doing it for the same reason she did everything: because it needed to be done, and she was the only one who could do it. Whether she was happy or not was meaningless, but was it too much to ask not to feel like she was sinking? Like her whole future was nothing but one long road of paperwork and lonely nights interrupted only by occasional fights to the—

"Bex?"

She shot off the log with a jolt, sword already in her hand as she whirled to see Iggs standing at the edge of the trees.

"Whoa," he said, raising his hands in surrender. "Just me."

The *sorry* was already on her lips when she quashed it, because queens didn't say that word. She'd gotten slack about that, too, but no more. She was committed to this, dammit, so Bex put her sword away and focused on looking like the queen she was supposed to be despite the mud on her jeans.

"What is it, Iggs?"

She hadn't realized how tired her voice sounded until her wrath demon winced.

"Are you okay?"

"I'm fine," Bex answered, determined to make that not a lie. "What do you need?"

"Me? Nothing," he said, hopping off the eroding bank where the forest met the beach to land in the rocky mud beside her. "It's Adrian. He finally figured out the Anchor thing, and he wants to get everyone together for a meeting."

Bex had started working on an excuse the moment she'd heard Adrian's name. Then she realized the rest of what Iggs had said.

"Does this mean the attack on the Anchor is back on?"

When Iggs nodded, Bex grabbed her leather jacket off the driftwood log's skeletal branch. "Finally! Let's get everyone rounded up. When does he want to meet?"

"Right now," Iggs said, rubbing the back of his neck. "And everyone else is already there. You're, um, the last one, actually."

Bex's arm froze inside the sleeve of the jacket she'd been putting on. She told herself she should be glad, that this saved time, but all she could think was that *she* used to be the first one Adrian told everything to. Now, she was the last.

Which was, of course, exactly how she wanted it.

"Good," she said in a voice that was anything but. "Let's go."

Iggs got out of her way as Bex stormed off the beach and up the densely forested hill to the clearing at the top.

Sure enough, everyone was already there, gathered in a semicircle around Adrian's porch. Lys was lounging in Iggs's folding chair like they'd been waiting for ages. Nemini was crouched on a root, watching a beetle. Desh was off to the side, leaning against a tree like he was too cool for all of this, and Adrian was sitting on a stool in front of his door, talking to Boston.

As always, he looked up the moment Bex got close, nearly making her miss a step. He must have just gotten out of the shower, because his curling hair was wet, and he was in his shirtsleeves rather than his coat and hat. He also looked terrible, like he'd just woken up from a four-day bender. It was so unexpected Bex forgot not to meet his eyes, which was where she got her next surprise, because Adrian didn't look mad at her. He looked sad and strangely determined, which was upsetting in an entirely different way.

"Excellent," he said as Bex and Iggs walked over. "Now that we're all here, we can begin."

"This isn't a board meeting," Desh muttered, fiddling with his sin iron knife. "Just spit it out already."

Adrian shot the fear demon a look that was so over-it, Bex almost laughed before she remembered she wasn't doing that sort of thing anymore.

"I called you all together because I've finally figured out what the Anchors are for," Adrian said when Desh quieted down. "Our initial assumption was correct: they *are* incredibly important to Gilgamesh, possibly the single most important piece of his entire infrastructure. Destroying even one will do lasting harm to our enemy."

"You say that like it's easy," Desh complained. "In case all of Seattle seething like a kicked beehive wasn't enough of a clue, Anchors are fortresses. How are you going to—"

"Would you shut up?" Lys interrupted, glaring at the fear demon until he raised his hands in surrender. When he didn't open his mouth again, the lust demon nodded and turned back to the porch.

"Go ahead, Adrian."

"Thank you," he said, sitting up straighter on his stool. "But Desh isn't wrong. The Anchors are Heaven's outposts in the living world. They're *insanely* guarded. I used to think that was to protect all the Heavenly citizens who did business there, which is why I had us go in through the office door, but I had it backward. The sorcerous aspect of the Anchor is the *most* important and the most protected. The Anchor's inner workings are guarded by a prince and princess who seem to be on duty there all the time."

"Bex can kill a prince," Iggs said proudly.

"I know she can," Adrian said with a sad smile that stabbed straight into Bex's soft underbelly. "But fighting in the Anchor's base would put her at a horrible disadvantage. Even if she could get through the door this time, the inside is a toxic sandbox of sin iron dust. That's why we'll be going in through the top."

Lys was in their neutral form today, but they flipped into a grim-faced, bearded warrior to give Adrian a scowl. "That sounds an awful lot like you mean to assault the Anchor Market directly."

"Not assault," he said with a smile. "Infiltrate. Attacking the Anchor itself is a fool's errand, but as someone who would know just reminded me, an anchor is nothing but a weight. It's useless without the chain that connects it to the thing that's being anchored, and to break a chain, you only have to cut through one link."

Iggs raised his hand. "I thought you said the chain was in that weird desert place."

"The base of it is," Adrian said. "But a chain has to run all the way between Heaven and Earth if it's going to work, which means there's no reason we can't cut it at the top."

"You want to cut the chain to Heaven?" Desh asked, his pale face aghast. "The highway all the denizens of the Holy City come down to buy their party food and trinkets?"

Adrian's head had barely dipped in a nod before the fear demon stomped forward.

"Are you out of your witchy skull?" he cried. "Have you ever been on a chain? 'Cause I have! Every demon taken from the Hells to become a warlock's slave has to walk down one to be sold. Damn thing's the size of a highway. How do you plan to cut that?"

"With her," Adrian said, pointing at Bex. "The queen's sword can cut sin iron, right?"

I can cut anything, Drox replied before Bex could open her mouth.

"Drox says he can do it," Bex replied since no one else could hear her sword's bragging. "But how are we getting there? The Anchor Market's open to the public, but the chain is what connects Earth to the Holy City. They don't let just anyone walk up it."

"That's the part I haven't figured out yet," Adrian confessed, his face falling into a scowl. "I'm also not sure how we're going to prevent a folded-space collapse."

"A what collapse?" Iggs asked.

"The Anchor Market is a sorcerous construct much like your RV," Adrian explained. "I learned a lot about them trying to figure out how the Anchors worked, and I'm pretty sure the fake Paradise the Anchor Market sits inside is built using a suspension matrix. There's just no other way to make a space that huge that isn't in constant danger of collapse. Think of it like a big canopy hanging from a pole. Cut the pole, and the whole thing falls down."

"And the chain would be the pole in this metaphor?" Lys asked.

"That's my guess," the witch replied, running a hand through his drying hair. "I could be wrong, but I'm going to go ahead and work on finding an alternative support. It'd be really unfortunate if we succeeded in cutting the chain only to die when the Anchor Market's false sky falls on our heads."

"Agreed," Bex said, squaring her shoulders. "You work on that—we'll figure out how to get me onto the chain."

"Might also want to add in how we're going to avoid the princes," Desh suggested. "Or Gilgamesh's armies since the Anchors are close enough to Heaven for those to come into play."

"We'll. Figure. It. Out." Bex told him through clenched teeth.

"Yeah," Iggs said, lifting his chin. "Are you a fear demon or a pessimism demon?"

"I'm a realism demon," Desh snapped. "I'd've thought you'd all appreciate that, given how much shit I've eaten about my reckless behavior getting people killed."

He finished with a glare at Lys, who was uncharacteristically silent.

"We'll figure it out," Bex said again, speaking the words hard to make herself believe. "How soon do you need us to be ready?"

Since she was doing her damnedest to avoid looking his direction, it took Adrian several seconds to realize that question was for him.

"Don't rush on my account," he said, looking around at his forest like the answer was hidden in the trees, which, for all Bex knew, it was. "The plan I'm thinking of takes a while to set up. Once it's ready, though, it'll go off quickly. I think that's going to be important given the concerns Desh raised."

"Yes, *thank* you," Desh said, giving Bex's demons a superior look, which they all ignored.

"We'll get to work, then," Bex said, waving for her crew to follow her back to the RV. She glanced at Adrian out of the corner of her eye as she left, bracing for the next step in the avoidance dance that had become her whole life over the past week. For once, though, he wasn't looking at her. His eyes were on his hands, his face scrunched up in furious thought as Bex led her demons across the clearing to start making a plan.

Preparing for the assault on the Anchor took the better part of a month. For once, though, the delay wasn't Adrian's fault. Despite what he'd said about a lengthy setup, his phase of the plan—rigging a backup support for the Anchor's folded space to prevent collapse—came together relatively quickly. The hardest part was figuring out where to put it.

He found his answer inside the demons' RV. For all that they made their spells out of ancient Sumerian poetry, sorcerers tended to be very literal in their actual application. Once he'd gotten Nemini to translate the cuneiform into something he could read, Adrian was able to pick out the most important magical concepts that had allowed a sorcerer to stretch a 1989 Winnebago Warrior into a moving palace.

From there, it was only a few more logical leaps to figure out how to place a support that would keep the much larger magical space of the Anchor upright. There was actually a structure-locking spell inside the RV's closet that

Adrian could have simply copied and enlarged, but it would have required an enormous amount of quintessence to pull off, and Adrian was never touching that stuff again if he could help it. Fortunately, there was nothing sorcery could do that witchcraft couldn't, and fourteen days later, Adrian had everything figured out. He could have been ready to march on the Anchor right then, but Bex was still busy.

Busy and *gone*. Her part of the plan required help from the demons she'd freed, and since revolutions couldn't be pitched over the phone, Bex, Lys, and Iggs had stolen a car from downtown Bainbridge and set off on a road trip across the Pacific Northwest, leaving Adrian alone with the RV he was studying, Nemini, and Desh. He had no problem with two-thirds of that company, but Bex had barely been gone for two days before Adrian was forced to admit an uncomfortable personal truth.

He missed her. Now that he wasn't busy being angry or worried, Adrian missed Bex like an ache, which was ridiculous. He'd spent twenty-five years of his life without her, but now, suddenly, the lack of her nightly phone calls felt like he'd been cut off from food. He missed having someone who actually listened to his schemes. His family never took his plans seriously. Bex took him *too* seriously, but Adrian missed that as well. He missed making her laugh, missed her smiles, missed the way she lit up whenever he came into view. He missed the way she reacted to his food like taste was a sense she'd never experienced before him, and he *dreadfully* missed sitting next to her. He missed things he hadn't even discovered about her yet because he was starting to fear he'd never get the chance, and it was driving him insane.

The affliction wasn't so bad during the day when he had work to keep him distracted, but he'd been forced to start sleeping again now that his stock of bottled nights was dwindling, and Adrian's brain had always been a traitor in the dark. No matter how late he went to bed, it refused to let him sleep, churning his thoughts around and around the same question:

How to make this right?

There seemed to be no answer. This wasn't some early-stages-of-the-relationship misunderstanding that could be cleared up with honest communication. The enemy had learned they could use Bex's caring for him against her, so, like the good queen she was, she'd cut him off. Adrian couldn't convince her not to do that without changing who she was, which he wouldn't—and *couldn't*—do. But if he couldn't change her mind, that left only two options: never be a liability again or win the war and render the whole issue moot.

It was a sign of just how high a wall he was up against that Adrian considered the second option to be his best bet. Not being a liability was impossible for someone who was only human, but the Morrigan had all but told him that the Anchors were the key to ending Gilgamesh's rule, and they had a good plan for how to bring one down. One led to two, and two led to many. Exactly how many was impossible to say, but he didn't think the number would be that high. Gilgamesh had thousands of Anchors, but Adrian had seen the pressure those chains were under. It wouldn't take more than a few popped lines before the bound wheel exploded back into motion and the gods returned. Once Gilgamesh's Heaven fell, Bex would go from being a lone rebel shouldering the fate of all demonkind to a normal queen who was free to do normal things, like have an affair with a common witch.

It was still a *big* stretch, but Adrian had always found it easier to face the impossible when he had a concrete goal. He threw himself into the Anchor project with maniacal fervor. Even Boston couldn't keep up with his work schedule, which was how Desh was able to catch Adrian alone.

"Morning."

Adrian nodded and kept his attention on the tree he was working on—the second tallest in his forest after his heart tree and the only reason he'd known Desh was coming. The fear demon could make himself nearly invisible to human eyes when he wanted, but the roots felt everything.

"Can I help you?" Adrian asked.

"Not unless you can conjure up some entertainment," Desh grumped, stalking past him to lean against the tree. "I don't recall fighting with the Queen of Wrath being so *boring*. We've done nothing but sit in this forest for weeks!"

He looked at Adrian for commiseration, but the witch just tapped the demon's arm with the stick he was using as a tester.

"Move, please."

Desh sighed and moseyed out of the way. "You're going at this awfully hard for someone with no horns in the game," he observed, walking over to sit on a fallen log instead. "This is the fifth morning in a row you've been up before dawn. Do you never sleep?"

"Not if I can help it," Adrian said, digging his fingers into the rich soil to check the thickness of the local mycorrhizal fungi network. "And just because I don't have horns doesn't mean this isn't my fight. Gilgamesh's regime hurts everyone, my family in particular."

"There are a lot fewer witches these days," Desh agreed, studying Adrian with glowing eyes that felt much less friendly than Bex's. "But is the rest of your family on board with this? I thought the Blackwood survived by staying *off* of Gilgamesh's shit list."

"It does," Adrian replied, keeping his eyes on his work. "But we're not in the main Blackwood. This is my forest. I do what I want here."

The fear demon arched a pale eyebrow. "So you're working yourself into an even earlier grave than most humans fighting for a family who won't back you up?"

Adrian saw no reason to respond to that, but before he could tell Desh to go be cynical somewhere else, his phone buzzed in his pocket. Adrian brushed the dirt off his fingers and pulled it out at once, smiling in relief when he saw the name on the text.

It was Bex letting him know she was in Portland. She'd been keeping him updated on her location ever since she left—her way, Adrian suspected, of making amends for worrying him so badly after the Anchor. The short, curt texts were nothing compared to the ones she'd sent before, but he still treasured them as proof that she still cared. Adrian had a lot more he wanted to say back, but he didn't want to push her even farther away, so he made do with *Be careful*. He was still smiling at his phone screen when he realized Desh was smirking at him.

"Thought so."

"Don't you have something else to do?" Adrian asked testily as he put his phone back in his pocket.

"Not at the moment," the fear demon replied, getting more comfortable on his log. "I got left behind as well, don't forget. We're just a pair of sods with nothing to do but wait on the queen's convenience."

Adrian shook his head and turned back to his tree. He'd almost managed to put the fear demon out of his mind when Desh said, "You'll never win, you know."

"Never win what?"

Desh shrugged. "Her, the war, any of it. Bex is the daughter of a goddess fighting the Eternal King in a divine conflict that's been raging for eons. Mortals don't fare well in stories like those. You'd do better to bow out while you still can. Forget Bex and go find some pretty witch to brew your potions with. You'll live a lot longer."

Adrian harrumphed at his tree. "And I suppose this advice is entirely selfless?"

"Oh no, it's extremely selfish," the demon said. "Though not for the reasons I'm sure you're thinking. I'm not some jealous ex-lover come back to ruin your chances. Your Bex is cute and all, but she's not a patch on mine."

Adrian knew he was being baited, but he still couldn't help asking, "What's different?"

"It'd be easier to say what's not," Desh said, looking up at the branches waving against the morning sky. "Lys claims she's the same every life, but that's bollocks. My Bex was hard as flint and tough as an old boot. She'd cut open a warlock's stomach just to choke him with his own intestines. The one time we killed a prince, she had me hold his head still so he'd be forced to watch while she cut it off."

Adrian winced. He liked a good retribution as much as the next witch, but he was glad he'd never met the Bex Desh described. The fear demon, however, looked heartbroken.

"She was a sight to behold," he said wistfully, "a true divine terror. We ran in Europe back then, and every warlock on the continent was scared shitless of her. I used to be the only one who could make her smile. Now she smiles at everyone. Makes a man feel less."

"I'm sorry," Adrian said.

"So am I," Desh said bitterly. "She was the love of my life, and now she doesn't even remember I existed. It'll be the same for you, so from one castoff to the next, here's some advice: Don't bother. She'll never be yours any more than she was mine. She's already married to her doomed crusade. Even if you win her heart, she'll just die and forget, so do yourself a favor and get out now, before she gets you killed too."

Adrian shook his head. "That's not going to happen."

"Why not?"

It was on the tip of his tongue to tell Desh about the bonfire and how this was Bex's last and greatest life. He was certain it'd give the bitter demon hope that things were different this time, but Lys had made him swear on his forest not to tell Desh anything before they left, so Adrian went for another approach.

"Because we're not just rehashing the same old tactics," he said. "All of Bex's previous rebellions focused on freeing demons, which was noble but did nothing to alter the state of the war. This time, we're attacking the foundation of Heaven's power directly, which should have a very different outcome."

Desh snorted. "You really think that's all there is to it? Picking a different target?"

"Better than doing the same thing over and over and expecting different results," Adrian said angrily. "But the fact that Gilgamesh has been in power for so long works against him in this case. He's become too reliant on his princes and warlocks and forgotten how to deal with an enemy who isn't afraid to attack him head-on. He's also never had to deal with a Blackwood on the offensive. Maybe all of that still won't be enough to bring down Heaven, but we've already scared the Eternal King into throwing two of his princes at the problem, so I feel like we're on the right track."

Desh rolled his eyes. "If you say so, mate."

"Why are you so pessimistic?" Adrian asked, legitimately curious. "You've got no reason to believe in me yet, but you must think Bex has a chance, or you wouldn't have come back."

"I came back because I wasn't done," Desh said, rising from his log, "but I'm not delusional. I saw the lot of you freaking out over a pair of princes. How in the Hells do you think you're going to manage when you have to face all seven at once? Or Gilgamesh himself?"

"I don't know yet," Adrian confessed, turning back to his tree. "But I trust us to figure it out when the time comes. You don't need to know how you're going to win every battle to start fighting back, but I think you should have more faith in your queen. She might not be the Bex you remember, but she's still tough, and she's not alone. We're all in this together, and the more we win, the more people will join us. That's how revolutions work. We don't have to beat everything by ourselves. We just have to light the match."

"If that's how you think this is going to go, you're nuttier than I used to be," Desh said, shaking his head. "No wonder Bex latched onto you. She always liked the crazy ones."

"Like you?" Adrian asked with a smile.

Desh's expression grew bitter. "Not anymore. Crazy gets you killed. I'm a pragmatist these days. Much higher life expectancy."

Now it was Adrian's turn to scowl. "If that's really how you feel, why are you here?"

"Because I made my Bex a promise," Desh said, "and despite what Lys would have you believe, I keep my word."

Adrian nodded, waiting for him to continue, but the fear demon just strolled away, whistling a tune Adrian

didn't recognize as he vanished into the bright morning
forest like a ghost.

Chapter 13

Despite how their conversation had ended, Adrian and Desh's relationship became much more civil after that. The fear demon went from bothering him every few hours to avoiding him entirely, leaving Adrian plenty of time to put the finishing touches on his part of the Anchor plan and move on to other projects, like replenishing his stock of curses. It'd be autumn before his new karma wasp was done curing, but there were lots of other spells to refill in the meanwhile. He'd just about restocked his entire coat when he got a message from Bex that they would be attacking the Anchor next Saturday evening.

"Why Saturday?" Boston asked when Adrian told him. "Isn't that the market's busiest night?"

It was a lot more than that. According to Lys—who'd pulled Desh, Adrian, and Nemini into a group call right after Bex's text to explain the plan—this Saturday night was shaping up to be one of the biggest in Seattle's history.

To prove the Anchor was safe and put to rest any whispers of weakness after the queen's attack, the divine committee in charge of all Anchor Markets had declared this Saturday to be the Seattle Anchor's grand reopening. Heaven was pouring money into the project, sponsoring a beer festival, bringing in specialty vendors from all over the west coast, and most importantly, hosting the biggest slave auction in a century. Fresh demons were being rounded up from every corner of the Hells for the event, including rare specimens not normally available for auction.

The announcement had only gone out yesterday, but warlocks from all over the world were already putting down deposits. Even for those who weren't interested in purchasing demons, it was shaping up to be a massive event, which was, of course, the entire point. The whole thing was a gratuitous display of wealth and power to prove that the Eternal King was still in command here. So, naturally, Bex had decided to hit it.

That wasn't just hubris. The huge crowds would help mitigate the heightened security, and all those demon slaves would turn into reinforcements if Bex could free them. She'd already rallied volunteers from her safe houses, which had turned into a pretty big recruiting pool now that all the California demons were together with the ones they'd freed after the Spider's assault.

The plan was to take that small army along with Iggs, Nemini, Desh, and Lys disguised as Bex, and stage an attack on one of the Anchor Market's outer doors. This would draw security away from the chain, where the real Bex and Adrian would be waiting. Once the guards ran off, Bex would chop the chain, disabling the Anchor and cutting off reinforcements from Heaven. After the deed was done, Adrian would keep the Anchor Market's folded space from collapsing while Bex freed the auction slaves, reinforcing their numbers to clear out the rest of the guards, warlocks, and anyone else who tried to stop them.

Assuming everything worked, they'd cut the chain, free hundreds of demons, and seize a ton of quintessence and other wealth to keep their army funded so they could do it all again. Even more importantly, they'd destroy Heaven's connection to the Seattle Anchor, making them the only people in history ever to take territory *back* from Gilgamesh.

It was exactly the sort of bold, daring, status-quo-destroying upset that Adrian had joined Bex to pull off, and aside from being miffed that he was hearing about it through Lys rather than from Bex herself, he couldn't have been happier. He'd gotten to work making himself a costume at once. He made one for Boston as well since there was no way he was leaving his familiar behind this time. This was war, which meant Adrian needed every weapon at his disposal, including his gardening knife: a big hacking blade as long as his hand that could cut through bone as easily as wood. He had no intention of using it, but a witch was always prepared, so the blade joined the rest of his materials in his costume's spelled pockets.

The final week seemed to drag on forever. That was normally a good thing for a witch who thrived on preparation, but Adrian was so ready to go that he was starting to second-guess himself, so when Friday night finally arrived, he forced himself to take it off. He took a bath, ate a good dinner, and went to bed early so he'd have time to toss, turn, and fret and still get a good night's sleep.

Finally, on Saturday evening at six o'clock sharp, Adrian put on his costume, slicked back his hair, collected Boston from his napping place on the windowsill, and went outside to fly everyone over.

Nemini was already sitting on his front porch. She stood up when Adrian opened the door, rising to her feet without a sound. Desh was nowhere to be seen, but by the time Adrian finished loading the evening's supplies onto the wings of Bran's raven form, the fear demon was standing right behind him.

Considering what they were about to attempt, Adrian had expected Desh to be kitted out like Iggs had been for the original Anchor run, but the fear demon looked the same as always. The only concession he'd made to tonight's attack was switching out his usual white-and-orange motocross jacket for a somber black turtleneck. He wasn't even armed except for his ever-present black knife, which Adrian had learned during Lys's briefing was actually a sin iron dagger and, thus, a Very Big Deal.

He'd had no idea. Desh's knife looked like pot metal to him, but Adrian was apparently garbage at feeling sin iron, and a special weapon would explain why Lys had made such a point of putting Desh in the main attack group. Apparently, in addition to being horribly toxic, sin iron knives could cut through anything, including a prince's golden armor. No one knew if the dagger would be able to poison the bastards yet, but just having another weapon that could hurt a prince was a game changer.

No wonder Bex had been so eager to bring Desh back into the fold. Still, Adrian had high hopes it wouldn't come to that. If their plan went smoothly, Bex would have the chain cut and be back on the ground before any princes showed up. He wasn't sure what would happen after that, but between Bex's fire, Desh's knife, his curses, and all the other demons, Adrian was certain they could weather whatever Gilgamesh threw at them—especially since, without the chain, there'd be no reinforcements from Heaven. That wouldn't save them if all seven princes decided to show up simultaneously, but there was no point in planning for annihilation, so Adrian kept his focus on getting his equipment loaded.

When everything was strapped onto Bran's crow form, Adrian took his usual position at the head. Nemini was already sitting on the broom's tail next to Boston, who was still fussing with his costume. Desh got on last, his face uncharacteristically pensive as Adrian lifted them into the air.

It wasn't quite dark enough yet to activate his broom's camouflage, so he kept them above the clouds, swooping across the bay as fast as he could to land on the roof of one of the big new condo developments that overlooked Puget Sound. Since the weather was dreary, no one was out on the rooftop balcony, giving them a kick-free path to the elevator that would take them down to the street level. Adrian was still wheeling his equipment through the building's marble lobby when he spotted Bex waiting for them outside the glass doors.

He almost lost his grip when he saw her. Like him, she was dressed for infiltration, but while Adrian had gone for the skeezy-warlock classic black suit and slicked-back hair combo, she was wearing a sleeveless purple sheath dress with a slit that went all the way up one leg. Her horns were decorated with crystals that made them look like pins for her elaborate hairstyle, and her fingers were covered in onyx jewelry to disguise her ring.

It was far and away the sexiest thing he'd ever seen her wear. Thank the Forest her glowing eyes were hidden behind brown contacts, because if she'd actually looked like herself, Adrian would have said something stupid for sure. He was already dangerously distracted, gawking openly while she directed Nemini and Desh to the rendezvous for the rest of their forces. Then the other demons were gone, and suddenly, it was just the two of them for the first time in weeks.

"Hi," he breathed as she held open the door for him.

Rather than answer, Bex passed him a black leather wallet.

"That's your ID," she said in a no-nonsense voice. "They're checking everyone at the doors. We're Mr. and Mrs. Ashford from Palo Alto. You're a sorcerer tasked with monitoring new technological developments for the Eternal Throne, and I'm your housewife. We've come up to see the spectacle and possibly purchase a new house demon."

"Excellent," Adrian said, reaching back into the lobby for the equipment he'd forgotten all about when he saw her. He'd just gotten everything arranged for the walk down to the Anchor Market when he realized Bex was staring at him.

"Adrian," she said, clearly trying not to laugh. "Why do you have a baby stroller?"

"It was the easiest way," he explained, stepping aside to show her the large and luxurious stroller he'd modified for tonight's operation. "The spells I'll be working tonight require a lot of accompanying materials. Strollers draw less attention than handcarts or wagons, and they're big enough to put Bran in without crushing any bristles." He opened the stroller's greatly expanded rear pocket to show her where he'd stashed his broom. "It also gave me somewhere to put Boston."

Bex frowned. "Boston?"

"Hello," said a voice from inside the bassinet.

She jumped nearly a foot, then her face spread into the biggest smile Adrian had seen on her since before everything had gone wrong.

"You turned your cat into a *baby*?"

"I turned myself into a baby, thank you very much," the chubby-faced infant huffed in Boston's voice. "And I assure you, it was the option of last resort. Tonight's announcement included a strict no-animals policy, and any high-security area is bound to be crammed full of anti-invisibility and anti-concealment spells. A simple shape change is much harder to detect, and no one ever thinks to check a baby."

"Sounds like you two have done this before," Bex said, clearly trying not to crack up.

"Once or twice," Adrian admitted, biting back a smile of his own. "It's simple and extremely effective. The only downside is the cost to Boston's dignity."

His familiar sighed dramatically, and Bex frowned.

"Why not just leave him at home?" she asked.

"He can't *leave me at home!*" Boston cried, grievously insulted. "You think a witch can do magic this big without their familiar? Preposterous! Even if Adrian could manage without me, I wouldn't allow it. The last time I let him go into the Anchor alone, he nearly died. I won't risk my witch like that again!"

"Keep it down," Adrian hissed, kicking the stroller with the toe of his boot, which he'd polished to a mirror shine for the occasion. "Babies can't talk."

Boston harrumphed, but he lay back in his bassinet without further complaint, allowing himself to be pushed down the sidewalk toward the market.

"So," Bex said, looking Adrian up and down with her disguised brown eyes. "You ready for this?"

"As ready as I can be," Adrian said, patting his disguise's gaudy coat to make sure all the extra pockets he'd put in were still where he'd left them. "Are *you* ready?"

"Oh, I'm ready," Bex replied, cracking her knuckles in anticipation.

Adrian looked down at the sidewalk to hide his frown. He couldn't explain what it was, but something about the way she'd said that sounded off. Her scent was odd as well, all flowers and vanilla without a hint of fire or smoke. Adrian was trying to determine if the change was due to some kind of concealment magic or if she'd just been really liberal with the perfume bottle when Bex picked up the pace, practically dragging him down the sidewalk toward the crowded street below.

It was obvious from three blocks away that something big was going on. Pike Place Market was normally dead after six, but the place was packed tonight with odd-looking, extravagantly dressed people. Adrian had worried that Bex's huge, horn-hiding hairstyle would draw attention, but she actually looked demure compared to some of the other ladies. Nothing was obviously magical yet—they were still on a public street—but the crowd looked *way* too nice for their surroundings. Even the demons were dressed up, trailing behind their masters like decorated pets as the whole parade made its way past the closed-up fish counters and florist stalls and down the wide cement stairs that led into the market's tangled bowels.

The Anchor Market must have opened extra entrances for the event. All the doors Adrian knew about were located at the bottom of the main building, but this crowd only went down one floor before filing into what appeared to be a large sports-memorabilia shop. When Adrian and Bex ducked behind the curtain of gray Seahawks and teal-blue Kraken jerseys, however, the mundane trappings fell away to reveal an entry hall much taller and grander than the vendor door they'd used on his first night in Seattle.

There were crystal chandeliers hanging from the high ceilings and an expansive marble floor crisscrossed with velvet ropes attached to ornate brass poles. Seven eight-foot-tall arched doorways marked the entrance to the Market itself, but the wide tunnel connecting the real world to the Anchor's false fields of Paradise was blocked by a platoon of golden-armored Anchor Guards.

There had to be a hundred of them checking IDs and running illusion-disrupting wands over the crowd. That last one in particular was causing an uproar since practically everyone here was using some kind of appearance-enhancing magic. Thankfully, Adrian and Bex were both wearing mundane costumes. Boston was enchanted, but as he'd predicted, no one bothered to check the baby. The security line was also very long, causing the harried guards to give them no more than a cursory scan before waving them into the Anchor Market, which looked totally different from the time Adrian had come here to buy Lot's Salt.

It was still a grassy field full of colorful vendor tents with a giant golden statue of Gilgamesh at the center. But while the basics remained unchanged, everything else had been altered for the event, starting with the fact that it was dark. Every other time Adrian had been to an Anchor Market, the sunless sky had been bright and blue. Tonight, though, the summer day had been replaced by a velvet night filled with glittering stars. Strings of magical lanterns decorated every tent, illuminating the grassy paths between the sales tables in a rainbow of colors. It reminded Adrian of the Christmas markets he used to visit as a child back when he could still leave the Blackwood without being hunted, but unlike those happy, festive events, this gathering put out an aura of pure malice.

You didn't need the spotlights bathing Gilgamesh's giant statue in heavenly radiance or the armored Anchor Guards who stood at every intersection to know that this was a display of power. The Eternal King wasn't just celebrating the Anchor's reopening. He was reminding everyone of who was in charge, showing them that last month's attack meant nothing in the face of true divine strength.

"We must've scared him more than we realized," Adrian whispered to Bex as they pushed Boston's stroller through the crowds. "Even for Gilgamesh, this is a lot of compensation."

"Or it's a trap," she whispered back, her disguised eyes roving everywhere. "How close do you need to be to the middle?"

"Nearer is better," he said, craning his head back to look at the glittering chain that rose like a golden kite string from the giant statue's upstretched fist. "But I'm flexible. I just hope I can get it tall enough. I swear the top of this place goes halfway to Heaven."

"I'm sure you've got it," Bex assured him, but it didn't sound like her heart was in it. She was busy glancing over her shoulder, something she'd been doing constantly since they got inside.

"What are you looking for?"

"Everything," she muttered, moving a little closer. "Let's just get you into position."

That was easier said than done. Adrian had planned to set up in the receiving lot, a dark bit of land hidden behind Gilgamesh's statue that was used as temporary storage for large purchases before they went up the chain to Heaven. Since people probably wouldn't be buying dining tables or smart fridges during the biggest slave auction of the century, he'd had high hopes it would be empty. Unfortunately, those hopes didn't pan out.

"Damn," Adrian said, pulling the stroller to a stop. "There goes that idea."

When Bex arched a questioning eyebrow, he pointed through the crowds at the base of Gilgamesh's statue, where the golden doors to the chain were located.

The place where the road to Heaven let out into the public market was normally a pretty low-key affair with just a few guards and a desk for the scribes who recorded the comings and goings of Heavenly denizens. Tonight, however, the receiving area had been expanded into an enormous VIP section that wrapped all the way around the

statue's base. There were sitting areas, a seven-course buffet
with champagne bar, private bathrooms, and an entire
roped-off section of velvet-padded bleachers, presumably
so Gilgamesh's chosen could participate in the slave auction
without having to mingle with the common rabble.
Fantastic for them, terrible for Adrian's plan.

"Damn, damn, damn," he said, holding the stroller
tight against his legs as he scanned the crowd. "We'll have
to set up somewhere else."

"We can do it from the edge," Boston whispered from
where he was pretending to nap under the baby blankets.
"It'll be lopsided, but a lopsided support is better than no
support."

"That will put more horizontal stress on the central
elements than we planned for," Adrian argued, but he
already knew his familiar was right. Changes in stress could
be managed, but the only hard requirement for the spell
they'd designed all of this around was space, and there was
none of that here.

"Change of plans," he murmured, leaning over so
that he was speaking right next to Bex's ear. "We need to get
out into the fields."

"Follow me," she said, turning on her high heel to
lead him past a line of vendors selling novelty pastries
shaped like demons in cages.

Adrian stuck as close as possible, using his stroller to
part the crowds, which were getting thicker by the second.
It looked like every non-scaled person on the West Coast
had showed up for this event, but while the throng was
enormous, everybody was angling to get spots with a view
of the demon auction stage. Since he and Bex were going
the opposite direction, the crush thinned out quickly, and
by the time they reached the dark stretch of grass beyond
the market's last ring of tents, there was no one at all.

"The edge of the Anchor is there," Bex said, pointing at the line where the neatly trimmed turf that carpeted the Anchor Market gave way to the waist-high swaying grasses of Paradise. "Will this work?"

"It'll have to," Adrian said, examining the crates the vendors had stashed out here for extra storage. There were a lot of them scattered around, but after a bit of rearranging, Adrian managed to secure himself a nice clear swath of grass. When he was satisfied he'd made enough room, he reached under the baby stroller for his bundle of premade Neverminds.

"Can you even support that many?" Boston asked, hopping out of his baby disguise, which was tied to the carriage.

"I can do Neverminds in my sleep," Adrian assured him, brushing the last bits of the shape change off his familiar so Boston wouldn't have to work magic looking like a hairless cat. "It's the first spell I ever learned."

He had three going already, big shimmering spiderwebs that he draped over the stacked boxes like tarps. He added still more on top, overlapping the edges until he'd curtained off a ten-by-ten square in a double layer of Neverminds and Lookaways.

"There," he said, adjusting the spells to make sure there were no gaps. "It won't stop a determined drunk, but unless someone watched us go back here, we should be both invisible and inaudible."

At least to start. Once the spell got going, nothing would be able to hide it. He was wondering if he shouldn't hang a few more Neverminds higher up to buy them more time when Bex's head whipped around.

"What are you doing here?"

Adrian didn't see who she was talking to at first. It was very dark out here away from the festival lights. He'd just pulled a small, battery-powered lantern out of his pocket when a familiar figure stepped through the haze of the Neverminds.

"Desh?" Adrian said, surprised. "I thought you were supposed to be with main group."

"He *is* supposed to be with the main group," Bex snapped, her face furious. "You're their blade, dammit. Get back in position!"

"I *am* in position," Desh said, crossing his arms over his chest. "You were taking forever to call in, so Lys sent me over to make sure you two weren't getting distracted."

Adrian wasn't sure whether to be flattered or offended by that, but Bex narrowed her eyes.

"How did you know where we were?" she asked suspiciously. "This isn't our planned location."

"I followed you," the fear demon said with a shrug. "Would've announced myself earlier, but it's hard enough getting around this mess as a free demon without making a scene by tapping fancy ladies on the shoulder."

That sounded reasonable enough to Adrian, but Bex was still glowering. Then, without another word, she turned around and started shoving a large vendor crate full of wine bottles farther away from Adrian's casting area.

The sight made him go still. Not because he was surprised she was helping, but he'd seen Bex throw a police car. She should've been able to move that wine crate with one finger, but she was shoving the wooden box with both hands like it weighed a ton. Adrian didn't believe for a second it was actually giving her trouble, so why the act? What was she trying to—

Desh moved before Adrian could finish his thought. One second, the fear demon was standing at the edge of the Neverminds, the next, he was on top of Bex with his black dagger in his hand. By the time Adrian realized what was happening, Desh's sin iron knife was nearly buried in her back—*would* have been buried, but something had caught the demon's wrist at the last second.

Not Bex's hands—those were still on the crate. Desh had been caught by a *tail*. A long, thin, extremely flexible tail belonging to a demon who was not Bex.

"Got you," Lys said, their amber eyes gleaming in Bex's face before the illusion fell away.

All of it. The fake Bex with her ridiculous updo and slinky dress vanished in the blink of an eye to reveal a new figure who was even taller than Desh. They were neither male nor female but still incredibly beautiful with dusky pink skin, a pointed, prehensile tail, and large batlike wings. Adrian had never seen anything like it because, unlike war, fear, and other combat demons, lust demons were usually forbidden from showing their true forms. Lys's was a lot bigger than he'd expected, but the fury in the amber eyes was Lys to a T.

"How long have you known?" Desh asked, seemingly unconcerned that a homicidally angry demon had his wrist in a tail-lock.

"From the beginning," Lys said, taking off Bex's tall horns—which were actual fakes made from plastic—as they looked down on Desh from their new imposing height. "I knew you'd never come back willingly, not unless there was something in it for you. I didn't want to believe that was stabbing your queen in the back, but I wasn't willing to put it past you, so I had Bex switch places with me. Not that you would have gotten her with that sloppy—"

They cut off with a gasp as Desh broke free. At first, Adrian thought he'd slashed Lys with the sin iron dagger. Then he saw the tip of Lys's tail hit the ground, cut off by the razor-sharp scales that suddenly covered Desh's body.

In the space of a heartbeat, the fear demon was armored from his head to his clawed feet in overlapping plates as black as demon blood. The scales covered his face like a visor, leaving his orange eyes glowing like candles in the darkness behind his armor. His fingers were tipped with scythelike claws that didn't seem to impede his hold on the black dagger in the slightest as he flipped it backward into a knife-fighter's grip. Lys responded by pulling their own knife from the sheath hidden under their left wing, but as their delicately clawed feet edged across the grass toward Desh, the fear demon lurched toward Adrian instead, his free arm moving like a whip to wrap around the witch's neck.

"Give it up, Lyssy," Desh ordered as he pressed the sin iron dagger into Adrian's ribs. "One scratch with this, and your precious witch dies."

Adrian stopped struggling at once, and Lys's eyes narrowed to slits.

"Bex will incinerate you if you hurt him."

"That's the whole idea," Desh said, his voice oddly chipper, as if he were smiling behind his armored mask. "My orders were simple: poison the queen, or if that fails, capture the witch."

"And who gave those orders?" Lys asked, their eyes never leaving the black knife Desh was holding against Adrian's side.

"Who do you think?" Desh taunted. "It was a sodding prince."

Lys jerked in horror. "You *didn't*."

"I damn well did," Desh snapped, squeezing Adrian's neck tighter. "You think I actually spent all those decades after Bex died wandering around as a free demon? Bollocks. The warlocks picked me up after only three months and banished me back to the Hells. The *lowest* Hell, where I rotted in agony until last month, when a prince had me brought up. He offered me my freedom—*actual* freedom, as in walking papers—and all I had to do was get him the Coward Queen. Preferably by tossing her sin-iron-crippled body at his feet, but the witch boy she'd do anything to protect was also deemed acceptable."

"If those were your orders, then your prince is a fool," Lys said. "Bex would never betray us for Adrian."

Adrian opened his mouth in a rush, but it was too late.

"She already did," Desh said with a sneer. "During the last fight for the Anchor, your sweet little baby queen traded a defeated prince *and* his sword to save her pointy-hatted boyfriend. You could've had a bleeding Blade of Gilgamesh! But she gave it away...for *him.*"

Adrian cringed in Desh's grip, waiting for Lys to blow up, but the lust demon just sighed.

"Gotta hand it to you, Desh," they said, getting a better grip on their knife. "I always knew you were a selfish prick, but I never expected you to sell out your queen over jealousy."

"You think that's what this is about?" Desh roared. "My Bex is *dead*! I'm not desperate like you, following copy after copy. I knew my queen was gone. That's why I didn't come back to help you raise the next one. Did you ever think about how sick that is? Growing a child into a soldier just so they can die in the same war over and over? It's disgusting! Not to mention pointless, 'cause you're never going to win. Bex has been suffering through this shit for five thousand years, and it hasn't changed a thing. It's *never* going to change, no matter what this cocky bastard thinks."

He squeezed Adrian harder, making him choke.

"My Bex understood that," Desh said, his voice cracking behind his mask. "I used to be just like the rest of you, lapping up the drivel, thinking this time would be different. I'd tell her 'No, no, luv, we're special. We can win. We've just gotta go bigger, think outside the box, hit 'em where they don't expect.'"

His orange eyes flicked to Adrian. "Sound familiar? You're not the first arrogant prick to think *you* were what this revolution was lacking. Why do you think I talked her into baiting that prince? I thought there was nothing we couldn't do so long as we were together, that we were the ones who could win it all and bring everyone home to Paradise. It wasn't until she died in front of me that I realized she'd been right all along. There is no victory, never was. We're just all playing our parts so demons like *them*"—he snapped his glare back to Lys—"don't have to give up their delusions of hope."

"Of course," Lys said with a sneer. "You loved her *so* much, which is why you just tried to stab her in the *back*."

"Yes," Desh said without missing a beat. "Because she told me things she couldn't tell the rest of you—*actual* truths, like how tired she was and how much she hated the war. She never wanted to fight and die. The only reason she did any of it was because she couldn't bear to let people like you down."

His story made Adrian wince because those were the same words Bex had said to him. She'd told him, too, that she was tired, hopeless, and worn out, right before she told him the bonfire had changed everything. He was scrambling for a way to communicate this to Desh that wouldn't reveal the secret of Bex's last life to a proven traitor when the fear demon cut through Adrian's coat and shirt to press his knife against the witch's bare skin.

"I should've listened to her," Desh said angrily, glaring at Lys. "I thought I was helping by insisting we could do it, but I was being just as bad as the rest of you. It wasn't until my Bex died and you called me in to help raise the next one like we were changing a burned-out lightbulb that I finally realized what my love had been trying to tell me all this time. She wanted me to help her stop, to find a way to quit the war."

The look on Lys's face grew deadly. "And you chose to hand her over to *Gilgamesh*?"

"There's no other way," Desh argued. "We can't win, and if she dies, the whole nightmare starts over again. Defeat is the only way she gets out, and I think she's earned a rest after five thousand years."

"Oh, yes, you're doing it *all* for her," Lys sneered. "And the fact that you're also getting your walking papers has nothing to do with it."

"You forgot screwing you over," Desh said, dragging Adrian with him as he took a step back. "That was also a big check in the plus column."

He took another step, and Adrian decided it was now or never.

"Don't do this, Desh," he said in the calmest voice he could manage. "I understand how you feel. Bex told me those same things, but she'd never want—"

"Shut up," Desh snarled, pressing the sin iron knife harder against Adrian's side. "Believe it or not, you're the one I *didn't* want getting involved in this mess. You're not a soldier like them. You're just an innocent sap caught up in things too big for your witch hat. I tried my damnedest to get you to bail back in the woods, but *no*. You wouldn't listen, and now—"

His rant cut off with a pained yelp, and Desh's arm vanished from around Adrian's neck as Boston—who was now the size of a jaguar—yanked it down with his jaws. Lys moved at the same moment, going for Desh's dagger, but the fear demon was too quick. He spun away, vanishing through the Neverminds like a shadow, though not before his sin iron dagger sliced a long, shallow cut across Adrian's torso.

"*Shit!*" Lys swore, running to his side, but Adrian shook his head.

"I'm fine."

"You can't be *fine*," Lys hissed, tearing back his ripped shirt. "That's *sin iron*, and you're *human*! Even a scratch like this could—"

"If I couldn't handle poisons, I wouldn't be much of a witch," Adrian told them stubbornly as he pressed his hand over the wound, which was bleeding like a waterfall despite its small size. "All that matters right now is keeping Desh away from Bex. You go after him. I'll bandage this and start taking down the—"

"Nothing gets taken down," Lys ordered, rising to their feet. "Stick to the plan."

"But we've been compromised," Adrian argued. "If Desh is taking orders from a prince, then he's undoubtedly been reporting everything we—"

"Desh doesn't know shit," Lys said, sliding their dagger back into the sheath under their wing. "I didn't trust him from the start, which is why every plan I've told him has been a fake."

"But..." Adrian said slowly. "Those were the same plans you told *me*."

"Because you only had to do one thing," Lys assured him. "Your part was the only real bit. The rest was a lie to cover our asses in case my instincts about Desh were on the money, which they *were*." The demon gave him a cocky smile. "Looks like the Ballad of Lys the Always Right gets another verse. Now bandage that cut and get back to your spell. I'll take care of Desh."

Adrian nodded nervously, but Lys was already gone, shifting into the shape of a war-demon bodyguard as they charged through the same Nevermind Desh had disappeared behind. He was still staring at where they'd vanished when Boston nosed under his arm.

"Let me see your wound."

Adrian removed his hand with a grimace. "How does it look?"

"Pretty normal, actually," the giant cat replied, giving the cut a sniff. "Either sin iron isn't as toxic as advertised, or you are *very* resistant."

"I am my mother's son," Adrian said proudly, digging into his pockets for his first aid kit, which wasn't nearly as easy to reach in this ridiculous coat as it was in his usual one. "I'm more upset that he was able to grab me so easily."

Boston looked smug. "Sounds like your Aunt Lydia and I were right all those times we badgered you to learn some self-defense."

"I was going to hit him with a curse," Adrian grumbled, slapping a sticky gauze pad over the cut. "But all the pockets in this stupid jacket are in the wrong places."

"Excuses, excuses," Boston said, shrinking back to his usual size so he could stick his head into the storage pocket under the baby stroller. "Shall we resume? I don't want to be late for our part in whatever the plan actually is."

Adrian lifted his eyes to the golden chain trailing like a comet through the sky. If Desh was telling the truth about being under a prince's orders, then this whole event was a setup. That sounded like a good reason to pull the plug, whatever Lys said, but if the plan was still going, then Adrian was determined to play his part. He did take out his phone and send a message to the real Bex, though, letting her know that Desh had turned on them and Lys was in pursuit before hauling himself off the grass to get to work.

"Craaaaaaap," Bex groaned when she saw her messages.

"What?" Iggs asked beside her.

"Lys was right," she replied, handing over her phone so the wrath demon could read the bad news for himself while she turned to face the crowd.

"Our witch is in position," she announced to the cavernous room full of demons. "We're proceeding according to Plan B. Everyone get ready. We move out in three."

The demons nodded, shifting nervously. They were holed up inside a truck garage just across the gum alley from the Anchor's vendor entrance. Not a great invasion point, but also not the one the enemy was expecting them to use.

"I always suspected Desh was up to no good," Iggs said quietly as he handed Bex's phone back. "How else does a free demon end up with a sin iron knife? I'm only surprised he didn't try to stab you earlier."

"Me too," Bex said with a sad sigh. "Guess he didn't want to poison me until I was in a convenient pickup location, and doing things this way made sure his prince would get all my demons as well. Not a bad setup for a double-cross. I just hope Lys ganks him before we go inside. If I have to do this with a knife at my back, things are gonna get ugly."

"Are you sure Lys can handle him?" Iggs asked, tugging nervously at his black combat armor. "I know they're old and salty, but fear demons are tried-and-true monsters, and lust demons aren't exactly known for their combat prowess."

Bex chuckled. "If you think Desh is the monster in that matchup, you haven't been paying attention. Now let's get this done before the prince realizes his inside man's been caught and we lose our advantage." She pressed the button on her earbud to activate her mic. "Ready, Nemini?"

"As ready as anyone can be in a world where the only certainty is chaos," came the monotone reply.

"Do it," Bex ordered, transforming her sword just before she rolled up the garage door.

That was the signal. Her own fear demons had already cleared the gum-covered alley outside, making sure all the kick-happy humans were frightened away when Bex led her volunteer army across the street to the innocuous door on the other side. Thanking Ishtar she'd thought to wear gloves, Bex yanked the gum-covered door off its hinges and jumped through, coming up with her sword ready, only to see that Nemini had already taken care of everything.

"Nice work," she said, grinning at the pile of golden-armored guards twitching at Nemini's feet. "But I thought you said there were only four."

"Another patrol came in right after you gave the order," the snake-headed demon replied. "Unfortunately for them, they were also ensnared by their egos. Once I ripped the illusion of self-importance away, there was nowhere for them to go except into the abyss." She leaned down to tap the closest comatose guard on the helmet. "I had to drop them hard. I'm not sure if they'll get out."

"Hazard of war," Bex replied, pushing the bodies out of the way to clear a path for her troops. She hopped on top of a pallet full of caviar next, using the extra height to get her short frame into view of the crowd that was rapidly filling the Anchor Market's vendor entrance.

"I told you when I freed you that you would get your chance for vengeance," she said, looking over the determined faces of the hundred and fifty demons who'd answered her call to war. "Tonight is that chance, but we have to do it right."

She pointed over her shoulder at the long brick tunnel that led into the Anchor Market.

"There are no innocents beyond that door, but we're not here to slaughter and ravage like the monsters Gilgamesh paints us to be. Our objectives tonight are to take over the Anchor and free our enslaved brothers and sisters. Nothing is more important than those two goals, so if a warlock runs, you let them. Every soldier of Gilgamesh that leaves the field is one less person to outnumber us. Don't waste time on pride fights, listen to your squad leaders, and look out for each other. I'll be leaving on my own mission once we get inside, so Iggs is in charge until I return."

Iggs saluted the crowd with the grenade he'd just pulled out of his bag.

"For the glory of Ishtar," Bex said, raising her black sword.

"*For the glory of Ishtar!*" the demons yelled in reply, showing their fangs as Iggs winged his grenade—a normal one, not a sorcerous one, but still highly effective—down the tunnel into the Anchor Market. For several seconds, the *ping ping* of bouncing metal was all Bex could hear. Then the grenade exploded, spewing an enormous cloud of hot thermal smoke all over the darkened fields of Paradise.

Bex was moving the moment it went off, darting through the smoke like a silent shot. She leaped as soon as she was clear of the tunnel, sailing over the heads of the confused, coughing crowd on the other side. A roar followed her as the free demons rushed down the tunnel, the narrow walls bouncing their battle cries until they sounded like a thousand instead of a hundred and fifty.

The packed market screamed in reply. What had been an orderly crowd of well-dressed shoppers transformed into a mob as everybody started trying to run for the exits at the same time, resulting in no one getting anywhere as Iggs and the first wave of demons slammed into the people at the back.

Chaos exploded when they hit. All of Bex's demons were armed with grenades—cheap, low-ordinance poppers that made a lot of noise and smoke but did little actual damage. Not because these slave buyers deserved mercy but because casualties would slow them down. Their goal was a stampede: a wave of blind, thoughtless fear that would turn Gilgamesh's faithful into an extension of their army.

So far, it was working beautifully. Like a rock chucked into a pond, the surprise attack sent waves of panic spreading to every corner of the crowded market. Screaming humans running for their lives collided into yet more people, who also began to scream and run. A few brave standouts tried to hold their ground, shouting spells or ordering their demons to protect them, but no one individual was stronger than a panicked mob, and this mob was even more panicky than Bex had hoped. Maybe their attack on the Anchor last month really had made a difference. She wasn't even on fire yet, and people were already screaming that the Queen of Wrath had come.

Good, she thought as she ran over the tops of the merchant tents. Let them shout her name. Let them *fear.* It'd make her next job easier as she circled around the spotlit statue of Gilgamesh, darted past the golden doors to the chain they'd told Desh was their primary objective, and leaped over the crowded VIP bleachers to barrel straight into the slave auction.

The panic hadn't reached this far yet, but Bex could feel it coming. The demons' roars echoed all over the Anchor Market, and the air was already growing hazy with the smoke from their grenades and the fires her arson teams were setting. The war-zone atmosphere made the warlocks on guard nice and nervous, *so* nervous that they were all facing the wrong direction when Bex landed on the stage behind them.

She did so like a cannonball, shooting through the smoky darkness to land right on top of her own stone head. The statue of the Coward Queen that stood above the auction stage exploded into powder as the real thing came down on top of it. Bex ignited the moment she landed, her flames leaping ten feet into the air to paint the stacks of sin iron cages in blazing firelight as the Queen of Wrath lifted her sword.

"Children of Paradise!"

Her voice sliced through the chaos, ringing with command. No one had ever taught Bex to speak that way. It was one of the things her body just knew, an ancient habit ingrained from back when she'd been an actual queen. That time was long dead and gone, but its power still remained, fanning Bex's flames even higher as her light flickered back at her from the eyes of the demons huddling inside the slave cages.

The sheer number shocked her into silence for a second. She'd known this was going to be a big auction, but now that Bex was actually standing in front of them, she was stunned. There had to be a thousand bodies crammed into the sin iron cages the warlocks had stacked like shipping crates on the grass surrounding the auction stage. Every one of them was collared, too, with big sin iron rings over their slave bands, proof that these weren't demons who'd volunteered to serve in return for a ticket out of the Hells. They'd been dragged up here by force, their necks noosed with poison to keep them weak and biddable. All of them were young, bordering on *very* young, and as she stared at them staring back at her in terrified awe, Bex's anger surged so hot her orange flames turned white.

"People of the Riverlands," she said, her voice soaring over the clamor of the warlocks, who'd started shouting orders to their own demons. "I am the Queen of Wrath, Blade of Ishtar, and I have come for you. Our days of slavery and humiliation at the conqueror's hands are over. Tonight, we fight *back*!"

She brought her sword down as she finished, slicing the slave auction stage in half. She cut the wall of cages behind it next, sliding Drox through the sin iron bars like they were cardboard. When one of the warlocks' war demons tried to stop her, she cut his slave band just as easily, calling out his true name as her sword sliced him free. He staggered as the control spell broke, and then he turned on his former master with a roar, leaping onto the warlock with a surge of righteous fury that hit Bex like a lightning bolt.

The pulse made her stagger. She hadn't been prepared for that, but she'd also never cut a slave band when her target was that angry. It felt uncomfortably like when her demons had poured their wrath into her in Limbo, but while Bex's fire leaped to consume the new fuel, Bex herself shied away. She couldn't afford to lose control here. Every demon in the Market was counting on her, so she pushed the unfamiliar rage aside to focus exclusively on her own fury as she started cutting the slave bands off the other demon guards.

She didn't even have to be close when she was burning this hot. The slave bands curled to ash the moment Bex yelled out the names Drox was feeding her, commanding them *Be free*.

The result was pure chaos. Not every slave turned on their master, but even when the demons did nothing but run away, the warlocks' control was weakened. Soon, there was no resistance at all, leaving Bex free to turn her sword on the cages again. She sliced them open like a box cutter through cardboard, sending the demons that had been crammed inside bursting into the market.

"Here," she said, jumping off the rubble of her statue to grab a ring of keys off the head warlock's dead body. "Use these to unlock the sin iron collars."

The demon she tossed the keys at—a bright-eyed lust demon who looked very much like Lys must have when they were young—caught them in midair.

"Yes, great queen," they said, their amber eyes glowing with excitement. "But what will you do?"

Bex pointed her sword at the fresh slave band that had been seared with magic into the young demon's graceful neck. "I'm going to set you free."

The lust demon lifted their chin in readiness, but Bex didn't cut their band off yet. She gave them a salute and turned away instead, charging through the wall of Anchor Guards that had started swarming out of the VIP section toward her next objective:

Gilgamesh's golden statue.

She leaped onto the base the moment she got close, scrambling over the ugly stone effigies of her kneeling sisters onto the king's shiny boots. Like his princes' armor, Gilgamesh's statue melted under her burning grip, but only on the surface. The main body remained untouched because the king's statue wasn't solid gold. Its glittering surface was nothing but a front, a gold-plated fake covering up the black mass of sin iron that was the statue's core.

Seeing the ugly truth beneath the melting gold fanned Bex's flames even higher. She *knew* Gilgamesh was a fraud! She climbed his spotlit statue with a roar, shoving her red-hot hands through the gilded plating as she hauled herself to the top of the traitor king's head. When she was as high above the screaming crowds as she could get, Bex kicked the molten gold off her flame-wreathed boots and grabbed the edge of Gilgamesh's crown to look down at the auction stage she'd cut in half.

The lust demon she'd given the keys to had done fast work. Fully a quarter of the demons had their sin iron collars off now, and the free ones were searching the warlocks' bodies for more keys to help uncuff the rest. All of them were out of the cages, and those who weren't frantically unlocking their fellow slaves were gazing up at Bex with the exact mix of hope and fear she'd been counting on. She needed to look down and see what had been done to her people, needed to get madder than she'd ever been because the next step was going to take everything she had.

This was the crux of the plan she, Lys, Drox, and Iggs had come up with after they'd left Desh in the Blackwood. Bex had sworn up and down that she could do it, but she hadn't actually been sure until she got up here. Now, though, looking down at the poison cages Gilgamesh's slavers had made for Ishtar's children did the trick. All she had to do was witness the terror on their faces, the wild hope sparked by even the tiniest chance to be free, and her anger roared up like the flames of Gilgamesh's Hells, building the Bonfire of Wrath higher and higher until Bex was shining like the sun.

Now! Drox cried, his booming voice almost lost in the thunderous noise of her flames. *Do it now before you burn out of control again!*

She didn't need his orders. The Queen of Wrath had already lifted her sword, sending liquid gold pouring down the Eternal King's face as she raised her voice to the market's false night.

"Witness me, victims of Gilgamesh!" she cried. "I am Rebexa the Bonfire, Queen of Wrath and daughter of Ishtar! By my own sacred name, I command you: *be free.*"

It was the same trick she used to make Drox use on her. Only a queen could command the demons of Ishtar, which was why Gilgamesh had captured her sisters instead of killing them. It was their stolen power that allowed Heaven's servants to enslave her people, but Bex was a living queen doing what she'd been born to do. Her Bonfire was burning right in front of them, and her name had been given to her by Ishtar herself. When Rebexa named herself, every word that followed became divine law, and everywhere her fire touched, that law was enforced, burning through the slave bands forged by a lesser authority until every demon neck in the Anchor was scorched clean.

The power left like a thunderclap when it was finished. Bex's fire vanished with it, dropping her into the pool of bubbling, molten slag she'd melted into Gilgamesh's skull. The heat didn't bother her, but the toxic fumes from the statue's freshly exposed sin iron core made her gag. She rolled away in a coughing fit, hacking the poison out of her lungs as she slid off the statue's head to land on the king's golden shoulder. But even with her eyes stinging and her fire gutted, nothing could stop Bex from leaning over the edge to see what she'd done.

A miracle seemed to be the answer. Now that she was no longer blazing like the sun, Bex had to squint through the statue's spotlights to see the crowds below. The panic their opening attack had kicked off at the service door was still spreading, but her army of demon volunteers was no longer outnumbered. Bex's invocation hadn't just freed the demons brought in for the slave auction. She'd freed *every* demon in the Anchor Market—the house slaves, the warlocks' entourages, even the demons working the food stalls—and the result was just as disruptive as they'd hoped.

The entire market was in chaos. Some demons turned on their masters instantly, attacking with a ferocity fermented over decades of humiliation. Others took their freedom and ran, knocking over everything in their path as they charged toward the exits. A few were still standing in shock, staring up at Bex like she was a meteor coming down to destroy them all.

No matter how they used their freedom, though, all of them contributed to the cause. With so many panicked humans and demons running in every direction and fights breaking out all over, the Anchor Guards were completely overwhelmed. The ones guarding the tunnels to the big front entrance couldn't even move. They'd been trapped against the doors by a screaming mob of their own people. It was all going exactly to plan, in other words, which meant it was time for Bex to move on to her next target.

You have to reignite, Drox said as Bex started climbing up the statue's arm toward the gold chain that was clutched in Gilgamesh's upstretched fist. *We hid as much from the traitor as possible, but he still knows our end goal. We should expect at least one prince when we reach the chain, possibly more. My blade can cut through anything, but only if you're capable of swinging me hard enough to—*

"I know, I know," Bex said as she hauled herself up the king's golden sleeve. "I'm working on it."

She was, too, but it wasn't going well. For the first time since she'd fought the prince in Adrian's forest, Bex's flames weren't coming when she called. The spark was still inside her—would always be inside her—but stoking her bonfire big enough to burn off so many slave bands at once had left her too exhausted to work herself back to the ignition point.

You can rest later, Drox promised, his ring biting into her finger to spur her on. *But right now, you* have *to cut that chain before reinforcements—*

"I *know,*" Bex snapped. "This is my plan, remember? I'll do it. Just shut up and let me focus."

To her great surprise, Drox did as she asked, leaving her head in silence as Bex hauled her unlit body toward the chain that extended off the statue's giant golden fingers.

Chapter 14

Desh was the fastest demon he knew, but even he couldn't run upstream through a panicked crowd.

"Move, Ishtar damn you!" he shouted, digging his claws into the mob of terrified people pushing him back like a river.

It would've been easier to run with them. Even Anchor Guards couldn't give him trouble under these conditions. He could let the mob take him, gut a path through the packed doors, then flee out into the city. The only reason he didn't was because Desh had already been down that route.

There was nothing for a solo demon out there. Even if he ran to the ends of the Earth, the warlocks would just pick him up again and send him back to the Hells. His only ticket out of this was Bex. Fortunately, Desh had heard her yelling somewhere over by the slave pens. He just had to get through this sea of screaming idiots before she—

A blast of light knocked the plans right out of his head. Fire was exploding through the Anchor's sky, and Bex's voice was roaring through it, calling out some nonsense about her name and freedom. Seemed she hadn't lost her love of grandstanding, but when in Ishtar's name had she learned to do that? His Bex had only been able to produce fire when her life was in danger, but this one was standing on top of Gilgamesh's golden head, burning like a bloody torch.

The sight was so impressive Desh actually stopped to gawk for a moment. Then he shook his damn self back to his senses and changed direction, slashing his way through the blast-shocked crowd toward the statue's base.

He'd have to approach this carefully. Lys had no doubt already rung the warning, but every version of Bex had a soft spot for demons of any stripe, even traitors. She wouldn't attack first, and Desh didn't have to beat her to win. He just had to cut deep enough for the poison to work. Then he could drag her comatose body to the prince, and this hell would finally be over for both of them.

That thought made Desh smile as he cut a fleeing man's legs out from under him. He'd just charged into the hole when one of the sorcerers who'd been running past in a panic suddenly turned on a dime and tackled Desh to the ground. They landed in the grass with Lys on top, the last of the sorcerer's shape vanishing off them as they stabbed their dagger at Desh's heart.

The blade sank into the ground as Desh rolled to the side. By the time he got his hands under himself, his body was covered in scales again, protecting his back from Lys's next strike as Desh shoved himself into them.

Lys's real form was taller than Desh's, but like all flying sorts, the lust demon was made of nothing. One good hit was all it took to knock Lys off their feet. They caught themselves with a flap of their wings, but Desh was already on them, grabbing their still-healing tail in his fist to slam them back into the ground.

"You traitorous *bastard!*" Lys roared, kicking up with their clawed feet. "When I'm done with you, there won't be a piece big enough to send back to the Hells, you—"

They cut off with a hiss when Desh stabbed his knife at Lys's neck. The sin iron's black point was supposed to punch through their windpipe, but the pink git was faster than Desh remembered. They flitted out of the way at the final moment, raking his face with their clawed fingers as they went. That move no doubt worked wonders on their usual lust-stupid prey, but Desh was armored like a tank, and he had everything to lose.

"You can't win this," he warned, whirling around to take another swipe at Lys's face. "Decades of war have sharpened you up, but I'm not some besotted human waiting patiently for my stab in the back. No matter how many times you trick Bex into making you her second, you'll never be anything but a lust demon whose only real talents are looking pretty and inflaming hormones. I was born to be what humans fear."

"You were born to *cleanse* fear," Lys corrected coldly, switching their knife to their left hand. "But you never bothered learning any of that. You never cared about our history or our purpose or what we're fighting for. All you wanted was to kill warlocks and impress Bex, and when the water got too hot, you ran away like the coward you've always been."

"If you want a coward, look in the bloody mirror!" Desh roared, letting out the anger he'd nursed for decades in the Hells. "She was like a daughter to you, and you still raised her to die, knowing she never had a chance! Now I'm trying to break the cycle, and you're too caught up in your bloody history lesson to care. You *never* cared that Bex was suffering! All you wanted was your damn queen!"

"Don't you dare speak of her to me," Lys snarled. "I've served Bex longer than you've been alive! She's been my savior and my queen and my sister and my daughter. There's no one who knows her better than I do! You think I didn't see how worn down she was? How hopeless? I knew. I *always* knew, but unlike you, I didn't put words in her mouth. I didn't do what I wanted and then make up some bullshit afterward about how I was doing it for her sake, because no Bex I've known would *ever* agree to surrender to Gilgamesh just so she could have a rest."

"She wouldn't tell you, would she?" Desh cried, lashing out with his dagger to force Lys into the tent behind them. "Do you know how terrified she was of disappointing you? Of not being the queen *you* needed her to be so you could get your damn revenge?"

"That's what you think this is about?" Lys shrieked, kicking out the tent pole to drop the tarp on his head. "My revenge died the day Bex—*my* Bex—slit my warlock's throat! I've fought at her side every day since for the good of *all* of us, so that other demons can know what it's like to believe that things will get better. *That's* what the last free queen is: our promise, our hope. She's the light leading us to better days, and I will die before I let you put her out!"

"And that's why you failed her," Desh said, slicing open the colored fabric before it could entangle him. "You chose your queen over Bex."

"They're the same, you idiot!" Lys yelled at him. "Whatever Bex complained about in her private time, whatever fears she unburdened onto you, she never turned her back on us. Not because she's the Queen of Wrath, but because the Queen of Wrath is *Bex*."

They lowered their knife with a scowl. "Dammit, Desh, you *know* this. You two were only together for ten years during one of her most brutal lives, but she still found it in her heart to die saving your arrogant ass. She put your life ahead of her own because that's what Bex does. She saves us."

"I do know it," Desh said desperately. "That's why I have to do this. Bex will never quit on her own. She'll just keep giving and giving until there's nothing left! She gave for *me*. Now it's my turn to give her something." He gripped his knife hard. "I'm ending this. If Bex is doomed to serve for eternity, then I'd rather she be Gilgamesh's slave than yours. At least he never claimed to love her."

Lys stepped out of the ruined tent with a glower. "If that's how you feel, then it seems we have nothing more to discuss. I'd hoped to talk some sense into you. You're a damned good fighter, but your judgment's just as terrible now as it was back then, and I'm sick of dealing with it."

Desh flipped the poison knife over in his hand. "Then why don't you shut your—"

The insult cut off as Lys spun, avoiding the stab Desh had been about to land in their side. Their arm flew up as they went, knife gleaming in lantern light as they slashed at Desh's neck. He dodged with room to spare, kicking his leg out to trip them instead. Lys leaped over the kick with a beat of their wings, but Desh's free hand was already wrapping around their wrist to yank them into the knife he held ready in front of his chest. He was just about to skewer them when Lys's long arm reached over his shoulder to slide their long, sharp dagger perfectly between the protective scales of his back.

Desh stumbled forward with a gasp. He didn't know if it was a lucky shot or if Lys had stabbed so many people in the back that it was second nature now, but their blade landed in the perfect position to skewer the top two chambers of his heart. His regeneration—the blessing Ishtar, goddess of life, had left to all her children—kicked in at once to repair the damage, but Desh couldn't get his heart going again while Lys's knife was still lodged inside it. He stabbed wildly, trying to drive them off, but Lys grabbed his knife hand and bent it backward, driving his own razor-sharp scales back into his skin until Desh was forced to let the sin iron dagger go.

He grabbed for Lys next, clawing at their wings, their arms, their face, anything he could use to push them off him. But while Lys had never been particularly fast or strong, they'd always been squirmy. Their body moved like water, slipping out of Desh's grasp wherever he tried to hold, leaving him with nothing as his heart spasmed around the knife they were *still* holding in his back. His vision was starting to go dark when the cold metal of Lys's blade finally slid out of him.

Desh's heart thundered to life with a spasm that hurt worse than getting stabbed. He rolled over with a gasp, coughing into the bloody grass as his regeneration forced the ruptured flesh back together. Desh was still trying to decide if he'd just dodged a bullet or been lined up for another one when Lys's foot landed in his chest, kicking him onto his back again.

He lay sprawled there for several seconds, waiting for the finishing blow. Using the sin iron dagger to kill him with his own poison would have been a trademark Lys finale, but the attack never came. Lys just shoved his body to the side and grabbed the sin iron knife out from under him. They were cutting a piece of canvas off the fallen tent to wrap the poison blade up when Desh finally managed to wheeze, "Why?"

"Because I'm not letting you die before you know you're wrong," they said, using their clawed foot to turn Desh's face until he was staring up at the melted crater Bex had left in the skull of Gilgamesh's statue.

"There's a lot you missed out on when you ran away," they said, shifting into a small female body with a belt pack at their waist that was a perfect fit for the bundled sin iron dagger. "I'm not telling a traitor more than that, but suffice it to say, we're doing things that would've made even your bitter old Bex hope again. This war's nowhere close to over, so maybe don't be so quick to sell us out to Gilgamesh."

Desh shook his head. "Oh no. You're not getting me with that line again. My hope bridge was burned ages ago."

"That's your problem," Lys said, giving him a superior look. "I can't force you to believe, but I *can* keep you alive to watch her win just like I always told you she would. That's my gift to you, Deshazor, so I suggest you take it and run. I'm done with you, but Iggs knows you tried to stab Bex in the back by now, and that kid's got a temper you don't want to be in front of."

Desh lay back in the bloody grass with a curse. Lys could call it bullshit all they liked, but plotting how he was going to set Bex free someday was the only thing that had kept him sane in the Hells. It was all he could do to make up for getting her killed in the first place. Lys, of all demons, should've understood that, but when he opened his eyes again, the lust demon was gone, vanished into the panicked crowd with his sin iron dagger.

Bex still hadn't reignited by the time she made it to the statue's fist.

She told herself it was fine, that she'd get her second wind once she was actually in danger, but the exhaustion was weighing on her like it had after Limbo. She'd burned too hot. Her body needed to recover before it could do it again, but there was no time. This was why everyone was here tonight, what they'd fought so hard to reach. If she didn't cut the Anchor chain, the armies of Heaven would march down it and recapture everyone she'd just freed. Fire or no fire, she had to see this through, so Bex stepped forward, walking off the edge of Gilgamesh's golden fist onto the chain his statue lifted into the sky.

The golden road to Heaven had looked as slender as a power line from the market side. The moment Bex put a foot on it, though, the whole view changed. Suddenly, the Anchor Market full of chaos was gone, leaving Bex standing on an interstate-sized golden bridge that spanned a glowing sea.

No, she realized a moment later, *not a sea*. She was standing over a river. A massive, swollen river of deep-blue water filled with the rainbow lights of human souls. It was a River of Death, but not one of the slow swells that had once braided through the Riverlands. This was a headwater, the flow of souls that surged up from the living world, and it wasn't alone. From her vantage on the chain, Bex could see hundreds of rivers flowing under hundreds of golden bridges that all went to the same place, a towering white city that filled the sky in front of her:

The Holy City of Gilgamesh.

For a long moment, Bex could only stare. She'd never seen Heaven with her actual eyes—not in this lifetime, at least. But even as her brain identified what she was looking at, a deeper part of Bex rejected it. That was not Paradise. That was an abomination, a lifeless white-and-gold tomb without trees or wind or water. The sacred rivers didn't even flow into it. They vanished before they got there, falling into a dark hole in the rock that formed the Holy City's foundations.

Falling to *where*, Bex didn't know, but the wrongness of it was enough to get her smoking again. How dare Gilgamesh channel the sacred rivers under his city like a sewer! She should smash the whole gaudy place to rubble. But while Bex was happy to get angry over it, she couldn't actually go on a rampage. She still had a job to do, and she'd better do it fast. Now that she was standing on the chain itself, Bex could already see Gilgamesh's golden-armored soldiers massing at the top of the bridge, getting ready to march on the demons' rebellion.

Any other time, that would have sent her into a panic, but dealing with the army had always been part of the plan. The only actual surprise was that the soldiers weren't closer. The panic had been going on for nearly ten minutes now. Bex had expected spears in her face the moment she stepped out, but while the army was clearly trying to advance down the chain, something was blocking their way.

Bex almost laughed when she saw what it was. The denizens of Heaven must have bolted from their VIP area when the attack started, because there was a wave of richly dressed humans gumming up the front lines of Gilgamesh's army. That hadn't been part of the plan, but the greatest thing about chaos attacks was that the anarchy seeped into everything. Bex hadn't even realized just how many people had come down from the Holy City until she saw them running back to it. Now, Gilgamesh's troops were mired in his own panicked citizens, which meant if Bex did her job quickly enough, they might not have to deal with the army at all.

That happy prospect snapped her into action. Whipping Drox back into her hand, Bex ran a few feet up the bridge and gave the golden paving an experimental *whap*. She still wasn't on fire, but she'd cut plenty of big things without her flames in the past, and the chain didn't look so bad from this angle. It didn't even look like a chain. She could feel it moving slightly under her feet, but the fancy bridge covered up all the links, making it look like an elevated highway made of solid gold.

If she hadn't just melted Gilgamesh's statue, Bex might have been fooled. But while she couldn't see anything but shiny, buttery yellow, she could feel the malicious aura hovering beneath the glittery plating like the stink of a buried body. There was a *lot* of sin iron down there, way more than she could cut through with a single strike even if she'd been burning like a blowtorch. Her test hit hadn't even broken through the golden coating, but knowing it was hard didn't change the job. What had to be done still had to be done, and Bex was raising her sword to get started when a bell rang out over the waters.

She swore when she heard it, pulling Drox back into a defensive position just in time as the prince appeared in front of her.

It was the tall one from before, the gaunt prince who'd held Adrian hostage, except he was no longer swordless. A princess stood at his side, clinging to his arm like she was afraid to let him go. She had the same ivory body and golden eyes as the one Bex had fought twice before, but otherwise, she looked totally different. The Princess of Greed had had wavy hair and a sneering, cocky smile. This princess looked frail and sad with long, straight hair that parted around her face like a waterfall. As with all of Gilgamesh's dolls, her dress was carved into her body, but this princess had a blue scarf draped around her narrow shoulders, the only clothing besides the glove that Bex had ever seen one wear.

She searched the princess's face next, looking for some hint of who she'd been. A name, a voice, anything would do. As ever, though, the only thing Bex saw was kinship. Somewhere behind that bone-white alien face was a daughter of Ishtar just like her, and that was enough.

"*Sister!*" she cried, throwing out her hand. "Don't worry, I'm here. I'll get you away from him!"

"You are no sister of mine," the sword replied, her calm voice totally different from the screaming princess Bex had faced in Limbo. "And I have no wish to leave my prince's side." She gazed adoringly at the tall man beside her. "Leander is the only thing in this world that matters to me. If you hurt him, I will destroy you."

The gaunt prince beamed back at her, leaning down to kiss the ivory woman on the forehead while Bex fought not to gag. She might not be screaming and clinging to his boots, but this princess was clearly just as brainwashed as the first one. Bex *had* to set her free, but before she did anything, she needed to know what she was up against.

"Where's your backup?" she asked, flicking her eyes away from the prince she could see to search for the one she couldn't. "I can't believe Gilgamesh sent you out to face me alone after the thrashing I gave your brother."

"Father didn't send me anywhere," the prince replied in an annoyingly condescending voice. "This is my operation now, and I've sent my brother to hit you where it hurts." His mouth curled in a smile. "Right in the witch."

"Then you got fooled," Bex bluffed, forcing her voice to stay calm as she watched the prince's feet for the attack she knew was coming. "We fed your spy a load of bullshit. You have no idea what we're actually doing."

"Couldn't have been that far off," the prince said, nodding at something behind her.

Bex knew better than to look, but her eyes moved before she could stop them, and her breathing stopped. Behind her, the Anchor Market sat on the glowing river like a perfectly circular island, and on its edge was an enormous tree, one she recognized. That was the big oak next to Adrian's clearing, the one she used to sit in while she kept watch and played guitar.

The realization made her panic. She hadn't thought Adrian would be using his own trees to prop up the Anchor. Stupid assumption in hindsight. Adrian used his forest for everything, but it meant the prince was right. That oak was as good as a flagpole for showing where their witch was, and now that she'd seen it, Bex was deathly afraid.

"Terrifying, isn't it?" the prince said as he wrapped his arm around his princess's shoulders. "Having someone precious to you threatened. But it's not too late. All you have to do is surrender, and I'll call my brother off."

"*Never*," Bex snarled, but her foot inched back down the chain.

"There's no need for posturing," the prince said, his voice uncommonly understanding. "I'm not here to break you or make you grovel. My only objective is to bring you back to Heaven so we can finally end this farce, and I'm willing to be very generous to achieve it. Lay down your sword, and I'll order my forces back. I'll let your rebels and all the demons you freed tonight live—the Blackwood boy too. You can be a good queen and save everyone, or you can fight me and be dragged before Gilgamesh's throne in defeat, achieving nothing. Your choice, Bex of the Bonfire, but make it quick. What you did in Limbo left my poor brother in quite the state. Once he starts killing, nothing I say will stop him."

He smiled at Bex like he had her, and it was hard to say he was wrong. If the scarred prince she'd fought in Limbo was back and going after Adrian, then her witch was as good as dead. Bex had only been able to beat him by pulling on the wrath of her entire population. Adrian wasn't even in his forest. She might still be able to reach him in time if she went now, but if she turned her back on the prince and left the chain, everything they'd fought for tonight was lost. There was no way she and Adrian could beat the mad prince before Gilgamesh's army reached the Anchor Market. Even if she managed to kill *both* princes, the endless armies of Heaven would eventually overwhelm their forces and drag everyone back to the Hells. There was

no way out of this unless she stayed and did what she'd
fought her way up here to do.

Rebexa.

"You don't have to say it," Bex told Drox as she turned
away from Adrian's tree to face the prince again.

"There will be no surrender," she announced. "You
can't bait me into the same trap twice. I came here to do a
job, and nothing you say will put me from it."

"Then you've left your witch to die," the prince said,
giving her a disappointed look. "But I shouldn't have
expected better from a heartless demon."

He paused, waiting for Bex to deny it, but she forced
herself to be as hard as the sword in her hands. This was
what she'd committed to when she'd left Adrian in the
forest. This was how it had to be, so she stomped down on
her traitorous, breaking heart and lifted her sword into
position.

The prince's frown deepened at the sight.

"I'd hoped you'd listen to reason," he said as he
stepped away from his princess. "I'd hoped you'd recognize
actual generosity when it was offered. Alas, it seems you are
exactly what the stories say, and so you leave me no choice."
He switched to Sumerian. "Bounty of a Thousand Winters."

Bex was still translating when a chunk of ice the size
of a truck crashed into her face, sending her flying off the
chain.

Adrian had never grown a tree so fast in his life.

Technically, he still hadn't, because this tree wasn't
actually growing. It had already done that work, rising to

become the second-tallest tree in his forest before Adrian rewound it.

That was a very shorthand description for an *extremely* complicated bit of magic. So complicated that Adrian never could have managed it if the tree hadn't been so eager to help. Most hardwoods were reluctant to take a risk of any sort, but this was a brave young oak. Once Adrian had explained they were doing this for the good of everyone but especially Bex, who'd sat in its branches and played it music, the tree had thrown all in, shrinking itself practically back to a sapling. Adrian had taken it the rest of the way, folding the tree down gently until it was nothing but a sprouted acorn.

He'd transported it to the Anchor inside a wet cloth wrapped in leaves. He'd even brought his own soil from the Blackwood, which he'd stowed in cloth sacks under Boston's baby carriage. Once the acorn was planted, all he had to do was undo what he'd already done, which was a not-so-shorthand way of saying that he needed to perform an extremely complicated bit of magic *backward*.

"Steady," Boston said, his voice shaking with the effort of holding everything together. "Steady."

Adrian couldn't have been steadier if he'd been carved from stone, but he didn't tell his familiar to stop. They had to unfold the tree perfectly. One wrong move, and the whole planting could go crooked. He was already worried about stress distribution this close to the Market's edge. If they went off-center even a little, the whole tree could fall over when Bex dropped the Anchor.

"Pause for branches," he ordered, trusting Boston to hold the trunk steady while Adrian got on his broom and flew up to unfurl the branches that had gotten stuck. He was still getting them arranged when a crow squawked in his ear, making him jump.

"Where did he come from?" Boston called from below.

"Must have gotten caught in the rewind spell," Adrian called back, shaking the branch the crow was perched on to scare it away, but the bird refused to budge. It clung with its talons, giving him a surly look, so Adrian let it be, smacking the other branches open with his palm before swooping back to the ground.

"Resume."

The word was hardly necessary. He and Boston worked in perfect tandem, restoring the tree a foot at a time. Other than pausing every ten feet to make sure the branches unfurled properly, nothing stopped its growth. Every time Adrian checked his watch—the same watch he'd bought for his stakeout date with Bex—it was looking more and more like they were going to get the oak up with time to spare. Good thing, too, because the rest of the market seemed to be going insane.

Since he'd been part of the fake-out, Adrian had no idea what the actual plan to take down the Anchor was, but it looked like all-out war. There were fires, explosions, and what sounded like Iggs throwing a lot of someones through something that wasn't meant to be broken. He was pretty sure Bex had made a speech from the top of Gilgamesh's head at one point, but he'd been too consumed with his tree to listen. When the stakes were this high, he didn't dare focus on anything but his work, which was why he didn't hear the golden sound of a bell until it was nearly too late.

"*Adrian!*"

Boston's shout was the only reason he got out of the way in time. A split second after Adrian jerked back, a three-foot-wide wooden crate of fancy honey jars went flying through the empty space where he'd just been. The near miss made his heart thunder back in the Blackwood, but what really scared him was how close that crate had come to hitting his tree. If the oak took a knock at this stage, they'd never get it straightened back up in time, so Adrian grabbed his broom and swooped sideways, getting as far from the oak's wide branches as possible before looking down to see what he'd been most afraid of.

A prince was standing inside the ring of his Neverminds. Not that the concealments were much use now that the tree was towering over them, but Adrian hadn't thought anyone would bother inspecting a little extra foliage when the Anchor Market was under attack and free demons were running everywhere. He was about to try a lie about how he was a sorcerer doing emergency maintenance and would His Majesty mind staying to guard him rather than going after the demons when Adrian realized *which* prince he was looking at.

It was the short man with the scars he'd seen in the Walking Memory, the one who'd gotten himself hit by a car just so he could go to Limbo. Adrian thought he'd died in there. He'd certainly looked like a corpse when Bex had returned to the living world with his scorched body at her feet, but Bex had said princes could recover from death.

If that was true, then this one hadn't done a very good job of it. He still had both his mirrored eyes, but the rest of the prince's face was a mottled, twisted mess of burn scars. Adrian didn't know if that was because he hadn't finished healing yet or if the Bonfire of Wrath burned so hot that even Heaven couldn't repair the damage, but the prince looked ready to take his fury out on everything as he jerked his head at Adrian.

The witch gripped his broom, ready to dart in whichever direction got him farthest away from whatever the prince was about to do, but nothing happened. The prince wasn't attacking. He just stood there, jerking his burned head toward Adrian over and over like he was trying to give him a signal.

Frowning in confusion, Adrian landed his broom on the wall of boxes he'd build to protect his tree. "What is it?" he asked, slipping his hand into his jacket pocket where he'd stashed his new curses. "What do you want?"

The prince shook his head, snapping his fingers at the witch like Adrian was a misbehaving dog. But while that was insulting, it wasn't violent. Adrian was racking his brain trying to figure out what the man was attempting to communicate when a cowed figure stepped out of the prince's shadow.

"He wants you to come."

Adrian nearly fell off the crates. That was the same princess who'd tried to kidnap him two months ago, but her attitude was entirely different. That princess had been arrogant and cruel. This one cringed like a beaten child, her hunched body leaning away from her prince, who seemed to be growing more agitated by the second.

"You have to go with him," she begged, looking at Adrian with pitiful golden eyes that clearly would have been weeping rivers if ivory dolls could cry. "Prince Leander ordered him to bring you back alive to use as a hostage against the Queen of Wrath. If he fails again, they'll send him back to the Sleep!"

She clasped her hands in front of her, which was how Adrian saw that her right one wasn't gloved or made of ivory. It was dark-skinned and human-looking, the same hand that Bex had traded for his life.

"You're the Princess of Greed."

"And you're the only one who can save my prince's life," she begged, falling to her knees. "Please, witch of the Blackwood! Your rebellion is doomed, so please give yourself up. If you help bring the Coward Queen to heel, I'm sure the Crown Prince will overlook your heretical magic and spare your life."

She smiled as she finished, clearly expecting him to leap on such a fantastic offer, but it was all Adrian could do not to roll his eyes.

"I'm not giving myself up so you can corner Bex again," he said, crossing his arms over his chest. "Why don't you surrender to me instead? You're Bex's sister. She's desperate to save you, and it doesn't look as if Heaven's been treating you very well."

"You dare speak such heresy in the presence of a divine son?" the princess cried, sounding more like her old self as she shot back to her feet. "My beloved is a hero of the purges! It is the honor of my existence to serve at his side, and I am no family to the Coward Queen. I was forged by Gilgamesh's hand to live and die for my prince. Even a witch like you should know that, so bite your sinning tongue!"

"So much for diplomacy," Adrian muttered, glancing around for Boston, but his clever familiar was nowhere to be seen. What Adrian *did* see was the crow. It had hopped down the tree during his conversation with the princess and was now perching on the branch directly above him, looking down at Adrian with calm, beady eyes. Adrian stared back at it for a long moment, then his mouth pressed into a hard line as he returned his attention to the princess.

"What happens if I refuse to come with you? You can't use me as a hostage if I'm dead."

"You need only be recoverable," the princess said, pressing her not-ivory hand against the shoulder of the scarred man beside her. "But you play a dangerous game, witch. My prince is quite agitated. His mind was already delicate from centuries of battle, and being burned alive by your monster queen eroded it further still. The only way I can guarantee your safety is if you surrender now, before he loses the last of his control."

"I think I'd rather die," Adrian replied, reaching into his coat for the gardening knife he'd placed there for just such an emergency. "Boston, hold the tree."

"I've *been* holding the tree," his familiar answered in a strained voice. "Please, Adrian, don't be hasty. You're not in your forest. You can't beat a—"

"I know," Adrian said. "Don't worry. I won't be fighting."

He saw Boston's alarmed face pop out from around the tree trunk. "What is that supposed to—"

The cat cut off with a hiss as Adrian whipped his knife out of his pocket and brought it down on the little finger of his left hand.

The heavy steel gardening blade went through his flesh and bone as easily as it hacked through wood, cutting his finger off in a single chop even though his hand wasn't braced against anything. It happened so quickly the pain didn't have time to register with Adrian's brain before he grabbed the severed digit in his fist.

"*Morrigan!*" he cried, his voice blending with the caws of the crows that suddenly filled the oak's branches. "I offer you my flesh, soul, and bone! By the three made one that is the root of all witchcraft, I beseech you: help me strike down the son of our enemy!"

Adrian poured himself into the words as he spoke them, squeezing the bloody finger in his fist. It wasn't as good as a proper offering buried in the ground, but his body was also the Blackwood, and the sacrifice of a witch was the most powerful magical component he could create. If the Morrigan wasn't satisfied with this offering, Adrian had nothing.

For three long heartbeats, there was no answer except the cawing of crows. As the stillness dragged on, Adrian began to worry that the Morrigan hadn't been serious when she'd invited him to call upon her again. He was considering dropping the finger and going for one of his own curses instead when the warm, bloody weight vanished from inside his clenched palm, and the cawing crows became a woman's cruel laughter as the Morrigan flapped down from the oak tree to stand in front of him.

"Your prayer is answered, son of the Blackwood!" the goddess said gleefully, pointing her bloody spear at the disfigured prince. "Is this the one who shall die?"

"Yes," Adrian said, grabbing a handkerchief out of his pocket to bind his bleeding hand. "And bring me his sword, please."

The goddess did not answer. She just opened her mouth, laughing in huge, hoarse croaks as her body began to change. It looked just like when she'd turned back into a bird after their conversation in the Walking Memory, only the Morrigan wasn't getting smaller this time. She was getting bigger, her bloody armor sprouting feathers until there was no woman left inside. There was only a crow—a giant, elephant-sized crow with eyes like black glass, talons like scimitars, and a huge black beak so hard and sharp it snipped the prince's golden helmet right off him before he could jump out of her reach.

"Is this the best the great Gilgamesh can offer?" the giant crow cawed, its croaking voice thick with the Morrigan's laughter. "How sad he has grown! How cowardly! Hiding in his stolen Heaven, ruling over a world he can no longer touch."

She punctuated each insult with a snap of her razor-sharp beak, driving back the prince, who roared like a wounded animal. His princess clung to him the whole way, weeping and begging for him to take her hand. But whatever was broken inside this prince must have been well and truly shattered, because he didn't spare her a look. He just threw himself at the Morrigan, screaming in wordless rage as he grabbed her feathers to rip them out, only to scream again when his hands came back bloody.

"Oh ho ho," the Morrigan cackled, delivering a peck that went through the prince's armored chest like a spear. "I'm sharper than I look."

She snapped her beak again, snipping the prince's arm off like he was a paper doll. The prince howled when his arm fell to the ground, splashing white quintessence blood up his legs, but he didn't stop. He just charged again, swinging wildly at the Morrigan with the arm he had left.

"You're nothing but a raging bull," the goddess chided, shaking her feathered head as she turned a beady eye back toward Adrian. "Are you sure this is the fight you want to spend your finger on?"

Adrian nodded wildly. The goddess might be dancing circles around the prince, but a raging bull was actually the hardest thing for witchcraft to counter. If even one of Adrian's curses missed, all that mad, thoughtless strength would slam into his body and turn him into paste.

He still wasn't sure it wouldn't happen. The prince couldn't touch the Morrigan, but his flailing fist and stomping boots were destroying everything else. The ten-foot square of grass Adrian had picked to grow his tree in already looked like someone had driven a plow through it, and the wooden crates he'd used as cover were being knocked to the ground just from the wind off the prince's missed punches. If any of those clipped the oak's branches—or worse, if the prince's stomping feet crushed its developing roots—the whole tree might topple over.

Adrian didn't want to draw attention to Boston's hiding spot or any of the actually important parts of their plan, but standing and gawking wasn't helping anything. They didn't have time to waste, so he leaped off the crates he'd been watching from and ran back to the oak's base, tying off his wounded hand so he could grab the textured bark with all nine of his remaining fingers.

"Resume!"

Boston's face was terrified when it peeked around the trunk, but he didn't say a word. He just matched his hold to Adrian's and resumed pushing, the two of them working in perfect tandem to raise the tree another ten feet.

It was unspeakably bizarre, growing a tree with the horrific sounds of the Morrigan's battle going on behind him. The prince's bellows got more and more frantic as the minutes ticked by, his princess's screams more and more desperate before they cut off entirely. The prince went quiet shortly thereafter, his final howl cut short by a wet *snap* Adrian recognized as the sound of a spine breaking. There were a few moments of silence, then Adrian heard something hit the ground at his feet.

He paused the tree and turned around to see the Morrigan's giant crow looming over him. Her beak was dripping with the prince's white blood, and her beady eyes were gleaming with delight as she nudged a small object closer to Adrian's polished shoe.

It was a hand. The same feminine, dark-skinned hand Bex had been clutching when she came out of Limbo, covered in the prince's white blood.

"He was most delicious," the Morrigan announced, puffing out her feathers. "Gilgamesh won't be getting *that* prince back!"

The Anchor rang with her croaking laughter as Adrian snatched the hard-won hand to his chest. "Thank you," he told the goddess most humbly. "Thank you very much."

The Morrigan nodded her acknowledgment, lifting her beak to look up at the oak that now towered overhead.

"You grow lovely trees, son of the Blackwood," she said, her voice softer now. "Your finger was lovely, too, steeped in power from many sources." She lowered her beak again, turning her giant head from side to side to look at him with each of her beady eyes in turn. "I see now why the Witch of the Future hitched the Old Wives' hopes to you. You will be a devastating weapon when your time comes."

Adrian swallowed against the sudden dryness in his throat. "What does that mean?"

"You'll see," the crow promised, giving him a wink. "Take care, little witchling, and don't hesitate to call on me again should you wish to sacrifice something else. Your flesh was most delicious. I look forward to eating more of you."

"I'll keep that in mind," Adrian said weakly.

She patted him on the head with her gory beak and vanished—just poofed into thin air with a smell of bloody feathers, leaving Adrian staring at the torn-up grass. He was still gawking when Boston's noise of distress snapped him back to his senses. He returned to his post in a rush, pausing only to stuff the princess's bloody hand into his most secure pocket before he grabbed the tree and resumed helping his familiar haul it into the sky.

And far away, unseen beyond the starry dome of the Anchor's false night, Bex started pulling herself back onto the chain.

Chapter 15

You need to be faster.

"I realize that," Bex grumbled, stabbing her fingers into the soft, buttery gold of the bridge that covered the chain.

It was a lot harder than when she'd climbed the statue, and not just because she *still* had no fire to melt the metal. Where the statue had been full of carved details that doubled as hand- and footholds, the gilded bridge over the chain was a smooth, slick drop straight down into a raging river of souls. The only reason Bex wasn't going for a swim right now was because gold was soft enough to dig her fingers into whether she was burning or not, but that wasn't going to be the case with the prince.

I can cut his sorcery, Drox promised, *but only if you get me in front of the spell before it hits you in the face. It seems like the prince still has to say a few words before he attacks. That should give us plenty of time to counter if you reignite and get your speed back up.*

Those felt like pretty big *ifs* at the moment. Iggs had warned her, but Holy Ishtar, how in the Hells did the prince throw spells so *fast?* Normal sorcerers had to give a damn recital before they cast their magic. The fastest one Bex had fought before this had still had to say at least a full sentence, but one phrase? It was ridiculous.

Complaining gets you nothing, Drox scolded. *Eyes front, guard up. We're about to clear the top of the chain.*

Bex was surprised the prince hadn't come over to shoot them off. When she rolled herself back onto the chain's wide expanse, though, he was still standing exactly where she'd left him, looking down his nose at her while his princess smirked in the background.

"The offer to surrender is still open."

Bex made a show of thinking it over as she shook the climb out of her aching hands. Her fire was still a dud, but she was pretty fast even without it these days, and this prince didn't look like much of a swordsman. Being quick with his spells didn't mean he'd be quick on his feet, and while she didn't know the new princess's powerset, Bex doubted Gilgamesh had two blades capable of reversing fatal damage. If she could dodge his sorcery and get in close, she could cut the prince's head off and end all of this, no bonfire necessary.

Whatever you decide, do it quickly, her sword urged, drawing Bex's attention to the top of the chain. *They're starting to get through.*

He was right. The traffic jam caused by Heaven's stampeding elite was finally starting to clear out, leaving Gilgamesh's army free to march down the chain. They'd already made it a quarter of the way to the Anchor, but they seemed to be stopped at the moment, probably waiting to see what their prince would do.

Once he went down, they'd only have a few minutes to finish cutting the chain before the soldiers overran them. Bex wasn't sure if that was doable even with her fire, but she'd burn that bridge when she got there. For now, she flexed her fingers around Drox to draw the prince's attention to her hands so he wouldn't see her bracing her feet. The moment his eyes flicked to her sword, Bex charged, flying down the golden bridge like a bullet. It was a damn good burst of speed for having no fire, but she still only made it halfway before the prince opened that mouth Bex was learning to hate.

"Seven Walled City."

Walls shot up from the golden bridge, huge ones made from the same white stone as the Holy City above them. The first popped up so close Bex nearly slammed straight into it, but she jumped at the last second, leaping straight up to land on top of the wall as it shot into the air.

She jumped again the moment her feet made contact, bounding from wall to wall as they grew. Sure enough, there were seven of them, but they were all rising at the same rate, giving Bex a stepstone path straight to the prince in the middle.

Happy to finally have a stroke of luck, Bex grabbed her sword with both hands and jumped for the final wall. Each one was a concentric circle just like the walled city in the spell's name, but because the bridge was only so wide, the last wall's inner ring was no bigger than a closet. When Bex landed on top, she saw the prince had covered the space inside with an iron pavilion to form a pillbox. She smirked at the sight because a metal roof wouldn't stop Drox. It was only when she jumped down for the swing that was supposed to go straight through the iron pavilion and into the prince beneath that Bex realized the shield hadn't been meant to stop *her*.

"Star's Lament."

Bex swore as thousands of gleaming arrows began streaking out of the sky like shooting stars. Each one was the same pearlescent white as quintessence, but they hit like red-hot drills, pulverizing the stone walls and her shoulders before she spun out of the way, but there was nowhere to take cover. The prince's metal pavilion was the only thing that seemed immune to the piercing stars, forcing Bex to move her unlit body faster than it was really able to dodge between them.

This is ridiculous, Drox said as blood began to soak the black canvas combat suit Bex had put on for tonight's operation. *If you don't ignite in the next thirty seconds, you'll be turned into a sieve.*

"I know, I know!" Bex cried, turning her head away with a hiss as a razor-sharp star sliced open her cheek. "I've been trying! But I'm just out."

Impossible. The Queen of Wrath can never run out of anger.

Bex wasn't out of anger by a long shot. Just hearing the prince try to use Adrian against her for a second time had pissed her off so much that she should have been melting the bridge in half. Her wrath was doing fine; Bex was the one who was out of juice. She could rage until she drowned in it, but someone still had to shovel all that fury into the fire, and after lighting up the whole Anchor Market earlier, Bex didn't have the strength. The only reason she was still dodging was because she'd die if she didn't, but what was she going to do?

What kind of question is that? Drox demanded. *You will do what you were made to do and burn for your people!*

"My people aren't here!" Bex cried, shaking her head to sling away the black blood that kept dripping into her eyes. "I'm going to bleed out alone up here while that idiot watches from under his metal umbrella!"

She needed to cut it down. The prince wouldn't be able to keep raining stars if he was getting hit too. One slice off the top, that's all it would take. The challenge would be getting over there without the falling stars punching her full of holes. She'd stayed alive so far by focusing all her attention on dodging. If she had to dodge, move, *and* swing her sword at the same time, Bex was pretty sure she was going to get Swiss-cheesed, but she didn't have any other ideas. She was about to just go for it and hope her regeneration could outpace the bleeding when Drox grew heavy in her hands.

Stop panicking and listen, he ordered, his voice stabbing through her mind like an iron spike. *You are a Blade of Ishtar, but you are also still flesh and blood. I'd hoped we could overcome that, but we played too deep and lost our tactical advantage. If you cannot ignite, we must retreat.*

"No!" Bex roared, chopping a hail of falling stars out of the sky. The broken pieces still cut her, though, and she cried out in pain.

You see? Drox said angrily. *You cannot win this as you are. If you keep pushing, you'll lose your last life, and all of this will be for nothing.*

"If I step back, it's already for nothing!" Bex cried, spinning just in time to avoid a falling star that would have sliced off her left ear. "Everyone in the Anchor is counting on me to cut this chain! I didn't leave Adrian to face a prince by himself so I could be stopped by a bunch of *stupid glowing arrows!*"

Then ignite, Drox commanded. *Conviction means nothing without action. If you would stand here as the Queen of Wrath, become the Bonfire and prove it.*

She was trying. Bex had been shoving wrath at her bonfire since before she'd set foot on the chain, but it wasn't taking. Her body was too overextended, her magic too exhausted, but that didn't mean she could give up. Bex had suffered a hundred and ninety-eight lifetimes just so her people could keep hoping for a victory. She wasn't about to quit now that she had a chance of actually giving it to them.

Rebexa, please *be sensible. If you truly cannot ignite, then you must run. Retreat is not defeat.*

"It is today," she said, planting her feet to keep them from slipping on the golden bridge made slick by her blood. "This isn't just another battle. It's a turning point. If we run away now, then everyone who said we were stupid to keep fighting because Gilgamesh always wins will be right, and our army will fall apart. But if we do this, if we win even once, we'll prove that the Eternal King *can* be beaten, and the whole world will change."

She looked back at the bubble of the Anchor Market, whose fake night sky was now orange from the fires. Those were *her* demons fighting and dying down there to buy her this chance. Adrian might already be dead because of her. How could she run and waste that?

You don't have a choice! Drox yelled as a glowing arrow clipped her shoulder. *All the will in the world doesn't matter without the power to back it up, and you have no fire!*

"There is always fire," Bex said, clutching her sword. "I just need someone to help me get it going."

She felt Drox's confusion bubble through her mind, but Bex had already reached back toward the battle she could still hear roaring behind her in the Anchor Market, holding out her fingers for the jolt of power she'd felt when the war demon she'd freed had jumped on his master. She'd been frightened at the time because the surge had reminded her of Limbo, and she didn't want to go out of control again, but Bex didn't care about that anymore. She'd already bet everything on this, so she bet herself as well, laying her bonfire at her people's feet in the hope their fire could ignite what hers was too weak to burn alone.

Don't do it, Rebexa! Drox shouted. *You're not ready! You can't control it!*

Bex didn't listen. Refused to listen, because his warning made no sense. She was the Bonfire of Wrath, but no bonfire burned for just one person. They were built to be a light for all, so Bex shared hers with the people she'd been made to burn for, welcoming their wrath with open arms.

Just like in Limbo, their fury consumed her. Unlike in Limbo, though, these demons didn't have five thousand years of pent-up rage ready to blow. There were also a lot fewer of them, barely two thousand in total. Bex could feel every one like a little match inside her. Theirs was a tiny light compared to the sky-consuming firestorm she'd been before, but it was still more than she'd had on her own, and the moment she welcomed them in, Rebexa the Bonfire burst into flame.

Nothing had ever felt so good. There was no overwhelming madness like there'd been in Limbo, because these weren't starving, enraged kick demons. They were soldiers fighting for a common cause, demons fighting back just like she'd always dreamed, and their fire felt like coming home.

I—I stand corrected, her sword whispered as the flames settled over them. *I thought you would burn out of control again, but...* Drox's weight shifted in her hands, almost as if he were lowering his head. *Forgive me for doubting you, my queen. I should have had more faith.*

"We both should've," Bex said as her flames burned the glowing arrows out of the sky. "I'm the one who asked everyone to put their lives in my hands. The least I can do is trust them back."

A queen lives for her people, Drox agreed, his hilt growing steady in her hands. *Ready when you are.*

Bex responded by launching them down the bridge. Her fire was roaring around them, incinerating the falling stars and boiling her spilled blood as the Queen of Wrath cleared the distance to the prince's iron pavilion and chopped it in one motion. Flames shot off Drox's blade as he sliced the protective shield in half, melting the prince's armor before he could finish the spell on his lips.

"Fifty Steps of the Pilgrim!"

He vanished an instant before Drox stabbed into his chest. He reappeared a second later, staggering back into existence with his princess fifty feet down the chain toward the Anchor Market.

That suited Bex just fine. The closer she was to her people, the hotter her fire burned, melting the bridge beneath her boots as she shot down it like a comet to take the prince's head. The prince opened his mouth before she started moving, but he still barely got the spell out in time.

"Bounty of a Thousand Winters!"

Bex's eyes went wide. She remembered that one, but knowing what was coming didn't do anything to stop the house-sized boulder of ice that was suddenly rocketing toward her face. If he hit her with that again, she'd be blown all the way up the bridge into the army. That might be more than even her new fire could handle, so Bex braced her feet instead, swinging her sword hard to meet the ice head on.

A little too hard, it turned out. She knew Drox could cut sorcery, but Bex had never swung with this much power before, at least not while she was still herself. It wasn't just the strength in her arms, either. The Bonfire itself raced up Drox's blade, turning his swing into a blast of fire that crashed into the ice with so much force the whole block cracked in half.

Bex almost cracked with it. Breaking the prince's giant ice cube was one of the most epic things she'd ever done, but the equal and opposite reaction from all that force hit her like a train. The blast threw her backward, bouncing her down the golden bridge like a skipped stone. If Drox hadn't dug his blade into the golden ground, they would have bounced straight into the river, but he caught her just in time, slicing a ten-foot gouge through the gold plating into the sin iron chain beneath to grind them to a halt.

"Thanks," Bex panted as she pushed back to her feet.

You're welcome, Drox replied, his voice grim. *This is more fire than you've wielded since the fall of Paradise. You'll need to be more careful.*

"Or more clever," Bex said with a smile, putting her hand behind her. "Watch this."

Before Drox could ask what she was doing, Bex fired another blast of fire at the ground behind them, launching herself like a rocket straight at the prince. It wasn't a controlled flight, but Bex didn't need to stick the landing. She just needed enough speed to drive her sword through the prince before he got another spell off. She'd just about made it to him when he whirled around, his mirrored eyes wild as he frantically shouted.

"Ishtar's Raging Bull!"

A shadow appeared in front of him, taking the form of a gigantic bull with the same straight stabbing horns as Bex. If it had finished growing, it would have been the size of a charter bus, but for once, Gilgamesh's son was too slow. The bull was still pulling itself out of the shadows when Bex flew right through it, scattering the gathering magic as she drove Drox's black blade straight at the center of the prince's chest.

"*No!*"

That shout came from the princess. She'd been quiet at her prince's side this whole time, watching the fight with cautious golden eyes. The moment it became clear that Bex was going to stab him, though, she threw herself into the sword's path, taking the hit on her own ivory arm. The force cracked her white limb, but while she looked like a delicate doll, she was still a Blade of Gilgamesh. Even cracked, her body held, knocking Bex's flying thrust aside to send her slamming into the ground.

The whole bridge shuddered when she hit. If Bex hadn't felt like her insides were being liquefied, she would have rejoiced that she'd finally hurt the chain. Her crash had destroyed the golden plating and bashed a two-foot-deep gouge into the sin iron below. Bex was able to heal the damage to her organs instantly thanks to her people's fire, but she still felt punch-drunk when she hauled herself out of the crater to see the princess clutching her panting prince.

"Enough!" she cried, tearing off her white silk glove to thrust her bare-skinned hand—which was still as pale as plaster—into the prince's golden one. "This demon cannot be defeated with sorcery. Use me, Leander! We'll take her to the king together!"

"No," he said, pushing her hand away. "I won't put you in danger."

"Don't be a fool," the princess told him, shoving her fingers right back into his. "This is what I was made for! In this as in all things, we should be together!"

The prince shook his head. "I can't."

She scowled at him, and the prince's eternally calm face melted into something like panic.

"I can't risk you," he pleaded, pressing her bare fingers to his lips. "I just got you back!"

"That's exactly why you should use me," the princess said, reaching her ivory hand up to brush the curls of his dark hair back under his helmet. "I am your sword. If I don't help you fight for our future, what am I good for?"

The princess's somber face lit up with a smile as she finished, and Bex's heart began to pound. She knew that smile. She couldn't remember where or when or what her face actually looked like when it wasn't made of ivory and gold, but the same part of Bex that had always known how to swing Drox knew that this was her sister. Her own flesh and blood. Her...

Mara.

The name hit Bex as hard as her own. That was Mara, the Queen of Sorrow. Mara, who wandered the riverbanks and watched the glowing waters flow between the reeds. Mara, who would hold her weeping demons as they ate humanity's regrets. Mara, who used to smile all the time because her work made the world a happier place. Mara, the sister who'd loved her.

"*Mara!*" Bex shouted, pulling Drox back into his ring. She quenched the flames on her sword arm next, holding out her bare, unburning hand.

"It's me, Mara!" she yelled frantically. "It's Rebexa! I can get you out of here! *Leave him!*"

The princess looked up at her name, and the smile vanished from her face.

"What makes you think you have the right to speak in a prince's presence?" she demanded, clutching Leander closer. "Your endless rebellion is why we have to fight in the first place! Without your troublemaking, the whole world would be united under the Eternal King's peace, and my love would not have to suffer!"

"He's not your *love*," Bex spat. "That man is Gilgamesh's son, the spawn of our conqueror!" She pointed at the princess's living hand, which was still clutched around the prince's. "Your *love* helped his father chop your hand from your body so they could steal your sword and turn you into a weapon against your own people, but you don't belong to them. You're a queen like me, a daughter of Ishtar! Don't help her murderers!"

"It is you who are the murderer, Coward Queen," the princess proclaimed with a haughty lift of her chin. "You killed my prince's divine brothers. You've spent five thousand years killing your own demons when you goad them into fights they cannot win. Your hands are the bloodiest in all creation, and you have the gall to call my prince a villain?" Her golden eyes narrowed. "You are not worthy to kneel at his feet."

Bex dropped her hand with a grimace. She knew Mara wasn't really saying those things, that she'd been corrupted just like the Princess of Greed, but it didn't take the sting out of hearing Gilgamesh's words from her sister's mouth. The sound made her want to scream and beat things, but she couldn't afford to lose focus. She still had to defeat this prince and steal her sister's hand back so she could start working on a way to restore her. It *had* to be possible. Bex's own soul had survived almost two hundred reincarnations. Surely, her sister could survive this. But as she covered her sword arm in fire again for the blow that would cut prince and princess apart, Mara raised Leander's clasped hand to her lips.

"Do it for me," she whispered against his knuckles. "Use me to end this, and then we'll be together for all eternity."

"For all eternity," the prince promised, clutching his fingers around hers.

His princess vanished as he moved, her carved body disappearing to leave only a fluttering piece of blue silk falling from the white sword that was now in the prince's hand. It looked very different from the Blade of Gilgamesh Bex had faced before—a slender thrusting sword rather than a heavy blocking one—but that was to be expected. Greed was all about defending what was yours, but sorrow was a spear that pierced without warning. The prince knew it, too, stepping into a fencer's position with his long, light blade balanced as delicately as a butterfly between his fingers.

Be careful, Drox warned. *These two are as close as we are.*

Bex nodded, raising her own sword, which had been worn thin by time rather than design. She couldn't remember what Drox's original blade had looked like anymore, but his battered hilt felt right against her palms as Bex wrapped her roaring flames around them both.

She would do this quickly, she told herself. She'd goad the prince into an attack, parry his thrust, and then get in close for the burn just like she'd done to his brother in the Blackwood. With her fire going this hot, she could turn him to ash in seconds. She just had to get into range.

Bex moved the second the plan was clear in her mind. The prince would be fast, which meant she had to be faster. She would make no mistakes, allow no weakness. She was a sword forged in fire, and she would strike—

Her mantra cut off as the prince went for the thrust. It was exactly the move she'd expected, which meant Bex already had her own sword in the perfect position to defend. But when she slammed Drox's black blade against Mara's white one for the parry that was supposed to open the prince's middle and let her in for the kill, Bex felt the horrible, cold pain of a sword stabbing straight through her heart.

Rebexa!

She sagged against the blade, but there was no blade. The prince's white sword was still locked against her own. She'd landed the parry perfectly, so how—

The prince kicked her in the chest. Bex tried to catch herself, but the invisible sword was still stabbed through her, and the pain made her clumsy. She went down hard on her back, slamming the crown of her head against the chain's golden surface.

The hit sent black spots dancing across her vision. Bex tried pushing up anyway, but her muscles wouldn't obey. There was no physical sign of injury, no gaping wound or geyser of black blood spilling onto the ground. Just pain strong enough to leave her whole body spasming. Wetness began pouring down her face next. Bex's first thought was that she'd cut her head during the fall, but the drops running down her cheeks weren't blood.

They were tears.

She was *crying*, weeping in huge, racking heaves. Her limbs felt like rubber, but she couldn't have moved them no matter what they'd felt like. All she could do was curl into a sobbing ball as the prince stepped over her.

"Now you see my princess's strength," he said, his voice sounding far away even though he was right above her. "No matter how good you are, there is no defense against sorrow."

He knelt next to her, grabbing Bex's shoulder—which she only now realized was no longer on fire—to roll her onto her back. Drox was screaming at her to kick him away, but Bex couldn't move. She was drowning in sorrow, sinking under a sea of it as the prince leaned down to grab her horns.

Bex didn't fight him. There was no point. She'd already lost. All her promises about making this last life count, the demons she'd freed, her training, her plans, none of it had mattered. She was as much a failure now as the day Gilgamesh had swatted her out of the sky. How had she ever thought it'd be any different?

The recriminations washed over her in waves. Each one stabbed like a knife in her chest, but they were old, familiar sorrows, which made their pain far less terrifying than the new abyss that was opening beneath her.

Adrian.

Bex's breathing hitched as the sea of sorrow dragged her deeper. She'd tried to push it down, tried to be responsible and make the hard choices and be a good queen. She'd told herself she was fine so many times that she'd actually started to believe it, but the blade of sorrow cut through her lies.

She wasn't fine. How could she possibly be fine? She'd left Adrian to die, and it hadn't even mattered. She was starting to think it never would have mattered because even if she'd won—even if she'd killed the prince and cut the chain and led everyone back to Paradise—there was nothing to look forward to.

Bex was used to being her people's hope, but being with Adrian was the first time in her life that *she'd* had hope. He'd made her feel giddy and excited about the future—*her* future, not the war or her demons or taking back Paradise. He'd made her happy, and he'd died for it because the Queen of Wrath was a sword, and that's what swords did. They killed, they *hurt*, and even when they won, they didn't get to rest. There would always be another battle, another precious person sacrificed for victory, and as steely as Bex had tried to make herself, that thought shattered her like glass.

She was crying so hard by this point Bex didn't even notice that Leander was dragging her until they were halfway up the bridge. She struggled a little then, mostly out of habit, because she didn't even care about the battle anymore. She just wanted to die, to fall into that beautiful river where she wouldn't have to lose any more. She was about to tell Leander to cut off her head and get it over with when she saw something flicker over the prince's shoulder. It happened so fast Bex didn't even recognize the fast-moving object as Lys until the lust demon plunged Desh's sin iron dagger into Leander's back.

The prince screamed when the blade went in, dropping the white sword he was keeping pressed against Bex's chest. The crippling sorrow vanished the moment his hand let go, leaving Bex blinking on the ground. She was still trying to figure out how much had been real and how much had been the Blade of Sorrow when Leander reached over his shoulder and grabbed hold of Lys, who was still twisting the dagger frantically between his ribs.

"Reflection of Malice."

A squeal of metal on metal followed his words, then Lys's face went blank in surprise as the sin iron dagger flipped in their hands, ripping out of the prince's sundered armor to slam its point deep into the narrow chest of the small female body Lys had used for the ambush. The lust demon didn't even scream when the knife went in. They just made a soft gurgling noise, their human disguise melting back into the tall, dusky pink of their true form as they collapsed on the bridge, black blood pouring from their lips.

"Lysanae!"

The name left Bex in a shriek. She lurched forward, reigniting in a torrent of flame as she shoved the prince out of her way and grabbed Lys's body. She paused only to yank the poison dagger out of their chest, then she was running as hard as she could, bolting back down the chain so fast that her flaming feet left molten craters in the bridge's gold plating.

She didn't slow down again until she reached the ornate doors where the chain met the Anchor Market at the base of Gilgamesh's statue. She kicked her way through and dropped to her knees in the grass on the other side, snuffing out her flames so she wouldn't burn anything by accident as she checked Lys's wound.

It was bad. The sin iron dagger was small, but its poison was spreading like wildfire. Bex could already see the blackness flooding Lys's amber eyes like ink as the toxic wave of concentrated sin began to saturate their body.

"No, no, no!" Bex cried, covering the chest wound with her hands. *"Live, Lysanae!"*

Lys's body jerked in her arms, then the lust demon flashed her a small, bloody smile.

"You know you can only order me to do things I'm capable of doing, right?"

"Do it anyway," Bex snapped, tearing the sleeve off her combat suit to bind the stab wound that should have been closing by now. *"Iggerux! Come to me!"*

Her scream was lost in the chaos of the battle that was still going on around them, but it didn't matter. True names always got through, and sure enough, Bex heard Iggs's roar a moment later. He was coming.

"Don't call him over here," Lys wheezed. "He's leading your troops. You can't take a commander away in the middle of—"

"I'll call the whole army if I have to," Bex said, pulling the cuff of her remaining sleeve over her hand to wipe the toxic blood off Lys's lips. "I'm not letting you die!"

She couldn't. Lys couldn't die saving her, not when this whole mess was her fault. Bex was the one who'd let herself get trapped. The prince's sorrow sword could never have taken her down like that if she hadn't given it so much to work with. She refused to let Lys die because of her stupid issues. It was too unfair. She had to—

"Stop," Lys wheezed, reaching up to touch her face. "I can see you blaming yourself, but this isn't your fault."

"It's all my fault," Bex sobbed, pulling Lys's bandage tighter with shaking fingers. "I'm supposed to be the queen. I'm supposed to keep you safe!"

"Not all by yourself," Lys said with a weak smile. "Soldiers die in war. Even a daughter of Ishtar can't stop that."

"But you shouldn't have had to do it," Bex whispered, lowering her head to Lys's shoulder. "The Blade of Sorrow didn't bring me down through our people's suffering. It got me with Adrian. I left him to die so I could stay and cut the chain. I thought I was doing the right thing, but then the sword hit me, and I just..."

Her voice trailed off as her throat grew tight. "I wanted to quit," she choked out at last. "No matter how hard I try, I can never get it right. I'm always a failure in every life, but this time you're the one who—"

"You are not a failure," Lys interrupted, grabbing Bex's face and wrenching her head up to make her look them in the eyes. "You have *never* been a failure. Ishtar made you perfect."

"But I couldn't do it!" Bex cried, grabbing Lys's hand. "I'm supposed to be Ishtar's Sword, the blade that protects her people, but when the Princess of Sorrow hit me, all I could think about was myself. I let my own selfish feelings get in the way of—"

Lys cut her off with a shake of their head. "If Ishtar wanted an emotionless weapon, she would have made you out of metal like Drox, but she didn't. She created you from her own body, because you're *not* a heartless sword. You're a queen, Ishtar's treasured daughter made from her own flesh and blood. You're *supposed* to feel sorrow and regret and attachment because how else could you love your people?"

"But I *didn't* love them," Bex argued, her voice shaking. "I abandoned them! I—"

"You abandoned nothing," Lys insisted. "I felt you in my head. I saw you on the bridge. You reached out to us, fought for us, took a sword for us."

"Because I was trying to be better!" Bex cried, closing her burning eyes. "You don't know how bad I've been. I—"

Lys placed a bloody finger on her lips. "If this is about saving Adrian from the princes while he was unconscious, I know. Desh spilled the whole story while he was betraying us, but I'd already guessed it was something like that. You've always been an idiot about these things, but you did nothing to be ashamed of."

"Nothing to be..." Bex jerked away from Lys's touch. "I gave up a Blade of Gilgamesh!"

"You chose a life over a weapon," Lys said, reaching for Bex again despite the shakes that were starting to rattle through their body. "You're beating yourself up because it was Adrian, but I know you would have done the same for me or Iggs or Nemini. That is *not* weakness. That's what makes you a good queen."

"But I'm *not*!" Bex cried. "I always make the wrong choice! I threw Adrian to the princes this time so I could stay and cut the chain, and it didn't even matter! I still lost."

"You haven't lost yet," Lys said. "And you didn't throw Adrian anywhere. He chose this fight the same as the rest of us because he believes you can win. We *all* believe."

They clutched her hard then, using Bex's grip to lever their spasming body off the bloody grass until they were nose to nose.

"I believe," they whispered, their sin-blackened eyes boring into hers. "From the moment you kicked down my warlock's door all those years ago to this second right now, you've been my hope. I don't know what lies the prince's sword told you, but I *know* what you are. You're my queen and my pride, so stop wasting tears on me and go show that prince what I've always known: that you're the one who will defeat Gilgamesh and return us all to Paradise."

Their grip was slipping by the end. Bex laid them back on the ground with a sob, kissing Lys's cheek as she cried and cried. She was still crying when Iggs finally made it over. He was fully transformed, his red skin bloody and ash-streaked from the fighting. He didn't look injured, though, and his red eyes were clear when they widened at the sight of Lys.

"What in the Hells happened to them?"

"Sin iron," Bex croaked, passing him Lys's too-cold, too-still body. "Get them to medical. Don't stop for anything."

Iggs nodded as he clutched Lys in his arms. "What are you going to do?"

Bex wiped the poisoned blood off her face and pushed back to her feet.

"What Lys told me to."

Iggs looked scared for a moment, but then he bowed his horns.

"Ishtar guide your sword."

Bex nodded in acknowledgment, waiting until Iggs sprinted away with Lys's body before she turned and walked back through the golden doors, her flames roaring over her like hellfire as she stepped back out onto the gilded chain.

Chapter 16

Bex marched onto the chain like an invading army. Unfortunately, she wasn't the only one. While she'd been saying goodbye to Lys, Gilgamesh's soldiers had advanced almost all the way down the bridge. The front line was only fifty feet away, a wall of golden armor similar to what the Anchor Guards wore, except there were no humans inside these suits. Their helmets held only a single golden eye, and they moved in synchronized formation, clanking down the bridge like a metallic tide.

We took too long.

"It's not over yet," Bex growled, stoking her flames higher.

She didn't reach for her people's anger this time. The fighting in the Market was dying down. Bex didn't know if that was because they'd won or lost, but the battle anger was dying out with it. That was good. Her people should know peace, and Bex didn't need them for this. Lys's blood had filled her with all the rage she could ever need as she thrust her hand behind herself and unleashed a blast of flame just like she'd done before.

The move worked even better now that it was only her fire. The Anchor Market demons' wrath had been easier to manage than the kick demons', but nothing beat her own. After so many weeks of practice, Bex could control the burn of her own rage like a muscle, putting out just the right amount of fire to superheat the air behind her. The resulting explosion launched her like a missile, sending her sword-first into the armored front line.

Drox carved through the golden soldiers like a scythe through wheat. Unlike the Anchor Guards, who usually put up a stiff defense, these were mass-produced sorcerous constructs, disposable troops. Their purpose was to overwhelm and subdue. They could still crush a rebellious demon slave, but Bex was a queen, the daughter of a goddess, and she cut them down with barely a blink.

Archers.

Bex nodded and dove, grabbing one of the golden monstrosities by its legs and hoisting it over her head for cover as a monsoon of golden arrows began to rain down. The shots bounced off the soldier's armored shoulders, but the barbed heads were made to tear through flesh, and they flew far. Bex couldn't even see the archer line through the waves of shock troops, but she shuddered to think what those arrows would do to her demons.

"We can't let them reach the Market."

Then you must cut the chain, Drox said, his blade steady in her hand. *The armies of Heaven are infinite, and even you can't hold this bridge forever. You must cut off their ability to attack before we're overwhelmed.*

It was already happening. The golden soldiers went down like paper under her sword, but Bex could destroy only so many with each swing, and the bridge was wide. The edges of the front line she hadn't been able to reach were already starting to move past her. Soon, she'd be encircled, so Bex swung one more time to clear the closest soldiers and turned her attention to their real objective.

The chain.

The sin is thick here, Drox warned as Bex took aim. *It will take multiple hits to get through.*

"Then I'll swing fast," Bex said, grabbing his hilt with both her hands as she drove the black sword into the ground.

Drox landed with a *clang* she felt all the way to her shoulders. The bridge's golden plating split like an onion skin under his sharp edge, but the black core beneath was a different story. Driving her sword into the sin iron felt like trying to cut a steel pipe with a kitchen knife. Bex wasn't even sure she'd made a mark when she felt Drox's hilt heat up in her hands, and the black blade began to cut through.

Again! the sword cried. *Harder!*

Bex obliged, yanking her smoking sword out of the metal and swinging it all the way over her head before bringing it down again like a sledgehammer. The blow shook the entire chain this time. All around her, Heavenly soldiers stumbled and fell, their giant limbs clicking like ratchets as they struggled to catch themselves on the bridge's slick surface. Some even slid into her, but Bex barely spared them a glance. She just blasted them away with her fire and hit the chain again, screaming as she drove her sword deeper into the cursed metal she'd come to hate even more than Gilgamesh.

"Stop!"

The command echoed down the bridge. The army obeyed at once, freezing in place, which suited Bex just fine. She was already reeling back for another strike when Prince Leander's sword appeared in front of her.

Bex had to twist her own blade to avoid hitting it. She could have driven the white sword into the ground, but she didn't want to risk a second blast of that debilitating sorrow. That was the only reason she stopped, pulling Drox back to her side as she raised her head to see Prince Leander standing right in front of her with a panicked expression.

"Stop," he said again, pulling back his sword and putting up his hands. "Please, Queen of Wrath, I understand that you hate us, but you have no idea what you're endangering. That chain is part of a system that protects the entire world. You can't just—"

The rest of his words were drowned out by the crash of metal on metal as Bex brought her sword down again. She saw the prince's face go pale with terrified rage as he brandished his own blade again, but he couldn't get close. This was the prince who'd killed Lys. The rage Bex felt toward him was personal and deep, and it hit her fire like bellows on a furnace, building her flames so hot that the sin metal began to boil under her feet. Within seconds, the air was choked with toxic fumes, but Bex was too far gone to care. All she felt was the fire of her wrath as she swung her sword again and again, driving Drox's black blade to the hilt into the softened sin iron.

"*No!*" Leander roared, struggling to keep his balance as the whole bridge rocked in time with Bex's hits. After a few more swings, it began to sag, sending the construct soldiers sliding over its golden surface like toy cars. They would have crashed right into Bex, but she was burning so hot now that their empty armor melted before it could reach her, the gold dripping like wax down the bridge's black heart as Bex swung again.

She was still hacking away when Bex felt something wrap around her legs. A dozen feet away on the part of the bridge she hadn't slagged yet, Prince Leander was screaming sorcery at her, binding her limbs in huge metal rods. Each one began to melt the moment it touched her, but he just kept adding more, wrapping Bex in log after log of molten metal until the sheer weight of it all sent her to her knees. The prince moved the second she gave him an opening, charging into her flames to tap his sword against her neck.

He could have easily cut her head off, but they'd never told Desh this was her last life, which meant the prince didn't know either. He was clearly still trying to take her alive so Heaven could enslave her people. Bad decision on his part because that realization just made Bex angrier. So angry that even the spear of sorrow couldn't drag her down as Bex pulled one hand off Drox's hilt and reached through the tangle of melting metal to grab the prince's white sword.

She heard Mara scream when her burning fingers bit into the blade. The prince screamed too, a howl of terror and rage as he tried to pull his beloved to safety, but Bex held on like a badger. Sorrow beat at her like waves as the princess struggled to free herself, but Bex knew her game now, and she fought back in kind, pouring the fire of her wrath into the abyss until, with a burst of light, she heard the white sword snap.

"No!"

Leander's scream was so ragged she hardly recognized it. He yanked his broken blade out of her hand, slicing Bex's palm open in the process. By the time her fire-fueled regeneration healed the cut, the prince was gone, vanished in a clang of golden bells with the two halves of his snapped sword clutched against his chest.

Bex waited a moment to see if he'd reappear, but Leander's princess must have been more important to him than the chain, because he didn't come back. The manacles he'd buried her in melted off a few seconds later, leaving Bex free to rise back to her feet in the center of the sagging bridge choked with the melting golden bodies of Gilgamesh's empty soldiers.

Let's finish this.

Bex nodded and stoked her fire hotter until she was melting through the sin iron she stood on. The boiling toxic metal ate through her combat boots and burned up her clothes. Its fumes filled her lungs, sending streaks of black across her skin and making her head spin. Too much more of this and Bex would pass out, but she ignored the feeling and focused on the memory of Lys's voice speaking what might've been their last words:

"You're the one who will defeat Gilgamesh and return us all to Paradise."

She would. Bex would not fail. She would be the queen that Lys deserved, the one who took her people home. That was the only thing that mattered, so she built her bonfire bigger still, filling the chain with her flames until the metal started to give.

She felt Drox's fear as he went back into his ring, but her sword didn't say a word. There was nothing to be said in the face of the queen's wrath as Bex stoked her fire until she was shining like a cutting torch, an unstoppable force melting her way through foot after foot of solid sin until, with a groan like a dying breath, the black chain gave way.

The link she'd been burning through let go like fingers slipping off a cliff, but the chain itself must have been under high tension, because it snapped like a rubber band. The unleashed force flung Bex backward, then she was falling through the empty air, plummeting past the snaking end of the broken bridge into the river below.

She crashed into the blue water like a red-hot stone. All light vanished when she hit. Her roaring flames, the white gleam of the Holy City, even the beautiful blue glow of the river itself, they all disappeared like snuffed-out candles, leaving Bex in the dark. The water's chill sucked the fire's heat right out of her, leaving her cold and heavy and filled with the strangest feeling of nostalgia.

This had happened to her before: falling into the water, her flames going out. Bex had no memory of what came next, but her body knew this deathly feeling. She had to get to the surface, had to light back up, but the water quenched her fire every time she called it, leaving her tumbling helplessly in the freezing current.

She fought it with the same fury she'd fought the prince, seething with betrayal. She couldn't drown in a River of Death. These were her mother's waters! How could something that had kept Bex alive for five thousand years be killing her now?

But as she raged and struggled for air, Bex began to understand. She'd been born in these waters, but she was no longer a creature of Paradise. Adrian had relit her with the fire of life. As Ishtar's daughter, the Rivers of Death would always give her strength, but she couldn't breathe in them. If she wanted to live, she would have to swim, so Bex stopped flailing angrily and focused on figuring out which way was up.

The dark and the current made it harder than it should have been, but eventually, Bex's head broke the surface. For several moments, she alternated between gasping in air and coughing out water. When her lungs were finally working again, Bex pushed her drenched hair out of her eyes and looked around to see where she was.

The answer seemed to be *nowhere*. Maybe the prince hadn't been bluffing when he'd said cutting the chain was bad, because now that it was broken, everything was black. She couldn't see Heaven anymore or the other chains. Even the eternally glowing water of death was dark as sin iron. If it wasn't for the pressure of the current and the freezing cold numbing her limbs, Bex wouldn't have known she was in a river.

That last part was actually her saving grace. It was impossible to tell direction in this darkness, but Bex knew the rivers flowed toward Paradise, which meant if she swam against them, she'd get back to the living world. That was good enough to get started, so Bex plunged forward, swimming upstream with all her might.

It was hard to tell if she was making progress with no reference points. It felt like she was moving forward, but fighting the current was rapidly sapping her strength, and she was so *cold*.

Bex had always hated the cold. A bonfire wasn't meant to be submerged in freezing water, and hers was flagging hard. She didn't stop moving, but her head was dipping under the surface more and more as she began to tire. Every time she went under, the water made her that much colder, but she couldn't stop. Even if she couldn't see the end anymore, this was still a river of death. If she let it sweep her away, she'd be carried right back up to Heaven.

That got her fire going again. Bex attacked the water in a rage, keeping herself warm with pure stubbornness as she thrashed her way upstream. She swam until she could no longer feel her hands and feet. Swam until her whole body burned with exhaustion. She was telling herself she'd swim until she died when a beam of light split the darkness.

"Bex!"

Bex's head shot up from where it had been sinking under the water. A door had opened in the blackness above her, letting in a blinding blast of light around a towering silhouette Bex recognized as well as her own reflection.

"Iggs!" she yelled back, half drowning herself in the process. *"Iggs!"*

Her voice was pathetically small in the dark, but it must have been good enough, because something huge splashed into the river next to her a second later. Bex was paddling toward it when Iggs's massive arms wrapped around her, pinning her to his chest in a bear hug.

"Got you!" he cried, buoying Bex so she could finally stop treading water. "Pull us up!"

Bex didn't know who he was yelling at, but they shouted back, and then Iggs's body jerked against hers as the rope he'd tied around his waist snapped tight, lifting them both out of the water. Bex coughed out buckets of river as they rose, clinging to Iggs's shoulders, which were still red and huge from his transformation.

"Lys," she gasped the moment she could speak without choking. "How is—"

"Alive," Iggs assured her. "They cut it pretty close, but Adrian caught them in time. He's got them bundled under his tree right now."

She stared at him, barely daring to hope. "Adrian's alive?"

"We're all alive," Iggs said, giving her a fanged grin. "I told you we'd win."

Bex pressed her face against his wet chest, trying not to cry. Crying in front of her subjects was inexcusable, but it was so overwhelming. She'd drown again if she let herself feel all the emotions hammering inside her skull, so Bex just focused on clinging to Iggs as he hauled her over the broken lip of something sharp.

The doors, she realized belatedly. They were going through the golden doors that had connected the Anchor Market to the chain. They didn't seem to connect to anything now, but there were dozens of demons on the other side, bracing their feet in the grass as they hauled the rope tied to Iggs and Bex back into the Anchor Market.

"Give the queen room," Iggs ordered as Bex stumbled into the light. The demons obeyed at once, backing off to let Bex breathe as she looked around at the smoking ruins that had been the Anchor's VIP area.

"What happened?" she croaked.

"Exactly what we planned," Iggs reported with a grin. "We kicked their butts! The folded-space-whatever-magical-thingy fell when you cut the chain, just like Adrian predicted, but his tree caught it before it could crush us.

We've cleared out all of Gilgamesh's remaining ground forces, and every demon in the Market is alive and free."

Bex gaped at him in disbelief, and Iggs's smile grew wider.

"We did it, Bex," he said, gripping her dripping shoulders. "We *won*."

She stared at him a moment longer, then the whole world went spinning as Bex keeled over in a dead faint.

She woke up under a tree.

It was beautiful and familiar, a towering oak with its green leaves lit up by the cheery light of a battery-powered camping lantern someone had hung from the lowest branch. Its roots were pleasantly lumpy under her back, and the grass was cool against her legs, her *bare* legs.

Bex sat up in a rush, staring in confusion at the soft woolen blanket covering her naked body. Where were her clothes? Where was *she*? The tree had made her think she was back in the Blackwood, but this wasn't the forest. She was sitting in what appeared to be a grassy lot walled in by stacks of wooden boxes. The night sky was spangled with more stars than could possibly be seen from Seattle, and she could hear hundreds of unfamiliar voices talking loudly in the distance. It sounded like a festival, but what—

"Welcome back."

Bex snatched the blanket to her chest, sword shooting into her hands before she spotted Adrian standing at a respectful distance.

"Sorry," she said immediately, yanking Drox back into her ring.

"Totally understandable," he assured her. "You've been through a lot. You were unconscious with moderate hypothermia when they brought you in. Lys said you might wake up aggressively, so I decided to wait over here."

Bex winced in embarrassment before her brain caught up with the rest of what he'd said.

"Wait, Lys is up? And talking?"

"Not *up* up," Adrian said, coming over to take a seat beside her in the grass. "They got a pretty severe dose of sin iron toxin. Fortunately, poison is one of my specialties. I'd just finished growing my tree, too, so I had an obliging set of roots close by and ready to help."

He patted the oak's trunk, and Bex swore the leaves rustled with pride.

"Anyway, Lys will be low for a while. Even demon constitution can't take a dose of poison straight to the heart without consequence, but I have no reason to think they won't make a full recovery."

He said this like it was nothing, but tears were streaming down Bex's face by the time he finished.

"I'm sorry," she whispered, scrubbing her eyes. "I don't mean to be like this. It's just... I'm *so happy* Lys isn't dead. When the prince stabbed them, I was sure I'd gotten them killed. I thought I'd gotten you *all* killed, and I... I..."

She trailed off, finally lifting her teary eyes to Adrian. "How are you alive?" she whispered.

"I was born that way," he replied with a laugh.

Bex was in no mood for jokes. "The prince sent his brother to kill you," she said, squeezing her fists tight. "He told me he'd save you if I surrendered, but I refused. I left you to die, so how are you not..."

Her voice faded off as she frantically looked him over, but other than a bandage around his left hand, Adrian seemed fine, which was impossible. The prince from Limbo was a monster. She knew her witch was strong, but for him to come out of that fight with nothing, not even torn clothes... That just didn't happen. They *couldn't* get this lucky.

"Take a breath before you faint again," Adrian suggested, giving her a warm smile. "The prince did come for me, and I had to make some sacrifices"—he held up his bandaged hand—"but I'm alive, and I got my tree up in time to keep the collapsing Anchor from killing us all, so I count them well worth it."

His words were light and cheerful, but Bex had spent hours on the phone listening to every nuance of Adrian's voice, and she could hear the mountain of what he'd left unsaid.

"How bad was it?"

"Terrifying," he replied, scooting a little closer. "Boston was furious, but seeing as we would have died any other way, I was able to bring him around. It's not something I'll be rushing to do again any time soon, but as I said, I count the price well paid. Especially since it means I get to give you this."

He pulled something large out of his enchanted pockets. It looked like a cracked-glass ornament the size of a basketball, but when Adrian held it out to her, Bex saw it was a spiderweb. A large, beautifully-patterned spiderweb spun into a globe, and hanging inside the globe like a snared bird was a woman's twitching, dark-skinned hand with a thick black ring on its third finger.

For several moments, all Bex could do was stare. She reached out to touch the spider-silk ball but thought better of it at the last second, clasping her hands over her heart instead.

"How did you get that?" she whispered in awe.

"Princes and princesses travel in pairs," Adrian told her with a smile. "I'm just sorry I had to wrap it up. I wanted to give you her hand in a way you could touch, but then I remembered what you told me about Heaven stealing it back after you beat her last prince, and I thought I'd better not take any chances."

"Will it work?" Bex asked. "I mean, can a spiderweb really stop the Eternal King?"

Adrian's face grew proud. "Never doubt the power of the forest," he said, reaching into his pocket again to pull out a glass vial with a large black-and-yellow spider inside. "Carlotta here is the best spinner I've ever raised, and the Blackwood guards its own. Gilgamesh himself couldn't break these webs so long as they're inside my witchwood, which we are, provided this ball stays within ten feet of my tree."

He wiggled his finger at the spider, who waved back with one of her eight legs before he returned her carefully to his pocket. It was all so charmingly Adrian that it should have warmed her heart, but Bex suddenly felt like she was drowning again.

"Bex?" he said, his face alarmed. "What's wrong? Are you okay?"

Bex had no idea how to answer that. She knew she should be screaming with joy, but it was hard to be happy when nothing felt real. She just couldn't believe that she hadn't gotten Adrian killed or that he'd gotten her sister's hand. She couldn't believe that he was talking to her again or that everyone was alive or that they were just sitting on the grass in an Anchor Market like they were having a picnic. It was too much. She couldn't handle it. She—

The grass rustled, and then Adrian was suddenly all around her, his warm arms coming up to encircle her shoulders as he pulled her close.

"It's okay," he whispered into her hair. "It's okay, Bex."

It was the same thing he'd said to her after she killed the prince in his forest. Those words had meant the world to Bex back then, and they meant no less now. She knew it was wrong to feel this way. That she should be going to check on Lys or putting on some clothes and going out to meet all the demons she'd freed or, or—

The pile of things she should be doing was as tall as the tree over their heads, but the only thing Bex *did* do was throw her arms around Adrian and bawl. She cried like she'd taken another hit from the sorrow sword, cried out all the fear and anger and grief. She cried in relief because she was alive and he was alive and *everyone was alive,* and that made her so happy that she cried some more. She cried longer and harder than she could ever remember crying in her life, but even though Bex knew she had to be making him horribly uncomfortable, Adrian didn't let her go.

"Sorry," she said when she finally finished.

"It's okay," he assured her again. "Stress builds up, and given what Iggs said about how you fainted the moment things were over, we figured you were due for some catharsis."

"I'm just glad no one else saw that," Bex muttered, gripping her blanket with both hands so she wouldn't start clinging to him again like a weepy idiot. She was just about to try standing up when she realized her legs felt weak.

"What the—"

"Oh, don't move yet," Adrian said, flipping back the bottom corner of her blanket to reveal what looked like a cast made from green mud plastered around both of Bex's bare ankles.

"It's my own special blend," he explained. "You had a pretty severe dose of sin iron poisoning on top of the hypothermia. It wasn't as bad as Lys's, but it still needed treatment. Fortunately, I'd already ground up a poultice of my own special strain of broadleaf plantain developed right in my garden. There's nothing better for removing poison, but this variety does have a numbing effect that can get pretty intense. The toxicity should be gone by now, though, so let me get it off you."

"I've got it," Bex mumbled, blushing as she reached down to scrape the leaf mash off on her own. "I'm going to feel like an invalid if you keep doing stuff for me, though I could use some new clothes if you've got them."

She didn't have much hope. Fresh, dry clothing seemed like a lot to ask in a war zone. To her surprise, though, Adrian popped up and walked over to the wall of boxes stacked just beyond the reach of his tree's branches. He dug through the crates for a bit then came back carrying a set of men's long-sleeved black silk pajamas.

"Where'd you get that?" Bex asked, grabbing the pajama pants and shoving her bare feet into the wide, slick legs.

"From your war spoils," Adrian replied, sweeping his arm over the piles of crates. "You captured an Anchor Market, which means you also captured all the things *inside* the Anchor Market. There's four more boxes full of sets just like that if you want another size, not to mention all the electronics, fancy chocolates, caviar, fresh fruit, wine, liquor, furniture, and several tents' worth of magical materials."

Bex's jaw was on the grass by the time he finished. She'd been planning this operation for a month, but it hadn't occurred to her until just now that assaulting an Anchor Market was the same thing as *stealing* an Anchor Market. All that fancy crap merchants were always hawking to the denizens of Heaven—the designer clothes and expensive handbags and imported cheeses—it was all *theirs.*

"What are we going to do with all this stuff?"

"Don't worry," Adrian said, sitting back down beside her. "Iggs is on it. He's declared himself your Minister of Loot. He found a laptop and is making a spreadsheet of the inventory as we speak."

Bex stared at him in bewilderment. "Iggs is making a spreadsheet?"

Adrian shrugged. "Revolutions make heroes of us all."

"This I gotta see," Bex said, sticking her arms through the pajama top's long sleeves.

The set was way too big for her, but it was workable after she rolled up all the cuffs. The numbness in her legs was fading, too, now that the plants were gone, leaving Bex ready to move out. When she looked over her shoulder at Adrian, though, he shook his head.

"I have to stay by my tree," he explained, reaching up to hang her sister's spiderweb-encased hand from the boughs like a macabre Christmas ornament. "The roots are still settling, and Boston's asleep. I would never leave him alone in a strange place. You go ahead. I know you've got a lot to do."

Bex hesitated, unwilling to leave him, which sent her back into a mini panic. She'd been trying for so long not to think about Adrian, not to look at him or smell him or touch him. Now, she'd done all of that without even noticing, and it had felt so right, which was the most dangerous thing of all.

Adrian had tried his best to play it off, but Bex knew he must have done something dreadful to beat that prince, and if she kept clinging to him like this, he'd have to do it again. Lys claimed that having a heart was what made Bex a good queen, but not everything the sorrow blade had made her feel was wrong. Adrian might have chosen this fight, but if Bex held on to her feelings for him, Heaven would never let him go. They'd attack him again and again until they finally came up with something he couldn't witch his way out of, and then she'd lose him just like she'd almost lost Lys.

That scared Bex way worse than the thought of dying herself. She'd grown up knowing that her life belonged to her people, but Adrian wasn't hers. He was his own witch with his own precious life, and Bex had no right turning him into her weak spot. She loved how she felt with Adrian, but only a truly selfish queen would keep someone else in danger to make herself happy. Bex refused to be that person, which meant it was time to do what she should have done from the beginning. It was time to come clean and tell Adrian it was over. She was working up the courage to do just that when Drox's voice spoke inside her head.

I don't think that's wise.

Bex almost screamed. Her sword was the one who'd started this! Now he was telling her *not* to cut Adrian off? What did he think he was—

I was wrong.

Bex went still, staring down at her ring in shock as the black metal grew heavy on her finger.

We have been together for a very long time, he told her quietly. *I don't lose my memories like you do, but somewhere during all those centuries, I forgot my purpose. I am the queen's sword, forged by the great Enki at Ishtar's request to consider tactics and victory above all other concerns. You are the queen, born to rule, which is a very different battlefield.*

Her ring grew heavier still, sliding toward her knuckle almost as if Drox were hanging his head.

Your servant Lysanae reminded me of that. I'd grown so used to you being childish and foolish, I didn't realize you were no longer any of those things until you took your people's power and struck down Heaven's shackles like a true sword of the gods. And if I was wrong about that, then I must accept that I could be wrong about everything, including your feelings toward Adrian Blackwood.

"But you weren't wrong," Bex whispered, glancing at Adrian. "When the Blade of Sorrow hit me, I—"

It was the Blade of Sorrow that showed me the truth, Drox insisted. *I told you to forget Adrian because I thought it would rid you of vulnerabilities, but there is no such thing as a perfect defense. Your feelings for the witch distracted you and gave the enemy leverage, yes, but denying those feelings left you weaker still. I felt your misery like my own when the Queen of Sorrow's blade struck you, saw your grief over what you thought you had to give up to be queen. I live inside your head, and yet I had no idea you felt that way.*

Bex sighed, but Drox wasn't finished.

The failure on that bridge was mine, not yours. I gave you ignorant advice based on the flawed premise that I knew you better than you knew yourself. By not trusting your judgment, I failed my most sacred duty and left you vulnerable to your enemies. I have been an unworthy sword to you, Queen Rebexa. I sincerely apologize for my faults and humbly beg your forgiveness and patience as I work to correct them.

"Apology accepted," Bex said after a stunned silence. "Does that mean you're okay with..."

Her eyes slid back to Adrian, who was giving her the slightly alarmed look he always wore when listening to her one-sided conversations with Drox.

I leave such things to your majesty's discretion, her sword replied. *I'm shutting myself down for a bit. Call on me if you need something cut. Otherwise, I think it's time I got out of your way.*

His presence vanished from her mind after that, leaving Bex blinking in amazement.

"Is everything all right?" Adrian asked as he started to get up from his tree.

"It's fine," Bex said. "Better than fine." She held up her ring, which just felt like a ring for once, with a grin. "It seems today is a day of miracles."

"And that's a good thing?" he confirmed nervously.

"Very good," Bex assured him, rolling the cuffs of her black silk pajama shirt even higher up her arms. "I've gotta go check on Lys and talk to Iggs and probably a billion other things, but would it be okay if I came back and found you later?"

"I'd be sorry if you didn't," Adrian said, settling against his tree. "You know where I'll be."

Bex flashed him one last smile and hopped over the wall of boxes stacked around his tree, which was how she nearly landed on Nemini.

"Whoa," Bex said, twisting out of the way just in time to keep her bare feet from getting tangled in the void demon's snakes. "What are you doing?"

"Existing," Nemini replied, rising from where she'd been sitting cross-legged in the grass. "And keeping the others away."

Bex frowned. "Others?"

"The line to see the queen is long," her demon replied stoically. "I've been encouraging them to wait. It won't kill them to sit on their gratitude, and I know you don't like people seeing you cry."

The rush of relief Bex felt at that nearly took her off her feet. "Thank you," she said, leaning in to give her demon a hug. "You are a queen."

Nemini froze in her embrace. Bex was about to let her go when she felt the taller demon's arms come up to wrap gently around her shoulders.

"I know death is inevitable," she whispered, "but I'm glad it didn't come for you today."

"Me too," Bex said, squeezing harder even though Nemini's void was consuming her vision. "Let's go check on Lys."

Nemini nodded and let her go, following Bex as close as a shadow into the barely organized chaos of a victory party five thousand years in the making.

Chapter 17

Despite everything she wanted to say to him, Bex didn't get to see Adrian again for several hours.

She found Lys rolling around shouting orders from an ancient blue-and-chrome hospital wheelchair someone had snagged from who knew where. After making sure they were really *really* okay and barely managing not to dissolve into tears again, Bex put Lys in charge of making a master list of all their new recruits.

There were a ton to keep track of. Bex's invocation of her royal name had freed *every* demon in the Anchor, from sorcerers' house slaves to warlocks' combat slaves to the old merchant slaves working the food trucks. Some had run after getting free, but the initial counts Bex had gotten from Anka—the sorrow demon she and Lys had freed in California who was now managing one of their biggest safe houses—showed that the majority had stayed, including *all* the demons from the slave auction, many of whom were children. They also had a surprising number of domestic slaves who'd come down with their masters from the Holy City and had no interest in going back up.

No one was going back up. When Bex rechecked the doors at the base of Gilgamesh's statue that used to lead onto the chain, they still opened into the same black nothing she'd been drowning in when Iggs saved her. She could still hear the river, but she couldn't see a thing. Bex wasn't sure what was outside the Anchor now, but she didn't think an attack would be coming from that direction any time soon. She still ordered a team of fear demons to keep watch on the doorway, though, just in case.

Back at the line of vendor tables they'd commandeered for registration, Lys was badgering all the Holy City demons for interviews since intel about Gilgamesh's capital was a rare and precious commodity, but it wasn't going well. The new demons were perfectly willing to spill their former masters' secrets, but they were far more interested in meeting Bex, asking other slaves for news about lost family and friends, and celebrating their newfound freedom.

That last part was in full swing by the time Bex got Lys and Anka settled. The lobster craze was long over. It was officially September now, which meant everyone who was anyone in Heaven needed beer, pumpkins, and pumpkin beer. One of the big events the sorcerers running the Anchor had planned for tonight other than the slave auction was a not-quite-Oktoberfest beer garden. They'd set up a special area with tables, drink carts, and everything, though most of those had been shoved aside to make room for a massive drunken dance party. Many of the demons had never heard the Earth songs someone had figured out how to play over the Anchor's sound system, but they danced anyway, laughing and flinging each other around in the sheer joy of being free.

Bex had never been a slave, so she didn't know how they felt, but she'd freed enough people to imagine. She tried to slip by unnoticed so as not to interrupt the celebration, but the dancers spotted her horns and rushed her.

She spent the next hour being thanked by scores of weeping demons. This was normally the part of being queen Bex hated most. She never knew what to say to crying people, and she always felt unworthy of their praise when there were still so many demons left to save. Tonight, though, it wasn't so bad. It was still awkward having someone she'd never met weep over her hands, but for the first time Bex could remember, she felt like she'd actually done something worthy of all that thanks. The throngs of happy dancers, the demons hugging friends and family they'd thought they'd never see again, that was her doing. She and her demons and Adrian, *they'd* made this happen. And if they could work a miracle this big, then even Heaven itself didn't feel out of reach.

That was a heady thought for someone who'd spent the last fifty centuries losing, and it got even crazier when Bex finally made it to Iggs.

She found him at the market manager's tent. Bex hadn't realized there *was* a market manager's tent until Iggs dragged her inside to show off the four laptops linked to a full security suite of cameras overlooking the entire Anchor Market. He was bouncing like an excited kid as he demonstrated the control panels that changed the Anchor's sky from night to day and worked the sound system that was currently blasting Billboard's Hot 100 dance hits.

"We got the whole thing," he told her for what had to be the thousandth time. "After we fished you out of the water, I deputized some responsible-looking demons and took them to clear out the sorcerers' offices. All the sorcerers were long gone by the time we got in, the cowards, but they left a ton of good shit behind. I don't read cuneiform, so I couldn't make heads or tails of it, but I found a pair of greed demons who used to work in the Holy City and set them loose on the place. You should have seen them! They went after the filing cabinets like piranhas. They said they'll have an initial report ready by tomorrow, but they want to present it to you personally."

"That's fine with me," Bex said. "Are you sure we can trust them?"

"As sure as I can be," Iggs said, flashing her the most excited grin she'd ever seen on his face. "It's crazy, Bex! No one's even looting. They're all too happy, and they all want to help. They want to help *you* specifically. You're the one they've heard stories about all their lives, and I'm not talking about Gilgamesh's 'Coward Queen' bullshit. According to the demons I've talked to, every slave in Paradise whispers about the escaped queen who'll come back to save them one day. That's *you*! You're a legend to these people, and now that we've taken over an Anchor, they really believe you're the one who'll burn down Heaven and take us all back home!"

"One victory at a time," Bex said, sliding her hands into the pockets of her pajama bottoms so Iggs wouldn't see how badly they were shaking. "Now, tell me about the loot."

That got Iggs off the subject of her savior role nicely. Adrian had hinted at their new wealth earlier, but five minutes of listening to Iggs taught Bex that she hadn't been thinking nearly big enough. They hadn't just taken over an Anchor Market. They'd taken over an Anchor Market stocked for the biggest shopping event of the decade. The place was stacked to the sky with goods from almost a thousand vendors, all of whom had been forced to abandon their stock when they fled. A lot of it had been damaged in the fighting and the fires, but there were still piles upon piles of super-nice stuff to go through, not to mention all the quintessence they were finding.

"It's freaking everywhere," Iggs said as he showed her the glowing bucket he'd found behind the manager's desk. "Every vendor brought a sack to use as change, and we're still counting the take from the money-changing booths. The warlocks who died in the chaos also had a bunch on them, but most of that went into their demons' pockets."

"Then let's leave it there," Bex said. "I'm more concerned with how we're going to fence all this stuff. We need weapons and transport, not caviar and designer handbags. We also need to relocate. The Anchor Market's safe for now, but we don't have the know-how to run a place this reliant on sorcery, and all of us together make a big target."

"Respectfully, Your Majesty, I disagree," Iggs said, turning his new office chair around to face her. "I think we should keep the Anchor."

Bex boggled at him. "*Why?*"

"Because it's a fortress," her wrath demon explained, pointing at the camera feeds. "We've got the best mundane and magical security money can buy here, and with the chain cut, Gilgamesh can't send his armies at us unless he wants to march them through Seattle. He can still attack with sorcerers, warlocks, and princes, but I'd much rather fight those from a single defended position than spread out across a bunch of safe houses. Also, keeping everyone together lets us be a community. That's really important."

He pointed through the tent flap at the dance party that was still raging outside. "Those people have been separated from their families and traded around like tokens their entire lives. It'd do them good to have a safe place where they can finally be free together. You know, like a town."

"We can't keep everyone in one place," Bex argued. "It'll be like shooting fish in a barrel."

"Not if the fish shoot back," Iggs said, holding his ground. "Running was all we could do when it was just the four of us, but we've got numbers on our side now, and we're not weak. You and Adrian beat *two* princes tonight, remember? And once we start trading all this junk for weapons, the rest of us will get our teeth as well. We'll be an *army*, Bex! And an army needs a fort."

Bex blew out a nervous breath. She was still trying to decide how to reply when Iggs added, "We also need to do something about the local vendors."

"What about them?"

"They're useful," he explained. "I'm sure they're mad as crap at us right now since we took all their stuff, but there's no reason it has to stay that way. I've been talking to some of the demons who worked the merchant tents, and they say most of the people who sold here aren't actually loyal to Gilgamesh. They're independents, usually people born into sorcerer or warlock households but who didn't want to swear their lives to Heaven. Some of them are even witches! Not famous ones like Adrian, but they do their own magic and sell in the Anchor Market to make ends meet. Those people still need their businesses, and I see no reason why that business can't be done through us."

Bex stared at him. "Are you suggesting we reopen the Anchor Market?"

"Not an Anchor Market," he corrected with a grin. "A *Free* Market! We'll take a cut just like Gilgamesh used to and give the merchants some of their stuff back in return for doing business with us."

"Who's going to want to do business with us?" Bex demanded. "No one who works for Gilgamesh can come in here without being branded a traitor."

"That's just it," Iggs said. "Most of the merchants who ran these tents *don't* work for Gilgamesh, but they do need a market, and we can give them a better one than Heaven did. We'll let them sell all the stuff Gilgamesh didn't, *without* his high taxes. Do that, and we'll have people coming from all over the country to sell through us! That kind of power makes us legit, and legitimate organizations get allies.

There's tons of people who hate Gilgamesh out there, they've just never had anyone to rally behind. We can be that. We don't have to be a ragtag group of demon insurgents anymore. We can grow this thing into an *actual* rebellion! And by the time Gilgamesh peeks out of his golden castle, we'll be too big to stop."

"Wow, Iggs," said Bex, legitimately impressed. "You've really thought this through."

"I play a lot of empire-building games," Iggs said proudly. "Taking over the centers of commerce and using the power of joint economic interest to build a war machine is always an OP strat. It'll also be great to have an actual stronghold. The Blackwood's amazing and all, but we can't put thousands of demons in Adrian's forest. They deserve somewhere they can feel safe too."

"You make a lot of good points," Bex admitted, tapping her fingers on the manager's desk—Iggs's desk, now, she supposed.

"I'm not a hundred percent sold on running our own market yet," she said, "but I'm willing to give it a try. See if you can get in contact with some of those vendors—the ones who didn't own slaves—and find out what it'll take to get them back. We also need to figure out what we're going to do for food."

"Lys is way ahead of you on that," Iggs promised. "They're already setting up a feeding schedule and a buddy system so no one has to go out alone. Fortunately, we're in the middle of a major city, which means there should be plenty of food to go around."

"I'll talk to them about it, then," Bex said, adding yet another item to her mental checklist, but Iggs was shaking his head.

"You've already done more than your share tonight," he insisted, getting comfier in his new chair. "Go get some sleep. We've got this."

"But—"

"*Go,*" he said. "Or I'll sic Lys on you."

That was not an idle threat. Leaving a situation this precarious went against every instinct Bex had, but Iggs was already pushing her out of the tent. The party outside was raging harder than ever, so no one noticed her leaving this time. She thought about heading back to Lys's table anyway just to check, but it was really crowded, and Bex didn't actually feel up to dealing with logistics. Now that Iggs had mentioned sleep, her body wanted nothing else, but there was still one thing she had to do.

With a final look at the Anchor Market that had somehow become their fortress, Bex turned away from the hordes of celebrating demons and started walking back toward Adrian's tree. Lots of people waved at her as she passed, but most were too nervous to approach the queen on their own, which suited Bex just fine. She couldn't deal with any more bowing or crying tonight, so she waved regally and broke into a jog, dodging clusters of happy demons until she was back at the wall of stacked boxes on the market's edge.

Just as he'd promised, Adrian was right where she'd left him: sitting under his tree, whittling something with his pocketknife. Boston was perched on a root nearby, talking to his witch in a hushed voice that stopped when Bex appeared. She was about to ask if she should come back later when the cat pressed his paw against Adrian's hand in what looked like the feline equivalent of a high five and darted off between the boxes.

"Where's he going?" she asked.

"Exploring," Adrian replied as he returned to his whittling. "Boston is the most responsible of familiars, but he's still a cat. Keeping him penned up in such an exciting new environment is cruel, so I gave him the rest of the night off."

"That's nice of you," Bex said, coming over to sit on the grass beside him.

"It was the least I could offer after everything I've put him through," Adrian said with a shrug. "I could go with him now that my tree's situated, but I've already found what I'm looking for."

He smiled at her as he finished, and Bex rapidly looked down at her lap.

"So, um, what are you working on?"

"A finger," Adrian replied, holding up the wooden object he'd been shaping so carefully.

Bex frowned. "Why are you carving a finger?"

"Replacement parts," he answered. "Wood's my favorite material to work in, and the tree was most obliging. I should be able to make something nearly as strong and responsive as the original with a little effort."

She gave him a baffled look, and Adrian held up his bandaged left hand, which Bex just now realized was short its little finger.

"You're making that finger for *you*?" she cried.

"Of course," Adrian said. "I make all my own things. It is called witch—"

"Craft, I know," Bex interrupted impatiently. "But *how* did you lose a finger? Did the prince cut it off?"

"No, I did," he replied, returning his eyes to his knife as he began cutting in the curve that would eventually become his pinky nail. "And before you say anything, I have zero regrets. Cutting off a body part for power is a rite of witchhood. My mother's missing three of her toes." He frowned suddenly. "Actually, all of the Old Wives are missing parts. My Aunt Muriel's had a fake liver for as long as I've been alive, and I think I just figured out why."

He scowled a moment longer, then he shrugged and went back to his woodwork. "It might sound drastic to you, but I count this a cheap price. I'm the one who pushed to attack the Anchor, and we won just like I hoped. Look at it that way, and I got a bargain, especially when you consider I gave up one finger to get a whole hand."

He glanced up at her sister's hand, which was still hanging safe in its spider-silk ball above their heads. Bex, however, clenched her fists.

"I can't let you do this."

"I'm not yours to let," he reminded her, setting his knife and the half-done finger aside so he could focus on her fully. "I'm not one of your demons, Bex. Fighting alongside you was my choice, not my duty, and it's one I'd happily make again. We changed history tonight. No one's ever taken territory back from Gilgamesh, but we *did it*. It's a different world now! A better one, because of *us*. If my little finger helped buy all of that, I've got nine more to bargain."

"Please don't," Bex begged, dragging her hands over her face. She stayed like that for a long second, then she turned around in the grass to face him.

"I owe you an apology."

"I don't want one," Adrian assured her. "It was my finger."

"That's not what I'm talking about," she said, forcing herself to look him in the eyes. Here it went.

"I'm sorry for how I've treated you. Freezing you out was selfish and cowardly. I should have told you the truth from the start, but I wasn't brave enough to say it to your face, so I didn't say anything at all. That was wrong, and I apologize. You did nothing to deserve this. It was all me, not you, and I'm sorry."

Adrian looked down at where she'd folded her hands in her lap. "It did hurt," he said quietly. "But I understand why you did it."

Bex blinked. "You do?"

"Desh told the story of how you traded a Blade of Gilgamesh for my life while he was holding me hostage," he explained. "That's why he went for me after he tried to stab you and got Lys instead. The prince thought he could leverage me against you a second time."

She looked down at her hands. "I'm sorry."

"Stop apologizing," Adrian said angrily. "None of this is your fault."

"Then whose fault was it?" Bex demanded. "I'm the one they used you to get leverage against."

"That doesn't make you responsible for their actions," he argued. "Death is always a risk in war. I don't get to put myself in your army and then blame you when I get shot at. I knew what I was getting into when I signed up for this, and I have no intention of getting out. I *want* to fight beside you. I *like* being here. I like *you*. And if you'd stop trying to make that into something to be sorry for, I'd very much appreciate it."

"I wasn't trying to insult you," Bex said, heart jackhammering in her chest. "I..."

She stopped just before she stepped off the cliff. Drox had apologized for it, but nothing her sword had said was actually wrong. Even if queens weren't meant to be emotionless killing machines, having feelings for Adrian still opened more fronts than Bex could defend. Those holes in her defense would only get bigger if she let this keep going, but Adrian was right too. There was no way to fight a safe war. Even Drox had said it was impossible, but that didn't mean Bex could take this step without making sure Adrian knew exactly what it meant.

"I like you too," she admitted in a tiny voice. "A lot. And that's dangerous. You've borne the brunt of it twice already, and it's going to keep happening so long as you're with me."

His lips quirked. "If you're trying to scare me away, it's not going to work. I grew up in a witchwood, remember?"

Bex laughed despite herself. "How could I forget? If you got any witchier, you'd be a Halloween decoration. But I'm not trying to scare you. I just need to be certain you know what you're getting into."

"I've known that since I came out of my forest and saw you sitting in a crater full of slagged gold that had been a prince," Adrian said, placing his five-fingered hand under her chin to tilt her head up. "And my answer now is the same as it was back then: I'm in this to the end. You're the only person I've ever met who's willing to stand up to Gilgamesh. I want to stand up with you, to fight for a world where it isn't a crime to be us. If doing that gets more princes lobbed in my direction, so be it. I'll face Gilgamesh's entire murderous family before I go back to hiding in the woods, or before I let them take me away from you."

Bex squirmed under his gaze, face blazing. "Only if you're sure."

"Absolutely sure," he said, then he flashed her a wicked smile. "Though, if you *really* want to make amends for giving me the silent treatment, I'd be happy to revisit that kiss now that I'm awake."

She jerked in horror. "How did you know about that?!"

"I have my ways," Adrian replied cryptically, leaning in very close.

Too close. Bex had always loved the way Adrian smelled, but now, it was like he was enveloping her. She couldn't think when he got this close, which was bad. They were still at war, and she had a whole Anchor full of demons to worry about. She needed to stay alert, not sit here getting lost in—

"Bex."

Her eyes flicked back to his, and Adrian smiled—just smiled at her like he always did—as he leaned in and pressed his lips to hers.

Bex jolted. Not counting the one she'd stolen while he was unconscious, which she didn't, this was her first kiss, at least in this life. It barely was a kiss at all to start. Adrian's mouth was as light as a falling leaf against hers, giving her plenty of opportunity to pull away, but Bex didn't want to go. She wanted more of this, wanted more of him, so she took the advice of Lys the Always Right and went for it, slanting her lips against his to kiss Adrian Blackwood like she'd been secretly wanting to since the very first day she'd met him.

And it was *glorious*. He must have been waiting for her signal, because the moment Bex started kissing him back, Adrian's fingers were suddenly in her hair, pulling her against him with a soft, hungry gasp that she felt all the way to her toes.

Bex was pretty sure first kisses were supposed to be awkward, but Adrian kissed masterfully, because of course he did. He was a Blackwood Witch of the Flesh. She understood now why Iggs had been so excited about that, because kissing Adrian was a magical experience. There was no war when he touched her, no fears, no responsibilities, no past or future—just this perfect, floating moment where Adrian was kissing her like she was the only thing in his world.

"There," he whispered when they finally broke apart. "Apology accepted."

Bex rested her forehead against his with a dazed smile. "Can I apologize again?"

"As many times as you like," he promised. "But now we've cleared that up, there is something I've been meaning to ask you."

"What?"

He glanced at the top of her head. "May I touch your horns?"

"Oh," she said, surprised. "Yeah, sure."

His face lit up in an elated smile, like she'd just given him a present he'd been wanting forever, and Bex's cheeks began to heat.

"You could have asked earlier," she said, lowering her head to give him full access. "They're just horns."

"I didn't know the etiquette," Adrian explained, reaching up to test the sharpness of the black points with the pad of his thumb.

"It's not lewd or anything," Bex assured him as she held very still. "Not that you should go around touching random demons on the horns, but they're not sensitive."

At least, she'd never thought so until Adrian brushed his fingers along her inside curve. The slight pressure was enough to make Bex's whole body shiver, which had never happened before. It could have been another of the changes from getting her fire back, but Bex was pretty sure it was just Adrian.

"They're warm," he said, his voice bright with that excited Adrian curiosity she'd come to treasure. "What does it feel like?"

"Like you're touching my horns," Bex replied, blushing furiously. "It's kind of hard to explain."

"Do they have nerve endings?"

"I guess?" she said with a shrug. "They're less sensitive than skin but more sensitive than fingernails. Mine are special, though, so I don't know if that's what it feels like for everyone else."

"What makes them special?" he asked. "Aside from being taller than average?"

Bex laughed. "That *is* what makes them special. My horns are big because they're my crown. They're how other demons know I'm a queen."

"Oh," he said, sounding slightly sheepish. "I didn't think it would be that simple."

"The important stuff is always simple," she said, lifting her head again to give him a nervous smile. "So… Can I touch you too?"

He opened his arms in invitation, and Bex scooted closer, leaning into his chest like she'd wanted to do since forever.

"Ahh," she sighed, closing her eyes in bliss. "This is much nicer now that I'm not crying."

"That's a low bar, but I'll take it," Adrian said, wrapping his arm around her shoulder as they settled against the tree. "Go ahead."

"Go ahead what?" Bex asked, confused.

"Talk to me," Adrian said, his voice rumbling pleasantly through her. "We went from talking every night to not talking at all. I feel cheated and demand recompense. I particularly want to hear about how you freed every demon at the same time, what happened on the chain, and what we'll be doing next."

Bex chuckled. "That's a lot."

"I'm fine with a lot," he said, hugging her tighter. "I missed you."

"I missed you too," Bex said, snuggling close as she began the long process of answering all his questions.

Epilogue

The Princes' Sanatorium, Highest Heavens, beneath the Divine Palace of the Eternal King.

Leander woke in a void of white. He couldn't breathe but didn't need to, couldn't feel but had no desire to. There was nothing but calm and emptiness, which wasn't right. He should be upset. Something was missing, something very important to—

He sat up in a rush, startling the crowd of white-robed servants surrounding the tank of quintessence his body had been floating inside. He was in the Sanatorium. In a renewal sarcophagus, which made no sense. He hadn't been critically injured during the fight—Mara had. He'd brought her broken blade here to be restored, so why was he the one floating in a tank? Where was his—

"You're up sooner than expected."

Leander's head snapped toward the sound just in time to see the Crown Prince step through the golden doors. The servants bowed before his divine presence, but he waved them away, emptying the room.

"What am I doing here?" Leander demanded when it was just them. "Where is Mara?"

"The Princess of Sorrow is still being reconstructed," his brother replied, leaning against the closed door, well out of Leander's limited reach from inside the sarcophagus. "You were causing a scene, so I had them put you somewhere you'd be more comfortable."

"I'm not yours to bottle up," Leander snarled, pulling the golden tubes out of his body to free himself from the tank's grasp. "Take me to my princess."

His brother heaved a long sigh. "That's why I put you in the tank, Leander. She's not your princess anymore."

Leander froze with one dripping leg out of the sarcophagus. "What?"

"Father has spoken," the Crown Prince explained, his one-eyed face closed and cold. "She is being reassigned."

Leander dropped to the floor in front of his tank, liquid magic dripping off his naked body as he closed his hands into fists. "He can't do that."

"He can do whatever he damn well wants," his brother snapped, finally showing some emotion as he stepped forward. "I gave you this job on a platter. You were supposed to capture the Coward Queen and prove you were still an asset to the Eternal King. Then I'd have an excuse to give you back your princess and regain a sane member of my family, but *no*. You had to go and abandon your post. If you'd let the Coward Queen kill you, I might have been able to smooth things over, but you *ran away* in the middle of a battle. Now the whole Anchor's lost, and father's blaming you."

"She broke Mara in half!" Leander cried. "What was I supposed to do? Stand there and watch her die?"

"*Yes!*" the Crown Prince shouted. "Because your 'Mara' is a Blade of Gilgamesh! We could put her back together even if the Coward Queen smashed her to splinters. Have done so, in fact. You *know* that, but you let your emotions overrule your reason, and now everything's out of control."

"I can fix it," Leander promised, squeezing his fists tight. "Just give me Mara, and I'll take care of every—"

"You've taken care of enough," the Crown Prince said bitterly, raking a hand through his dark, curling hair. "I let you run this operation because I thought you had a plan. You've always been the cleverest of us, so when you said you needed a fear demon released from the Hells, I saw it done. I let you organize that ridiculous reopening festival. I even got you a sin blade, and you *lost* it. Do you have any idea how bad that looks?"

"It was just a small sin blade," Leander hedged. "I needed to give the Coward Queen something so she'd let my spy in, but I was careful. That little knife isn't big enough to cause any real damage, and princes are immune to the effects of sin iron, so it's not like—"

"I don't care if it was a sin iron needle!" his brother yelled at him. "I stuck my neck out for you! I went to *Father* for you, and you threw it back in my face! You don't care how your actions reflect on the rest of us. All you care about—all you've *ever* cared about—is your precious Mara, and now you've lost it all. She's being reforged with a complete memory wipe. She won't know you from a servant, and it's all your fault."

Leander began to shake. "Please," he whispered, falling to his knees. "Please, brother, *Alexander*, don't do this. Don't take her from me."

"I'm not doing anything," Crown Prince Alexander said, his one mirrored eye as cold as steel. "You lost an Anchor, got an entire legion of the Holy Army dropped into the Rivers of Death, and allowed a chain to be destroyed. Your sins have far outstripped my ability to fix or forgive. I'm afraid this matter is in Father's hands now."

"No," Leander whispered, shaking on the white floor. "You can't give me to him. You *can't*—"

He cut off with a gasp as a set of cold, hard fingers latched onto his shoulder like a bear trap. When Leander raised his head, the Princess of War was staring down at him, her mismatched eyes sharp with hateful triumph as she yanked him to his feet.

"I tried to warn you," Crown Prince Alexander said, following at a safe distance as his princess dragged his little brother into the hall. "My princess did as well. We told you the price over and over, but you chose to be stupid anyway. It's the same mistake you've been making since the beginning, and I can't defend you anymore. I'm sorry, brother, but this is the end."

"*No!*" Leander screamed, clawing at the white floor in a desperate attempt to reach his brother. He even tried sorcery, but the words did nothing without the Eternal King's blessing, and the Crown Princess was impossibly strong. No Blade of Gilgamesh was supposed to be stronger than a prince, but his brother's sword picked Leander up like a doll, carrying him howling up the long spiral stair that led to the golden throne at the pinnacle of Heaven.

Thank you for reading!

Thank you for reading *Hell of a Witch*!

If you enjoyed Bex and Adrian's story, I hope you'll consider leaving a review. Reviews, good or bad, are vital to every author's career, and I'd be extremely grateful if you'd take a moment to write one for me.

The third book in the *Tear Down Heaven* series is written and out now, with the last book launching in early 2026. You can be the first to know when it drops by signing up for my new release mailing list! (Over at rachelaaron.net) List members always get first dibs on my books, and I only email when I've got something new, so there's zero spam. Signing up is free and easy, so come join the fun!

Again, thank you so, *so* much for being my reader. There would be no books without you. Thank you from the bottom of my heart, and I'll see you in the next story!

Yours sincerely,
Rachel Aaron

Want More Books?

Tear Down Heaven is only the latest addition to the Rachel Aaron library. I have plenty more titles of all sorts for you to enjoy, including five finished series! Keep paging forward to see my top picks for new readers or visit rachelaaron.net for the full list, and, as always, thank you for reading!

Nice Dragons Finish Last

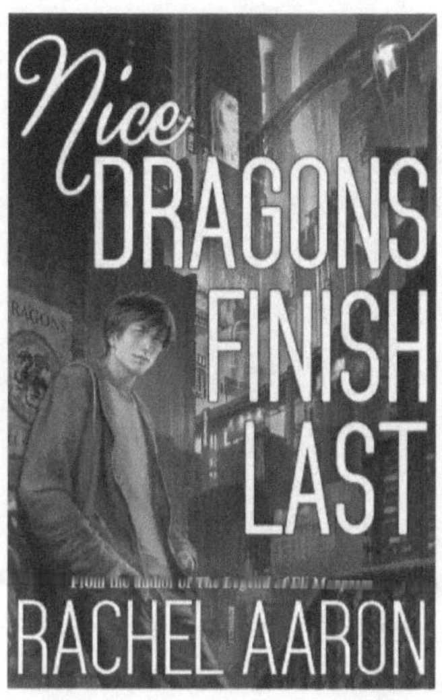

"Super fun, fast-paced urban fantasy full of heart, and plenty of magic, charm and humor to spare, this self-published gem was one of my favorite discoveries this year!" - **The Midnight Garden**

"A deliriously smart and funny beginning to a new urban fantasy series about dragons in the ruins of Detroit...inventive, uproariously clever, and completely un-put-down-able!" - **SF Signal**

As the smallest dragon in the Heartstriker clan, Julius survives by a simple code: stay quiet, don't cause trouble, and keep out of the way of bigger dragons. But this meek behavior doesn't cut it in a family of ambitious predators, and his mother, Bethesda the Heartstriker, has finally reached the end of her patience.

Now, sealed in human form and banished to the DFZ--a vertical metropolis built on the ruins of Old Detroit--Julius has one month to prove to his mother that he can be a ruthless dragon or lose his true shape forever. But in a city of modern mages and vengeful spirits where dragons are seen as monsters to be exterminated, he's going to need some serious help to survive this test.

He just hopes humans are more trustworthy than dragons.

My first and most popular DFZ series, complete at 5 books.
Available in **audio, print, eBook, and Kindle Unlimited**!

By a Silver Thread

"By A Silver Thread *is
exquisitely trademark Rachel Aaron.
Immensely readable & instantly
engaging, with new characters that you
can't help loving. The inclusion of fairy
lore just leveled up the already
fascinating world of the DFZ. So good,
so fun!"* - **Novel Notations**

"*A superb return to the world of
the DFZ. This is a heroic story that is in
parts heartwarming, in parts
mysterious and just a fantastic read all
the way.*" - **Fantasy Book Critic**

In the world's most magical metropolis where spirits run
noodle shops and cash-strapped dragons stage photo-ops for
tourists, people still think fairies are nothing but stories, and
that's exactly how the fairies like it. It's a lot easier to feast on
humanity's dreams when no one believes you exist. But while this
arrangement works splendidly for most fair folk, Lola isn't one of
the lucky ones.

She's a changeling, a fairy monster made just human
enough to dupe unsuspecting parents while fairies steal their real
child. The magic that sustains her was never meant to last past
the initial theft, leaving Lola without a future. But thanks to Victor
Conrath, a very powerful--and very illegal--blood mage, she was
given the means to cheat death.

For a price.

Now the only changeling ever to make it to adulthood,
Lola has served the blood mage faithfully, if reluctantly, for
twenty years. Her unique ability to slip through wards and
change her shape to look like anyone has helped make Victor a
legend in the DFZ's illegal-magic underground. It's not a great life,

but at least the work is stable... until her master vanishes without a trace.

With only a handful left of the pills that keep her human, Lola must find Victor before she turns back into the fairy monster she was always meant to be. But with a whole SWAT team of federal paladins hunting her as a blood-mage accomplice, an Urban Legend on a silent black motorcycle who won't leave her alone, and a mysterious fairy king with the power to make the entire city dream, Lola's chances of getting out of this alive are as slender as a silver thread.

The newest standalone series set in the DFZ, complete at 3 books!
Available now in <u>ebook, print, KU, and audio</u>!

About the Author

Rachel Aaron is the author of almost thirty novels both self-published and through Orbit Books. When she's not holed up in her writing cave, she lives a nerdy, bookish life in the suburbs of Denver, CO with her perpetual-motion son, long-suffering husband, and mountains of books. To learn more about Rachel and read samples of all her work, visit rachelaaron.net!

© 2024 by Rachel Aaron. All rights reserved.

Cover Illustration by Luisa Preissler
Cover Design by Rachel Aaron
Editing provided by Red Adept Editing

As ever, this book would not be as good without my beta reader Linda Hall, the keenest typo-hunter of all time.

www.ingramcontent.com/pod-product-compliance
Lightning Source LLC
Chambersburg PA
CBHW021237190726
48289CB00005B/1366